MAXIMUS
THE KEY TO HEAVEN
A SERAPHIC NOVEL BOOK ONE
CHRISTOPHER M. SHAMOUN

For my best friend,

Erik Ahad

11-03-89 – 12-26-11

"In the end what matters
Isn't how long we've lived
But how fully we've lived.
The good we've done,
The friends we've made
And the love we've shared
Along the way..."

A Note from the Author

Dear Readers,

Thank you so much for picking up my book. I don't take your time or interest for granted, and I'm honored to share this story with you. Before you begin, I want to offer a quick note of care and transparency.

Although the novel is categorized as New Adult because of the characters' ages, it does touch on some darker and more mature themes, including:

- Torture (characters being harmed for information)

- Attempted sexual assault

- Underage drinking and the purchase of fake IDs

- War-related violence and demonic elements

- Occasional foul language

These moments are never written to shock for shock's sake or to glorify harmful behavior. Instead, they are included to reflect the struggles my characters face and to deepen their growth. They are described with intention, not excess, and I've taken care not to make them gratuitous.

I encourage you to read with awareness of these themes and to take breaks if any scene feels overwhelming. Your comfort and well-being matter most to me.

With gratitude,
Christopher M. Shamoun

"There once was an angel who came from heaven
and fell in love with a girl.
He gave her a key
and called it his soul and then he disappeared."

Prologue

The Key

She awoke in pain. Her body was bound, her eyes blindfolded. She struggled against the restraints, the metal around her wrists and ankles biting viciously into her skin.

"I see you're awake now, little Nephilim," a deep, familiar voice said.

"What do you want with me, demon scum?" she spat. "Let me go, and I'll ask Maximus to kill you quickly when he comes for me."

"We want your Angel Key. Gift it to us, or we'll make your torture long and sweet."

"Take off my blindfold so I can see you for the coward you are," she demanded.

"Fine," the voice replied, untying the blindfold from behind her head. "As you wish, child."

Her vision cleared, revealing the sinister face of Azazel, his flaming irises burning with malevolence.

"Now gift me your key or die," he said, flashing his wicked smile.

"Maximus will have your head for this," she said and spat at him.

His eyes narrowed into thin, angry slits, and he slowly wiped the spit from his face.

"Maximus won't be coming for you. No one's that stupid. Now gift me the key!" He reared back and struck her across the face with his open hand.

Her vision blurred again, and she saw stars. Dammit. The bastard.

"I'll never give you my key, and you know as well as I do that you can't torture someone into gifting it," she chided. "First rule of Angel Keys: the owner of the key may only gift it with an open heart, and I would never open my heart to a bottom-feeding lowlife like you," she growled.

"Have it your way then," he reared his hand back and struck her again, and again.

She spat blood onto the floor.

"You'll learn humility, abomination," Azazel hissed, his voice rising with rage. "You'll break. They all do."

"And yet here I am," she muttered, just before he struck her hard enough to rattle her bones. Her eyes rolled back.

"Just wait until Abaddon has his turn. He enjoys making angels scream." He smiled wickedly. "You'll die here, girl. That coward will never come for you."

Her limbs trembled. The pain, the heat, the fatigue—it was all too much. Still, she forced herself to speak.

"He's no coward. He'll come for me," she breathed. "And when he does, you'll be the one with regret," she said, staring into his eyes with a challenge. "You'll regret the day you sold your soul," she said, smiling weakly.

"Abaddon, it appears she has some fight left in her." Azazel called behind him. A burly demon approached, his form hulking and menacing. He was huge, maybe even larger than Darius, whose grizzly form had become a comfort to have around.

"It appears she does," Abaddon smiled. revealing a mouth of sharp, metal fangs.

He was nothing like Darius. His pale, bald head and thick, caterpillar-like eyebrows were the opposite of Darius's beautiful dark mocha skin and smooth, endearing features. This creature was made this way. She refused to believe he was ever an angel.

"Break her." Azazel ordered as he turned to leave.

Abaddon stalked toward Cecelia's limp form, cracking his knuckles as he went.

"It'll be my pleasure."

What followed was agony. Real, raw, endless agony. He tore her down—bone from socket, nail from flesh. He burned her, whipped her, drowned her, always stopping just before she slipped beyond reach. Her Nephilim blood healed her faster than he liked—mending too quickly, stitching too neatly—but that didn't matter.

Because after every brutal session, just before her body fully restored itself, he brought in mystics—twisted remnants of once-holy beings—who healed her with dark magic. Not to save her. To reset her.

So he could start again.

And again.

She lost track of time. Minutes felt like hours, hours like days.

And when he was done—when he finally tired of his game—he left her hanging, her arms chained above her head, body bruised and trembling, discarded like trash.

Her throat was raw from screaming. The silence that followed felt almost crueler than the noise.

She cried then. Truly cried. Not just from pain, but from despair.

How had she let it get this far? How had she been so stupid, so reckless, so hopeful that love could rewrite her fate? She'd led them right to her. And now here she was.

Because she fell in love with a fallen angel.

Because she believed she could outrun prophecy.

Her mind drifted to her father, to what he would think if he saw her like this—torn, bleeding, and broken.

But still, she held onto hope, waiting, wondering. Where was her angel now? Where was Maximus, and would he come for her?

Cecelia White

Chapter 1

Break in

She'd been reading late again. Last time she checked, the clock said 2:00 a.m.—now the power was out.

Typical.

She would've preferred another hour of reading. The book was just getting to the good part: the heroine was about to uncover a secret tomb buried beneath a forgotten city. Instead, Cecelia sat wide awake in bed, wrapped in anticipation—not just from the book, but from tomorrow's move. Her whole life was about to change, and she couldn't calm her thoughts long enough to sleep.

Her fingers absently twisted the antique key hanging from the chain around her neck. She sighed and shut the book, laying it gently on her nightstand.

Stupid power.

She hated how the house always waited until her parents were out of town to get creepy. She cracked open the drawer and fumbled for the box of matches, lighting one with a practiced flick. The flame hissed to life.

Why can't this stuff ever happen when Dad's home?

Annoyed, she padded across the dark room to her desk and lit the half-used candle perched on a stack of books. Its soft glow pushed back the gloom, casting golden light over the walls and shelves.

This'll do… until I find the stupid flashlight.

Note to self: Leave flashlight on nightstand. Right next to book. Like a normal person.

She tucked her necklace beneath her shirt, grabbed a blue hoodie from her desk chair, and zipped it all the way up to her chin. The chill in the air was almost theatrical.

Foreshadowing, much?

Candle in hand, she cracked open the door and stepped into the hallway. It was long, quiet, and too still. The shadows stretched strangely along the walls. She moved carefully past the closet and bathroom—both closed. Her parents' room was shut, too. No surprise there.

They were away on business. Again.

Cecelia was used to being alone. Ever since she'd been old enough to manage on her own, her mother—New York's favorite French-imported fashion icon—had packed her off to an all-girls boarding school. Something about "discipline" and "elegance" and "developing a personal brand."

Her mom chased fashion like it was some kind of holy grail. Cecelia barely registered on her radar.

Her dad, on the other hand… he used to be different. An archaeologist. A dreamer. They used to sit on the couch for hours while he showed her ancient maps and photos from digs halfway across the world. She loved those days. But after she got shipped off in middle school, he sort of… drifted. Fell deeper into his work.

He was always there—but never really *present.*

How poetic, she thought, *that two people obsessed with discovering the world completely forgot to raise one.*

She moved down the stairs and into his study.

During the day, this room was her favorite in the whole house. Floor-to-ceiling bookshelves, stone sculptures, relics and replicas from every era. It smelled like old paper and coffee grounds. It was like stepping into another time.

But at night?

Total haunted museum vibes.

The candlelight made the sculptures look like they were breathing. Watching.

Ugh, pull it together, Cecelia. You're not some trembling damsel in a haunted house. You're the girl with the key around her neck and destiny in her veins.

She passed through the family room and reached the kitchen, rummaging through a drawer beneath the TV. She found a yellow flashlight. Of course, it was dead.

She rolled her eyes and slammed the drawer shut.

Useless.

Just as she crossed toward the garage, a sudden crash shattered the silence. Glass.

She froze.

Her heart slammed once—twice—then went still.

Intruder.

Do I call the cops? No. Useless. They'd take forty-five minutes just to find the house. And what if it's nothing? What if it's just the wind or a bird or—

Another sound. Scraping.

Nope. Not the wind.

Alright then. Time to be the main character.

She squared her shoulders, lips pressing into a thin determined line.

She didn't panic. She didn't scream. She calculated. First thought: weapon. Cecelia wasn't stupid. She knew the difference between paranoia and danger. She also knew how to handle herself.

Some loser picked the wrong house to rob.

She grabbed the nearest blunt object—an golf club—and gripped it tight.

If this is the start of my origin story, she thought, *then fine. So be it.*

She slipped into a low stance, heart pounding as she darted across the kitchen.

Boomsville, population: you, idiot.

She raced back toward the study—the noise definitely came from there.

"I've got you now," she whispered, barely above breath.

As she entered the study, candle in one hand and golf club in the other, Cecelia kept her back to the wall.

Always protect your back. Check all exits. Don't be an idiot.

Just like she'd been taught—by karate instructors, by spy novels, and by every late-night action movie she ever fell asleep watching.

She reached the bay doors by the patio and checked the handles. Locked.

No sign of forced entry. But the alarm wasn't blinking.

It should be blinking.

She frowned. That meant it had been disabled—somehow.

Dammit. The windows.

She made her way to them, checking each one like a detective on a case. Locked. Locked. Still locked. Not a single pane shattered.

What the hell?

Something didn't add up. That crash wasn't in her head.

She pressed her back to the shelves and began moving slowly along the room, golf club raised. She wasn't just wandering—she was clearing the space, aisle by aisle.

Come on, Cecelia, think. The sound had to come from somewhere. Look for clues. A broken vase, an open drawer, anything.

If she found what the intruder broke or where he came in, she could track him. Yes—him. That made it easier. Visualizing him gave her something to focus on.

Tall, clumsy, underestimating her. Probably in for the shock of his life when a girl in a hoodie and pajama pants came at him swinging a golf club like a cursed relic hunter.

She could take him.

She'd dropped guys twice her size in sparring. This wouldn't be any different.

Her eyes swept the shelves.

"I know you're in here, thief," she called out, voice steady—mostly. "And I'm letting you know now that I'm a second-degree black belt in karate, and I have a samurai sword with me, ready to cut you up!"

…Shit. *Why did I say that?*

She cringed. Idiot. She'd just lost the element of surprise. What was this, a comic book? She might as well have screamed *"Prepare to die!"* while dramatically removing her glasses.

Still, it was too late now. She made one last pass through the ground floor before heading to the staircase that led to the second level of the study.

She moved slowly, toes barely making a sound on the wooden stairs. Her candle flickered, casting tall shadows against the walls.

Despite everything, Cecelia felt her heart racing—not with fear.

Excitement.

She was kind of loving this.

That was messed up, right? Probably. But adrenaline was a hell of a drug.

It wasn't that she wanted danger. Not really. But… this was something. Something she could *do*.

This is your moment, Cecelia White. Main character energy. Agent Carter meets Indiana Jones. Time to channel your inner Peggy and get it done.

She imagined herself in one of those grainy 1950s spy thrillers—slipping around potted plants, rolling past doorways, lips painted red and confidence even sharper than her eyeliner.

All that was missing was the theme music.

She made it to the upper floor and worked her way toward the far back wall, where the last set of bookshelves met the fireplace.

As she reached the lounge area, she used the club to poke beneath the couches, one cautious nudge at a time.

Silence.

Still… something felt off.

She got down on her knees, candle held low.

If this were a movie, this would be the part where the monster lunges.

Her eyes caught something strange—one of the shelves had shifted. The bookcase next to the fireplace had been pushed aside, revealing a narrow, dark doorway.

Her father's hidden liquor room.

He always got such a kick out of showing it off to his friends. Slide out the book, cue the *click*, Bond-style entrance revealed.

Secretly, she loved it. It made her dad feel… cool.

James Bond would know what to do right now, she told herself, climbing to her feet using the coffee table for balance.

She gripped the golf club tighter and moved toward the opening, candle stretched in front of her like a sword of light.

She hesitated just outside.

Just a peek. Nothing to freak out about. I've got this. You've got this. Cecelia White does not back down.

She extended the candle, leaned in for a quick look—

Nothing.

She took a breath.

Then another.

Fingers curling around the key at her neck, she whispered a prayer.

Please don't have a gun. Or a knife. Or… anything sharp.

She stepped inside.

"Last chance, loser," she muttered. "You better hope I don't find you."

She slowly swept the candle across the room, casting light into every corner.

And then—

Her breath caught.

Eyes.

Bright gold. Watching her. Not blinking.

Her soul briefly departed her body.

She screamed, dropped the candle, and started swinging.

She slashed left, then right—hacking the air like she was in a showdown in feudal Japan. She spun, raised the club overhead, and brought it down with a crack. Something shattered. Maybe glass. Maybe a statue. Probably something expensive.

Didn't matter.

She kept swinging.

"Come on then! You want a fight? LET'S GO!"

Eventually, when nothing leapt at her throat, and she realized she was shouting into empty air, she stopped.

Breathing hard, she fumbled for the matchbox.

One strike. Two.

The third flared to life.

She lit the candle again and held it out with trembling hands.

The room was empty.

"…Meow."

She froze.

"…Maslow?"

She swept the candle's glow around again.

And there he was. Her black cat, slinking from the shadows like a smug little demon prince, tail high, utterly unbothered.

"MASLOW! You little *shit!*"

She nearly collapsed from the flood of emotions—rage, relief, embarrassment.

"How did you even get in here?"

Maslow blinked at her with the callous grace of royalty and strutted past her out of the hidden room like *he* had just saved *her.*

She took in a long, slow breath.

And then she smelled it.

Whiskey.

"Oh no. Dad's gonna kill me."

After cleaning up the broken glass and soaking in a hot bath for what felt like an hour, Cecelia finally collapsed into bed.

She left the golf club beside her nightstand.

Just in case.

That was her new motto: Never sleep unarmed when home alone.

She had four hours until her first day of college. A fresh start. A new adventure. Time to be a freshman all over again.

As she drifted off to sleep, one final thought bubbled to the surface.

How did Maslow even get in there…?

And then—

Wait. Aren't his eyes green?

Chapter 2

The Fall

That night, Cecelia White had a dream.

It did not feel like a dream. It felt like a memory.

A strange, ancient place unfolded before her—alabaster statues looming like silent judges, fountains that sparkled like starlight, and rose bushes blooming in impossible colors. In the center of it all, shackled between two towering marble columns, hung a man.

He was lean, olive-skinned, and barefoot, his arms stretched above him in brutal restraint. His head drooped low, ebony curls tangled and matted like a broken crown. The light bathed him in gold, but there was no divinity left in his posture—only ruin. His entire being sagged beneath the weight of defeat.

Three men emerged from a set of massive cathedral doors. Their armor gleamed gold beneath the heavenly light, Romanesque in design, more ceremonial than functional—yet fearsome all the same. They moved with precision, boots echoing against the stone with dreadful finality.

As they approached the prisoner, they called his name.

He didn't respond.

He only stared down at the floor, as if the stone itself had judged him more mercifully than the ones who came.

The first of the trio stepped forward—a tall, broad-shouldered figure with striking blond hair and an air of celestial authority. When he spoke, it was with the voice of command, of judgment, of fate.

"Ceruleus, you have failed in your divine mission.
You have broken your oaths, and in doing so, forsaken Heaven.
How do you plead?"

No answer. Ceruleus remained still, unmoved, as though the words were distant echoes from a life already lost.

The silence unsettled the second man, whose long chestnut hair framed sharp features twisted in fury.

"Ceruleus Maximus," he barked, "you will show respect when addressed by your superior—Archangel Michael, divine commander of Heaven's Host."

Still nothing. Not even a flicker of recognition.

Infuriated, the man stepped forward and struck Ceruleus across the face with the back of his gauntlet. The crack rang through the air like a gunshot.

Golden ichor sprayed from Ceruleus's lips, spattering the marble.

At last, the fallen angel looked up.

His once-radiant eyes—those piercing, golden orbs that had once blazed with brilliance—were dim now. Hollow. Resigned.

The third angel, quiet until now, stood behind the others. He was younger, with blonde hair and an innocent face that did not belong in a place of such cruelty.

Michael raised a hand to stop the next blow.

"That is enough, Gabriel," he said quietly, placing a hand on his brother's shoulder. "We are not here to punish in anger. We are here to fulfill the will of the Creator."

Gabriel clenched his fists but obeyed.

Michael turned to the third.

"Uriel. Gabriel. Hold him down."

They moved swiftly. Gabriel took one arm. Uriel, hesitating for a moment too long, took the other. Together, they braced Ceruleus in place.

Michael reached behind his back and drew his sword.

It was a thing of beauty. Terrible beauty. Gold-forged and impossibly bright, with an obsidian hilt that shimmered like volcanic glass. Ancient seraphic runes blazed along the blade's length—symbols of power, of judgment, of divine execution.

Michael raised it high.

In a burst of blinding light, Ceruleus's wings unfurled from his back. They were breathtaking—massive, flawless, pure as morning snow. They flapped violently, as if trying to break free of this moment, to lift him back to glory.

"Hold him still!" Michael shouted.

Uriel flinched.

"This doesn't feel right…" he said, barely above a whisper. His voice trembled. "Michael, this feels—"

"Hold. Him. Still." Michael's tone was cold. Absolute.

There would be no defiance.

Gabriel tightened his grip. Uriel, after a pained pause, did the same— grasping the base of each wing with trembling hands.

Michael stepped forward, placed a boot to Ceruleus's back, and in a single motion, drove the sword down.

Ceruleus screamed.

The blade cut clean through the left wing, severing it with a spray of golden ichor. Then again—his right. Another scream, more ragged, more broken. His body convulsed and collapsed to the floor in a heap, twitching, bloodlike ichor pooling around him in molten halos.

Michael exhaled. Silent. Stone-faced.

He wiped his blade clean—on the severed wing itself—and returned it to its sheath with finality.

Ceruleus did not move.

He lay curled on the floor like something no longer human. Breathing, but barely.

"It is done," Michael said quietly. "Uriel, gather the wings and leave us. Gabriel, with me."

Uriel hesitated—then stepped forward, unraveling a silken cloth. With reverent hands, he wrapped the wings, folding them gently. He didn't look at Ceruleus again. He couldn't.

He left without a word.

Michael and Gabriel removed the chains from Ceruleus's wrists. He didn't resist. He couldn't.

"You are no longer one of us, Ceruleus," Michael said, his voice devoid of emotion.

"You are damned," Gabriel added.

They dragged him across the courtyard.

The rose garden they passed through was a vision of divine beauty—blooms of scarlet, gold, violet, sapphire. Each petal glowed faintly, kissed by the light of Heaven. The air was perfumed, sweet, serene.

It should have felt like paradise.

Instead, it felt like mockery.

Every bush they passed was stained with a smear of golden ichor, a trail of suffering against perfection.

They reached the edge of the garden.

A single, towering apple tree stood before them. Its fruit shimmered with divine knowledge, glowing with the memory of Eden.

Michael looked down at the broken body in his arms.

"Do you remember this tree?" he asked, as if to no one. "This is where Adam and Eve tasted the fruit of truth… and were cast out of paradise for it."

He knelt, just long enough to whisper:

"This is where all who fall from grace say their last goodbyes."

Then, without pause, he and Gabriel lifted Ceruleus by the arms.

They cast him from the edge of the world—into the blinding white abyss below.

No final word.

No glance back.

Just silence.

And the echo of wings no longer there.

For a while, there was only darkness.

Then—wind.

It screamed past him in violent gusts, tearing at his skin, howling in his ears like a beast unchained. But it wasn't the wind that broke him.

It was the voices.

He could hear them now—all of them. Screaming. Sobbing. Wailing in agony. A thousand tormented cries ripping through his mind with the fury of a storm. Each voice a wound. Each shriek a memory.

And somehow, impossibly, he could feel them—their pain. Their sorrow. It seeped into him like smoke, like poison.

His eyes clenched shut, but it didn't help. The faces were still there. Twisted by grief, distorted by rage and despair. As if the suffering of every fallen soul had been etched onto the inside of his eyelids.

He had never imagined this. Not truly.

He had never known instability. Never tasted chaos. Never believed that such pure, unrelenting madness could exist beneath the order of Heaven.

And now—it consumed him.

He was spinning. Spiraling. Tumbling down through endless white, air rushing past him in a maelstrom of sound and fury. He couldn't breathe. He couldn't scream. He couldn't stop it.

Everything was moving too fast.

And the harder he tried to brace himself—mind, body, spirit—the more it slipped through his grasp.

This was damnation.

And of all the agonies clawing at him, none compared to the inferno blazing between his shoulders.

The wound where his wings had been.

It wasn't just pain. It was loss.

A hollow, searing emptiness that radiated out like a second heartbeat—one that pulsed with absence. With shame.

With finality.

The knowledge that he would never fly again hit harder than the sword had.

He would never rise. Never soar. Never feel the wind beneath his wings or the hum of celestial power flowing through him.

That part of him was gone.

Ripped away.

Torn from his body and soul like it had never belonged.

And he would carry that void with him wherever he went—every step, every breath, a reminder.

He was broken long before he ever hit the ground

Evie

Evette Renee
Angelique
Lamoureux

Chapter 3

Move in Day

Cecelia awoke thrashing in her sheets, breath ragged and skin slick with cold sweat.

Nightmares did that to you.

It took a moment for her eyes to adjust. Her heart was hammering in her chest like she'd just run a mile barefoot in a thunderstorm.

The dream still clung to her like static.

She rolled over, trying to catch her breath—and promptly face-planted onto the hardwood floor with a thud.

Still tangled in her sheets.

"Great," she muttered into the floorboards.

Wiggling free with the grace of a stuck caterpillar, she stood, tugged down her wrinkled shirt, and pushed the hair from her face. Her room was quiet. Ordinary. Safe.

But the dream still lingered.

She crossed to her window, lifting the curtain to check the sky. Still dark. Early, but the horizon was starting to blush. Her eyes flicked to the digital clock beside her bed.

7:03 a.m.

Only three hours of sleep.

She rubbed her face. It felt like she'd lived through a century. Her body was here—but part of her still felt like it had fallen straight out of Heaven.

Coffee.

That was her first real thought.

Coffee will make this better. *Coffee makes everything better.*

Cecelia had a theory: the mood of your entire day could be predicted—no, *dictated*—by the size and artistry of your breakfast.

And today? Today was her first day of college.

The breakfast gods would be pleased.

Now in the kitchen, having raided the fridge like a strategic general, she stood surveying the ingredients she'd lined up across the counter: strawberries, bananas, blueberries, pancake mix, waffle mix, farm bread, eggs, chocolate chips…

It was about to go *down.*

She connected her smartphone to her blue tooth speaker, dialed up *The Format,* and let *"The First Single"* fill her kitchen with positive vibes.

Cue transformation montage.

Cecelia cooked like she trained—precise, passionate, and with far more flair than necessary. She tossed berries into batter, poured smoothies like a mad scientist, and danced from waffle iron to frying pan like a culinary ninja in fuzzy socks.

Spatulas clanged, syrup flowed, and the air filled with the rich aroma of vanilla, cinnamon, and hope.

This was her kind of therapy. This was sacred.

When it was done, she stood before a table fit for a champion.

French toast dusted with powdered sugar. Scrambled eggs fluffed to perfection. Chocolate chip strawberry pancakes stacked like golden towers. Blueberry waffles glistening with melted butter. A tall glass of strawberry-banana smoothie.

And a very large cup of coffee.

She sat down, eyes closed for a moment, breathing it all in.

Breakfast: the truest form of self-care.

People always asked how someone her size could eat like a linebacker.

The answer? She trained like one.

Between karate, gymnastics, swimming, and a rotating door of seasonal sports, Cecelia was always moving. Her nutritionist once estimated she burned close to 6,000 calories a day. She called it *balance*. Her friends called it *magic*.

Cecelia just called it living.

BEEP! BEEP!

A car horn honked from outside.

"Guess my ride's here," she said with a sigh, taking one last look at the breakfast buffet and pushing her chair back with quiet grace.

She was always polite. Even when no one was around.

As she passed under the staircase toward the front door, the doorbell rang.

DING DONG.

"Impatient today, are we Edward?" she said aloud as she opened the door.

Standing there, tall and stately in a pressed suit and driver's cap, was Edward—family chauffeur, personal hero, and longtime guardian of White family sanity.

"Good morning, Miss Cecelia. I see you're all ready for your big move."

"Of course I am. Why wouldn't I be?" She waved her arms theatrically. "I mean, what girl *wouldn't* be overwhelmed with joy at the thought of starting Uni completely alone, without so much as a goodbye from her parents? Truly, a moment to treasure."

She spun dramatically in place, peering around the front entry like she expected someone to jump out from behind a ficus.

Edward gave her a look—half concerned, half amused.

"Is that sarcasm I'm sensing?"

"No, Edward," she said sweetly. "That's called *coping.*"

He tilted his head with a soft frown.

"You know your parents are away on important business… and if they were here all the time, well—then I'd be out of a job."

"Oh please," she smirked. "You've been with this family longer than I've been alive. If anyone deserves a retirement package and a private island, it's you."

She paused. "You don't actually think I'd ever let you go, do you?"

A rare, genuine smile crossed Edward's face.

"Of course not, Miss."

"Good." She nodded firmly, then glanced around the hall. "Now where is that ridiculous cat of mine?"

"Maslow?" Edward asked.

"Yes, Maslow. Furry little traitor. I wanted to say goodbye."

"He's probably chasing shadows or plotting the downfall of mankind. You know how cats are."

"Too true," she muttered. "Alright, where are my bags?"

"That's what I came to ask."

She stepped aside and gestured to a pile of coordinated blue Coach luggage stacked neatly near the door.

"Right over here. And Edward—seriously, can we drop the 'Miss'? I'm eighteen, not a twice-divorced heiress recovering from her fifth wedding in Capri."

"Yes, yes, of course," he chuckled, hoisting the luggage with practiced ease.

By the time he reached the trunk of the sleek black Lincoln Town Car, Cecelia was already in the back seat, smartphone in hand, bluetooth headphones on, fingers poised to press play.

"Getting ready for the long drive, Miss Cec—" he corrected himself mid-sentence, smiling in the rearview mirror.

"Yup. Got my playlist locked and loaded," she said with a grin.

Then paused.

"Hey… Edward?"

"Yes?"

"Did your power go out last night?"

"I suppose it did," he said thoughtfully. "But I must've slept through it. The electric company was already outside fixing the line when I woke up. Something about a blown transformer."

Cecelia frowned.

"That's weird. There wasn't a storm or anything. Could that mess with the alarm system?"

"Possibly. I'm not sure how all those security systems work, but I'll have the company come out and check everything tomorrow."

"Please do," she said softly.

Then she slid her headphones back on and pressed play.

Let Me In by Grouplove flowed through the tiny speakers, filling her world with melody.

She closed her eyes and leaned her head against the cool glass of the car window.

Time to let it go.

Last night was just a power outage. That's all.

Just a dream.

She inhaled deeply and let the music wash over her.

Time to sit back, relax, and start her next chapter.

Cecelia had always liked the idea of taking the long drive into the city—especially in the fall.

There was something about autumn that made goodbyes easier.

The vibrant reds and golds outside the window softened the edges of her small, quiet town: the prim, too-perfect homes with trimmed hedges; the country club golf course her parents never used; the overpriced restaurants that all served the same three pasta dishes.

Wrapped in fall's warm palette, even the suburbs looked almost poetic.

Goodbye, suburbia. Thanks for the existential dread.

She welcomed the shift as the city skyline began to rise in the distance. Where Long Island ended, possibility began.

Cecelia loved the city.

The noise, the chaos, the sheer scale of it all. The skyscrapers reaching skyward like they were trying to touch Heaven itself. New York wasn't just a place—it was a story waiting to be lived.

And Cecelia White was determined to be its main character.

Somewhere between Montauk and Manorville, drowsiness caught up with her. She let her head rest against the window and closed her eyes. But peace didn't come.

The dream crept back in.

It was hazy now, like fog curling around the corners of her thoughts—but still there.

Those eyes.

Golden. Otherworldly. Familiar in a way that shouldn't have been possible.

That angel. The fallen one.

There was something about him that wouldn't let go of her. Not just the pain in his face, or the way he collapsed after they took his wings—but the way he looked right before. Resigned. Beautiful.

It had to be a dream. Just leftover adrenaline from the power outage and Maslow's late-night scare.

Still… it didn't feel like something her brain just made up.

The angels in her grandmother's stories had always been radiant, righteous, merciful. Not cruel. Not detached. Not… monstrous.

These weren't the kind of angels who wept over humanity. These were soldiers. Executioners.

And that one—Ceruleus, was it? She wished she could remember. He didn't belong in that nightmare. He looked too human in his suffering. Too real.

Why did they do that to him?

She turned the thought over and over in her mind, even as sleep pulled her down again.

And in her dreams, she tumbled through clouds and memories and fractured biblical metaphors—visions of golden eyes, broken wings, and way too many waffles.

She stirred at the sound of her stomach grumbling.

Of course. Even her subconscious couldn't distract her for long when food was involved.

"We're just entering the city now, Cecelia," Edward's voice drifted in from the front seat. "Are you still sleeping, Miss?"

"What?" she blinked awake, rubbing her eyes. "Wait—we're here already? How long was I out?"

"Oh, not long," he chuckled. "Just the last hour or two. Sounded like you were dreaming up quite the storm back there. I'm amazed you didn't wake yourself."

"Are you saying I snore?"

Edward chuckled, "possibly."

"I *do not snore*, Edward."

"Of course not, Miss Cecelia."

"And don't call me 'Miss'!"

He only smiled.

They were getting close now. Buildings wearing NYU banners zipped past.

Cecelia perked up, pressing her face lightly to the glass. A narrow bookstore caught her eye—*Ray's Books*, tucked beside a cozy-looking coffee shop. Definitely a place she'd return to.

She loved small bookstores. Back home, the indies were all devoured by corporate giants. But in the city? They could survive here.

Here, hidden gems had a fighting chance.

They passed restaurants, cafes, a Chipotle she could live with, and no less than seventeen pizza joints.

Noted. Pizza situation: stable.

Her stomach gave another warning growl.

Then they slowed near Washington Square. The trees lining the plaza had started turning—their yellowing leaves catching the morning light like soft fire.

Edward pulled the Lincoln to the curb outside a tall brick building.

"Alright, Cecelia. This is Goddard Hall. I'll help you with your luggage and then find a place to park. Would you wait for me in the lobby, please?"

"Right," she said, still a little groggy.

As the car came to a stop, she caught sight of other students—some unloading suitcases, others wrapped in long, tearful hugs from their families.

Her stomach twisted—not from hunger this time.

Where were *her* parents?

They should be here. This was supposed to be one of those milestone moments. One of those scenes you look back on in scrapbooks. She hadn't expected a parade or anything—but… something.

Anything.

"Come now, Miss," Edward said gently, opening her door. "I already set your luggage out. Let's bring it in and get you settled somewhere comfortable while I find parking."

She stepped out and looked around at the flurry of goodbyes and family snapshots.

No one was waving at her. No one was wiping away proud tears.

But Edward was here.

And honestly? That meant more than most things.

The lobby of Goddard Hall wasn't quite what Cecelia expected.

No soaring ceilings. No dramatic chandeliers. Just a modest check-in desk and a handful of worn-in sofas—most of them already occupied by students and their overly emotional parents.

Edward helped her move her luggage to a small corner near an empty couch. With a quick nod and a promise to return, he disappeared to find parking.

Cecelia plopped onto the couch, already tired again despite the nap. She pulled out her copy of *Obsidian* by Jennifer L. Armentrout, popped on her headphones, and hit play on her waiting playlist.

Nothing like sexy aliens to erase the weirdness of de-winged angels.

The music kicked in, and the words of the book wrapped around her like a warm blanket. Within minutes, she was fully absorbed—her hunger forgotten, the nerves gone, the world narrowed to the flirtatious chaos on the page.

Time passed without her noticing.

Until she felt a tug on her sweater.

"Miss Cecelia," Edward said softly. "I just got off the phone with the movers. They'll be here shortly, but I'll need to stay downstairs to meet them. Why don't we bring your bags up to your room in the meantime?"

She looked up from her book, blinking.

"That's alright, Edward. You've already done so much. I'm a college girl now—capable, mature, fully independent," she said, flashing him a squint-eyed smile. "I can handle it."

"No doubt," he replied, amused. "But what kind of gentleman would I be if I let you drag all these bags up on your own?"

"Oh, *quit it*." She rolled her eyes with a grin. "Tell you what—walk me to the elevator with the heavy stuff, and I'll take it from there. That should satisfy your noble instincts."

"Fine, fine," he said, already lifting her two largest bags like they were full of pillows and dreams instead of books and shoes.

Cecelia packed up her things—book back in the bag, smartphone stashed, headphones around her neck—and shouldered her backpack and gym bag. She grabbed the handle of her rolling suitcase and followed him to the elevator.

As the doors opened, she quickly pulled a folded paper from her jacket pocket.

"Room 407C," she said, handing it to him. "Don't forget. I'll see you up there." She gave him a quick wink and stepped inside.

The doors slid shut, and she hit the button for the fourth floor.

The elevator dinged, and she stepped out into a hallway that smelled faintly of detergent and new beginnings.

A tall, lanky guy with messy brown hair and glasses stood at the other end of the hall, a red flannel shirt tied lazily over his NYU staff lanyard.

Definitely a film major. Or a very tired barista.

She waved to catch his attention.

"Excuse me! Could you help me? I'm trying to find 407C, and these room numbers are doing their own thing."

He turned toward her with a crooked smile.

"Ah, freshman," he said, mostly to himself. "Hey! I'm Lucas. RA for this floor. You're in luck—I was heading that way anyway. Let me help you with those bags."

Before she could even respond, he hoisted her two largest suitcases like they were nothing.

Okay, not just film major. Secret gym rat. Noted.

She followed him down the hall, passing a laundry room and a pair of vending machines.

"Ooh, snacks on standby," she said aloud, mostly to herself.

"This place just earned bonus points."

"You got lucky," Lucas called over his shoulder. "Room with a street view. Those usually get scooped by returning sophomores before freshman housing gets assigned."

They reached a door with a silver number plate: 407C.

Above it was a dry-erase marker board that read:
 Welcome Evette & Cecelia!
 Written in cheerful red and blue bubble letters.

Roommate confirmed. Extroversion status: pending.

"Do you have your room key from your welcome packet?" Lucas asked, setting her bags down.

She slipped off her backpack and dug through it for a moment before pulling out the card.

"Sorry—here you go."

He slid the white Goddard Hall keycard into the electronic lock. The light flashed green, and the door gave a satisfying *click*.

He pushed it open and carried her luggage inside.

"Well, here you are. Home sweet home—at least until midterms break your spirit," he said with a grin.

"Thanks so much, Lucas."

"No problem. If you need anything, my door's at the end of the hall—can't miss it. Says 'Resident Advisor' in obnoxious red letters."

He gave her a little wave and vanished back down the hallway.

"Nice meeting you too." Cecelia called after him as the door clicked shut.

The room wasn't exactly small, but for two people, Cecelia wasn't sure it would feel spacious for long.

Being an only child, she'd never had to share a space—at least, not one this personal. Still, she found herself quietly relieved. Her new roommate clearly had taste.

Purple and black taste.

The entire right side of the room was practically dipped in it. Purple comforter, matching pillows, beanbag, even the leather desk chair. The desk was sleek and black, the headphones and laptop both a clean mix of violet and midnight.

The band posters were what really caught her attention.

Fall Out Boy. Motion City Soundtrack. The Early November. Something Corporate.

Okay, I can work with this.

This girl wasn't just into the genre—she had *taste*. Cecelia felt a small grin tug at her mouth. She suddenly felt very validated for taking that roommate questionnaire seriously.

Andrew McMahon was Cecelia's all-time favorite artist. She had a Jack's Mannequin poster rolled up in her bag that she'd been planning to hang. Now it felt like more than decoration—it felt like a silent nod across the room.

She even noticed a few surfing posters tucked near the desk. Cecelia had never tried it before, but maybe—just maybe—she'd finally have someone to go with.

With Edward returning soon, and her mystery roommate out somewhere, Cecelia knew she had limited time to get her side of the room set up. She dropped her largest suitcase flat and unzipped a small compartment.

First things first. Poster goes up.

She retrieved a box of thumbtacks, unfurled the Jack's Mannequin poster with care, and climbed onto her bed to pin it above her headboard.

She stepped back, hands on her hips, proud.

"Rad poster you've got there," said a voice behind her.

Cecelia jumped, nearly falling off the bed. She twisted around, startled, and scrambled off the mattress awkwardly to face the speaker.

A petite brunette with big brown eyes stood in the doorway. She was wearing purple Nike runners, black leggings, a matching sports bra, and a loose purple hoodie.

"Is that a real autograph?" the girl asked, stepping inside. "That's really awesome. I love him."

"Yeah! I saw him in concert two summers back. He was *incredible!*" Cecelia said, her voice lighting up.

"Really? Two summers ago? At Bowery Ballroom?"

Cecelia blinked.

"Yeah, actually… how'd you know?"

"I was there," the girl said with a casual shrug. "Sat backstage. My brother opened for him that night. No big deal."

Cecelia's jaw dropped.

"WHAT? That's amazing. You're so lucky! Wow. I'm Cecelia White, by the way. Your… uh, roommate."

"Figured as much," the girl said, extending her hand with a confident wink. "Evette Renee Angelique Lamoureux. But you can call me Evie."

"Nice to meet you, Evie."

"Likewise. I gotta jump in the shower. Probably smell like a wet dog. I just came back from a quick run." She turned toward the bathroom. "When I'm done, I'll help you finish setting up, cool?"

"Yeah, that'd be great. Thanks."

As the bathroom door clicked shut, Cecelia reached into her luggage again and pulled out her Bluetooth speaker, plugging it into the outlet near the nightstand. Then, from her backpack, she grabbed her phone and scrolled through her playlists.

She tapped *"Shimmy Shimmy Quarter Turn"* by Hellogoodbye and let the bubbly synth-pop fill the room. It was the exact energy she needed to get in the zone.

She unzipped the rest of her bags and got to work—bed first. She smoothed her navy-blue comforter over her mattress, fluffed the baby-blue pillows, then moved on to her drawers. Jackets and dress clothes were hung neatly in the closet, while everything else found its place in the dresser.

By the time Evette emerged, her hair wrapped in a towel and a fresh outfit on, Cecelia was lounging on her bed, flipping through a book while *Of Monsters and Men* played softly in the background.

"Wow. You move fast, little missy," Evette said, tossing the towel over her desk chair. "Almost done without me."

"Had to keep myself busy."

"Great music choice, by the way. Not gonna lie—I was totally rocking out in the shower. I always play music when I'm cleaning too."

"Everything's better with music."

"Amen to that. So what's left?"

"Not much. Just waiting on the rest of my furniture."

A knock sounded at the door.

KNOCK KNOCK

"Who is it?" Evette asked with a mischievous grin, pressing her ear to the door.

"Oh, just me, Miss Cecelia," came a familiar muffled voice.

"Evie, open it," Cecelia giggled. "It's just Edward."

Evette flung the door open.

"Well, hello there Edward," she said in a mock-sultry tone.

"Hello, Miss. You must be Evette."

"That's me." She turned and grinned at Cecelia. "Your grandfather is *adorable.* I didn't know you were British!"

"Oh but I'm not—" Edward began, confused.

"British. He's actually Welsh," Cecelia jumped in quickly. "From my mom's side. Evie, this is… Grandpa Edward."

Edward gave her a sidelong look but didn't question it.

"Grandpa Edward, do come in," Cecelia said with forced formality.

He tilted his head but obliged, stepping inside.

"We're down here," he called into the hallway. "Bring everything over this way."

"You got it, English!" called a raspy voice from somewhere beyond.

Cecelia had made a decision before ever stepping foot on campus: no one needed to know she came from wealth. Not unless she told them.

Sure, her last name held some weight. Her mother was a fashion icon, her father a renowned scholar. But this—college—this was hers. She earned her scholarship. She applied. She wrote the essays. She wasn't about to let anyone dismiss her for being privileged.

Even if… well, technically, Edward *was* a family driver.

"Where you want this, lady?" asked a stocky man with a thick beard, already sweating through his shirt.

"Desk goes by the closet, sofa near the window," Cecelia said, pointing.

Another mover appeared, carrying a large wooden trunk.

"Where you want the treasure chest?" the tall balding man asked.

"It's books," she blushed. "Please just place it at the foot of my bed."

"Man, I thought *I* had a lot of stuff," Evette joked. "That's why I showed up early—I didn't want you to think I was a total pain."

"I'd never!" Cecelia said quickly.

"I mean, my brother and his friends carried my stuff in, and they were *not* going to smile doing it. So I figured better to be the early bird." Evie added.

"Smart move. How long was your drive?"

"Just under four hours. We came in from Avalon—Exit 13 on the Garden State."

"Jersey Shore? Huh. I pegged you for a California girl… maybe Florida, with that tan."

Cecelia nudged her. "Seriously though, you have great skin."

"This?" Evette gestured at herself. "Au naturel. Half Colombian, half French."

"Wow. I'm part French too. My parents met in England. My mom's got a little Welsh in her, but that's about as exotic as it gets." She smiled genuinely. " Half Colombian, how cool."

Evie grinned, "thanks!"

Another mover leaned in.

"Hey, lady, where you want the TV?"

"In front of the sofa, please. Thanks."

"Alright, boys," the man called. "You heard the boss."

"Trucks all empty," said the stocky one. "Anything else we can do for you?"

"No, everything's perfect. Thank you," Cecelia said with genuine warmth.

Edward handed the man a few large bills and nodded.

"Just give me a moment," he told them, then turned back to Cecelia.

"Leaving already, Grandpa Edward?" she teased, touching his shoulder.

"You're all moved in now, love. Time to break in the place. Explore. Have those adventures you're always talking about." He rested a hand on her shoulder. "Take good care of yourself. Call me if you ever need anything."

"Take care of Maslow, please."

"Of course. I'll treat that bloody cat like royalty."

"You *like* him."

"Not by choice," he said, smirking.

"I'm going to miss you."

"Always a phone call away."

"See you soon?"

"You will. And it was lovely meeting you, Miss Evette. You ladies enjoy your evening."

With that, he turned and left, the door clicking softly behind him.

"What a charming old man," Evette said, still staring at the door.

Cecelia stood silent for a beat longer.

"Well, all this moving has me *starving*," Evette announced, hopping onto her bed and cracking open her laptop. "I heard there's an all-you-can-eat sushi place around the corner."

That snapped Cecelia out of it.

"All you can eat?"

"YES. Unlimited sashimi, sushi, special rolls—*everything*. And trust me, I trolled their menu *hard* before my run this morning."

Cecelia blinked at her, caught between awe and hunger.

"Don't look so shocked," Evette laughed. "We'll just burn it off tomorrow. You're going to be my workout partner. Running, lifting, boxing—I do it all."

Cecelia grinned.

"Do you now? Well, I think I can keep up. Bring on the sushi."

"No backing out tomorrow. I don't accept food comas as excuses."

"Please. I'm a second-degree black belt. I'll teach *you* a thing or two."

Evette beamed. "Great taste in music, bottomless pit for sushi, and you can kick ass? I think this is the start of a beautiful friendship."

She threw an arm around Cecelia's shoulders.

"Now let's go eat that place out of business."

He sat across the street, half-hidden beneath the awning of a quiet noodle shop, watching them through the window.

Tan skin. Black hair that fell over his brow in soft waves. Hands tucked into the pockets of his dark hoodie. He blended in with the crowd well enough. Just another guy on the sidewalk, killing time.

But his eyes—sharp, gold, impossible to ignore—were locked on *her.*

At first glance, she looked like any other college freshman: slightly overwhelmed, trying not to show it. Laughing too hard at dumb jokes. A little wide-eyed, a little too confident.

But after a minute, he knew better.

Because the way she laughed—really laughed, head thrown back, squinting with delight as she obliterated another sushi roll—it hit something in him he didn't expect.

It was disarming.

He stood there, watching her hold court at the table with her new roommate, waving her chopsticks around like drumsticks and devouring sashimi like a personal challenge.

And damn if he wasn't impressed.

She's not what I expected.

She was smaller than he imagined. Blonde. Light eyes. Quick to smile.

Not the kind of girl you'd expect to carry something like *that.*

He glanced at the chain around her neck, mostly hidden beneath her sweatshirt. But he knew what it held. He could feel it—faint, but unmistakable.

Why does she have the key?

Did she even know what it was? What it could do?

Did she know what it might bring with it?

His brow furrowed. He didn't think so. She didn't look like someone who had answers—just questions. And probably too many library cards.

But that only made it worse.

She doesn't know.
She's walking around with something she doesn't understand.
And she's not ready.

He shifted his weight against the post, scanning the restaurant again—casual, relaxed. But the tension in his shoulders never really left. There was always someone watching. And now, *he* was the one watching her.

And yet, he couldn't bring himself to walk away.

There was something about her. Something unexpected. Something honest.

He was supposed to be gathering intel. That was it. Just watch, confirm, report back.

But he'd been standing here for twenty minutes now, watching her smile, watching her come alive over seaweed salad and sarcastic banter, and he had no answers. Just more questions.

So how do I approach her?
What do I tell her?
Hi, I'm the wingless celestial being who's been watching you eat
sushi like a heathen and by the way, you might be in danger? Yeah.
That'd go over real well.

He shoved his hands deeper into his pockets and sighed.

He had a lot to think about on the ride home.

Christoph Maximus

Chapter 4

Making plans

Turning the key to the three-inch-thick, steel fireproof door, Ceruleus Maximus stepped into the garage of his Brooklyn apartment, still wearing the same clothes from the night before.

He barely thought of that name anymore—Ceruleus. And when he did, it never felt like his. Not since what Michael did to him.

The dream had shaken him more than he wanted to admit. But that was the past.

These days, he was just *Christoph*.

Heavy rock blasted from the stereo above the worktable where his roommate was half-buried under a blue Honda Civic. He recognized the band. Four Years Strong.

Christoph dragged himself past his black Camaro, weaving through two dirt bikes. until he reached the other side of the garage. He dropped his black duffle bag against the red tool chest with a loud *thud*.

From beneath the car came a dull *clang* followed by a curse.

"You jackass," Erik groaned. rubbing his forehead. "What the hell?"

"I didn't get the key." Christoph said flatly, his head hanging in defeat.

"Ah," Erik deflated. "Did they beat you to it?" he asked, tightening a bolt with the wrench in his hand.

"No. It just wasn't there. I searched the whole house… It wasn't empty, by the way." He sounded annoyed as he leaned against the edge of the worktable.

Erik slid out from under the car and looked up. "What do you mean?"

"There was this girl," Christoph said, sharp and annoyed.

"There's always a girl," Erik sighed. "She give you trouble? I want the rundown."

"No, of course not. She didn't even know I was there. I did everything as planned." Christoph scratched the back of his head, pacing. "Cut the power, bypassed the alarms, got in through a second-floor bay window. Didn't even need to use a spell."

"So where does the girl come in?"

"I'm getting to that." He peeled off his leather jacket and slung it over his shoulder. "I was trying to feel for the Angel Key's energy when I ran into her cat." He let out a dry chuckle. "One look at me and the little shit panicked. Bolted into a table and knocked over a vase. Shattered before I could catch it."

"Man, you're getting slow in your old age. What happened to the magnificent Christoph Maximus that robbed the Vatican all those years ago?" Erik shook his head. "That guy would've caught it midair and had time to pose for a photo."

"Slow, maybe. Never sloppy." Christoph smirked and pointed at the duffle bag. "The vase is in there. Had to clean it up—heard the girl coming."

"With the cat?"

"No. With a golf club. Kept muttering stuff about karate and cutting my head off with some sword." He chuckled.

"But you said it was a golf club?"

"It was. She was improvising."

"That girl's got some balls. She find you?"

"No chance." Christoph laughed. "But she came close. I kept searching the house and found a secret room. And I mean some real James Bond shit."

He folded his arms. "Cornelius White—her father, I think—kept his whiskey stash behind a sliding bookcase. Looked like the VIP lounge at the club. Found a safe behind a portrait of some guy with a handlebar mustache. But no relics. Just money and a fossilized dinosaur claw. That's when she walked in."

"What'd you do?"

"What do you think?" Christoph raised a brow. "Used a quick glamour and kept to the shadows. She was waving around a candle when she spotted me. I'll never forget the grey of her eyes—and I *know* she caught the gold in mine. Almost lost it."

He ran a hand through his hair and resumed pacing. "It was strange. When our eyes locked, it felt like something inside me just… snapped. Like all the air had been sucked out of my lungs. I think she sync'd with me."

Erik blinked. "What? Humans don't sync with us. That's not possible."

"I'm telling you, it happened."

"Was she a looker or are you just being dramatic?"

"She was the most beautiful human being I've ever seen," Christoph said flatly. "Blonde hair smooth as silk. Full lips that whispered promises. Skin that looked so soft it hurt to not touch it."

"Alright, Romeo." Erik muttered. "Douche, hand me that Allen key."

Christoph tossed him the tool.

"Think she was wearing it?"

"I. Am. An idiot," Christoph muttered.

"Tell me something I don't know," Erik grinned.

"Didn't even cross my mind. It'd explain the white aura."

"So? We go back. Tonight."

"Can't." Christoph shook his head. "I stuck around all night. Watched her butler load the car and followed them into the city on my bike. I've been trailing her all day."

"Good thinking. Where'd they go?"

"NYU. She's a freshman—Goddard Hall."

He smirked. "I know I sound like a total creep, but I even followed her and her roommate to dinner. Watched them demolish sushi like it was an Olympic sport. It was like watching two black holes devour the galaxy."

Erik burst out laughing. "Did you get her name? We could go pay her a visit." He wiggled his eyebrows.

"Cecelia. And no, we're not torturing some poor girl to get the Key. That's not who we are."

"Relax, man. Joking. Mostly. But we need a plan. We need her to *give* it to us. Willingly. Before Azazel gets wind of this."

"Right." Christoph nodded. "A plan."

"And? You got one?"

"Yeah. A philosophy degree."

Erik stared. "You're a jackass."

"I don't have one yet, and I need to be close to her. What better way than enrollment?"

Christoph grinned, smug.

Erik smirked back. "Let's *both* enroll."

"And who's watching the club?"

Erik shrugged. "We'll figure it out. I'm in."

"Good. I'll call in that favor with the Board. See if I can fast-track registration."

"We did make a generous donation last time."

"Ten years ago. But who's counting?"

Erik punched him lightly in the shoulder. "Tomorrow morning, then. We're going back to school."

Christoph slung the duffle bag over his shoulder. "I need to get some sleep. Don't wake me unless the house is on fire."

"Pizza's in the fridge."

"Appreciated." Christoph disappeared up the stairs.

Erik leaned against the hood of the Civic, watching the spot his friend had stood.

"White aura," he muttered. "Now that's something new."

RAY'S
COOL CAFE

Chapter 5

New Routines

"Wow. You girls sure got quite an appetite!" said a balding, middle-aged man in a deli apron, his thick Brooklyn accent making Cecelia smile. He chuckled to himself while placing six heavy bags of food on the counter. "You got me all hungry just ringing you up!" he said, patting his belly.

"Yeah, yeah, keep it to yourself, Chubs!" Evie called back with a malicious grin. "Come on, Cecelia." She handed her three of the bags. "Let's grab a table."

They sat down at a corner table now buried in a mountain of breakfast. Bacon, egg, and cheese sandwiches; buttermilk pancakes; fruit cups bursting with pineapple, strawberries, and blueberries; waffles drowning in syrup; a box of bacon and hash browns—and three different syrup bottles stood like condiment sentries. Cecelia was elated. Finally, someone who matched her breakfast energy.

She watched Evie peel open her sandwich and slide a crispy hash brown inside. Cecelia raised an eyebrow.

"What are you doing with that?"

Evie looked up, mid-chew. "What, you've never had a Zebra?"

"No… and now I'm worried. There's not, like, actual zebra in that, right?"

Evie snorted. "New Yorkers, man. Okay, a Zebra is a fat sandwich. The kind they made at the Grease Trucks at Rutgers. You at least know what a fat sandwich is?"

"Of course." Cecelia lied.

Evie gave her a look but kept going. "So this one's got cheese, hash brown, eggs, more cheese, Taylor ham, and bacon—my signature touch. Salt, pepper, ketchup. Layers like a zebra, get it?"

"Got it. Making one now." Cecelia giggled, already rebuilding her own sandwich.

After inhaling the sandwich in record time, Cecelia took a sip of her coffee and cleared her throat. "So after this, I wanna check out that bookstore I passed yesterday."

"Good thing we showered at the gym before we came here. I would've died going anywhere else looking like we just ran from a crime scene."

Their morning had started at 5:30 AM—thanks to Evie. By 6, they were running laps at the gym. Then ten rounds of pushups, sit-ups, and squats. An hour of machines. Another ten rounds of mountain climbers, bicycles, and lunges. Five rounds of boxing drills. And finally, a half hour of what Evie dubbed "Hatha Yoga, but meaner."

"I was impressed you kept up." Evie said between bites.

"Told you I'm a second-degree black belt," Cecelia replied, slurping her smoothie with satisfaction.

"If you weren't so tiny, I'd say you should go pro. I've never seen anyone move that fast."

"I've won a few tournaments in my day, but what's a case full of trophies prove when you've never been in a real street fight?"

Evie laughed. "Girl, you're insane. I love it." She raised a hand for a high five, which Cecelia gladly met.

"Today was fun," Cecelia said. "But tomorrow, we do *my* routine. Deal?"

"Bring it on," Evie smirked, standing and brushing crumbs from her shirt. She chucked her empty tin into the trash and lazily waved to the man behind the counter. "Later, Chubs!"

Cecelia laughed as she followed her out.

Once outside, they rounded the corner of University Place, headed to 8th Street, walked two blocks, then turned left. In front of them stood a quirky, colorful building with a hand-painted sign:

Ray's Bookstore & Cool Café.

Cecelia hadn't noticed it yesterday, but now, standing in front of Ray's Bookstore, she was completely charmed. The window displays were genuinely impressive. Her favorite was the one labeled Ray's FAVES of the Month, painted in crisp white script. In its center hung a poster that read:

"My problem isn't that my favorite characters aren't real. It's that I'm not fictional… I don't want them to be real. What I desperately wish is that I could be fictional with them. It's not that I want them here with me, in this mundane and ordinary world… it's that I want to join them in their extraordinary one."

Now *that*, she thought, was a quote.

Flanking the poster were two spiraling towers of hardcover books—artfully arranged, almost sculptural. A few titles immediately caught Cecelia's eye: the latest from Cassandra Clare, Jennifer L. Armentrout, Sarah J. Maas, Pittacus Lore, Tahereh Mafi, Alexandra Bracken, and Laini Taylor. Ray had excellent taste. The YA Fantasy was strong with this one.

"After you," Evie said, holding the door with a mock bow.

"Why thank you, good sir," Cecelia replied in her best regal British accent.

Inside, the shop opened up like a storybook. It was packed but cozy, somehow managing to be cool *and* magical. Every section felt like its own immersive world.

They strolled into an aisle marked *Medieval & Renaissance*, complete with a full suit of armor standing guard beside the bookcase like some chivalrous literary knight. Blue silk tapestries hung in gentle waves from the ceiling, and a shield with crossed swords gleamed overhead.

Beneath the armor stood a barrel of foam swords, beckoning like treasure. Above it hung a cheeky sign:

"I think the world would be a much better place if there were no guns. Then we could finally focus on important things, like sword fighting, and how to kill a man with one punch."

Evie grabbed a foam sword and pointed it dramatically at Cecelia. "En garde!" she shouted in a terrible French accent.

Cecelia gasped. "Touché!" She dove for the barrel, yanked out a foam sword, and parried with theatrical flair.

They clashed with the grace of caffeinated toddlers—Evie lunged, Cecelia spun. She twirled in a full circle and tapped Evie in the ribs with the tip of her sword.

"You have *wounded* me!" Evie cried, staggering back into a bookshelf. She pressed a hand to her chest and collapsed dramatically like a Shakespearean queen. "Tell my story!"

Both girls burst into giggles.

"You're ridiculous," Cecelia wheezed, brushing hair out of her face.

"You're the one who spun like a damn ballerina!"

They glanced around to make sure no staff had witnessed their duel, then returned the foam swords like two kids who definitely weren't just play-fighting.

"Hey, I like your necklace," Evie said casually, nudging Cecelia. "Saw you tuck it in before our run. Figured you'd take something that pretty off before working out."

"Oh, my key?" Cecelia tugged it out from under her shirt. "I never take it off. It's a family heirloom. I'd die if I lost it."

"Can I see?"

"Sure." Cecelia held it up.

It gleamed even in the bookstore's soft light—a silver key with an ornate design and a blue gem in its center.

"That's the prettiest key I've ever seen," Evie murmured. "What do you think it opens?"

"Oh, I dunno… the gates to Heaven?" Cecelia teased, slipping it back into her shirt.

They passed through a tunnel of leaning books into the YA Fantasy section.

"Did you get your books for class yet?" Evie asked.

"Ha, yeah. Ordered them two weeks ago on Amazon. Online syllabus, Prime shipping—two days, boom, done. Didn't you?"

Evie grimaced. "I may still need to grab a few."

"No biggie. Open your school email and hand me your phone—we'll see what Ray's got before you get robbed at the campus bookstore."

She grabbed Evie's hand and pulled her toward the front desk.

A guy in his late twenties stood behind the counter shelving books under a sign that read *Autographed Copies*. He had brown hair, a beard, and a faded Adema band tee.

"Hey, buddy," Evie called out.

He didn't respond.

Evie rolled her eyes. "EXCUSE ME! WE NEED SERVICE!" she shouted, leaning dramatically over the counter to wave her arms.

"Whoa, Evie, chill," Cecelia whispered, reaching to pull her back.

Just then, the man turned around, startled. He blinked at them like a deer in headlights, then quickly recovered, pulling wireless earbuds from his ears.

"Hi there—sorry. Didn't hear you with these in. Can I help you girls with something?"

"I'm sorry about my friend," Cecelia said quickly. "She didn't mean to climb over the counter—"

"Yes I did," Evie cut in.

Cecelia elbowed her. "She *did* mean to be dramatic, but she's sorry."

The guy laughed. "It's no biggie. What can I help you with?"

"We're looking for books for class," Cecelia said. "Evie's got her list."

She read off the titles while he searched the database.

"I'll print out the locations for you," he said. A moment later, he handed her a still-warm paper. "This tells you which floor, which genre section, and how to find them alphabetically. If you need help, come back—I'll page someone. I'm Ray, by the way."

He scratched his beard.

"Of course you are," Cecelia smiled.

"And hey, before you go, try the café. People say we have the best smoothies in the city. You can pay up there too."

"Thanks, Ray," Cecelia said.

Evie gave him a playful salute, and the two girls disappeared deeper into the stacks.

It was some time before they found everything, but there they were, standing in line at the café, a stack of books in both of their hands.

"Hey Evie, smoothies are on me. Okay?"

"Aw, thanks Cecelia! Do you know what you want to get yet?"

"Oh, most definitely. Have you seen their 'Movie Inspired' menu? Ever since I saw *Zoolander*, I've wanted to try an Orange Mocha Frappuccino. I've never been able to find it anywhere. Yet here we are, and there it is!" she said, pointing excitedly to the poster above the counter.

"I loved that movie," Evie squealed. "Check it!" She spun around and struck a pose, channeling her inner Ben Stiller. "Blue Steel," she winked.

Cecelia chuckled. "That's terrifying."

"Next!" the cashier called.

"Ooo, that's us!" Evie bounced to the counter. "Okay, I think I'm ready for you," she said to the cashier, determination in her eyes.

"I've never seen anyone so excited to order before," the girl laughed. "Alright, what'll it be?"

"I want the Cotton Candy Pop Rock Swirl from *Back 2 the Future*! Extra whip. Make it a large. Go big or go home, baby."

"Oh man, that sounds incredible." Cecelia sighed. "And I'll have a large Orange Mocha Frappuccino—with extra whip, please."

"Are either of you a member of Ray's Cool Club?"

"Ray has a *cool club*?" Evie giggled.

"She means a membership card," Cecelia deadpanned. "No, we're not."

"That's alright," said the cashier. "You can sign up here. It's just ten bucks for the year and you get 20% off books and 15% off all café stuff. Honestly, you'll probably make it back today—especially with that stack your friend has."

"Alright, you've convinced me. I'll do it. And the shakes are still on me. Is it okay if Evie uses the discount on her books too?"

"Totally fine."

After paying, Cecelia handed Evie two bags for her books, and the two of them made their way to a small table at the back near a stage with a piano and full drum set.

"They must have live music here at night," Cecelia said.

"That's not all they have!" Evie shoved a flyer in her face. "Open Mic Night. Every Wednesday and Saturday! We *have* to go."

"Didn't you say your brother's in a band or something?"

"Yup. I used to tag along with him and his friends every week back home. This place is perfect."

"Then yeah," Cecelia smiled. "We're going."

Evie grinned. "So what'd you end up buying back there?"

"Just a few books. I finished *Obsidian* last night, and I had to know what happens next, so I picked up the rest of the series."

"Damn, it was that good?"

"You have no idea."

"What's it about?"

"Okay, there's this girl, Katy. She's a blogger who just moved next door to this hunky alien named Daemon—who's a total jerk at first but secretly in love with her—"

"Wait, an alien? Like green and slimy?"

"No, like *Roswell*-style aliens made of light who can take human form. It's cooler than it sounds, I swear. You can borrow the first book while I binge the rest."

"All three? This week? You're nuts."

"I read books like people binge Netflix. If I can find out what happens next, I *need* to."

Evie laughed. "Alright, deal. I'll check it out. I secretly loved *Roswell*. Katherine Heigl as Isabel Evans? Iconic."

"She was amazing. But hey—we've gotta go if we want to make that 12 PM class."

Evie glanced at her phone. "It's already 11:15? How?! Time flies in this place. Let's move."

They grabbed their bags, tossed their snacks, and power-walked back to the dorms—books in hand, smoothies in tow, and hearts full of caffeine and YA drama.

She hadn't been there long, but Cecelia was already realizing how different college was from high school. They were passing around a sign-in sheet. Guess they figured if you wanted to go to class, it was on you. This never would've flown in boarding school. Though, it was kind of cool that she and Evie shared their first class together. What were the odds? It was Modern European History. They even found seats next to each other. That's where it stopped being cool.

She felt a sharp poke in her back and instinctively spun around, fists half-raised. Behind her, grinning like a cocky game show host, was a guy with short curly brown hair and a wide nose. Not exactly hot, but clearly thought he was.

"Hey sweetie," he said with a lisp, twirling a pen between his fingers. "Name's Brian Watterson. What's yours?"

"Looks like we've got a smooth operator over here," Evie snorted.

Brian oozed confidence like cologne in a locker room. Cecelia pegged him for the type who'd never pass a mirror without flexing.

"I'm Cecelia, and this is Evie," she replied, nudging her friend.

"Where you girls from?"

"I'm from—"

"Why do you wanna know? You a stalker?" Evie asked, deadpan.

"Evie, filter," Cecelia muttered.

"So where are you from, Brian? Ogre Swamp?" Evie smiled mischievously.

He ignored her. "What's your major? Electives suck. I only picked this one because Rate My Professor said this guy's a breeze."

He leaned back, hands behind his head like he was posing for a dorm poster.

"I'm International Business, by the way."

"Wouldn't European History help with that? Understanding different regions, culture, economy? I'm Art History. I love this stuff," Cecelia replied.

"Yeah, totally. Same thought exactly."

Evie snorted. "Hey Cecelia, I think that's the professor."

Brian's feet hit the ground. He straightened instantly.

A tall, skinny man in a button-up and black tie was writing 'Professor Peterson' on the whiteboard.

"Hi class! Sign-in sheet?"

"Over here!" said the guy next to Brian, raising it high. He had a thick southern drawl.

"Has it made it around yet? If not, see me after class. What's your name?"

"Andrew, sir."

"Mind bringing it up here, Andrew?"

"Course," the boy stood and handed it over.

"Thanks. One sec. Here—can you hand these out? Ten per row."

"Pleasure, sir."

"That's my roommate," Brian whispered. "Andrew. If you're free after class, maybe we all grab a bite. I know spots."

"Too bad we've already got plans," Evie replied before Cecelia could speak.

"Shame. Your loss. Maybe tonight?"

Cecelia picked up on Evie's vibe. Her friend never turned down food. Something about Brian rubbed her the wrong way.

"Why don't you give us your number? If plans change, we'll let you know."

Brian scribbled something on a page, tore it out, and handed it over. "My number," he grinned.

"Thanks," Cecelia said.

"What's your problem?" she whispered once he turned around.

"Not so loud." Evie scribbled in her notebook: *I know his type. Big creep. Don't make those friends your first week.*

Cecelia slid the notebook back. *What type?*

Cecelia raised her brows but let it go.

Professor Peterson went over the syllabus and said they'd cover the first three chapters Thursday. Then class ended early.

Evie grabbed Cecelia's arm and led her out before Brian could open his mouth again.

As they crossed campus, Cecelia spotted a familiar face: jet-black hair, olive skin. She couldn't place it. But she *knew* that face.

Erik Taylor

Chapter 6

Being sneaky

"That's right, Jacob. I know all the classes I want to enroll in are closed, but you're going to find me a place in them anyway."

"Mr. Maximus, I understand your family's significant contributions to the school. We've allowed you late registration in recognition of that, but I simply can't create space that isn't there."

Christoph leaned forward, resting his forearms on Jacob's desk. His golden irises glimmered faintly like sunlight dancing on glass. When he spoke, his voice lowered into something melodic, almost musical—each syllable soaked in calm assurance. "Jacob... I really need you to understand how important this is to me. I trust you'll make the space."

Jacob blinked slowly. His fingers hovered over the keyboard. "Yes... absolutely, Mr. Maximus. I'll make it happen."

"Well, that was easy," Christoph said, slipping his phone from his pocket as he left the registrar's office. His golden eyes dimmed back to their usual hazel glow. There was a little swagger in his step now, subtle and confident.

"You really are something else, bro." came a voice from the other end of the call. "Can't believe you just Jedi-mind-tricked admin."

"It was just a nudge. No memory fog. No harm done," Christoph replied coolly.

"You're the one always lecturing *me* about compulsion. And now here you are..."

"Rome." Christoph said simply.

Silence.

"Okay. Yeah. Point taken." Erik finally conceded.

"Anyway, are you on task? Or are you too busy flirting with every skirt on campus?"

"Hey, I am multitasking. Did you *see* that girl in the red skirt just now? Because *I* did."

Christoph rolled his eyes. "You're hopeless. I'm going to track down Cecelia. You tail the guy who tried to hit on her in class."

"What's so special about this dude again?"

"Because that's the plan. Just do your part."

"Fine. But I want lunch after this. Real lunch. Like, Meatball subs *and* dessert."

Christoph hung up without replying.

Erik slid his phone into his jacket pocket and smoothed his chestnut brown waves back with one hand. He adjusted his blazer and strolled across the quad like a model stepping off a runway—head high, shoulders relaxed, eyes casually scanning the crowd. The quad was buzzing with life—students sprawled on blankets, skateboarders weaving between benches, music thumping from someone's Bluetooth speaker.

"Hey, you!" he called.

A redhead in a fitted skirt turned, startled, then immediately smiled. How could she not? He had that dangerous, heartbreaker smile and the kind of swagger that should be illegal.

"Hi... do I know you?"

"Yeah, I'm Erik. We have Contemporary Math together," he said, nodding at the book in her hand.

"We do? I think I would've remembered you."

"Came in late. Real late," he said, flashing his signature grin—the kind that lingered in your thoughts. "What's your name?"

"Margot," she said, twirling a lock of hair.

"Cool name. So... Margot. I work for Max Lounge. You might've heard of it. Kind of a big deal."

Her eyes lit up. "Yeah! That place with the hidden VIP lounge? My roommate was just talking about it!"

"Perfect. I need a little favor."

He leaned in, lowering his voice like he was sharing a secret worth gold. Her laughter echoed a second later, loud and delighted.

Whatever the favor was, she was already sold.

Cecelia and Evette were standing in line at Chipotle, waiting patiently—until Evie dramatically sighed.

"I'm done."

"You're not hungry anymore?" Cecelia asked.

"No. I'm done *waiting*. This is taking forever, Cecelia! My stomach's starting to eat itself."

"You're being so dramatic, Evie," Cecelia giggled. "Relax, it's not that bad."

"No. It is, Cecelia! You don't understand the struggle. This hot bod needs *fuel*. Burrito fuel! Ugh!" She grunted and whipped her hair over her shoulder. "Time to turn on my A-game." She stepped out of line and looked back. "Follow me."

Cecelia hesitated, then trailed behind as Evie marched forward past a disapproving group of girls, a confused middle-aged couple, and a few others Cecelia couldn't bear to make eye contact with. Finally, they reached a cluster of four brawny frat guys.

"Excuse me," Evette said with a sweet smile.

The guys turned like synchronized predators, eyes scanning the two petite girls with instant approval.

"Hey, I'm Evie and this is Cecelia," she said, flashing a practiced smile. "Think we could cut in front? We're on the edge of starvation."

The largest guy grinned, clearly smitten. "Sure, that'd be cool. I'm Anthony. These are my boys."

They nodded their hellos.

"You guys from around here?" Evie asked, flipping her hair again.

"Yeah, we go to Pratt—couple blocks away. You?"

"Same," Evie lied smoothly.

"Next!" the cashier shouted.

Evie beamed. "That'd be me!"

"Burrito or bowl?"

"Burrito! Obviously."

Behind them, one of the guys elbowed Anthony. "I can't believe you let them cut."

Anthony shrugged. "What, you gonna say no to that? And it's not like they're gonna order much. Look at them."

Evie, meanwhile, was on a mission. "I'll need a round of tacos too. Oh—and double chicken," she said to the girl at the toppings line.

The girl gave her a flat look and barely added extra.

Evie popped her hip, leaned in, and sighed *loudly.*

"It's not coming out of your paycheck, girl. Goshhh... And yes, I *know* guac is extra," she added, spinning around to Cecelia. "You want that quesadilla or should I put it on mine?"

"Nope, I got it!" Cecelia chirped.

She smiled sweetly at the boys. "Thanks so much for letting us jump ahead. Seriously—such gentlemen."

The guys beamed. "No problem. Anytime."

The annoyed one grumbled once she turned away. "Yeah, not gonna eat much my ass. They're ordering like a couple linebackers."

"Shut up, man," Anthony muttered.

Cecelia turned to the guy at the start of the line. "I'll need a chicken quesadilla, a burrito bowl, *and* a regular burrito."

The server blinked. "You got it," he said, wide-eyed.

Evie leaned toward Cecelia, whispering through a grin. "A-game, babe. Works every time."

Brian Watterson and his roommate, Andrew, sat under an umbrella in the university courtyard, enjoying their lunch. Brian held a cheeseburger dripping grease all over his tray of French fries.

"That Cecelia girl totally wants me," he said, talking with a mouthful of burger, a streak of ketchup glistening on his chin.

"You're gross, bro," Andrew laughed. "And yeah, I could really tell by the way she casually shut down your invite like it was spam mail."

"Nah, I just need to think of something that'll impress her. A classy girl like that takes time to soak in the Watterson charm."

"Ha!" Andrew let out a loud snort. "Soak in the charm? You make it sound like you're a bubble bath."

"A luxury bubble bath," Brian replied smugly, licking ketchup off his fingers.

A table over, a group of attractive girls had just sat down to eat their lunch, laughing and smiling, chatting amongst themselves. Brian paused mid-bite and cleared his throat theatrically.

"Hotties, six o'clock," he said, nodding subtly.

Andrew turned his head. "Dude! Don't point with your burger."

"Hey, don't look, man. They'll know we're talking about them."

"And? We're a couple of fine-lookin' gentlemen. Want me to take the lead?"

"Nah, not yet. I'm gonna finish this burger first. Gotta keep my strength up for charm deployment."

"Ah, I see. Priorities." Andrew smirked.

Just then, a redhead at the girls' table perked up. "Hey, Erik!"

Brian and Andrew both looked up.

Erik strolled by like he'd walked out of a commercial for impossibly attractive people. Chestnut brown wavy hair, striking blue eyes, blazer fitted to perfection, and a smirk that made women reconsider their life plans.

He turned, spotted the redhead, and gave her a smile that could melt asphalt. "Hey, Margot."

He walked over, nodded coolly to the rest of the table. "Ladies."

The group of girls collectively giggled like they were on cue.

"Where you headed?" Margot asked, twirling a strand of her hair.

"Back to work," he said, adjusting the lapel of his blazer. "First weekend of the semester's always chaos."

"Well, *speaking of chaos*… think you could hook us up with some VIP passes? I really don't wanna wait in line Thursday night."

"I might be convinced… what's in it for me?" he asked, nudging her playfully.

"Oh, I'll think of something," she winked.

"You're all over twenty-one, right? Max Lounge doesn't play."

"Obvi," she said, rolling her eyes. "We're seniors."

"Alright," he said, pulling out a sleek leather wallet and slipping out five glossy black cards. "Just don't call me if Darius gives you trouble. First round's on me."

He handed them over with a wink, then turned to leave, tossing a casual "Later" over his shoulder like it was magic dust.

The girls burst into excited squeals.

"Oh em gee, Margot! *How* do you know that guy?"

"We have math together," she said proudly, fanning herself with the tickets. "Relax, Cynthia."

"He's like… stupid hot," one of the girls whispered.

"You don't even realize how amazing this is," Cynthia said, eyes wide. "That place is nearly impossible to get into on a weekend. Margot just scored us a miracle."

Margot grinned. "No big deal. Only the coolest people go there, and I just happen to be one of them."

Brian stood so fast his tray rattled. "I just figured out our plans for the weekend!" he said, shoving his chair back and brushing crumbs off his shirt.

"What? No, where are you going? Maybe you've forgotten, but I *still* want to talk to the girls!"

"You got this, man." Brian slapped Andrew on the shoulder like he was giving a pep talk to a quarterback. "Now I've gotta catch that guy!"

"Some wingman," Andrew muttered, watching Brian jog off after Erik. He sighed, straightened his collar, and turned toward the table of beautiful girls. Showtime.

In five, four, three, two, one...

Erik smirked to himself as the sound of hurried footsteps echoed behind him.

"Hey man, wait up!" a winded Brian Watterson called out, his breath ragged as he jogged up the sidewalk.

Man, I'm good, Erik thought, quickly replacing his smug grin with a surprised look as he turned around.

"Huh?" he said, feigning confusion. "Me?"

"Yeah, man!" Brian doubled over, hands on his knees, gasping like he'd just run a marathon. "Just... one sec... need to catch my breath."

"Heh. Take your time," Erik said, casually leaning against a bike rack.

"Man, you move fast. Thought I lost you for a sec."

"Do I know you or something?" Erik tilted his head, brows raised in mock curiosity.

"Nah, not exactly. I overheard you talking to some girls back in the courtyard. About Max Lounge."

Erik crossed his arms, his tone cooling. "Ah. I see."

"Yeah—well, no. I mean, yeah. Look," Brian fumbled, his excitement tripping over his words. "I heard that place is the hottest thing in the city, and I really wanna impress this girl I met today. She's a total fox, man. And I thought maybe, you know... some VIP tickets might help seal the deal?"

"So you came sprinting after me in cargo shorts for club tickets," Erik said dryly, rubbing his fingers together. "Forty a piece."

"WHAT? *Forty* a piece?!" Brian squawked. "Dude, I literally just saw you hand out a stack of them to those girls like candy!"

"Yeah," Erik said flatly, "because they're *hot*, and I *like* them. You? You're sweaty and desperate. Those don't exactly scream VIP."

Brian straightened. "Okay, okay, I get it. But come on, help a brother out. I only got a hundred on me—I just need four tickets."

Erik pretended to weigh the decision, tapping his chin. Then he sighed. "Fine. I'll do you a solid. Mostly because your vibe is so tragically thirsty, it's honestly painful to watch. But you owe me. Big tip Thursday night, or I'll tell Darius you're underage."

Brian brightened immediately. "Yeah, totally! You got it. I'm Brian, by the way." He stuck out his hand.

"Erik," he replied coolly, not bothering to shake it. Instead, he reached into his coat and pulled out a sleek stack of tickets.

"Here you go, man," he said, extending the tickets—but then pulled them back at the last second. "Ah-ah-ah. Cash first, chief."

"Oh! Right. Yeah, my bad." Brian scrambled to grab his wallet and handed over a crumpled hundred-dollar bill.

Erik inspected it briefly, then slid it into his blazer and handed over the tickets.

Brian's eyes lit up as he took them, like he'd just been handed keys to the kingdom. He flipped through them—then blinked.

"Wait… there's six here."

"I know," Erik said, already turning to leave. "Bring more girls. In places like Max Lounge, it's all about the optics. A guy rolling in with a squad of gorgeous women? Instant credibility. You're welcome—that tip was free." He snapped his fingers at him and pointed as he walked away. "Later."

Brian stood there, grinning like a kid on Christmas. He looked at the tickets again, eyes wide with excitement.

"Man, that guy was *awesome*. This is gonna impress the *shit* outta Cecelia!"

Brian Watterson

Chapter 7

Tickets

"Ladies, ladies, ladies... today is your lucky day."

The slurred voice came from behind like nails on a chalkboard.

Evie's eyes shot to the ceiling as she raised her hands in mock prayer. *Why me? Why, God? Why?!*

"Hey, Brian," Cecelia said politely beside her.

Evie groaned under her breath and slowly turned in her seat, already bracing for the verbal trash fire.

Brian Watterson stood there with his usual overconfidence, sporting a wrinkled jacket and an infuriating smirk. He waved a shiny black and gold stack of tickets in the air like he'd just invented charm.

"What is it?" Evie snapped, her tone sharp enough to cut glass.

Brian flinched slightly, but covered it with a lazy grin. "What's up your sand trap?"

Cecelia winced.

Brian held up the tickets like a magician revealing his final trick. "Whatever lame plans you girls had for tonight? Cancel 'em. Because *tonight*, we're going VIP at *Max Lounge*."

"Max Lounge?" Cecelia asked.

Evie had already pulled out her phone and was furiously typing. "Hold on—lemme check." She swiped quickly, then turned her phone to Cecelia. "Five stars. VIP Lounge. Speakeasy vibes. Celebrity DJs. Honestly? Kinda tempting."

"You actually *wanna* go?" Cecelia blinked in surprise.

Evie shrugged. "Could be fun. And look, I'm not giving Brian credit—but these tickets? Solid."

Brian beamed. "Boom. Told you. I deliver."

Evie rolled her eyes so hard it was a miracle they didn't detach. "Don't push it, Watterson. This is a one off, not a trend."

Brian ignored the jab. "You two got any friends you wanna bring? I've got two extra…"

"Oh! I met this girl Jen in figure drawing last night," Cecelia said excitedly. "She's hilarious. I'll text her!"

"I'll ask Phoebe," Evie added. "No promises though. She's more books than bass drops."

"Cool, cool. So what dorm are you guys in?" Brian asked. "Andrew and I will swing by around eight."

"Goddard Hall," Cecelia replied. "And Jen's down to go! Just call when you're close."

"Perfect," Brian said, sliding the tickets into his coat with a satisfied grin.

At that moment, Professor Peterson walked into the room, straightening his glasses. "Who's got the sign-in sheet?"

A girl with brown hair across the room raised her hand and stood to deliver it.

Cecelia turned to Brian with a smile. "I'm excited! We'll talk more after class."

Brian gave her a smug nod, watching her turn back to the front of the room.

Got this in the bag, he thought, grinning to himself.

Evie glanced over her shoulder and narrowed her eyes. *Keep dreaming, dude.*

Cecelia had invited Brian and his roommate Andrew to join her and Evette for lunch in the courtyard after class. Now the four of them sat around a table beneath a striped umbrella, plastic trays spread with half-eaten sandwiches and fries.

Cecelia held one of the black-and-gold tickets between her fingers, turning it over with a skeptical frown. "Brian… these say *twenty-one and up.*"

Brian leaned back in his chair, smirking. "Yeah, about that… You girls don't have fake IDs?"

"Excuse me?" Cecelia blinked, scandalized. "I don't—"

"—I usually just use my sister Lana's," Evie cut in smoothly, sipping from her iced tea. "But we probably don't have time to grab one for Cecelia before tonight."

Brian snapped his fingers. "No worries. There's this spot off Canal Street Andrew and I hit up yesterday. Took, like, an hour. We'll take you there after lunch."

"Wait, hold on." Cecelia said, eyes wide. "I don't need a fake ID. That's— *that's a federal crime.* You could literally go to jail."

"Relax," Evie said, waving a fry like a pointer. "We'll get your actual name and photo on it so it's not like you're pretending to be some random chick from Delaware. It's just... creatively fast-tracked documentation."

Cecelia hesitated. "That... technically makes me feel better, but I still don't like it."

"You'll be fine," Evie said with a grin. "It's only illegal if you get caught."

"That's... not how the law works."

"Details," Evie shrugged. "What matters is that you'll get into Max Lounge."

"Awesome," Brian cut in, slapping the table. "Settled. We grab the ID after this—right after I finish this glorious double cheeseburger." He lifted it like a trophy.

Evie raised her soda can in mock salute. "To fake IDs and poor decisions!"

Cecelia groaned. "This better be worth it…"

The group exited the subway on Canal Street, between Broadway and Centre Street. The street was alive and chaotic, riddled with vendors hawking knockoff goods and locals moving briskly.

"Golll-eee! Smells like a fish market on Satan's stovetop down eeere," Andrew said, holding his nose and shaking his head.

"That's because it *is* a fish market, genius," Evette replied, not even glancing his way.

"This part of Canal is right by Chinatown," Cecelia added, brushing her hair behind her ear.

"Well, it didn't smell like this yesterday," Andrew grumbled.

"Yeah, and it wasn't ninety degrees yesterday," Brian shot back.

"Darn global warming. That Al Gore feller's probably sittin' in a recliner right now, just laughin' his ass off. Watch it drop to fifty tonight!" Andrew declared, waving a dramatic finger at the sky.

"We're almost there, man. Calm your southern buns and look around," Brian said, arms out theatrically. "There's our landmark."

"Praise be! That Godzilla cutout—I remember him!" Andrew pointed to a cardboard monster standing proudly outside a storefront.

"Yeah, I saw you posted it last night. Seventy likes on Instagram. And thanks for *not* tagging *me,* by the way. Photocred goes where it's deserved, bro," Brian grumbled.

Evie nudged Cecelia. "This place always has the best bootlegs. My brother used to bring me here when we visited the city. We'd go on black market treasure hunts."

She paused at a cart and picked up a counterfeit Coach purse. "You could never tell from the outside. She's beautiful."

"My mother would scream fashion suicide and ask a priest to exorcise the bag if I brought one of those home," Cecelia laughed.

"Put that down, Evette. We're almost there," Brian called back, pointing to a storefront with a faded red awning.

Evie sighed dramatically but placed the purse down. She and Cecelia followed the boys into the store, the bell jingling overhead.

"It's really tight in here," Cecelia said, squeezing between racks.

"That's because this place is stuffed with treasure," Evie replied, scanning the walls. "Look at those bootleg anime figures. That one has Sailor Moon's face on Naruto's body—iconic."

"I like their bootleg watch collection. I'm not above a fake Rolex," Brian added proudly, tapping on the glass case.

"Focus, people!" Andrew called from the front. "We're here to get Cecelia a fake ID!"

He stopped at the counter, scanning the shop. "Hey, Brian. Do you see that little china ma—"

Evie narrowed her eyes. Danger.

"...uhh, guy from yesterday?" Andrew stammered, realizing too late.

"Andrew," Evie said, crossing her arms. "Were you about to say 'China man'?"

"I—no! I mean, yeah, I guess I was. Shit, I didn't mean anything by it. We always said that back home. I know it's not okay. I'm sorry, y'all. Really."

Cecelia placed a gentle hand on his arm. "It's okay, Andrew. It's just... maybe retire that one for good."

"Done. Retired. Gone. Forever," he said sincerely.

"You're good," Evie said, already wandering. "Cecelia, come on. Let's ditch the cavemen."

They slipped down a cramped aisle lined with bootleg DVDs, dusty anime figurines, and suspicious 'energy supplements.'

Then Evie stopped cold. Her eyes lit up.

"Jack. Freaking. Pot," she whispered, lifting a sleek black katana with painted blue petals on the sheath.

"Evie... I don't think you're supposed to—"

"CAN'T CHU READ SIGN?!" a voice boomed.

Both girls jumped and turned to see a man with slick silver hair, a dramatic curled mustache, and round sunglasses—indoors, of course. His accent was thick. *Too* thick.

"Sign say, 'No touch swords,' lady!"

Startled, Evette quickly sheathed the sword and placed it back.

"I'm sorry! I just thought it was really cool and wanted to show my friend."

"You like? Wu give good deal."

"How good?"

"Seventy dolla. Sword come with stand it sit on."

Evie squinted at him. "I'm a broke college girl with big dreams. I'll do fifty—and throw in the gold brass knuckles from that case."

"What are you going to do with brass knuckles?" Cecelia asked, incredulous.

"I don't know. Carry them in my purse? We live in the city now. I'm petite but I'm not helpless."

"Hmm, Wu say sixty five!" he countered.

"Fifty or no deal," Evie said, standing her ground.

Mr. Wu grinned. "You haggle like tiger-mama. You got deal."

"Yes!" Evie fist-pumped the air.

Mr. Wu shuffled over to the glass case, grabbed the gold knuckles, then carried the katana and accessories to the register. He wrapped the blade in cloth, placed it in a long box, and rang it all up.

"Okay, tough cookie. Fitty-five dollar."

Evie narrowed her eyes. "You said fifty."

Wu paused, deadpan. "Wu test you. You pass. You sharp lady."

He cackled, pleased, and handed her the goods with a wink. She took the bag pleased with herself and removed the golden knuckles and placed them into her purse. Then Mr. Wu turned to Brian and twisted the ends of his mustache.

"Okay, what can Wu do for you?" Mr. Wu asked, twirling one end of his mustache with a pinky.

"Well, you see, Mr. Wu, these fine ladies are actually with us," Andrew replied, puffing out his chest just a little.

"Ohhh, you boys got ladies with you?" Wu said, raising his eyebrows theatrically. "You cool guys, huh? You here to impress deez gurrrls?"

"Yes— I mean no— I mean—" Brian cut in before Andrew could dig a hole. "We're actually here for your… uh… special. The blonde over there needs your 'special.'"

"I see," Mr. Wu said, rubbing his hands together and wiggling his fingers like a cartoon villain. "Wu understand. Okay, everybody come with Wu to the back. Wu give Blondie the 'special.'"

He led them through a pair of dark blue curtains printed with white Chinese characters and ninja stars. The small room they entered was even tighter than the storefront, dimly lit, and smelled faintly of incense and plastic.

"Okay Blondie, you go stand over there and Wu take your picha."

"Oh, you mean me?" Cecelia blinked and stepped behind the camera nervously.

"Yes, yes. Right there. Now look at me—smile, but no teeth, okay? Wu like mystery in face."

He snapped a few pictures, muttering things like "Oooh, yes. Fierce. Like noodle warrior." Then he waved her over to his computer.

"Okay, now Wu load these up. You tell Wu which picha you like best."

"Oh, that third one's great!" Evie chimed in before Cecelia could even answer.

"Yeah," Cecelia nodded. "That one. Let's go with that."

"Good choice, very strong cheekbone. Okay, now: which state you want?"

"Well… I've always wanted to live in California. Do you make that?" Cecelia asked.

"Wu make *all* the states," he said proudly. "Even Delaware. No one ask for Delaware, but Wu still do it. You want to be Sandy? You look like a Sandy. Like from Grease movie with John Travolta." He chuckled to himself.

Cecelia smiled politely but shook her head. "No, I want to use my real name. And keep the same birthday—just make me twenty-two, please."

"Ohhh, so polite. Wu respect that. Okay polite Blondie. Wu make magic. Just fill out this sheet."

He handed her a clipboard and a chewed-up pen. Cecelia filled it out quickly and passed it back. Wu nodded with approval and got to work on his very illegal arts and crafts.

Cecelia joined the others, who were lounging on a cracked leather couch in the corner of the room.

"So, how'd you guys find this place?" she asked.

"Well, I overheard these nice girls talkin' about gettin' fake IDs Tuesday while Brian was gettin' the tickets," Andrew began. "Said they picked 'em up on Canal Street, so I told Brian and we came down yesterday."

"It was hilarious," Brian jumped in. "We were walking around aimlessly, about to start asking random strangers on the street—"

"—when suddenly out of nowhere, Mr. Wu appears like a vending machine genie," Andrew finished. "He's all like—" he cleared his throat and did his best impression: "'You boys need fake ID?'"

"And naturally, we followed him in like a couple of dumbasses," Brian laughed.

Cecelia tilted her head. "Wait, you called him old? He has silver hair, but he doesn't look older than his late twenties."

"Sweetie," Evie said, gently patting her arm, "you might want to get your eyes checked. Mr. Wu's old enough to be your dad. A *hot* dad, but still."

"I guess it's just dark in here… or he really takes care of his skin." Cecelia blushed.

Evie gave her a look, then turned to the boys. "—And wow. You two idiots are *lucky*. Do you even *realize* how much trouble you could've gotten into if you asked the wrong person?"

"Yeah," Cecelia added, thankful Evie was saving her from embarrassment. "Like I said before—federal offense."

"I *know*," Andrew said with a shrug. "But we were gettin' desperate."

"Didn't have to be," Brian added. "Wu found *us*. Divine intervention."

"OKAY!" Mr. Wu shouted from across the room. "Wu finish! Come here now!"

They stood as he waved them over.

"Now this one," Wu said, tapping the fresh ID card, "this one Wu no ring up. Cash only."

"Not a problem," Cecelia said, digging into her purse. "The guys told me. I came prepared."

She pulled out a crisp fifty-dollar bill.

"This enough?"

"Yeah, yeah, this good." Wu nodded and handed her the card. "Here Blondie. Take. Still warm."

Cecelia took the ID, inspecting it carefully. It looked flawless. Clean. Crisp. Exactly like the examples Evie had shown her online.

"Thank you so much, Mr. Wu," she said.

"No problem, Blondie. You come back next time you in city, Wu give you good deal. You bring Wu noodles from Joe's Shanghai, we call it even."

They all laughed as he escorted them out. The group waved goodbye and exited into the sun-drenched street.

"That was pretty cool, guys," Cecelia said, her voice bright. "Thanks for bringing us."

"Yeah, don't mention it," Brian said, puffing up a bit. "Tonight's gonna be epic. Andrew and I are gonna go grab some new threads uptown—if you ladies want to join."

"Yeah," Andrew said. "Made the mistake of not bringin' any dress clothes, but Pa gave me his credit card for 'eee-mergencies.' This qualifies."

Evie grinned. "Appreciate the offer, gentlemen, but Cecelia and I have some errands. Call us when you're back downtown."

"You got it," Brian said, visibly disappointed.

"Bye ladies! See you tonight!" Andrew said, tipping his invisible cowboy hat.

"Later, boys," Evie said with a wink, walking off as Cecelia followed, katana box swinging at her side like a fantasy heroine returning from a quest.

Wu walked to the back of the store behind the counter and picked up the phone. He dialed a number, and it was answered after just two rings.

"Hey, Sam," said a familiar voice.

"Alright, it's done," Sam replied, his heavy Chinese accent completely gone—his tone crisp and annoyed.

"Good. I'll be expecting them later tonight. Thanks."

"This is the *last* time I pull a favor for you. I *hate* playing up the whole 'mystical Chinatown guy' stereotype, and you *know* I like to keep this place low-key."

"Yeah, but you do it so well! Wait—hold up. Did you wear the fake mustache again?"

There was a long pause on Sam's end.

"...Well? Did you?"

"Two days of my life I'll never get back," Sam muttered. "You guys owe me one."

The voice on the other end exploded into laughter. "YOU *DID*! Oh man, that's too good!"

"Shut up, man. It's not just a mustache. I use a *very* complicated glamour when I do that bit, and you *know* it. Don't gloss over this. You owe me."

"Yeah, yeah, we know."

"I'm coming by the restaurant later. Free drinks and dinner. Tell Darius."

"You got it, bro. Later."
Click.

MAX LOUNGE

Chapter 8

"So... what do you think?" Evie declared, strutting out of the bathroom like it was a damn runway.

She wore a short magenta dress with a rounded black velvet collar that screamed retro rebellion. A tiny black leather jacket slid over her shoulders like second skin. She dropped down to lace up a pair of scuffed black combat boots—because of course she did.

"It's perfect, right?" she said, doing a little spin and then striking a dramatic pose in the mirror. "I look like a punk rock cupcake and I'm not mad about it."

"Oh yeah! You look hot!" Cecelia said, smiling from her bed. "I wish I could pull that off but—"

"Don't you *dare* finish that sentence." Evie's boots stomped across the room with purpose. She marched into the closet like she was conducting a fashion intervention. "This outfit needs... *something.*"

From deep within a cardboard box, Evie began launching accessories over her shoulder with wild abandon. Scarves. Gloves. One suspiciously sequined beret.

"Found it!" she shouted in triumph, spinning around with a bowler hat in hand. She popped it onto her head—a black bow perfectly perched on its rim—and beamed. "NOW I'm ready."

"I was going to say, 'won't you be cold?'" Cecelia said, laughing.

"Me?" Evie scoffed. "Cold? Please. Sass is a natural insulator."

But then she stopped mid-victory pose, tilting her head. "...Wait. Cecelia. Why are you still in your *bathrobe?*"

Cecelia stood awkwardly by her bed, eyeing three elegant dresses laid out like sacrificial offerings. Each one looked like it belonged at a royal garden party.

"I just don't know, Evie." She bit her lip. "I've never really been to a club before." Her voice cracked with nerves, and she clutched her robe tighter.

Evie softened. Then smiled.

"Girl. You leave that to me. But first—what *is* this lineup?" She picked up one of the dresses and held it against herself in the mirror, giving it a judgmental squint. "This is stunning. You look like you'd accept an award for Best Behavior in this."

Cecelia flushed. "My mom's a fashion designer. She picked out most of these for events. I'm not... used to choosing my own clothes."

Evie froze. "*That* explains the Coach purse comment."

By now, she was halfway inside Cecelia's closet. "No shade, babe, but you've got designer hostage vibes in here."

Then she gasped. "HELLO. What is *this?*" Evie emerged with a deep red dress, eyes wide like she'd uncovered a buried treasure chest.

"This," she declared, holding it up with reverence, "is what you're wearing tonight."

"What? No. Evie, it's freezing and that dress is practically *backless.*"

"We'll be inside. Dancing. Surrounded by sweaty college boys and overpriced vodka tonics. You'll be sweating in five minutes." Evie tossed her a pair of black tights. "Add these. Boom. Cozy *and* smokin'."

"And *this*—" she flung over a small black leather jacket, a twin to her own. "Now we're *twinning*, baby."

Cecelia caught it all in her arms, blinking. "Wait... I don't even have shoes that match—"

"Combat boots. I've got an extra pair. Size?"

"Seven and a half."

"Girl, say less. They're yours."

Cecelia gave her a look of total surrender, gathering the outfit and disappearing into the bathroom without another word.

Evie waited until the door clicked shut.

Then she grinned smugly to herself in the mirror.

"Mission: Hot Angel—*activated.*"

Evie flopped onto her bed and tugged her laptop onto her thighs. She pulled her legs in under her like a smug little tech gremlin and typed in: *Max Lounge NYC*. A glamorous, neon-lit site filled her screen.

"Oh *wow*," she said aloud, eyes scanning the homepage. "Cecelia! This place has five-star reviews for their *restaurant!*"

"That's great," Cecelia called from behind the bathroom door. "But I don't think Brian's taking us to dinner. He said the tickets were for the club."

Evie narrowed her eyes at the screen. "But they have *mac 'n' cheese balls,* Cecelia. MAC. N. CHEESE. BALLS."

She let out a dramatic sigh. "Ugh. I just got emotionally invested in carbs for nothing."

A beat passed. Then she called out, "Sooo... what do you think about Brian?"

Cecelia's muffled voice floated back. "I dunno. He's nice enough. Just not really my type."

"I know. I can't get past that Brillo pad he calls hair."

"What'd you say?"

"I said: How about Andrew? He's not bad. Slightly less tragic on the eyes."

Cecelia giggled. "He seems sweet. Still not really my type, though."

Truth was, Cecelia didn't *have* a type. Not yet. An all-girls' boarding school didn't exactly set you up for a healthy dating portfolio.

"How about you?" she asked Evie.

"Oh, I'd pick Andrew over Brian in a heartbeat," Evie said. "But that's like saying I'd rather stub my toe than step on a Lego."

Cecelia laughed. "What *is* your problem with Brian, anyway?"

Evie paused, her fingers hovering over the trackpad. "Honestly? He just… gives me a weird vibe. Like, try-hard energy. Something about him doesn't sit right."

BZZZZZZZ. RING RING.

Cecelia's phone buzzed from the dresser. Evie rolled off the bed and picked it up.

"It's that cheapo Brian!" she called.

"Just answer it!" Cecelia shouted. "And he's *not* cheap just because he's not buying us dinner!"

Evie rolled her eyes and answered. "Evette speaking, secretary to Miss White."

"Yo, I'm in the lobby. Grab Cecelia and come down."

Evie blinked. "Wait—you're *already here?*"

"Yeah. We gotta get there by eight, eight-thirty. Doors at nine. I don't wanna risk them charging us again if we're late."

She pulled the phone away from her ear. "Cecelia! He says he's *already here!*"

"What?!" Cecelia's voice pitched in panic.

"He says we're gonna be late and he doesn't wanna pay. Also—no dinner."

Cecelia groaned. "Ask him why he's here *so* early! We said 8:15!"

Evie brought the phone back up. "Brian, Cecelia wants to know why you're pulling this premature nonsense. And are we going to dinner or what?"

"What? No! Why would we be going to dinner?" he sounded genuinely confused. "The tickets say we can get in as VIPs if we're there by nine. I'm not risking it."

Evie hung up.

"Well," she said loudly, "he's here early *and* we're not getting fed. I *told* you he was a cheapo."

"I never said I didn't believe you!" Cecelia groaned. "Ugh, just tell him we'll be down in ten. I haven't even started my makeup."

Evie texted instead. *Be down in ten, Brillo head. Calm your ticket-greedy ass.*

She tossed the phone on the bed and muttered to herself, "I *really* don't like that guy."

Just then, Cecelia stepped out of the bathroom, and Evie's mood did a full 180.

"Oh. My. *God.*" she said, standing up. "You look like a red velvet dream."

Cecelia blushed. "Too much?"

"No. It's just enough." Evie circled her like a stylist on a reality show. "But we're missing one thing."

She reached into Cecelia's dress and pulled out the shiny vintage key pendant she was wearing and draped it gently over the front of her dress.

"This," she said, "is pure *eye candy*. It ties everything together."

A little invasive much but Cecelia smiled, a little more confident.

Evie grabbed her purse, slung it over her shoulder, and headed for the door. "Now come on, girl. Let's go before that walking red flag calls again."

As the elevator doors opened to the lobby, Evie and Cecelia stepped out— and immediately spotted Brian pacing like an angry gym rat. He wore a skin-tight black muscle tee that clung to his torso like shrink-wrap, his aggressively pointy man-nipples threatening to pierce the fabric. The shirt was tucked into dark blue True Religion jeans, accented by a shiny black belt and silver buckle. Polished black dress shoes completed the look.

He looked like he was about to get bottle service at a Jersey Shore reunion.

Andrew, on the other hand, was chatting up the front desk girl, looking perfectly pleasant in a baby blue button-down under a navy blazer, khakis, and neatly parted blond hair. He looked like a college catalog model. Brian looked like a club bouncer with bad opinions.

"There you are," Brian snapped the second he saw them. "Took you long enough. Evette, you said ten minutes—it's been almost *twenty*. We're gonna be late and if we don't get in, it's on you."

Evie smiled sweetly. "Don't you want us looking *cute* next to you, Brillo-head?" she batted her lashes. "Perfection takes time, and you're welcome." Then her voice turned cold. "Now why exactly do we need to be there *so early*? You been before? Is there, like, a secret handshake to get in?"

Brian shifted. "No, but I heard it's the best underground spot in the city. All the cool people go. And we've got VIP passes—only good if we get there before nine. I'm not risking that."

He looked around. "So where are Jen and Phoebe? We gotta go."

"Phoebe's not coming," Evie said flatly.

"And we were gonna pick up Jen on the way," Cecelia added, her voice quieter.

Brian huffed. "Ugh. This is *bullshit*."

Evie's eyes flashed. "Oh, *relax*, Nipzilla," she snapped. "You didn't say you were showing up twenty minutes early. You didn't say there wouldn't be dinner. You didn't say *anything*, so don't pin your lack of planning on us."

"Maybe you should just go without us," Cecelia offered.

"Nope. We didn't just get all cute for nothing," Evie said, slinging an arm around Cecelia's shoulder. "We're going, and we're gonna have a *great* time—"

She turned to Brian and gave him a razor-sharp glare. "Even if we have to drag your sorry ass along for the ride."

She held the stare for a beat, then turned back to Cecelia, all sugar again.

"We can always ditch him later," she grinned.

Brian scowled. "You *do* know I can hear you, right?"

"Oh no," Evie said mock-gasping. "Was I supposed to care?"

He folded his arms. "Well, then Jen's just gonna have to meet us there. We're not gonna make it if we stop for her."

"She doesn't know where she's going, Brian," Cecelia said, frowning. "And *you* didn't tell us we were taking the subway."

Brian's smug expression dropped. "Fine. Then we'll all have to split a cab."

Andrew walked over, still smiling. "That's fine by me. I don't see why this is such a big deal, Brian. No need to hassle these lovely ladies."

He turned to them, eyes twinkling. "And might I say—*dang*, y'all look stunning tonight."

"Why, thank you, Andrew," Cecelia said, brightening.

"I'll head out and hail us a cab," he offered.

"Now *that's* how you treat a lady," Evie said, glaring at Brian. "You should be taking notes."

Brian muttered under his breath, "Bitch."

Evie didn't flinch. "I *heard* that."

Cecelia quickly looked at her phone. "I'll text Jen. Tell her to wait in her lobby and come out when she sees us."

As she typed, Evie yanked Brian aside by the sleeve, dragging him toward the elevator and out of earshot. She spun, grabbed his collar, and yanked him down so they were nose to nose.

"Let me spell it out for you, Captain Spray-Tan," she hissed. "You're off to a *disastrous* start. And if you think for one second that after pulling this crap, Cecelia is going to fall for your discount cologne and dollar-store attitude— you're out of your Brillo-haired, Shrek-faced, cheap-ass *mind.*"

She shoved him backward and walked away without another word.

"Let's go help Andrew," she said sweetly, linking arms with Cecelia and leading her out the front doors.

Outside, standing proudly next to a yellow cab, Andrew grinned like a southern gentleman.

"Your chariot awaits, ladies," he said, opening the back door with a theatrical bow.

"Oh, Andrew, you're too good!" Cecelia said, giggling as she slid into the backseat. "Thank you!"

Evie followed behind her and gave Andrew a playful salute. "You're winning major points tonight, sir."

"You're riding shotgun, Brian," Andrew said, closing the door behind them.

"Fine by me," Brian muttered, clearly still salty.

The cab driver peeked at them in the mirror. "Alright, kids—where to?"

"Brittany Hall, 55 East 10th," Evie replied. "We're grabbing a friend first. Then Max Lounge—433 Broadway."

"Copy that," the cabbie nodded, pulling into traffic.

"So what've y'all heard about this spot?" Andrew asked, turning halfway in his seat.

"I heard they've got a hidden VIP room behind a fake bookshelf," Brian said, suddenly animated again. "Like, legit secret entrance. If you go on a good night, you can spot celebs."

"I read there's a five-month waiting list to even get in that room," Cecelia added, lighting up. "And apparently Billie Eilish has been spotted there a few times."

Everyone blinked at her.

"I mean—I only looked it up earlier today, so who knows?" she said, blushing.

"That sounds amazing," Evie cut in. "But I read the restaurant menu is *insane*. Lobster tacos, chili honey wings, and the mac and cheese balls of my dreams."

"Evette," Cecelia laughed, "for the last time, we're *not* going for dinner tonight."

"Don't ruin my fantasy," Evie huffed. "Let me pretend I'm going for the food and *not* for the sweaty dancing."

"Alright, kids. Brittany Hall," the cab driver said as he pulled up to the curb.

Brian lowered his window and leaned out. "Hey Jen, over here! Climb in the back—unless you'd rather sit on my lap?" he added with a greasy grin.

Jen didn't miss a beat. "Ha. Ha. Funny," she deadpanned, brushing past the window without looking at him.

"Creep," she muttered under her breath as she opened the door and squeezed into the seat beside Cecelia.

Cecelia lit up. "That's a gorgeous dress, Jen! You look amazing in purple—I wish I had the curves to pull that off."

Jen smiled, the compliment catching her off guard. "Thanks, Cecelia. Oh wow—your necklace! That key is *stunning*. Is it antique? That blue stone looks real."

"It was my grandmother's," Cecelia said, fingers brushing the key at her chest. "I think it's a sapphire. I always wear it, just usually tucked under my clothes. My dad says it's supposed to bring me good luck."

She glanced toward Evie with a grin. "Evie convinced me to let it show tonight."

Evie gave her an approving wink. "Damn right I did. That necklace is a vibe."

"Alright, next stop: Max Lounge!" she shouted, throwing a fist in the air. "WOO!"

"Somebody's ready to dance," Jen laughed.

"You *know* it," Evie said. "And maybe fight a man if necessary. Let's roll!"

The cab peeled off into the night, headed straight for neon lights, questionable decisions, and whatever secrets Max Lounge was hiding behind its polished doors.

"Alright, here we are. That'll be thirty-two-fifty," the cab driver said, tapping the meter.

Brian turned around, already in accountant mode. "Okay, five of us—that's seven bucks each with tip."

Evie stared at him like he'd just asked her to Venmo him for breathing air. "Are you *seriously* making us pay for the cab you insisted on taking? Because *we* were 'gonna make *you* late?' You're unbelievable, Brian. And by the way, seven bucks isn't even enough for a decent tip."

Brian scowled but didn't say anything.

"Don't worry about the tip, darling. I've got it covered," Andrew said, resting a reassuring hand on her shoulder and giving her a wink.

Brian stuck out his hand to collect the fare like a middle school lunch monitor.

"Alright, here you go, man," Brian said, handing the cab driver the wad of crumpled bills. He slammed the door with a little too much attitude, then turned toward the group waiting on the curb with both arms raised like he was hosting a game show. "Come on, everyone—let's get this party started!"

Evette crossed her arms and leaned in to Cecelia. "Oh look, now he's Mister Cool Party Guy. Whoopee."

Cecelia stared up at the building, her brow furrowed. "This doesn't look like a club. It looks like a hotel…"

"I dunno," Evie said, tilting her head. "It's giving me *elite prep school with a scandalous secret dormitory.* Like something straight out of *Gossip Girl*—but with less Chuck Bass and more bad decisions."

The building was sleek and imposing—walls of pale marble, tall black-tinted windows, and a brushed metal logo gleaming near the top left corner. It read *Max Lounge* in clean, serif font. The crest-shaped emblem next to it gave the whole place the feel of a private academy—or maybe a secret society headquarters.

"Not much of a line out here," Cecelia noted, scanning the mostly empty sidewalk.

"Yeah," Evie said, lowering her voice as they headed toward the entrance. "So remind me why we needed these *VIP passes of legend* again?" She raised an eyebrow. "We could've walked right."

Jen snorted. "Facts."

"I'm still not convinced this isn't just a very fancy trap," Evie added as they approached the front doors. "If we walk in and there's a guy in a velvet cape asking if we've accepted Max Lounge into our hearts, I'm turning around."

"Deal," Cecelia whispered with a smile.

Walking into Max Lounge felt like stepping into an alternate universe—one where prep school kids went to class to party. A set of tinted sliding doors greeted them, emblazoned with a black and silver crest that read *MAX* down the middle, and a ribbon at the bottom that said *Lounge*. Three fully bloomed red roses framed the emblem like a twisted coat of arms.

At the front desk stood a peppy redhead in a literal Catholic schoolgirl uniform, flanked by two mountain-sized bouncers. Her black blazer bore the same Max Lounge crest on the breast pocket, and her outfit was completed with a white button-up shirt, skinny black tie, short gray pleated skirt, and black knee-high socks. It was absurd—and Cecelia thought, somehow, totally awesome.

"Do you guys have reservations for dinner, or just here for the club tonight?" the girl chirped, eyeing them as her red curls bounced.

Everyone looked to Brian.

"Uh, I've got these five VIP tickets," he said, holding them up. "Some guy gave 'em to me the other day."

She accepted the tickets, side-eying him with a skeptical smirk. Then her expression lit up as she scanned them.

"Oh wow. You're friends of *Erik's*," she said with a little giggle.

Brian scratched the back of his head. "Oh yeah, that was his name. Kinda hard to read his signature—thought it said Cupid, ha."

"That's because it *does* say Cupid," she deadpanned, her smile dropping. "He signs everything that way. Guess he thinks he's God's gift to women." Her words dripped with acid. "Not like I care or anything."

She motioned toward the left. "Go on through."

Then, all sweetness again: "They're cool, Darius. They're with Erik," she said to the bouncer, who unclipped the red velvet rope and nodded.

As they stepped inside, Cecelia blinked. It was like her father's study had exploded into a Gatsby-themed rave. The walls were wrapped in ornate red-and-gold 1920s wallpaper, with antique gold sconces and heavy mahogany bookshelves lining the room. Twin staircases curved elegantly to an upper balcony, where more patrons gathered. Chandeliers glittered from above, and Cecelia couldn't stop staring at the one hanging directly in the center of the room.

"Evie—look at that!" she said, pointing.

Evie immediately pulled out her phone. "That's *going* on the feed."

Below the chandelier, vintage library desks had been repurposed for college drinking games. A glossy black tile dance floor stretched beyond them, surrounded by clusters of leather furniture that looked like they were stolen from an old-money mansion.

"You seeing this?" Brian shouted, arms outstretched like he built the place. "Isn't this awesome?"

Cecelia tilted her head. "Honestly? It kind of reminds me of my dad's study."

"Your dad has a study? What are you guys, British or something?" Brian snorted.

"Well, yeah—"

Brian cut her off and spun toward the bar. "So who wants a shot? You girls want a shot?"

"I don't really drink," Evie said flatly.

"Yeah, me neither. I'm good with dancing," Cecelia added.

"I'll take one!" Jen chimed in brightly. "Me!"

Brian grinned. "Ah, come on. Don't be shy. First time for everything, right? I scored you VIP tickets—I can score you drinks, too."

He led the way to the bar and called out, "Hey, Erik!"

A tall, handsome bartender turned around, brow raised. Chestnut brown wavy hair, striking blue eyes. He looked like he'd just stepped out of a dream and into a cologne commercial.

"Do I know you?" Erik asked, clearly confused.

"Yeah, man! Tuesday, remember? You gave me these tickets. Told me to come by tonight."

Erik stared a moment, then scratched his head. "Oh… yeah. That *does* sound like me."

He looked Brian over, unimpressed. "You do know it's only nine, right? The tickets say the party starts at eleven. You don't exactly look like you came for the beer pong tournament dressed like that..." He gestured vaguely at Brian's tight black tee and True Religion jeans.

"But the tickets said 'doors at nine!'"

"That's when we open," Erik said with a laugh. "Lemme guess. First time at a club?"

That's when Evie stepped forward and jabbed her finger into Brian's chest. "Wait a damn minute. *This guy* made us rush out of our dorm, tried to guilt trip *me* about being late, made *us* pay for the cab—and the club isn't even open yet?! *That's* why there was no line outside!"

She whirled to Cecelia. "Girl, some friend you've got."

Cecelia threw her hands up. "Don't blame me! You talked me into going!"

"Because of the five-star reviews!" Evie groaned. "And we're not even eating here! I *hate* you right now."

Brian raised his hands like a traffic cop. "Whoa, whoa—ladies! No need to get your panties in a twist." He chuckled at his own joke. No one else did. "Let's just take some shots and chill here with Erik. Bet he knows some great drinks. Right, bro?"

Erik stared back at him. "I'm not your bro."

Brian smirked. "Hook us up with a round of Fireball, yeah?"

Erik rested his forearms on the bar and gave Brian a slow, satisfied smile. "Not until I see some I.D."

Brian confidently pulled out his wallet and offered his card.

Erik took one look and barked a laugh. "This is *the worst fake I.D.* I've seen all year." He tilted it toward the light. "Seriously, where'd you get this? Chinatown? Canal Street?"

"It's *real!*" Brian protested, trying to snatch it back.

Erik pulled it away with a wag of his finger. "Nuh uh. Try again, McLovin."

Andrew leaned in to Jen. "Told him not to go with Hawaii."

Erik shook his head. "Yeah, I'm keeping this. Better me than the cops."

Then he looked to the others. "You guys got ID?"

Evie and Cecelia handed theirs over. He checked, nodded, handed them back. Andrew too. Jen had mysteriously vanished—smart girl.

"You're all good," Erik said.

He turned to Brian. "You know what? I'll do you a solid—just this once. One round, on me. 'A' for effort." He poured five shots of amber liquid and slid them across.

Brian, still sulking, handed over three twenties.

"Thanks, bro."

Erik narrowed his eyes. "Not your bro, doofus."

He turned to the girls. "You ladies have a good night." Then he winked at Evie before walking off to refill a pitcher at the pong tables.

Evie handed out the shots. Brian glared at her the whole time.

Then, predictably, Brian raised his glass first.

"To gettin' *crunk!*" he said proudly, as if he'd invented the phrase.

Evie rolled her eyes. "To 2am dollar slices."

Jen chimed in, "To a great night and new friends!"

Cecelia thought for a moment. "To getting back in one piece?"

Andrew grinned. "Just take the shot and think about Jesus—'cause we're all going to hell after tonight."

They clinked glasses, laughter bubbling around the circle, and threw back the shots.

"Woo!" Jen shouted. "That was *good!* Come on boys—beer pong time!"

She grabbed Brian and Andrew by the wrists and hauled them toward the game tables like a woman on a mission.

Evie and Cecelia stayed behind for a second, catching their breath.

"Well," Evie muttered, "that was a lot."

Cecelia nodded. "And it's only nine fifteen."

"'Bout time we were rid of them," Evie spat. "Remind me to thank Jen later. That girl's pretty cool for taking one for the team."

"They're not *that* bad," Cecelia said, smirking. "Okay—Brian's not the coolest, but hey, they got us in here. It's not like we have to be friends with them after tonight. Try to be optimistic, Evie. The night is young… and we're hot." She let out a laugh.

"Speaking of hot…" Evie turned toward the bar. "Let's go talk to that hottie Erik. Did you *see* those eyes? Ugh. I could just drown in them. They're blue like the ocean after a storm."

"Wow, never would've taken you for a poet."

"I'd jump his bones given the chance," Evie said bluntly.

"Aaand you ruined it. My goodness, Evette—you hornball," Cecelia giggled.

Right on cue, Erik strolled over.

"You know you don't have to just stand there looking gorgeous," he said, gesturing for them to come closer. "Other than the pong tournament, it's pretty dead in here. Pull up a seat."

"Yeah?" Cecelia asked, suddenly shy.

"Yeah," he smiled. "Also, sorry about putting you on the spot earlier. I just really don't like that guy."

"Didn't you *give* him the tickets in the first place?" Evie asked, eyes narrowing with curiosity.

Erik snorted. "First off, that tool stopped me outside Tuesday—definitely *not* my friend. Saw the Max Lounge logo on my blazer and wouldn't stop bugging me. Tried to haggle, too."

"Told you he was a cheapo," Evie muttered to Cecelia.

"So I gave him a few extras I had and told him to piss off," Erik shrugged. "Figured he wouldn't show up till the rush when I could pawn him off on someone else. And second? I *knew* he wasn't twenty-one. Some pricks need to be humbled. Builds character," he added with a grin.

"Pshhh, typical loser. Leave it to Brian to annoy his way into a club," Evie said. "Though it'll take more than a fake ID roasting to humble *him*."

"I like you," Erik said to her. "You're a funny little one." Then his eyes flicked to Cecelia. "So where are you girls from?"

"I'm from—" Cecelia started, but he cut her off with a hand up.

"Wait. Let me guess." His grin was boyish and cocky. "College girls, obviously. NYU, I'm betting—since you came in with that dork. But you're not *from* the city. Hmm…"

He leaned against the bar, eyes narrowing playfully at Cecelia. "You—the pretty blonde. Confident posture. Polite. Classy. You blush when someone even hints at anything dirty. And that outfit? Money. You're from Westchester. Or maybe the Hamptons."

Cecelia stared, stunned. "You're *good!*" she said, pointing. "Hamptons. But I'm *not* a priss."

"Now do Evie!" she added, excited.

"Oh would I…" he winked. "Let's see. Tan skin. Killer style. Loud mouth. Big energy. Not Cali, but you *do* look like you surf. You've got Jersey written all over you. And not just any Jersey—*South* Jersey. The classy part."

Evie smacked his arm. "Arrogant? Huh? It's not arrogance when you can *back up* what you put down, pretty boy."

"Oh, really? Not arrogant?" he grinned. "I bet you're the gambling type too."

"Are you challenging me, *boy?*" she laughed.

"Maybe." He shrugged. "I bet you couldn't beat me in quarters."

"You're looking at the total package. I could outplay, outdrink, and outdance you any day."

"Well, then." His smirk widened. "Pick your poison, *Eves.*"

"*Eves?*" she raised a brow. "No one's ever called me that... I kinda like it. And I like Captain Morgan."

"Let's do it then, *Erii,*" she teased.

Erik raised a brow. "Oh, *you* think you're funny. Where'd you hear that?"

She shrugged.

"Only my best friend calls me that. But I think I like how it sounds when *you* say it," he said with a low smirk.

Evie bit her bottom lip, holding his gaze. "Oh do you, Erii?"

A new voice cut in—smooth, amused, and teasing. "Does it make you feel all hot and bothered?"

The girls turned to see a tall, striking man in his twenties stroll behind the bar. Jet-black messy hair, golden skin, a black V-neck under a Max Lounge blazer—and the most dangerous smile Cecelia had ever seen.

Cecelia's breath caught. She *knew* that face. But from where?

"Ladies, meet my best friend and partner in crime—*the Magnificent Christoph Maximus.*"

Christoph gave a theatrical bow, then reached for Cecelia's hand.

"Just Christoph," he said, winking. "And what might *your* name be?"

Their eyes met. Cecelia froze.

She'd seen that face before.

In her *dreams.*

He looked *exactly* like that fallen angel.

"I'm—" she paused, stunned. Her brain scrambled with a thousand questions. Did they grow up near each other? Was he in one of those prep schools? Did their families know each other?

Instead, what came out was: "Are those… contacts?"

"Well, it's a pleasure meeting you, *Are Those.* That's quite a mouthful. Do you have a nickname?" he said with a grin that could melt glaciers.

Cecelia flushed crimson. "Wow. Rude. I'm Cecelia. Cecelia White. And I promise I'm not usually a jerk."

He laughed—a sound like wind chimes in the sun. "Nice to meet you, Cecelia. And it's alright." He winked. "Also? Not contacts."

She was still staring. At his eyes. At his lips. At *everything*.

"You've got quite the grip there." Christoph said, glancing down. She hadn't let go of his hand.

"His eyes are honey brown. Relax, Cecelia," Evie teased. "We get it. He's *pretty.*"

Cecelia snapped back and released him, laughing awkwardly. "Sorry. You… have really smooth hands."

"You know what they say about guys with smooth hands," Evie chimed in.

Christoph turned his megawatt smile on her. "And *what* might your name be?"

"Evette Renee Angelique Lamoureux," she said proudly. "The pleasure's all yours."

"Oh, *indeed* it is," Christoph grinned. "So what are you guys up to? Erii here challenging you to quarters? Hate to break it to you, but if you think you're winning, you're both delusional. He's never lost. No matter what *he* tells you."

"Excuse me?" Erik scoffed. "This spitfire *challenged* me, thank you very much."

"Oh, I most definitely did," Evie said, puffing her chest. "Now… how exactly do you play again?"

"*Wait*—" Erik burst out laughing. "I thought you were the *ultimate party girl?*"

"I *am!*" she said defensively. "I just need a refresher."

Shaking his head, Erik grabbed two beer glasses and filled them with an ounce of rum.

"Okay, rookie. Here's the game. This one on the left's yours, right's mine. I bounce a quarter off the bar. If it lands in *your* glass, you drink. If I miss, you go. We keep going until someone gives up or someone wins by whatever score we set."

He leaned across the bar, eyes locked with hers. "Still game?"

"Bring it on, pretty boy."

"This is going to end badly…" Christoph said, grinning at Cecelia.

"Oh, I don't know about that," she replied. "Kick his ass, Evie!"

Four shots later, Evie was growling with frustration.

Erik flicked the quarter again. It *almost* landed, but she slyly moved the glass.

"Hey! That's cheating," he laughed.

"I don't know what you're talking about." She gave him a grin that said she *absolutely* knew what she was doing.

"You've gotta take the shot. Cheater's tax."

"But you missed," she said, smug.

"Don't be a sour sport. Take the shot."

"*You* missed," she repeated.

"Take the shot. Do it. You won't."

Evie's eyes flared. "I won't do it?"

"Yeah," Erik smirked. "Do it, you won't.

She knocked it back in one go.

"Works every time," Christoph smirked to Erik, and the two burst out laughing.

"Hey—you *tricked* me!" Evie frowned, turning to Cecelia for backup.

Cecelia tried to keep a straight face. She really did. But a smirk snuck out… then a giggle… and then she was laughing too.

Moments later, they were all doubled over, laughing together like old friends.

And just like that, the night had *really* begun.

Hanging out with Erik and Christoph was an experience, to say the least. They were hilarious—telling the girls the most ludicrous stories about their adventures in the city, complete with reenactments and accents. They taught them new drinking games, shared inside jokes, and seemed genuinely excited just to be spending time with them. The hours flew by, and before Cecelia knew it, the place was packed. Music thumped overhead, the back of the bar was swarming with staff, and yet Christoph and Erik stood there like it was just the four of them—laughing, teasing, and vibing like nothing else mattered.

"Aren't you guys gonna get in trouble for not working?" Cecelia asked nervously, watching the flurry behind them.

"I don't think that'll be a problem, will it?" Erik said, glancing over at Christoph with a knowing grin.

"Nah," Christoph said coolly, glancing around the room. "I don't think so."

"What if your boss sees you?" Cecelia pressed.

"What do you think, boss?" Christoph asked, raising an eyebrow.

"Not at all," Erik smirked. "I'd say we're *exactly* where we need to be, boss."

Evie's jaw dropped. Her gaze bounced between them, finger raised like she was connecting conspiracy dots in real time.

"No. Way. *THIS* is your place?" she blurted.

"Well, his name *is* on the building..." Erik said, casually gesturing toward Christoph.

He just shrugged.

"Max," Cecelia whispered, the name settling in her chest like a spark catching fire.

Then, out of nowhere, a new song blasted through the speakers—something fast and familiar with a funky beat.

"Ohh, I love this song," Christoph said, perking up.

"Dude, this is *my jam*," Erik grinned.

"Show 'em the ping pong!" Christoph laughed.

Without hesitation, Erik jumped into a ridiculous dance move that mimicked an intense ping pong battle—back-and-forth paddles, hyper-serious face, exaggerated footwork.

"Take it away!" Erik shouted.

Christoph launched into an over-the-top *churn the butter* motion, clapping his hands together and moving his body around like he was an amish butter maker with rhythm.

The girls stared, wide-eyed holding back their laughter.

"Stand back, boys," Evie said, tying her hair up dramatically. Then she busted out a fierce *running man*, moving with surprising rhythm and flair.

"Come on, Cecelia," Christoph teased. "Show us what you've got!"

"Okay, fine!" Cecelia shouted, laughing. "You want moves? I *got* moves!"

She launched into her best version of the *robot*, her arms stiff and mechanical as she strutted past them like she was in a dance battle from another dimension.

Everyone burst out laughing.

"You guys are so weird," Cecelia giggled as she caught her breath.

"And yet, so charming," Christoph said with a wink.

When the song faded into another, Christoph leaned on the bar and asked smoothly, "Would you girls be interested in another drink?"

"I'm gonna take a break," Evie said, holding up her hands. "I know when I've had enough. *But* Cecelia would *love* one. Wouldn't you now?"

"You know what? Yeah," Cecelia grinned. "I'm gonna live a little. Let's do it. Make me your favorite drink, *Max.*"

"Alright, but this one's a dinger," Christoph said with a crooked grin, glancing at Erik before turning back to Cecelia. "And for the record, no one really calls me that—but it's okay if *you* do," he added with a wink.

"Bro, you're *so* corny," Erik said, smacking him on the shoulder. "Before he gets carried away, that's actually the name of the drink. But trust me, you don't want it. Tell him to make you one of his Berry Blast Mojitos. Now *those* are sexy."

Evie raised an eyebrow. "How can a drink be *sexy*?"

"Have one and you'll find out," Christoph replied, throwing her a wink of his own.

"Why don't you make both," Cecelia said with a sly grin, "and let me be the judge?"

"Alright, pretty girl. You got it," he said, flashing her a grin that could've stopped traffic.

As Christoph ducked away to gather ingredients, Evie leaned in close.

"This is perfect. I think he *likes* you," she whispered.

Cecelia blushed. "How do you know that? We *just* met."

Evie rolled her eyes. "I see the way he looks at you—like you're something *good* to eat. That boy is into you, Cecelia."

Before Cecelia could argue, Christoph returned with a tray full of berries, mint, limes, and liquor, placing it all in neat rows like he was prepping for a show.

"Alright, I'm gonna teach you how to bartend. Come around back and work with me," he said, gesturing her over with that same magnetic grin.

Cecelia's eyes widened. "Seriously? No, I couldn't."

"Yeah, you could. Come on, it'll be fun," he coaxed.

"Yeah, Cecelia!" Evie nudged her. "What happened to 'living a little,' huh?"

"Okay, okay!" Cecelia said with a laugh, pushing out her chair. Christoph opened the latch and guided her behind the bar, and suddenly she was standing next to him, face to face with muddling tools and bottles of rum like she'd just landed in an alternate universe.

"I've gotta give you credit, Christoph," Evie called out. "You're smooth."

"I try," he said with a playful wink over his shoulder.

Meanwhile, Evie wandered over to Erik and nudged him with a smirk. "I like your signature, by the way."

Erik looked puzzled. "What?"

"On the tickets," she clarified.

"Oh, that," he said, grinning.

"So… Cupid, huh?" she asked, crossing her arms.

"The angel of love and mischief, at your service," Erik replied, giving her a mock bow and his most devilish smile.

"Okay, Cecelia, first things first—hand wash," Christoph said with a playful grin.

He guided her to the sink, and she quickly washed up, nerves fluttering in her stomach like she'd just been invited to perform onstage.

"Alright. Strawberries go in first, then blueberries, raspberries, and finally, a few mint leaves. Grab that tool—it's called a muddler—and lightly mash the ingredients. You're not trying to smash them into paste. Think... coax, not crush. I don't use sugar in my mojitos. If you do it right, the berries are sweet enough."

"So like this?" she asked, pressing the muddler gently into the glass.

"Exactly. Nice technique. Mash those berries," he chuckled.

She laughed, clearly enjoying herself.

"Now grab that metal squeezer and juice two lime halves into the glass."

She did, yelping when a spray of juice almost caught her eye. "Ooo! That was close."

"Yeah, that happens. Just hold it over the glass, close your eyes, and squeeze like you mean it."

She squeezed the rest of the limes, then turned to him expectantly.

"Next," he said, "two ounces of white rum—use the big end of the jigger."

She reached for the hourglass-shaped tool, hesitating until he nodded. Carefully, she measured and poured the rum in.

"Now what?" she asked with a smile. "This is actually... really fun."

"Almost done. Top it off with that Mountain Dew Voltage and give it a good stir."

"Oh, I *love* this stuff!" she said, adding the vibrant blue soda and swirling it gently.

"Alright," he said, nudging her. "Moment of truth. Taste it and tell me I'm a genius."

She sipped.

Her eyes widened. "*Oh my goodness.* This is the most incredible thing my lips have ever touched."

She turned, waving urgently at her friend. "Evie! Come try this! Look what Max taught me!"

Evie took a greedy sip. "Okay. Wow. Cecelia, you're making this for me every weekend now. Christoph, I gotta hand it to you—this is one sexy-ass drink."

Cecelia beamed. "So what about that other one? The 'dinger'? You still gonna teach me how to make it?"

Christoph raised an eyebrow and grinned. "I think I'll save that for another night. Gotta give you a reason to come back and see me."

There it was again—that grin. That ridiculous, heart-melting, center-of-the-universe grin.

Caught in it, Cecelia forgot what she was about to say. Then reality snapped back.

"We should probably go check on our friends. But we'll be right back."

"Of course," Christoph said, leading her out from behind the bar and back onto the floor. "Didn't mean to kidnap you. Just swing by when you're ready—drinks on us."

"Will do!" Cecelia called back. "Come on, Evie."

Evie gave Erik a longing glance before joining her.

They wove through the crowd and beer pong tables until they found Jen and Andrew dancing nearby. A clearly annoyed Brian sulked beside them like a wet cat in a thunderstorm.

"There you are!" Brian called out, half-drunk and trying not to slur. "Where've you *been*?"

"We were at the bar—where you left us," Cecelia said. "We met the owners. Really cool guys. They offered a round of free drinks if we bring everyone over."

"Wait—how 'bout a dance first?" Brian said, grabbing her hand and spinning her around.

"Maybe later," she said, pulling her hand away. "I don't really dance." A lie—but a necessary one.

"FREE DRINKS! WOO!" Jen shouted, already on the move. "Come on, grumpy-pants!" She grabbed Brian and yanked him along.

"Wait, Jen! You don't even know where it is!" Cecelia groaned, chasing after her.

Back at the bar, Christoph and Erik were waiting with five drinks already lined up. The cocktails looked like melted sunsets—bright yellow swirling into blood orange.

"Welcome to Max Lounge," Christoph said smoothly, gesturing to the glasses. "This one's a Dinger. My favorite. Compliments of the house."

Brian looked around, confused. "Wait—I thought you said you *met* the owners."

Cecelia just smiled. "We did. Brian, meet Christoph Maximus. Max Lounge is his and Erik's club."

Brian blinked like a man trying to do math while drunk. Then, scrambling to save face, he stepped forward and extended a hand.

"I'm so sorry—I forgot my manners. Brian Watterson. Pleasure to meet you."

Christoph shook his hand briefly, forcing a smile. "Yeah. Pleasure."

He wiped his hand on his jeans and turned back to Cecelia, lowering his voice.

"Hey—after this, Erik and I are hosting a small after-party. You and your friends should come by. We're close by. Subway's easy."

Cecelia's eyes lit up. "*Really?* You want us to come with you?"

"Of course. That's why I asked." He smirked. "So... you down?"

She nodded. "*Absolutely.* I'm just surprised you're being so—"

"Nice?" he offered with a shrug. "Guilty as charged."

She turned to Evie, mouthed *OMG*, and whispered the news. Evie gasped, then shrieked with delight.

Cecelia turned back to the group. "Okay, everyone—it's official. We're heading to Max and Erik's for the after-party."

Brian spat out his drink.

"No. Freaking. Way."

Jen

Chapter 9

After party

Cecelia was feeling good—better than she had in ages. The city air was crisp, her heels clicked confidently on the sidewalk, and for once, she didn't care if her hair got frizzy or if her dress creased. She felt *alive*. Buzzed just enough to feel loose, bold, and wide open to whatever the night threw her way.

She and Evette had made fast friends with a pair of stylish girls—Margot and Cynthia—on the subway ride over. Both had thick New York accents, killer eyeliner, and a pineapple vodka flask they were more than happy to share.

Cecelia wasn't much of a drinker. Honestly, she couldn't even say she'd ever been properly drunk—unless you counted that one winter break when her best friend Blake convinced her to sneak a bottle of her dad's scotch into the dorms. She kept that bottle hidden like a national secret, and when they finally cracked it open weeks later, she nearly coughed up a lung. The stuff was disgusting. Molten gasoline with a hint of leather. She'd sworn off alcohol ever since.

But tonight? Tonight had changed everything.

That berry mojito Christoph taught her to make was divine. And the Pineapple vodka? Practically juice. It hit her now—she *definitely* had been missing out.

The group trailing behind Erik and Christoph had grown into a small, rowdy parade—nearly twenty strong. A mix of Max Lounge bartenders, club regulars, college kids, and new subway besties. They laughed too loud, took up the whole sidewalk, and didn't care in the slightest.

When they reached the apartment building, Cecelia blinked. It was... humble. A solid brick structure, six stories high, with a small gated drive and a compact parking garage. Not what she expected from the owners of a high-end speakeasy.

Christoph turned the key on a door marked *1*. "Welcome to our humble abode," he said with a mock bow. "It's not much, but it's home."

As the crowd poured inside, Cecelia hung back a beat—bracing herself for... well, something rough around the edges.

Instead, she walked into a scene straight out of a GQ home spread.

"Wow. Spiffy place you've got here, guys!" Evette called, clearly impressed.

"Thanks, Eves," Erik replied. "Let me give you the grand tour."

"Definitely. Lead the way, pretty boy," she said, smacking his butt and following after him.

Cecelia stayed near the door, momentarily stunned. The place was *gorgeous*. Antique velvet couches, a mid-century modern coffee table that Erik casually slid open to reveal a *mini fridge* full of drinks, and black leather electric recliners that looked like they belonged in a penthouse suite.

The walls were lined with clean art deco shelves, and every painting seemed intentional—like the boys had actually *curated* their decor. A series of seasonal tree landscapes hung above a sleek wine rack, and in the far corner, she spotted what looked like a replica of Salvador Dalí's *Meditative Rose*.

Music bumped through the room, low but magnetic. Darius—their bouncer—was now behind a compact DJ booth in the corner, wearing headphones and nodding to the beat like a professional. Cecelia had no idea when he'd arrived.

A sticker on his laptop read: *DJ No Requests.*

Weird stage name, she thought—but kind of iconic.

"Come help me in the kitchen?" Christoph's voice was soft at her side, warm like honey.

She turned, caught off guard by how close he was. "Sure."

He led her past the island and over to the fridge. "I made these with Erii the other night," he said, opening it with a proud smile.

Inside, the shelves were stacked dangerously high with trays of red and blue Jello shots. The boys had banished actual food to one shelf, and even that looked like it was one wrong move away from total collapse.

Cecelia laughed. "Oh my God. Did you *buy out* an entire store?"

Christoph scratched the back of his head, grinning sheepishly. "Might've overdone it. But I always say—there's no such thing as too many Jello shots."

She leaned closer, peering at the small condiment-style containers. "Wait— *there's alcohol* in these?"

"Of course there is," he said, grabbing one and holding it out. "They're dangerous. And delicious. Try the blue. It's my favorite."

She accepted the little cup like it was sacred. Blue was her favorite color. Her favorite Jello. Her favorite summer snack. She lifted it to her mouth and... nothing.

"Um... it's stuck," she said, shaking the container.

Christoph burst out laughing. "Right! Rookie mistake. You gotta use the *finger scoop.*" He demonstrated, expertly loosening the edge with his finger and flipping it into his mouth like a pro.

She copied him—and immediately melted.

Cool. Fruity. Just the right amount of kick.

"Wow," she breathed. "That's brilliant."

"I know," he said smugly. "But watch yourself. These things sneak up on you."

"I'll be fine," she replied, feigning confidence.

He handed her a tray. "Good. Take this and pass 'em out?"

"Absolutely."

"And when you're done—come back. I've got something else I think you'll love."

More winking. She didn't even like winks—but his? *Swoon.*

She strutted back into the living room like she owned the place. "Alright, who wants Jello shots?"

Within seconds, a small crowd surged toward her.

"Damn," she whispered, watching the tray empty like it was Black Friday.

With four left, she weaved toward the couch where Jen, Andrew, and Brian were playing cards.

"Hey guys, want one?"

"Hell yes!" Jen cheered, snatching one. "Where'd these come from?"

"Christoph," Cecelia said, beaming. "He's got trays in the fridge."

"I'm in," Andrew said, tipping an imaginary cowboy hat. "Thanks, darlin'."

Brian raised an eyebrow. "So... you're back. Guess you couldn't resist the Watterson charm."

"Mm, no. I just missed Jen's sparkling personality," she deadpanned.

"Delusional," Jen muttered, elbowing Brian. "Okay, how do we eat these?"

Cecelia held hers up proudly. "The *finger scoop.* I just learned this. Watch and learn."

"The finger scoop? Sounds dirty," Jen giggled.

"Only if you're bad at it," Cecelia replied with a wink.

They all followed her lead and downed their shots.

Jen's eyes widened. "Oh my *God.* These are dangerous. You realize how deadly these could be, right?"

"Yup. This is my third and last. But come with me after this and I'll get you a whole tray."

"You're the best," Jen grinned.

Meanwhile, Erik was observing Brian from a distance. He noticed Brian's unsuccessful attempt at flirting with Margot, the hot redhead Erik had used to convince Brian to buy the tickets to Max Lounge. Margot looked completely uninterested and was edging away from him.

Erik smirked and decided it was time for some fun. He twisted his fingers like he was weaving a mysterious thread in the air and Brian's shoelaces magically tied themselves together.

Brian, oblivious, got up and made his way across the room, spotting another girl to hit on. As he took a step, he tripped over his own feet and went sprawling to the floor, his drink flying out of his hand and splashing onto the ground.

Everyone around burst into laughter, including the girl he was heading toward. Erik couldn't help but chuckle at the sight. "Oops," he muttered to himself, trying to hide his grin.

Cecelia, meanwhile, looked over to see what the commotion was about and caught Erik's eye. He winked at her, and she shook her head, smiling.

Erik made his way back to the kitchen, where he found Christoph handing out more Jello shots. "Did you see that?" Erik asked, still grinning.

"Oh, I saw it," Christoph replied, laughing. "You couldn't resist, could you?"

"Hey, he deserved it," Erik shrugged. "Besides, it was hilarious."

Christoph shook his head, smiling. "Just try not to get us into too much trouble, alright?"

"No promises," Erik replied, grabbing a Jello shot from the tray and raising it in a toast. "To good times and better friends."

"To good times and better friends," Christoph echoed, clinking his shot against Erik's.

The night continued with laughter, pranks, and good-natured teasing.

Brian had been waiting for the right chance to catch Cecelia's eye, but that last trip left him a bit humbled. He couldn't understand how his shoe laces ended up tied together like that. There she was and he thought, now's my chance.

"Hey, you sure you don't wanna chill here with me?" Brian asked, reaching for her. "You can sit on my lap," he said, slapping his thigh.

"I think I'm okay—see you later!" Cecelia called, pulling away from Brian's grasp and wobbling her way back to the kitchen like a woman on a mission. God, he was a confident drunk.

As she turned the corner, her eyes locked on Christoph behind the island, pouring fizzy cocktails into tall glasses like a magician. Standing beside him was someone new—a guy with silver-black hair, sharp cheekbones, and a look that sparked a weird déjà vu. Her steps slowed. She squinted.

She *knew* that face.

"—Fallen were tailing your group, but we took care of them." the silver-haired boy said, low and serious.

What?

Cecelia blinked. Definitely didn't hear that right.

"Heyyy," she cut in, holding up the tray like a trophy. "All out! Should I get more?"

Christoph lit up. "Perfect timing. I made this for you." He handed her a glass filled with sparkling pink liquid. "I call it… Fizzy Bubbly."

She tilted her head at the name. "That sounds like a bath bomb."

He laughed. "Two strawberries, muddled. Champagne to here—" he pointed to just below the rim. "—dash of Pop Rocks, splash of strawberry Pucker. Light, fizzy, dangerous."

"Ooooh." She took a sip and her whole body smiled. "That is so good. Like—*stupid* good."

"Hey, what about mine?" the silver-haired guy asked, elbowing Christoph.

Christoph turned with mock offense. "How rude of me." He handed him a second glass. "Here you go, Sam."

Sam. That name rang a bell.

Christoph looked back at her. "Cecelia, I've been a terrible host. Let me introduce you properly. This is one of my oldest and most loyal friends— Samuel. Sam, this is Cecelia."

Sam smiled and offered his hand. "Pleasure to meet you."

She stared at him as she shook it, her buzz foggy but her gut sharp. That *was* the same face. Those same eyes.

"Wait a second…" she squinted. "Don't I know you from somewhere?"

"I don't think so," he said, all smooth and smug.

"No, no, I swear. I *just* met you. Maybe two nights ago?" She leaned in, peering closer. "You just… look really, really familiar."

He chuckled, eyes glittering. "People say that. Apparently we all look alike."

And there it was. Her brain clicked into place.

"OH. MY. GOD." She pointed at him with theatrical drama. "You had the moustache!"

Sam froze for half a beat.

"It's YOU! *Mr. Wu!*" she exclaimed, slapping his arm like they were old pals.

He laughed—but it was awkward now. "I really think you've got me confused with someone else."

"Nope. No way. I knew I wasn't crazy." She looked around like she needed backup. "Hang on—ANNNDREW!"

Across the room, near the DJ booth, Andrew turned, mildly panicked. He jogged over quickly.

"What's wrong, darlin'? These two givin' you trouble?" he asked, puffing his chest and shooting Sam a suspicious look.

"No! Nothing's wrong!" Cecelia giggled. "I just found Mr. Wu!"

Andrew looked between her and Sam. Slowly.

"Darlin', I think you might be… celebratin' a little *too* hard. This fella's definitely not Mr. Wu." He placed a gentle hand on her shoulder. "He's just some guy. Probably feels pretty awkward now."

Cecelia pouted. "I'm not drunk."

Her hand missed the edge of the island on the first try.

"Okay, I'm *a little* drunk," she admitted, then blinked hard. "Whoa."

Her stomach did a weird flip.

"Hey, Max?" she turned toward Christoph, trying to look composed and utterly failing. "Where's the bathroom?"

Christoph instantly moved toward her. "Just around that corner. But if it's full, there's another one upstairs. Want me to walk you?"

"No, no, I'm good. Totally good." She set her glass down carefully—like it was a bomb and looked toward her friend. "Take care of Jen, Andrew," she turned to leave toward the bathroom, accidently bumping into Sam.

"Sorry, Mr. Wu—I mean *Sam!* Ugh, whatever, I didn't mean to—"

She accidentally bumped into his chest on her way out. "Sorry again!" she winced.

He caught her gently by the elbow to steady her. "You're okay," he said softly, but there was something strange in the way he looked at her now.

She rushed to the bathroom and reached for the handle. The door was locked. "Shit." She turned and made her way across the room and through the front door.

Brian looked up from where he was sitting on the couch, just as she was leaving the room.

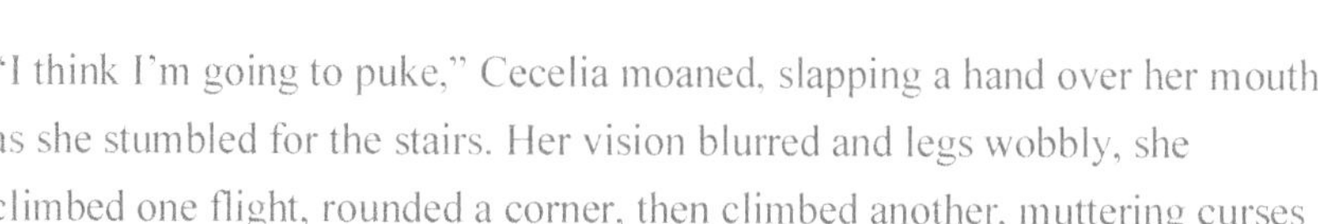

"I think I'm going to puke," Cecelia moaned, slapping a hand over her mouth as she stumbled for the stairs. Her vision blurred and legs wobbly, she climbed one flight, rounded a corner, then climbed another, muttering curses with every step.

"This must be it!" she cried, spotting an open door at the end of the hall like it was a holy grail. She staggered inside, passing an empty room that looked like a study or maybe a tiny library. A door on the left caught her eye— locked.

"Of course," she muttered, spinning around unsteadily. There, at the very end of the hallway—another door. She nearly crashed into it trying to grab the handle.

"YES. Thank Jesus!" she wheezed, practically falling into the bathroom as she flicked the light on and slammed the door behind her. Her stomach flipped violently.

She barely made it.

The toilet seat clattered up just as her body convulsed forward. Vomit sprayed across the lid and into the bowl in one explosive heave. It burned like hell.

She stayed there, slumped over the toilet, arms shaking, sweat pouring from her forehead.

Where did things go wrong?

She didn't think she drank *that* much. But then… three drinks at the club, two on the subway, three jello shots here.

"Dammit. I'm such an idiot," she groaned, forehead against her forearm. "Max is gonna *hate* me. His friend Sam probably thinks I'm a Jeerr—"

Another heave cut her thought short. Her whole body convulsed.

"Ughhh, dammit," she sobbed, chest heaving as she pulled back and looked at her sleeves, now covered in blue and red streaks. Her whole body was drenched in sweat.

"When the hell did it get so hot in here?"

She clawed at the sleeves of her leather jacket, yanking it off and throwing it onto the tiled floor with a wet slap—just in time for another three rounds of retching. Dry heaves, acid. Nothing left.

Spent, she collapsed sideways onto the bathroom floor, cheek pressed to the cool tile.

Just for a minute… just until the spinning stops.

Then came a knock.

Shit. Someone needed the bathroom.

She moaned, dragging herself up. Her legs were shaky but she made it to the sink and flipped the cold water on. Soap. Scrub. Splash. Rinse.

Another knock. Firmer.

"Just a second!" she called hoarsely.

She rinsed her mouth again. Fixed her hair with trembling fingers. One more deep breath—and then she opened the door.

Brian.

He leaned in the doorway, grinning too casually.

"Hey. You alright in there?"

"Yeah, I'm… cool," she said, trying to lean against the doorframe and missing it entirely. Her shoulder thunked against the wall.

"I was looking for you," he said with a crooked smile.

"Yeah?" she asked, voice soft.

"Yeah. Just wanted to hang out. I mean, I got the tickets for *us*, thought we'd be spending time together tonight. But you've been... avoiding me."

She blinked. "I wasn't avoiding you," she said, honest and tipsy. "There was just a lot going on. You ditched us for beer pong first, so Evie and I hung out with Erik and Christoph, and then we came here and Max—Christoph—asked me to help—"

"—Oh, so we're calling him Max now?" Brian interrupted sharply. His smile didn't reach his eyes anymore. "Got nicknames for him already, huh? What's that guy got that I don't? He got muscles like *these*?" He flexed, smug as hell.

She laughed, but it was nervous now. "Nooo, but he's charming, and witty, and classy, and—"

Suddenly his hands were on her face.

He kissed her—fast, sloppy, forceful.

She froze.

Panic flared. Her arms flailed as he mashed his lips against hers.

She shoved against his elbows, pushing him off. "Brian, no!" she gasped, voice cracking. "I don't like you like that."

"Oh come on, sweetie," he said, his grin gone predatory. "You know you can't resist the Watterson charm. Just relax. Let it happen. Let your body do the talking."

"No—Brian, *stop*—"

He grabbed her face again, rougher this time, pressing her back into the sink. His mouth crashed into hers, sloppier now, his tongue forcing its way inside. It tasted like stale beer and ash. She gagged.

She tried to push—her arms were too weak. Her stomach turned. She kicked feebly, but he was stronger. His hand slid up behind her dress.

Then instinct kicked in.

She brought two fingers up, wedged them just beneath his jaw, and *dug* into his throat with everything she had.

Brian gagged and stumbled back, coughing, his face red.

"You like it rough, huh?" he spat. "Or are you just playing hard to get?" His voice was darker now. He lunged again, slamming her back against the sink with brute force. "I *like* a little fight."

She screamed—but nothing came out. Her throat was raw. Her lungs too tired.

She whispered "No" again and again, but they were just whimpers now. Her body was too drunk. Too exhausted. She couldn't fight anymore.

And then—he unhooked her bra.

And then—

Brian was gone.

Just—gone.

One moment he was there, pinning her to the sink.

And the next... nothing.

Something had yanked Brian off her.

Cecelia heard it—the violent thud of his body slamming onto hardwood outside the bathroom. It echoed like a gavel falling.

"Do you have a problem with your hearing?" a deep voice demanded, sharp as steel.

She looked up.

Christoph stood in the doorway, shoulders squared, jaw clenched, a fire raging in his eyes.

"The lady said *no*," he growled, stepping into the hallway like a lion cornering his prey.

Brian was scrambling to his feet, disoriented. Blood already dripped from his lip. He raised his fists—sloppy, off balance.

But it didn't matter.

Christoph was *under* him in a blink. He seized Brian's arm and flipped him flat onto his back like he weighed nothing. Mounted him. Pinned him.

Then came the fists.

One.
Two.
CRUNCH.

The third punch landed with a brutal, satisfying pop. Brian let out a choked grunt, blood now pouring freely from his nose, soaking his black shirt.

Christoph rose, grabbed him by the collar, and *hauled* him to his feet with terrifying ease.

"You are never to talk to Cecelia again," he said, voice low and lethal. "*Ever.*"

Brian swayed in his grip, dazed.

"I so much as *hear* you looked at her wrong," Christoph snarled, "I'll hunt you down, find you, and make you regret the day you were born."

He shoved him hard into the wall. "And you're *banned* from my club. Permanently."

"Now get the hell out of my house, you piece of shit."

Brian turned, blood dripping down his chin. He paused at the stairs, glancing back with glassy eyes.

"Cecelia…" he croaked. "I'm sorry. I didn't mean—"

"—And I suggest you change your schedule immediately," Christoph barked, pointing toward the door. "*Now leave.*"

That did it. Brian broke into a run, stumbling down the staircase like a frightened animal. His footsteps echoed, loud and desperate, until they finally vanished from the building.

Silence.

Then Christoph turned back.

Cecelia was still on the bathroom floor, hugging her knees to her chest, eyes glassy and rimmed with red. She looked so small.

He didn't approach right away.

He knelt down a few feet away, voice gentler now. "Did he hurt you?"

She shook her head faintly, barely able to speak. "No," she whispered hoarsely.

Christoph slipped his coat from his shoulders and draped it around her. He sat down beside her, slowly, like she might break if he moved too fast.

She leaned into him.

"I didn't know what happened to you," he said softly, eyes still on the open door. "I thought maybe you got lost, so I came to look. But you weren't in the bathroom on the second floor… I didn't even realize Erik left this floor open."

He looked down at her, guilt etched across his face.

"Cecelia, I am *so* sorry. If I'd gotten here sooner—"

"No… Maaaxx," she said, teeth chattering. "Thank you."

She looked up at him with tears in her eyes.

"Thank you."

He pulled her into his arms.

And for a long time, they just sat there together on the bathroom floor, wrapped in silence and each other's warmth. Her trembling started to slow.

Finally, Christoph gave a small, sheepish smile. "I know this probably isn't the best time to ask… but I'm gonna go out on a limb and guess you threw up?"

Cecelia blushed. Nodded.

"Okay. That's okay," he said quickly, squeezing her shoulder. "No judgment. If you want, I've got some mouthwash under the sink."

He rose, moving with quiet care. "I'll just step outside and give you a minute to freshen up. When you're ready, we can head back downstairs. No rush."

She nodded again, silently, and he stepped out, closing the door behind him.

Cecelia stayed there for a moment longer, hands trembling as she wiped her face. She rinsed her mouth, straightened her dress, and smoothed her hair. When she finally emerged ten minutes later, Christoph was waiting for her outside, calm and steady.

Without a word, she reached for his hand.

He took it.

And together, they made their way back downstairs—out of the darkness, and into the light of the party below.

"Hey, where *have* you been, sexy lady?" Evie called from the couch, flashing Cecelia a teasing grin.

Cecelia didn't answer. She just shook her head.

Evie's smile vanished.

She stood abruptly, pushing through the crowd without hesitation. She reached Cecelia, placed both hands on her shoulders, and stared into her eyes.

"Tell me everything," she said, voice low and serious. "Did he hurt you?"

Cecelia's lips barely moved. "Brian."

That was all Evie needed to hear.

"That *fucking* bastard," she snarled. "We're gonna ruin him. Don't you worry."

Across the room, Christoph had stormed over to the long black leather couch, where Darius sat sipping a glass of Moscato, deep in conversation with Sam and Erik.

"Guys," Christoph said sharply, "that Brian kid? He's *done*. Never allowed into the club again. Got it?"

Darius and Erik both nodded, silent but firm. No one questioned it.

Christoph turned back, his eyes scanning the room until they landed on Cecelia and Evie, now locked in a quiet embrace. Her face was buried in Evie's shoulder.

He walked to them gently.

"Hey, Cecelia," he said, his voice warm again. "Come sit with us, yeah? I'll get you some water, and ask Erik to start clearing people out."

"Okay," she whispered.

He led her over to the couch where Darius sat, and helped her down onto the cushion opposite him. Evie followed and sat beside her, never leaving her side.

Cecelia looked over at the towering man beside her. Darius had intimidated her when she first saw him at the club—but now, seated with a calm presence and an almost fatherly energy, he reminded her of a giant teddy bear. A teddy bear built like a tank, but soft just the same.

He met her gaze and gave her a solemn nod.

"I heard what happened," Darius said quietly, setting his glass down. "Don't worry. If I see that kid again, I'll break his *goddamn* legs. You're safe here. With *all* of us."

Erik and Sam nodded from across the room.

"A friend of Christoph's is a friend of mine," Darius added with a small smile. "I'm Darius by the way."

"Cecelia," she said softly, offering a weak but genuine smile back.

"You want some leftover pizza?" he asked, already rising to grab a plate.

"Yeah," she said, her voice still hoarse. "My stomach could probably use something… solid."

Christoph returned just then, carrying a bottle of water and a paper plate stacked with reheated slices. Of course he already knew.

He handed them to her without a word, and she took both gratefully.

For the next hour, she sat curled on the couch, wrapped in Christoph's jacket, slowly sipping water and nibbling pizza while listening to the buzz of conversation around her. Evie never left her side, arms draped protectively around her shoulders, gently stroking her hair.

Eventually, Evie stood and stretched, and Cecelia leaned into Darius. Her head rested near his leg like a child curling up beside her guardian. And there, in the warm cocoon of voices and safety, she finally fell asleep.

Darius didn't move.

He stood slowly, retrieved a folded blanket from the nearby linen closet, and returned to gently drape it over her body. Then he sat back down next to her. Quiet. Watchful.

Evie never strayed far, her eyes flicking back to the couch every few minutes like a hawk.

"She's asleep," came Christoph's voice from behind her.

Evie jumped—she hadn't even heard him approach.

"If you'd like to stay the night," he continued gently, "we have guest rooms upstairs. I can set you up in your own. You both can leave in the morning. Erik and I would be happy to drive you home."

Evie looked at him for a long moment, then nodded.

"Yeah… that'd be cool. Thanks—for everything." She folded her arms. "I heard someone say Brian ran out of here covered in blood. Was that you?"

Christoph met her gaze without hesitation. "Yeah. That was me."

"*Good*," she said coldly. "That bastard deserved it. And then some."

"This is my fault, Evie," he said, voice heavy. "This never should've happened. Not in my house."

"Hey. Shut it." She pointed a finger at his chest. "It's no one's fault but *his*. Look… what happened was really fucked up. But if there's *one* good thing that came out of tonight, it's meeting you guys. I'm not letting that asshole ruin that too."

She hugged him, and then Erik.

"No one fucks with my best friend and gets away with it," she said, cracking her knuckles with purpose.

Christoph turned to Erik. "Go open up the blue room for Cecelia. I'll carry her up in a few."

"You got it," Erik replied, already heading toward the stairs.

"Hey, Eves," Erik said over his shoulder with a hopeful smirk, "you wanna go watch the sunrise after this?"

Evie raised an eyebrow. "Wow. Didn't peg you for the romantic type."

"So… that's a no?"

"Pshhh. That's a *yes,* you dork," she replied, giving him a playful shove as they disappeared up the stairs.

When Christoph reached the couch, he bent down gently and lifted Cecelia into his arms. She stirred but didn't wake. He carried her quietly to the room Erik had prepared—a peaceful guest room with soft blue walls, a queen-sized bed, and warm light coming from the nightstand lamp.

He laid her down gently, tucked the blanket around her, and turned to leave.

But her voice stopped him.

"Hey… Max?" she murmured.

He turned back.

"I'm glad I finally got to meet you."

He frowned slightly. "Finally?"

"I dream about you every night," she whispered sleepily. "My angel. My Cerul—"

And just like that, she was out again.

Christoph stared at her for a long moment, his hand still resting on the doorknob.

"…It's just Christoph now," he said softly, the sadness deep in his voice.

"Goodnight, pretty girl. I'll see you in the morning."

He closed the door behind him, leaving only the hush of night and the safety
of dreams.

Chapter 10

The Fall - Part II

As Cecelia slept, she dreamed again—the same dream she'd been having all week.

Ceruleus, wreathed in pain, had his great white wings torn from his back in a blaze of agony. They fell like ash behind him as Michael stood over him, silent and unyielding. Heaven opened a rift and cast Ceruleus out through the eastern gates of Eden. His scream echoed through the heavens as he plummeted downward, spiraling helplessly through realms of light and sky until the mortal veil swallowed him whole.

This time, though, the dream continued. She saw what happened next.

Ceruleus struck the sea.

The waters of the Mediterranean exploded around his broken form as he crashed into the waves off the coast of Athens. The force of his fall dragged him beneath the surface, where the world grew cold and quiet. Dark green seaweed rose from the depths like the hands of forgotten gods, tangling around his limbs, clinging to his skin, pulling him into silence. The blood from his back—where his wings had once been—dissolved into gold ribbons in the water. He stopped fighting.

He sank.

But fate, or perhaps mercy, had not abandoned him. A current rolled him through the kelp beds and toward the shore. Tangled, lifeless, and barely breathing, Ceruleus's body washed up on the sand at dawn—salt crusted in his lashes, the seaweed clinging to his ankles like chains. A broken angel, stripped of divinity, lying at the boundary between sky and sea.

That's when she saw her.

Barefoot and alone, a basket in one hand, Violette walked the beach as she did every morning, collecting driftwood and shells. Her sun-darkened skin glowed gold in the rising light, and her eyes were lined with weariness. She had known loss—Cecelia felt it in the way she moved, each step heavy with memory.

She spotted the body.

At first, she thought it was wreckage from a ship, or a dead animal tangled in kelp. But as she stepped closer, she saw his face. Even caked in sand and bruised by the sea, Ceruleus radiated an unearthly beauty.

"Are you alive, little sea beast?" she whispered cautiously, kneeling beside him.

Ceruleus stirred, groaning as he rolled onto his back. "I... I am no beast," he rasped. "And I will not eat you."

Violette flinched, her breath catching. His voice was cracked and low, like thunder heard from far away. But he was awake—barely.

"By the gods," she whispered. Her eyes scanned his face, softening as she took in his features. "You look just like my son..."

She pulled the seaweed away, cradled his face with trembling hands, and brushed the wet curls from his forehead. Her voice broke. "Christos?"

Ceruleus's head lolled to the side. "I... don't know that name."

With strength born of desperation, she heaved his body upright, draping one of his arms over her shoulders. "Come," she said, dragging him slowly from the shore. "If you are not my son, then you are my second chance."

Violette lived in a small cottage nestled on the edge of an olive grove. She laid Ceruleus on a cot near the fire, stripped off the seaweed and rags, and dressed his wounds with old linen soaked in herbs and honey. Days passed. Cecelia watched it all unfold as if through a veil, her dream tethered to Ceruleus's pain.

When he screamed in his sleep, Violette stayed by his side, whispering lullabies in Greek. When his fever broke, she wept in silence. And when he finally opened his eyes and asked where he was, she only said, "Home."

But the world was not kind to widows, nor to miracles.

Violette's village was small, ruled by superstition and poverty. Her husband had died years ago, and her only son had gone off to war. She had survived by tending her land and avoiding trouble—but trouble now came knocking.

They came one morning—three men, drunk on hunger and cruelty. One kicked down the gate while another seized her basket of olives.

"You owe us, Violette," one sneered. "Your husband left debts. You pay them—or we take what's due."

"I have nothing to give," she pleaded. "Leave me be."

One of them struck her.

Cecelia's heart thundered in her chest. No—she tried to scream through the dream. Not her. That poor woman.

And then he came.

Ceruleus stepped from the shadows of the cottage, his body thin but standing tall. There was no sword, no armor—just the righteous fury of something ancient and fallen. His fist shattered the first man's jaw in a blink. The second crumpled before he could draw a blade. The third ran.

The silence after was deafening.

Violette, still on the ground, looked up at him in awe. Blood streaked his bare arms, and his chest heaved with the weight of fury barely restrained.

"You... you're not human," she whispered. "Are you… are you Apollo?"

Ceruleus knelt beside her, his brow furrowed in pain. "No," he sighed. "They called me Ceruleus. I'm what they call a fallen angel. I'm not sure what they'll call me now."

Her breath caught. But she didn't run.

Instead, she reached out and touched his face, just like she had on the beach. "Then be my Christos. Be the son I've already lost."

Ceruleus hesitated—then nodded. "If you will have me."

Time passed in flickers.

Cecelia saw Ceruleus working the fields beside her. Fixing the roof. Laughing over burned bread. Sitting under the fig tree, painting symbols in the dirt.

He began to heal. Slowly. Not just his body, but his soul.

And Violette healed too. Her laughter returned. The light in her home came back.

A fallen angel and a grieving mother. Together.

Cecelia stirred in her sleep, tears wetting her pillow. She didn't want to wake. Not yet.

But as the sun rose, the dream faded.

Still, in her chest, something had changed. Her heart beat with a deeper truth.

Ceruleus had fallen—but he had not shattered. He had landed in a place where love found him again.

And now she knew the next chapter of his story.

And maybe… hers too.

Chapter 11

Discovery

He awoke to total darkness.

A crushing weight pinned him down. Chest tight, limbs trapped—his body braced for battle. *Michael. He's found me.* The thought slammed into him like lightning. If he could just free one hand, reach under the pillow for the dagger—he might stand a chance.

Just one solid thrust of the hips and—

"Rise and shine, sleeping beauty!" a familiar voice rang out, thick with smug satisfaction.

Erik.

With a sharp grunt, Christoph twisted and bucked, launching the weight off his chest. It hit the floor with a satisfying *thud.*

"OW! Okay! Rude!" Erik groaned dramatically. "You didn't have to *yeet* me across the room like yesterday's garbage."

Christoph groaned and flopped back onto the mattress, dragging a pillow over his face.

"Go away. Five more minutes."

"Nope! Not happening. You're already late to your own breakfast party."
Erik yanked the covers back with flair. "Now take a deep breath, my guy.
You smell that? That's divine intervention. Pancakes. Bacon. Syrup. Joy."

Christoph reluctantly inhaled—and froze.
Pancakes.

Warm vanilla, sizzling bacon, real maple syrup. It hit like a spell. He sat up,
rubbing his face.

"Okay. All right. You make a compelling case, my brother," he muttered
through a yawn. "Let's see if she's willing to share."

Still in his boxers, he moved toward the dresser.

Erik threw his hands over his face with mock horror. "OH NO. My *pure*
virgin eyes! I am too young and too good-looking to be scarred like this!"

Christoph rolled his eyes. "Please. You're the angel of mischief, not
modesty."

"Yeah, and even I know when to look away from a man undressing in broad
daylight," Erik quipped as Christoph reached for a pair of pants.

"Out," Christoph said flatly, already halfway into his jeans.

"Fine, fine, I'm going! But I swear I just saw penguins on your boxers." Erik
added with a grin, slipping out the door just before it slammed shut behind
him.

"Better hurry!" came the distant shout. "Before I eat *everything!*"

Little bastard, Christoph thought, shaking his head with a reluctant smirk.

He trudged to the bathroom sink and turned the faucet on. Cold water
splashed into the basin with a steady rhythm, the sound sharp against the
silence. He cupped his hands and dipped his face into the chill, hoping to
wash away the heaviness clinging to his thoughts.

What's going on with these dreams?

He exhaled through his nose, water dripping from his face in slow rivulets, down his jaw, onto his bare chest.

First the Fall—his wings torn from him, the Garden stripped from his grasp—and now Violette. That beach. Her voice. Her grief. Her hands wrapped around his broken body like a prayer.

He twisted the faucet off and reached for a towel, rubbing it briskly over his face and neck, trying to shake off the fog. But the images clung to him like the seaweed that once tangled around his limbs.

It's Cecelia. It had to be.
Somehow, she's gotten into my memories.

The thought wasn't entirely shocking—but it was unsettling. The dreams had always belonged to him. His pain. His shame. His past. And now, she was inside them, witnessing things no one else ever had.

But does she even know what she's doing?
That question burned more than the water ever could.

He stepped back into his room, his mind still buzzing as he opened a drawer and pulled out a fresh pair of boxers and a soft black V-neck. He tossed the towel aside and dressed in silence, his muscles tense, his focus scattered.

A cold shower's what I really need...
But he already knew no water could scrub away what lingered in his mind.

He stared blankly at the wall for a moment, then blinked it away. *The past is the past.* He clenched his jaw, forcing down the ache in his chest. *I need to live in the present. Focus on what matters.*

He ran a hand through his hair and exhaled sharply.

I need to find that key. No more stalling. No more ghosts. No more distractions.

He paused.

All right...

 A faint smirk tugged at the corner of his mouth.

Maybe just a little.

It had been a long time since Christoph Maximus was truly caught off guard, but stepping into the kitchen that morning? That did it.

The entire counter was buried under plates—fluffy pancakes, waffles dripping with syrup, omelets folded with spinach and cheese, fruit bowls, turkey sausage, a mountain of bacon, and at least three types of toast. Erik sat at the head of the table, gripping the edge like he was physically restraining himself.

He looked up at Christoph with wild eyes. "Dude. What took you so long?"

Christoph blinked. "It's been fifteen minutes."

"They told me I couldn't eat till you showed up!" Erik cried, like he'd survived an ambush. "Do you understand what that's like for someone with my metabolism? My soul almost left my body."

Christoph smirked. "So dramatic."

Erik released the table like it had been holding him hostage and flexed his fingers in exaggerated relief.

Cecelia stepped out from behind the fridge with a pitcher of orange juice. She still wore her party clothes from the night before, now paired with an apron that read *Hot Stuff Coming Through.* She blushed when she caught Christoph's eyes.

"We just wanted to say thanks," she said. "For… everything. The hospitality. The rescue. The not letting anyone die part."

Evie, dressed like she hadn't slept and didn't care, tossed a towel over her shoulder. "Also, your fridge was criminally empty. Seriously, three jello shots and a jar of pickles? That's not food. That's a threat."

Christoph looked around at the spread, then back at Erik. "Did you know we had all this?"

Erik shrugged. "Nope. They raided the corner store and took over the kitchen like it was a Food Network challenge."

"And somehow," Christoph said, dropping into the seat next to him, "this isn't even the weirdest part of my week."

"Go ahead," Cecelia said, nudging him toward his plate. "We'll finish setting everything out."

He leaned over to Erik and lowered his voice. "Is that French toast?"

"Stuffed," Erik whispered like it was classified intel. "With cream cheese and strawberries."

"And the bacon?"

"Applewood smoked. Crispy. I counted twenty-three slices. I've been staring at them for eleven and a half minutes."

Christoph grabbed a slice like it was sacred. "You are a strong man."

Erik nodded solemnly. "I know."

"Erik," Evie called from across the kitchen.

"Yeah, Eves?" he said, mouth already full.

"Don't forget—studio time. You promised."

"Right," he said, wiping his hands. "I got you."

"You have a studio?" Cecelia asked, surprised.

"Upstairs," Evie answered for him. "He gave me the VIP tour last night. It was very exclusive."

"Oh did he now?" Christoph said, raising an eyebrow at Erik.

Erik raised his hands. "In my defense, she threatened to cry if I didn't."

"Lies," Evie said, flipping a pancake with expert flair. "I *politely* blackmailed him."

Cecelia leaned toward Christoph, voice soft. "I want a tour too. Will you show me around, Max?"

He looked over at her, caught off guard by the way her eyes lit up when she smiled.

"Yeah," he said, trying not to sound too eager. "I'd like that."

"Oh, but fair warning," Evie added. "No singing from Cecelia. Trust me."

"Rude and uncalled for, but true. I'm tone-deaf," Cecelia confessed, laughing. "I can't even hum without offending someone."

"Good to know," Christoph said with a grin. "And just so we're clear, you'll never catch me cooking. That's Erik's thing."

"So you'd burn toast?/" Evie chimed in.

"He *has* burned toast," Erik added.

"Okay, alright!" Christoph waved them off, laughing. "I'm a disaster in the kitchen. I admit it."

"But," he said, leaning closer to Cecelia, "I can appreciate a good breakfast. And good company."

Cecelia's cheeks flushed, but she didn't look away.

The conversation continued, light and full of warmth. Christoph found himself laughing more than he had in weeks, watching Erik and Evie banter, listening to Cecelia talk about her art with that quiet kind of pride.

The food, it turned out, was perfect. But the company?

Even better.

"So this whole place is yours?" Cecelia asked as she and Christoph climbed the stairs to the third floor.

"Have I mentioned how incredible breakfast was?" Christoph offered with a hopeful smile.

"Flattery will get you nowhere, handsome man. Quit trying to change the subject and answer my question," she shot back.

He chuckled. "Yeah, the building technically belongs to Erik. But it's not something we advertise to party guests."

"Why not? I think it's kind of impressive."

"It's one thing to control a small party on the first floor. It's another thing entirely to worry about forty tipsy strangers wandering around your five-story apartment building. There's only two of us. We can't be everywhere at once," he said with a shrug.

"So what are you two, like… trust fund babies or something?"

"Something like that," he replied, not elaborating. "Erik makes most of his money through real estate, but we've got investments—like the restaurant. And a few side ventures."

She squinted up at him. "How'd you even get into all that? You can't be older than twenty-two, twenty-three."

She was watching his face, waiting for a flinch—anything to give away the truth. But he gave her nothing. Just a casual smile.

"We're just a couple of driven guys with a strong sense of direction," he said, tapping his temple. "What else can I say?" He winked at her.

By now, they had reached the top of the stairs and moved down a quiet hall. Christoph pulled a key from his pocket and unlocked a nondescript door. She recognized this floor—it was familiar somehow—but she couldn't place it.

"This is my favorite room in the building," he said as they approached a pair of sliding doors. "I don't bring many people up here."

There was something in his voice—something quieter, more open. Not a line, not a tease. Something close to vulnerable.

It caught her off guard.

She blushed again. Damn it. Her cheeks were getting sore from all the blushing around him.

He pulled the doors open and turned toward her, smiling.

"I'd like to formally welcome you to my world," he said with a flourish. "After you."

She stepped inside—and froze.

It was… beautiful.

There were no other words for it. Not impressive. Not cool. Not even romantic. Just—*beautiful.*

Towering shelves lined the walls, filled floor to ceiling with books of every kind. The scent of old paper, polished wood, and something warm and earthy surrounded her. On the far wall, a Dali original hung over a lit fireplace. Antique couches and armchairs were arranged in cozy groupings. A staircase spiraled up to a second level, where a window nook overflowed with soft pillows and a view of the city skyline.

She spun slowly, mouth parted in awe.

"This puts my dad's study to shame," she whispered.

"You like it?" he asked, suddenly sounding unsure. He scratched the back of his head, like a teenager showing off his room for the first time.

Row after row of shelves stretched along the walls, packed with books from floor to ceiling. Every genre, every era. Worn spines and crisp hardcovers. No labels, but everything was clearly organized with intent. Her heart skipped.

He had a *fantasy section.* Her pulse doubled.

"This… this is your *personal* library?" she asked, spinning in a slow circle.

"Cecelia," he said gently, drawing her gaze. He scratched the back of his head, sheepish. "What do you think?"

"Just wow. This is incredible," she said with such genuine amazement. "Do I need a permission slip to explore?"

He laughed. "You're holding the golden ticket. Knock yourself out."

She began wandering through the aisles, running her fingers along the spines. Fiction, nonfiction, poetry, history, medical journals—everything was grouped neatly, even without labels. Each book looked well-worn, well-read, well-loved. She could tell instantly: this wasn't for show. This was someone's sanctuary.

"I'm actually kind of overwhelmed," she admitted. "I still can't believe this is your personal library."

He nodded. "Every book in here, I hunted down myself."

"How do you have time to read them all?" she teased.

"I don't sleep much."

"Same."

She found herself smiling again. Of course he didn't sleep much. Maybe he was like her—up until 3 a.m., lost in another world.

She wandered toward the back wall where several glass cases lined the room, displaying rare objects: ancient scrolls, statues, and even weapons. She stopped in front of a glass case containing two golden daggers with black hilts covered in intricate leaf and swirl designs. Symbols—unfamiliar, possibly ancient—were etched into the base of the blades.

"Tell me about these."

Christoph joined her, arms folded behind his back. "I found them in Rome. They date back to about 70 B.C.—give or take."

"They're beautiful," she said. "They look like they could still slice through steel."

"They could," he said, a little too confidently. "I had a few… enhancements made."

"Of course you did," she said with a sly smile. "But why two?"

"I like pairs."

Cecelia raised an eyebrow at that, but let it slide. She moved to the next display—an ancient book, its pages brown and curling at the edges, bound in something that looked like pressed leather. Just looking at it made her fingertips ache to turn a page.

"And this one?"

"A papyrus manuscript," he said, stepping beside her. "From Alexandria. It's a first-century reprint of a lost Greek text. The real thing might've been burned during the fire."

"Wow," she breathed. "Do you ever read from it?"

He smiled. "Only when I'm feeling particularly poetic."

She turned toward him and said, "You're full of surprises, Max."

"You have no idea," he replied, and for once, he wasn't teasing.

"And this one?" Cecelia asked, stepping up to a glass case holding a large, aged tome.

"The *Codex Sinaiticus*," Christoph said, coming to stand beside her, hands in his pockets as he peered into the case. "One of the oldest surviving copies of the Old Testament."

"Can you read it?" she asked, tilting her head to study his face.

"It's handwritten in ancient Greek," he said with a smirk.

"That was a statement, not an answer."

"I know," he replied, lips tugging into something smug and playful.

She narrowed her eyes. "Is it open to any particular page?"

He glanced sideways at her. "Are you always this curious?"

"Always," she said without hesitation. "I like knowing why people do things. And something tells me you don't open an ancient book to a random page for display. You're definitely a 'everything has a reason' kind of guy."

He nodded, impressed. "Guilty as charged."

She smiled. She was starting to really enjoy peeling back Christoph's layers. Last night at the club, when he'd started talking about his adventures with Erik, she could've listened for hours. There was something ageless in the way he spoke. Like he and Erik had seen a thousand lifetimes between them, even though they didn't look a day over twenty-five.

"It's turned to the passage about Lucifer's descent. His fall from grace," Christoph finally answered, voice lower now, like the weight of the story had settled in.

Her brow creased. "That's... specific."

He nodded slowly, expression unreadable. "This version predates the political edits. It's closer to the source—before the corruption, before indulgences and revisions turned the text into something palatable."

She wasn't sure what to make of that. Maybe he was referring to the rise of Catholicism, or the church's long history of altering scripture to fit its agenda. Whatever he meant, it gave her a weird little chill. The kind that comes from hearing something you're not sure you were supposed to.

"What does this version tell you?" she asked softly.

He turned to face her fully. "Tell you what. You go first. You tell me the version you know... and I'll pick up where you leave off."

She raised an eyebrow. "You want the Sunday school version?"

"Why not? Could be fun."

She crossed her arms. "Fine. From what I remember, Lucifer was God's greatest angel—"

"False," he said, interrupting with a smug grin.

She stopped and gave him a withering look. "Excuse me. No interrupting."

He held up his hands in surrender, still grinning.

"Lucifer was one of God's most beloved angels," she continued with exaggerated patience. "But he became jealous of humans. He wanted power, wanted things to go his way. So he rebelled, got a bunch of angels to follow him, and Michael cast them all out of Heaven."

Christoph snorted. "Wow. They really gave you the SparkNotes version."

She elbowed him in the ribs.

"Alright, alright," he said, rubbing his side. "Let me give you the director's cut."

He stepped closer to the glass case, voice softening. "Before the fall, Lucifer discovered something powerful—dark magic. He used it to transform his most loyal generals into something beyond their angelic forms. That's where the first demons came from. The Greater Demons."

Cecelia's eyes widened slightly.

"He didn't just rebel," Christoph said, looking her dead in the eye. "He tried to overthrow the Creator by force."

She sank to the floor, cross-legged, chin resting in her hands as she looked up at him with a grin. "Okay. Now you have my full attention."

He smirked and took a seat beside her, back resting casually against the display case.

"Michael—God's champion, leader of Heaven's armies—fought back. He wiped out most of Lucifer's forces, captured the rest. Then he personally stripped their wings. After that, they were cast into the Pit."

"Yikes," Cecelia murmured. "Sounds… brutal."

"Oh, but wait," he said, eyes glinting. "Here comes the twist."

She leaned in.

"The Codex claims that the First Angel—older even than Lucifer—cast *himself* out of Heaven. Out of love. For his brother. He couldn't bear to see him punished alone. He chose exile."

She blinked. "Wait… what?"

Christoph nodded. "That act of free will—it was unprecedented. An angel disobeying God out of loyalty to someone else? That moment became the spark that justified humanity's free will. It was the blueprint."

Silence fell between them.

Cecelia felt like the floor had dropped out from under her. It made a kind of twisted sense. If one of God's own angels had chosen love over obedience…

it changed everything. Maybe free will wasn't born from divine generosity—but from heartbreak.

"Is that true?" she asked, her voice smaller now.

"In the truest sense?" Christoph said. "Yeah. I believe it."

"But it's not in our Bible."

"Nope."

"Why not?"

He shrugged. "Maybe the church couldn't handle the idea of angels choosing love over duty. Or maybe they just didn't want anyone questioning their version of control."

She stared at the case in front of them. "So mankind's entire concept of choice… came from an angel's act of grief."

"That's one way to look at it."

Cecelia shook her head. "This is insane. And amazing. And insane."

"Good stories usually are," he said with a smile. "Ready for part two?"

"Hit me."

"In Hell, Lucifer perfected the same magic he used on his generals. He created a new spell—a promise. It lured the newly fallen with the one thing they missed most: their wings."

Cecelia shivered.

"He called it a blessing. But the cost was everything. The spell consumed their blood, burned away the last of their angelic grace. What it gave them in return wasn't wings… it was transformation. A total rewrite of who they were."

"And they went for it?"

"They were broken. Desperate. Alone. Of course they did." He glanced at her, voice quiet. "Magic always has a price."

She watched him closely. There was something personal in the way he said that, like he wasn't just reciting myth.

"And the result?" she asked.

"They became his," Christoph said. "Utterly. Irrevocably. Lucifer wasn't just their leader anymore. He was their creator. Their god."

He leaned back and let out a long breath. "Bet they wish they'd read the fine print."

Cecelia pushed herself up and pointed at the glass case. "You're telling me *that* book says all that?"

Christoph gave her a wicked grin. "Something along those lines."

She narrowed her eyes. "You're messing with me."

"Am I?"

"You jerk!" she said, laughing as she shoved his shoulder. "You really had me going for a minute!"

He laughed too, low and warm, brushing his shoulder where she'd hit him. "You liked it."

"Maybe a little," she admitted, still grinning. "So what else are you hiding up here, Maximus?"

"Hmm," Christoph winked at her and reached for her hand. "Come with me," he said, his fingers warm around hers as he pulled her gently behind him. "I want to show you something," he added, glancing over his shoulder with that damn grin again—the one that made her chest flutter like a shaken snow globe.

They wandered deeper through rows of bookshelves and displays. She spotted another marble statue on a pedestal, followed by a striking Romanesque portrait hanging on the wall.

She slowed her pace just long enough to study it.

With a fresh haircut and maybe a pair of designer sunglasses, the man in the painting could *absolutely* pass for Christoph. She squinted. Dimples? Check. Brooding gaze? Check. Jawline you could use to sharpen pencils? Double check.

She narrowed her eyes playfully. *He did not.*
...He totally did.

The man was a *little* conceited, after all. She wouldn't put it past him to commission fan art of himself and then frame it like a historical relic.

They climbed the stairs to the second floor, deeper into the quieter corner of the room. Christoph led her behind a tall shelf to a tucked-away nook, almost entirely surrounded by books. The air felt warmer here—more intimate. Quiet. Still.

She stopped when he did, suddenly aware of how close they were standing.

Wait... hold on. Are we—
Oh my god.
OHMYGOD.

Is he going to kiss me?!

She instinctively leaned back against the bookcase, trying to look cool. Relaxed. Like this wasn't the moment her brain turned into a blender full of butterflies.

Okay, no big deal. He's hot. I'm cute. We're alone. Just act natural. You've got this. You haven't been kissed in forever, but who cares? He probably has lips like poetry. You're totally fine.

Her hands fidgeted behind her back.

 He stepped closer, leaning in. His chest pressed gently against hers.

I am absolutely not fine.

What if I'm terrible at this? What if I do that weird sideways head tilt thing again? Oh god, Tyler Summers. Ninth grade. He called me "teethy." AHHH.

She squeezed her eyes shut and puckered her lips in anticipation.

Then—

"Would you excuse me?" Christoph whispered against her ear.

Her eyes flew open, lips still stuck in kiss-mode. "Wait, wha—?"

That's when she felt the bookshelf behind her shift.

With one smooth motion, Christoph wrapped an arm around her waist, pulling her into him as the entire bookcase slid open behind her, revealing a secret room hidden inside the wall.

She stumbled, but he caught her like it was all part of the plan. Honestly? It probably was.

"What is this place?" she asked, stepping cautiously into the dimly lit room.

It was barely the size of a walk-in closet, but she immediately noticed the sleek wardrobe on the left and a narrow spiral staircase coiled in the back corner. It looked like it went both up *and* down.

Christoph leaned in with a grin. "Erik gave Evie the 'grand tour' last night," he said with mock seriousness. "But *you*, Cecelia White, are getting the *secret special tour.*"

She gasped with theatrical flair. "Oh my god, not the *secret special tour.* That's elite status, right?"

"The highest."

"Well then, I insist you carry on, tour guide." She gave him a mock bow. "Lead the way, handsome man."

He flashed her another grin—ugh, that grin—and turned for the stairs.

"So friggin' cute," she mumbled under her breath.

"What was that?" he asked, glancing back at her.

She blinked, startled. "Huh? I didn't say anything."

He gave her a knowing smirk and continued climbing.

She followed him up the spiral staircase, eyes darting around. Whatever was at the top had her heart racing again—and not because she thought he might kiss her this time (though, now that the surprise-door moment was out of the way, she wouldn't mind a *redo*).

When they reached the top, Christoph pressed a sequence into a discreet keypad mounted on the wall.

A metallic door slid upward with a hiss, revealing a space unlike anything she expected.

"You're gonna like this," he said. "I remember overhearing you were into martial arts."

She stepped in—and nearly choked.

"Whoa," she whispered, spinning in place. "Okay, this is... this is intense."

It wasn't just a training room. It was a black belt's fever dream.

Floor-to-ceiling mirrors, clean lines dividing polished hardwood from padded mats, and racks of gear that made her feel like a kid in a candy store. Wooden katanas, kendo sticks, batons—lined up like museum pieces but clearly used.

"This is all yours?" she asked.

"Welcome to the Elite Wing Dojo," he said, bowing playfully. She bowed back with a grin, barely stifling a laugh.

They moved deeper into the space, and Cecelia soaked in every detail like she was cataloging it for her dream journal. One room was split between a boxing ring and a practice zone with two heavy bags, two Wing Chun dummies, a pair of wooden torsos, and even a set of those fully-padded MMA dummies she'd seen on YouTube clock drill videos she'd secretly studied at 2 a.m.

Oh my god, they have everything.

Next was a private gym: rows of treadmills, free weights, machines, pull-up bars, and—of course—giant tractor tires. Why? Who knows. Who cares. They were beautiful.

"This whole thing," she said slowly, turning in place. "It's amazing, but like... what do you even need all this for?"

"We like to stay fit. Prepared."

"Prepared for what, the zombie apocalypse?" she teased. "Because I saw those wooden dummies back there, and there are holes in them. No way you're just hitting them with padded swords."

"Actually," he said, lips twitching, "they're for throwing knives."

That stopped her. "Shut up. For real?"

"For real."

"Okay, now I'm jealous. I'm decent with a katana, but throwing knives? That's like... assassin-tier. Can you show me?"

He raised an eyebrow. "You wanna try?"

"Oh, I definitely do," she said, arms crossed and smirking like she'd already beat him in a match.

"Well then," he said, looking her over with a smirk, "first we should probably get you out of that dress."

Her brain tripped over itself. "W-what?"

He laughed. "Workout clothes, pretty girl. Follow me."

She exhaled sharply and rolled her eyes, face flushing as she followed him. Of course he had to word it like that.

The changing room near the entrance looked straight out of a boutique gym: black tiles, built-in sauna, sleek showers, lockers.

"You and Erik train here alone?" she asked, spinning slowly in place.

"Mostly," he said, opening a locker and grabbing folded clothes. "But sometimes the guys come by—Darius, Sam—you met them."

He handed her a bundle. "Gi pants, black tee, hoodie. A little loose maybe, but they'll do."

She took the clothes, trying not to smile too wide.

"Thanks."

"I'll change in the next room. Meet you on the mat?"

"Hell yeah," she said, eyes sparkling.

She ducked into the changing room, heart hammering. Secret doors, ancient libraries, private dojos, flirty rich boy energy—what even was her life right now?

And more importantly: when did she get this lucky?

"Okay, so you want to hold it like this," Christoph said, gripping a sleek black throwing knife in his left hand. The blade glinted like it was waiting for a fight. He handed it to her, and she took it like it was a shiny new toy she couldn't wait to play with.

"You need to get a feel for the weight of it."

Cecelia held it in her hand, lifting it gently up and down. "Okay, what am I supposed to feel? The rage of a thousand fallen warriors? Or is this more like... 'just breathe and pretend you know what you're doing?'" she grinned.

"Not quite," he chuckled, stepping closer. "Here, try this." He adjusted her grip, his fingers brushing against hers. "Support the blade with your pointer finger and secure it with your thumb. Wrist straight, elbow bent."

"Like this?" she asked, tilting her head as she followed his lead.

"Yeah," he said, eyes flicking up to meet hers. "Just like that." That smirk of his? Criminal.

"I'll throw first. Watch and mimic my movements."

She watched him with laser focus as he raised the blade, twisted his hips, and sent the knife spinning through the air. It cut cleanly through the space between them and thudded dead-center into the bull's eye on the dummy's chest.

"Whoa," she said, wide-eyed. "You're, like... scary good at this."

"Knives are kind of my specialty," he shrugged, like it was no big deal. But Cecelia was screaming internally.

She stepped up with her own blade, bent her elbow, channeled her inner assassin—and chucked it like a javelin.

The knife wobbled mid-air, missed the dummy entirely, clanged off the wall, and skittered to the floor like a disgraced ninja star.

"Damn it," she groaned, stomping over to pick it up. "It didn't even stick."

"Hey, hey, that was a solid first try," he said, following behind her. "No one sticks it on their first throw. Trust me, this stuff takes time."

She huffed like an angry cat. "Fine. One more try. But if this one hits the fire alarm, I'm blaming you."

"Breathe," he said, placing a hand on her back gently. "Trust yourself."

She exhaled slowly, refocused, and let him adjust her grip again.

"Remember—where your elbow points, your wrist follows," he said, giving her hand a light tap.

"Got it," she nodded. "Ready to be impressed?"

"Oh, I'm counting on it."

She narrowed her eyes, locked on the target, and let the blade fly.

THWACK.

Right in the center of the dummy's chest.

"YES!" she whooped, jumping up and down. "I got it! Did you see that?!"

Before he could answer, she launched herself at him, arms wrapping around his neck as she hugged him tight.

"You rock, Max."

"Nah," he murmured into her hair, hugging her back. "That was all you."

She grinned into his chest. "Best first date ever."

He let her go and stepped back, a smirk tugging at his lips. "Oh no, pretty girl. This isn't our first date."

Her smile faltered slightly.

"We're just hanging out," he added with a playful nudge—but it hit different. The words left a tiny ache somewhere inside her chest.

But then he leaned in closer, voice softer. "Trust me... you'll know when it's our first date. That night will be something special."

Butterflies exploded in her stomach. And not the cute kind. The kind that wore tiny leather jackets and rode motorcycles.

"Alright, handsome man," she said, punching his arm. "Want me to show you some wicked karate moves? Or did I forget to mention I'm a second-degree black belt?"

She did a dramatic air-chop. "Kiya!"

He burst out laughing. "Wait—you were serious about that?"

She raised an eyebrow. "You think I'm small and harmless, huh?"

"Oh no, that's not it, it's just—"

That's when she stepped in, grabbed his shirt, and hip-tossed him flat onto the mat.

THUD.

"Ow," he groaned. "You really weren't kidding."

"Guess not," she said sweetly, offering her hand to help him up.

As he stood, his eyes caught on something—a glint of metal slipping from the collar of her shirt.

"Hey," he said, pointing. "You didn't take that off? Do you always wear that thing?"

"This?" she asked, instinctively clutching the key pendant around her neck. She tucked it back into her shirt. "Yeah... always."

"It's beautiful. Where'd you get it?"

"It's a family heirloom," she said, voice softening. "It was my grandmother's, and her mother's before her. It's passed down through the women in my dad's bloodline. He was an only child, so he held onto it until my 18th birthday."

Christoph stepped closer, curiosity in his eyes. "Tell me more."

Cecelia blinked, surprised. "Really? You sure you want the whole origin story?"

"Try me," he said, hand over his heart. "Promise not to laugh. Mostly because I'd prefer not to get slammed again."

She laughed and plopped onto the mat, patting the space beside her. "Alright then. Sit. It's story time."

He sat down cross-legged next to her, eyes fixed on hers.

"There's a legend in my family," she began, turning the pendant in her fingers. "About my great-great-great-grandmother... who fell in love with an angel."

He stilled, but she kept going.

"My dad used to say the angel gave her this key and told her it was his soul. That when he saw her, he no longer needed the key to Saint Peter's gates—because she was heaven to him."

Christoph's expression didn't shift, but something in the air between them did.

"They say he never aged. He stayed young while she grew old. They even had a child together."

His eyes flickered at that, but she played it cool.

"And when she died... he ended his life too. Said he didn't want to live in a world without her."

She looked away, her voice softening. "Romantic, right?"

Christoph shook his head slightly. "Nope."

She recoiled. "Oh great, you think I'm insane—"

"Nah, pretty girl," he said gently. "I think it's the most beautiful thing I've ever heard."

Her breath caught. And for a moment, the only sound in the room was the quiet thrum of both their hearts.

Cecelia kept talking about something but Christoph became lost in thought.

He didn't understand.

Fallen angels couldn't reproduce—not without darkness, not without consequence. Their offspring were twisted things—mules of the damned. But Cecelia… she didn't feel like a mistake. She felt radiant. Inherently good. Seraphic…

"Hey," she nudged him playfully, snapping him out of it. "Are you there? You looked like you were spacing out for a second there. You alright?"

He blinked, dragging his eyes back to her face. "What did you say this angel's name was again?"

"I didn't," she smirked. "But since you asked so nicely—Jed. His name was Jedediah."

His stomach dropped. That name. He remembered that name.

Jedediah.

The lost one.

Rumor said he'd vanished not long after the fall—never returned, never seen again. Some believed he'd been destroyed. Others whispered he chose love. But Christoph had searched for him once. And for the key he'd carried. Now here it was… around *her* neck. She wasn't lying. She *couldn't* be. Her blood sang with something sacred.

She wasn't demonic.

She was his opposite.

She was seraphic nephilim.

"I think it's about time I got you home," he said, standing and offering his hand. He masked the shake in his fingers by tightening his grip. "Can't leave your roommate waiting."

She took it slowly. "You sure you're okay?"

"Yeah." He forced a smile. "Just… processing."

She squeezed his hand and bumped her shoulder against his. "Well, if you're gonna mope, you better do it while showing me this so-called hot car of yours."

He raised a brow. "Oh, you like cars?"

"I like anything that moves fast," she grinned. "Bonus points if it makes my stomach drop."

He chuckled, tension breaking from his shoulders. "Then you're in for a treat, pretty girl."

The garage lights blinked on as he keyed open the side door, and Cecelia's jaw dropped. It wasn't just a garage—it was a *hangar*. Polished cement floors. Industrial lighting. And rows of serious machines.

"Holy hell," she breathed. "This is like… Fast & Furious meets Gotham."

He laughed. "You're not far off."

"These are all yours?"

"Not all," he said, motioning to the right. "The blue Honda's Erik's, so is the dirt bike and the Harley. That red one's mine. The Ducati under the tarp, too."

She crossed to the Ducati and gently pulled back the edge. "Damn," she whispered. "That thing looks like it could outrun the apocalypse."

"It probably could," he said proudly. "You ride?"

"I *dream* of riding," she said. "Does that count?"

"That's a start," he winked.

Then she caught sight of it—the black SS Camaro gleaming in the far corner, low to the ground, perfectly buffed, parked like it *knew* it was king.

"Oh. Oh my *God*." She took off toward it. "This… this is art."

He grinned as she circled it. "That's Icarus. My pride and joy."

"Icarus?" she tilted her head. "Thought you were supposed to name cars after women?"

"Amateurs do," he said smugly. "Icarus is my wingman. Helps me soar."

"Oh, does he now?"

"Every damn time," he said, walking around to open the passenger door with a flourish. "Climb in, pretty girl. Let me show you why."

The interior was blood-red leather—sleek, stitched, and warm. As she settled in, she let out a happy little sound, running her fingers over the console.

"I feel like I need a tux just to sit in this thing."

"No tux required. You're perfect like this."

She grinned as he slid into the driver's seat. "Okay, I take it back. You *were* bragging. But… you earned it."

"Glad you approve," he said, hitting the ignition. The car purred like a dragon waking up.

"I mean, you've got heated seats *and* rearview cameras. This is bougie muscle car perfection."

"You noticed," he smirked. "Impressed?"

She turned to him, all mock-serious. "Handsome man, I am deeply, soulfully, *shamelessly* impressed."

"Good," he said, eyes still on the dash. "Speaking of seeing more of each other… I'm starting back at NYU next week."

Her head whipped toward him. "Wait—seriously?"

"Yep. I cleared it with the Dean. Starting late, but all my coursework's done."

She narrowed her eyes. "You *would* be that guy. Secret genius-slash-mystery car god."

"I just like being prepared," he shrugged.

"Well," she said, nestling into the seat, "in that case… I'm really glad you're going back. I might even let you sit next to me in class."

"Oh? Is that how it works now?"

"Only for guys with cool cars and excellent taste in cocktails."

"Noted," he chuckled, pressing the garage button.

The door rumbled open, and the street lights outside glimmered across the hood of Icarus.

"I'm excited," she said quietly, looking out the windshield.

He glanced at her. "About what?"

She looked back at him, a soft smile tugging at her lips. "About this year. About you. About whatever this is."

He didn't answer at first. He just reached over, gently brushing her knuckles with his thumb.

"Oh, indeed it is," he said finally, voice low.

"Alright, handsome man," she leaned back, ready. "Let's see what Icarus can do."

"Hold on tight, pretty girl."

He hit the gas, and Icarus launched them forward—fast, smooth, and screaming into the city night.

Arch Duke
Azazel

Chapter 12

He had been running all night.

Not out of duty. Not even desperation.

Out of fear.

He was no stranger to death—had dealt it himself in creative, messy ways for centuries—but tonight was different. Tonight, he had witnessed something far worse than death. He'd seen judgment.

Golden blades that hummed with divine fury. Axes that sliced through demon flesh like butter through warm bread. Smoke and ash—his brothers reduced to vapor in seconds. He hadn't known the fear of God in eons, but tonight?

Tonight, it came roaring back.

He sprinted down the still-shadowed streets as the first light of dawn crept over the city. The sidewalks were empty. The world above remained blissfully unaware of the war being waged beneath their feet.

He glanced once over his shoulder before diving into the sewer grate.

The tunnels welcomed him with the stink of rot and the silence of the dead. He sloshed through the muck, zigzagging through the ancient arteries of the city, his breath ragged, his heart pounding. Left. Right. Left again. Through rusted iron doors and forgotten passageways only his kind knew.

The lair approached.

He barreled through the door, too frantic to acknowledge the guards, dodging swinging axes, arrows, and even somersaulting to avoid the snapping jaws of hellhounds

He burst through the final threshold, collapsing onto the scorched marble floor.

"*Arch Duke Azazel,*" he gasped, chest heaving. "We've found the key."

A long pause. Then, from the shadows, the voice came.

"*Report.*"

The voice was cold as steel and twice as sharp. Azazel stepped forward—tall, lean, and hard-edged, like a blade forged in sin. His raven-black hair hung in dark waves across his brow, and his eyes flickered with flame, two dying stars ready to collapse into fury.

"One of our scouts spotted a girl—on the subway," the demon panted. "She was wearing the Angel Key you've been looking for."

Azazel's expression did not change.

"Where is she now?"

"We gave chase. I was one of seven sent for backup. But she wasn't alone."

He paused.

"She was guarded."

Azazel's gaze narrowed. "By whom?"

"We saw only two at first… Ceruleus and Eros," he said, like the names themselves were a curse.

Azazel's jaw clenched. He stood still for a long moment, fire dancing in his irises.

"There were eight of you," he said slowly. "Is that correct?"

"Yes, my lord."

"And I am speaking to the *last*?"

The demon swallowed hard. "Yes, my lord."

"I don't believe I understand," Azazel said, his voice low and dangerous. "How can *eight* of my soldiers be torn apart by *two* fallen?"

"They weren't alone!" the minion blurted out. "We were ambushed. The girl was bait. Two more appeared from the shadows—Samuel and Darius. All four of the Elite Wing."

Azazel's eyes flared with molten fury.

"I watched them work," the demon continued shakily. "They moved like executioners. Silent. Precise. Golden light in their veins. I barely escaped with my life—I ran only to bring you this news. I made sure I wasn't followed."

Azazel paced the chamber like a caged animal.

"This is a problem," he growled. "The Elite Wing *are* a problem."

He didn't care for Samuel. Never had. Too noble. Too human. Darius was worse—quick with a blade, quicker with judgment. But Ceruleus and Eros… those were the ones that mattered. The girl, too.

She had *the Key*.

"What would you have me do, master?" the demon asked, trembling.

Azazel stopped pacing.

"I will dispatch new scouts. You'll travel in pairs. No more lone runs. I want *eyes* on that washed-up Archangel Ceruleus and that lunatic Eros. I want that girl watched night and day. I want surveillance on that club of theirs, every back entrance, every sewer, every goddamn shadow they crawl into."

"Yes, sir."

"And when the time is right, when she's *alone*—you take her. And you bring me their heads."

The demon hesitated. "But sir... we stood no chance. If the Elite Wing is watching her, we'll never—"

"I *said*," Azazel's voice roared, the air around him igniting in flame, "I WANT THEIR HEADS!"

The demon dropped to his knees, shaking.

Azazel turned, fire fading from his skin as he stared into the darkened corridor beyond.

"Send word to the others," he said, quieter now but no less deadly. "War is coming. And I intend to win it."

Andrew

Chapter 13

Shake it up

"Hey, Cecelia."

She turned, and Andrew slid into the seat beside her, tipping his baseball cap back with an awkward fidget.

"I just… I'd like to formally apologize for my roommate's disgustin', intolerable, and downright inexcusable behavior the other night." His voice was low but sincere. "I didn't hear the full story till Jen filled me in, but even before that—what Brian told me?" He shook his head. "Horseshit. I knew it was."

She opened her mouth, but no words came out.

"I'm angry, Cecelia," Andrew said gently. "Ashamed too. And I just hope me livin' with that bastard doesn't mess with our friendship."

"I—" Cecelia looked down at her hands. Her knuckles were pale. She hadn't realized how tightly she was gripping her notebook.

Evie leaned across the aisle. "Do you think he's going to show?"

"He's got an ego bigger than Manhattan, but after what that Christoph feller did to him?" Andrew gave a half-smile. "He might think twice about showin' his face. I reckon he learned his lesson."

"I doubt it," Evie muttered darkly, cracking her knuckles. "But if he does, he sure as hell better not sit anywhere near you. I'll knock his teeth out."

"Evie, I don't want to talk about it." Cecelia's voice was quiet but firm. "Or think about it."

She turned to Andrew, trying to smile, but her eyes betrayed her.

"And you don't need to apologize for Brian. You're not his keeper. He's my prob—"

The door clicked open.

Brian Watterson walked in.

It felt like someone hit pause on the whole room.

Cecelia's stomach dropped. Her chest tightened. Her breath caught somewhere in her throat. She hated that just the *sight* of him made her feel small. Weak. Dirty. The bruises on his face weren't enough. She should've been the one to give them to him.

He was wearing a hoodie and sunglasses—black Ray-Bans to hide what Christoph had done. His nose was still swollen, and he kept his chin tilted down as he took the seat at the front, close to the door. Coward.

"Well," Andrew muttered, "guess he didn't take Christoph's advice after all."

"I *cannot* believe he actually showed," Evie whispered, hand reaching into her purse fishing to grip something.

And then—perfect timing.

The door opened again.

Christoph strolled in like a storm in a t-shirt. Jeans. Max Lounge blazer. His shirt read *Avada Kedavra, Bitch.* His energy? Nuclear.

Cecelia swore she saw a flash of gold in his eyes.

He didn't say a word.

He just *looked* at Brian.

And then, in one clean, terrifying move, he walked up to him, grabbed Brian by the shirt with one hand, snatched his bag with the other, and yanked him out of the room like taking out the trash. His chair scraped loudly as it was pulled away from the desk, then silence followed.

No one breathed. No one dared move.

A full minute passed before they heard rapid footsteps echoing down the hallway—Christoph walking in. Alone.

He strolled right back in like nothing had happened.

"Hey, guys," he grinned, casual as anything, waving to them like he'd just come back from getting a snack. "Fancy seeing you all here."

Evie's mouth opened… then closed. Then opened again. Nothing came out.

Cecelia blinked. "Max… what are you doing here?"

"Told you I was starting late," he shrugged, plopping into the open seat beside Andrew. "Kinda cool we've got class together."

"It *is* cool," Cecelia said carefully. "But, uh… what just happened?"

Christoph leaned back and stretched his arms across the desk behind him like he owned the whole damn building. "Oh that?" he said innocently. "Brian just needed a refresher on our little chat from the other night. Guess I didn't hit him hard enough the first time."

"But you didn't have to do that," she whispered.

"I know," he said. "I did it anyway."

Then he smiled.

And *damn,* she thought. She would *definitely* never cross him.

"So," he added cheerfully, "what'd I miss?"

Andrew coughed, trying to pull the room back from its tailspin. "Not much really. Professor's just been ramblin' about China and their rising economy. Supposedly they're populations gonna outnumber the US in a few decades. I'm thinkin' of takin' Mandarin as a second language."

"Oh, *Nà tài hǎo le,*" Christoph said with a grin.

Andrew stared. "Uh… come again?"

"I said that'd be great."

"You speak Chinese now?" Andrew asked, laughing. "Damn show-off."

"Yeah, my friend Sam's been teaching me. Good for business."

"That's what I'm sayin'!" Andrew slapped the desk. "This guy gets it."

The mood finally started to lighten. Evie shot Christoph a grateful look across the aisle—*thank you,* mouthed silently. He nodded, no big deal.

The professor walked in, setting down a stack of papers and launching into his lecture like nothing had happened.

But Cecelia sat still for a long moment, her pulse still racing. The room had moved on.

She hadn't.

Her body still remembered the way Brian made her freeze.

And her heart—well, it was trying not to flutter every time Christoph looked her way.

"Now as you're all aware from your syllabus, this week we're to begin our first group project," Professor Peterson announced to the class. No one was aware. He just caused room-wide panic with that statement alone, and he didn't even realize it. "You are to separate into groups of four, and then you will be assigned countries at random to research and report on. Once you select your group, send a representative to the front of the class to get your packet."

"Nobody move," Evie warned. "You're all in my group. I don't feel like going around and introducing myself to anyone else."

"Uh, sure thing, sweetheart," Andrew said, standing up. "I'll just head up there and get our packet."

"What if I wanted to meet new people?" Christoph teased.

"Too bad. You're sitting with the only people you'll ever need to know in this room," Evie stated plainly.

"Well, alright then," Christoph chuckled. "I see this is a dictatorship, not a democracy."

"Of course it is," Cecelia giggled. "Welcome to being friends with Evie."

Andrew returned with the packet. "Says here we needa choose a group leader. Duties state they are responsible for coordinatin' our meetins outta the classroom."

"I could do that," Cecelia volunteered.

"I'm all for it," Christoph stated.

"Yeah, me too," Andrew agreed.

"What happened to this being a dictatorship?" Evie chided. "Fine, Cecelia can be group leader. I didn't want all the responsibility anyway," she pretended not to care.

"Evie and I know of this great bookstore near College Ave that we could all meet up at after lunch," Cecelia suggested. "I'd like to get a jump start on this. Everyone cool with that?"

"Oh yeah, I liked that place," Evie added.

"Why don't we all go together so no one gets lost?"

"Sounds like a plan," Christoph agreed.

"Why didn't you just say we were coming here?" Christoph asked as they approached the storefront. "Ray's actually a close personal friend of mine."

"Oh, of course you know the owner," Cecelia said with a playful eye roll. "You just *know* everyone, don't you, Max?"

"I see no harm in introducing myself and making friends whenever I find a new place I happen to like," he replied smoothly, like it was the most obvious thing in the world.

"Wait a sec…" Andrew tilted his head, squinting at the sign above the door. "Is this place *really* called *Ray's Cool Café?*"

"The name's a little cheesy," Christoph admitted, "but once you go inside, you'll see it fits."

"If you say so, Casanova," Andrew snorted.

"You've got the wrong guy," Christoph chuckled. "That would be Erik."

Andrew just looked confused.

"Let's just go inside and find a table," Cecelia said, tugging the door open.

"I'm gonna wait out here. I asked Erik to meet us," Evie added casually, taking out her phone to check the time.

"Oh *did* you now?" Christoph smirked. "Somebody's got a *cruuush*," he sang, winking.

She gave him a firm shove. "Just go inside, dork."

"See you in there, Evie. I'll grab your favorite."

"Ugh. You're too good to me, Cecelia. You're the best."

"I know." Cecelia grinned, holding the door for the guys.

"That didn't take too long," Cecelia said, handing Evie her smoothie once they were all seated around a corner table near the back.

"Nope," Evie said, slurping through her straw as she pulled out a chair. "I texted him before we even left class. *He's* actually late," she added, side-eyeing Erik as he strolled up.

"I came all the way from Brooklyn," he said, arms wide. "I think I made pretty good time."

"Nope. Late. Unacceptable," she said with a smirk.

"You're impossible, Eves," he groaned.

"Just sit your cute butt down already," she commanded, and he obeyed with exaggerated defeat.

"So, what'd I miss?" he asked.

"Everyone's been assigned a topic," Cecelia said. "Max's handling environmental issues, Andrew's taking the economy, I've got religion and culture… and you, Evie, are on population."

"Nice. I get the easy part," Evie said, pleased. Cecelia knew her too well. And they'd only been friends a few weeks.

"Alright then, let's get to researching!" Cecelia raised her fist in the air like she was rallying troops.

Everyone stared at her.

"What?" she blinked. "Too soon?"

"Just chill out a sec," Evie said. "We're here. We claimed our territory. Let's finish our smoothies before we go full academic warfare."

"I admire your work ethic," Christoph said, swirling his straw. "But I gotta side with her on this one." He held up his neon-blue smoothie. "Let me finish my *Blue Raspberry Pop Rock Swirl* in peace."

"Dang, they really *do* have the best smoothies here," Andrew said, nodding with respect. "I applaud Ray. And his Cool Café."

"Okay, *fine*," Cecelia sighed dramatically, sinking into her chair.

"Hey Eves, check this out," Erik said, holding up a flyer from the bulletin board.

"Oh yeah!" she said. "Cecelia, this is that thing I told you about—the Open Mic Night."

"It's tomorrow night," Erik added. "I think we should all go. Could be fun."

"Yeah, that sounds cool. Do you guys play anything?" Cecelia asked.

"Ha. I dabble," Erik replied with fake modesty. "Little drums. Little bass. Christoph here's the real show-off," Erik added. "Guitar, piano, violin. He's like a one-man band."

"What *don't* you do?" Cecelia asked, giving Christoph a half-laugh, half-eye roll. "You're *too much*."

He shrugged with a grin. "It's a curse, really."

"Do *you* play anything?" Christoph asked, looking at her.

"Ha!" she snorted. "Not a musical bone in my body. But that's okay. I prefer to *listen* and *judge silently*."

"You do that so well," Evie deadpanned.

"Hey, *nobody* asked if I play anything," Andrew chimed in.

"Oh! Sorry, forgot you were here," Erik teased.

"I'm sittin' *right next* to you, man!"

"Yeah, but you vanish next to Evie's spotlight," Erik said, pointing to her.

To everyone's surprise, she blushed.

"Aww heck, I can't blame ya, partner," Andrew grinned, nudging him. "She's got a gravitational pull."

"Wait," Cecelia cut in, "do you *actually* play anything?"

"You're darn tootin' I do. I play the fiddle."

"That's actually really cool," Christoph said, impressed. "You should come jam with us sometime. I've got a few covers that could really use a fiddle line."

Andrew's face lit up. "Wait—seriously? After everything that happened with Brian?"

"Of course," Christoph said without hesitation. "You're not him. I don't hold people accountable for other people's screw-ups. If Cecelia and Evie trust you, that's good enough for me."

Andrew blinked. "Wow. Yeah. I'm down. I'll run back to my dorm and pick her up."

"I'm sorry, *pick who up?*" Evie asked slyly. "Jen?"

"Nah, my sweet *Charlene*. She's my fiddle," he said proudly, puffing up. "Wait—why'd you ask if I was picking up Jen?"

"No reason," Evie said innocently, glancing at Cecelia with the world's most obvious smirk.

Cecelia grinned back. They didn't need words to coordinate mischief.

"Yeah, I heard you left the party with her," Evie teased. "Spent the whole night together. Something *must've* happened…"

She wiggled her shoulders and made a very un-lady-like hand gesture.

Andrew turned bright red. "Well, uh, a gentleman never kisses and tells…"

"Andrew, you sly dog," Erik whistled. "Eves, you better bring her tomorrow night."

"Don't tell me what to do," Evie snapped automatically. "But fine. I will."

"This is gonna be some night," Cecelia laughed, shaking her head.

"Alright, so," she clapped her hands with renewed purpose. "Smoothies are done. Time to get to researching."

Everyone groaned in unison.

"I won't allow any more procrastinating," she said, standing and gesturing like a general calling troops to battle. "Come on. Everybody up."

"Do *I* have to come too?" Erik asked, slouched deep in his chair.

"Yes, you dork," Evie said, grabbing his collar and hauling him upright. "You're with me."

Christoph stood, stretching his arms behind his head. "So," he asked, eyes sliding to Cecelia, "where to first, fearless leader?"

She smirked. "The history section. And no detours. I *will* be watching."

"Damn," Christoph muttered with a wink. "I love it when you boss me around."

Cecelia rolled her eyes, but her smile gave her away.

They were going to make a hell of a team.

"What happened to 'Time to get to researching, no more of this procrastinating' nonsense you gave us earlier?" Christoph said mockingly. "I'm pretty sure our research didn't involve the YA Fantasy section of the bookstore."

"We did our research," Cecelia said gesturing to the stack of books Christoph held in his hands.

"I would hardly call you pulling a bunch of random books from the shelf without even opening them research," he said condescendingly shaking his head at her.

"It was TOO research," she said frowning at him. "I told the girl at the desk what I was looking for and she pulled up a list of where to find them."

"But we didn't look through any of them yet."

"That's a technicality," she said, waving him off. "The first step of research is retrieving sources, thank you very much. See," she said emphasizing the 'E', "research done. Now it's time for a break," she smiled happily as she gingerly skimmed her finger along the spines of the books on the shelf she was looking through.

"You're impossible," he muttered, but there was a fondness behind it.

"Ooo I found it!" she said triumphantly pulling the shiny red book like it was buried treasure.

He rolled his eyes at her. "You treat books like they're sacred relics," he teased.

"They kind of are," she said, cradling the book like it might disappear. "This is a book I heard about online. This Booktuber I really like gave it a great review. It's called *Ruby Red* and it's about a Time traveling girl named Gwen Shepherd."

"Time traveling? Like Doctor Who?"

"No, not like the Doctor, but she does have a Time Gadget!" she said pointing her finger matter-of-factly, "But it's no TARDIS. Actually, it's not a ship at all, more like one of those small do hickeys, where you turn some nobs, set some dates and it transports you."

"Hmm. So like a Time Machine," he teased.

"Ugh, not a Time Machine. It's a compact gadget the size of a typewriter. No stepping into a machine, no flying around. You're in one place and time one minute, and then in the same exact place but at another time," she huffed in annoyance but then smiled at him. "Not a Time Machine."

"Sure, sure. Not a Time Machine," he said with a wink, enjoying every second of her nerd rage. "So what else happens in it? Does Gwen fight dinosaurs? Rescue Abe Lincoln?"

She smirked. "Nice try. You'll just have to read it yourself."

"Well, I'd love to hear more about this story," he said, scanning the shelf and pulling two more books. "I see it's a Trilogy," he showed her the other books in the series. "That shows promise. Could I see that one?" he asked indicating to the copy she held in her hand so happily.

She didn't get a chance to respond before he took it from her and walked away.

"Hey, give that back," she called to him. "Where are you going with those?"

"I'd like to get them for you," he said smiling at her when she caught up to him.

"Oh, you don't have to do that. I can pay for them myself."

"But I insist," he said reaching the counter at the front where Ray stood behind the register.

"Hey, buddy buddy," Christoph said nodding his head at Ray.

"Ah, Maximus! What do I owe this pleasure?" Ray said smiling. Ray had one of those genuine smiles that were contagious. It reached his eyes and tugged at his cheeks puffing them up like a chipmunk's. "I see you're back as well. How did you like those smoothies the other day?" he asked looking toward Cecelia.

"Amazing, absolutely incredible," she said beaming at him with joy. "So I brought back some friends," she said gesturing to Christoph and over to Evie and Erik who were back at the Café. "But apparently, they've already been here before," Cecelia said blushing.

"Well, thanks all the same! No better compliment than a referral," he snapped his fingers. "So will that be all today?" he looked to the stack of books Christoph laid on the counter.

"Those are actually for me," Cecelia said trying to cut in front of Christoph at the register, but he reached over her and handed Ray his card.

"Thanks so much," Ray said taking the card and charging it. He placed the books in the bag along with the receipt and handed it to Cecelia. He leaned over the counter as if to whisper in her ear. "A word of advice. If a guy offers to buy you a book, take it. That guy knows how to treat a lady. Books are much better than flowers," she looked up at him confused. "The words in a book are forever. The scent and beauty of a flower is only temporary. There one day, gone the next," he winked at her.

"Ray, never took you for the romantic type." Christoph said chuckling.

"Well, nothing out there quite as romantic as a good book," he chuckled. "What can I say? I love books," he coyly shrugged his shoulders.

"It was good to see you again bud. I'll be stopping by again tomorrow night."

"It's been a while since we've had the pleasure of hearing you perform. Look forward to it."

"Come by the restaurant this weekend and I'll treat you to something special," Christoph said putting his arm around Cecelia.

"Sounds good to me! See you tomorrow."

"Definitely," Christoph said and him and Cecelia headed back over to the café.

It was the next night. Christoph, Erik, and Andrew had left the girls at the Café to go straight home and practice following their study session. Now they all sat back at Ray's Cool Café awaiting the evening's performances to begin. It was a packed house.

Every table was taken. Strings of fairy lights glowed above the crowd, casting soft golden hues on faces full of anticipation. The smell of sugar, coffee, and fresh-baked pastries lingered in the air. The place was electric.

"I wonder what they're going to play," Cecelia asked, leaning slightly over the table. "I bet they're good."

"Oh they are, and they know it," Evie replied a little too smugly, leaning in like she held a secret. "Erik showed me their stuff."

"Hey, that's not fair."

"What?" Evie shrugged. "He did show me his recording studio after all."

"Fine, guess it is fair, but you didn't have to rub it in." Cecelia looked over to the stage, her lips pursed in mock jealousy.

Ray, the owner of the Cool Café, walked over and picked up the microphone.

"Geeks and Geekettes, welcome to our Wednesday Open Mic night."

The crowd applauded, a few cheers breaking through.

"So as most of you know already, the rules are as follows," he clapped his hands and pointed to the table in front of him. "Sign-up sheet is over there, sign your name and you'll be called up in order. You get three songs. Or poems, or whatever the hell you want to do, just have fun, and buy a drink!" He looked over to the table at the guy holding the sign-up sheet. "Yale, who's first?"

"It says Christoph Maximus," the boy with large glasses and bushy brown hair replied.

"Alright then," Ray nodded to his friend and walked back over to the center of the stage.

"Hey Maximus, are you ready?" Ray looked over to the boy holding his guitar, who grinned back at him proudly.

"Okay then, ladies and gentleman, first up, my good friend, Christoph Maximus."

Christoph walked up the stage and adjusted the microphone, then tested his guitar. Being satisfied with the levels, he tapped the microphone and looked at the crowd.

"Thanks Ray," he said and winked at the owner. "I'm Christoph Maximus and this first song goes out to that beautiful blonde over there with the wicked hip toss," he winked at her and looked back to Erik, already ready on the drums. Erik tapped his drumsticks three times and Christoph began strumming his guitar.

Cecelia, sitting next to Evie, turned beet red with embarrassment.

Her eyes widened. "He did not just—oh my god." But the smile tugging at her lips said otherwise.

"There's something about her smile that lifts me up," he sang.

"And I swear I've never felt this way before / There's something about the way, she looks at me, that makes me feel all warm / like there's a moving inside me and I swear my heart skips a beat EVERYTIME."

"Whoa, he is good," Cecelia said to Evie. "It's like *Dashboard* meets *Jack's Mannequin.*"

"I told you," Evie smiled and looked back to the stage.

"It's just you and me, we're like the colliding of two winds," he strummed. "It's just you, and me, we're like the colliding of two winds," and the beat picked up, "and you and me, we're like the colliding of two winds, and just you and me, we're like the colliding of two winds, we're a hurricane." DUN DUN DUN DUN DUN DUN DUN DUN "WOOO"

They were *really* good. So good, people got up and started dancing. The energy in the café shifted like lightning. Feet tapped. Heads bobbed. A wave of movement rolled through the room.

Evie pushed her chair out and took Cecelia's hand.

"Come on," she said to her. "We're dancing."

Cecelia laughed. "I don't dance."

"You do now."

And they made their way to the floor, shaking their heads, and moving to the music. Their hair swayed back and forth across their faces as they jumped up and down to the beat. For the next few minutes, they lost themselves in the crowd. Cecelia's ponytail bounced, and her cheeks flushed—not from embarrassment now, but from joy.

When she read *open mic night*, she wasn't expecting this. She was expecting some low-key acoustic stuff and lame poetry readings.

What she got… was Christoph Maximus.

"Erik sure can play the hell out of those drums," Evie said proudly.

"Yeah, a total badass." Cecelia giggled, breathless.

And then the song was over and they were catching their breaths while looking up to the stage expectantly.

"So I promised Erii here that I wouldn't hog all the spotlight." Christoph said and looked back at his friend on the drums. "I'd like to introduce our friend Sam who will be taking over on drums. Come on Erik, you're up."

Erik walked around the drum set and picked up a white Bass guitar off a stand. It was already plugged in before he swung it over his shoulder. He walked over to the mic and Christoph moved aside to stand at his left flank. Sam approached the stage and settled in behind the drum set, getting the feel for it by hitting the high hats and toms with the sticks Erik left behind.

"I'm Erik Taylor. I'm not much for singing but I wanted to play this cover tonight for this crazy broad I know. So Eves, this one's for you."

Christoph strummed the guitar, Sam picked up a beat on the bass drum and Erik sang.

"Am I more than you bargained for yet?
I've been dying to tell you anything you want to hear
Cause that's just who I am this week..."

"Oh my god, it's *Fall Out Boy*!" Cecelia squeaked.

"He really does like me." Evie smiled triumphantly.

"Drop a heart, break a name / we're always sleeping in, and sleeping for the wrong team!"

This was when the crowd started to sing along and at that moment, Erik knew he had her.

"We're going down, down in an earlier round / And Sugar, we're going down swinging / I'll be your number one with a bullet / A loaded God complex, cock it and pull it!"

"Look at you two staring all dreamy-eyed," Jen had startled them from behind.

"They're amazing, aren't they?" Cecelia asked her.

"This is all I've seen so far, but by the looks on your faces, you'd think they were rock stars," she laughed.

"They kinda are," Evie agreed. "What are the odds, Cecelia? We landed two best friends who are perfect gentlemen, got their shit together, and still finding new ways to impress us?"

"I never really thought about it like that, but now that you mention it, we're pretty lucky."

"You could say they're almost a little *too* perfect," Jen chided.

"Is that jealousy I'm sensing?" Evie chuckled.

"Max can't cook," Cecelia added. "He's good at basically everything else, but he *can't* cook. So there, he's not perfect," she said and stuck her tongue out at the other girl.

"So Jen," Evie chimed in. "Glad you could finally join us, what took you so long anyway?"

Jen took a seat and pulled out her phone trying to make herself look busy.

"Andrew said we had some time before he had to go on, so…"

"Oh snap, someone was *getting it in!*" Evie laughed and Cecelia nudged her.

"What?" she shrugged her shoulders and pointed at Jen. "She's the one saying we're staring all dreamy-eyed," she said mocking her. "But she's been missing out on all the fun because she's been sucking face with *Dreamboat*, Andrew."

"We've been in here dancing, watching the guys play and having an awesome time while you were outside. Pshhh," Cecelia laughed. "Evie's right, you have been missing out."

"Whatever," Jen said, shrugging her shoulders and looking back down at her phone.

Evie and Cecelia looked back to the stage as the song finished.

"Thank you," Erik bowed, then winked at Evie and stepped away from the microphone. Christoph walked back up to the mic stand and addressed the crowd.

"I know it seems like our band's been growing after each song but since this is our last, we wanted to make it something special. Hey Andrew, time to shine. Sweet Country," he said, nodding toward Andrew who was already making his way to the stage, his fiddle tucked protectively between his arms.

"We all learned this song last night so feel special," Christoph said and looked back at Andrew who now stood at his right flank. "Take it away, Andrew."

And Andrew did.

Wow could he play. He played that fiddle like it was an extension of his body. Like it was what he was born to do.

The notes danced across the room, wild and precise. It was just between the drums, and the crowd clapping along to a steady beat, that Cecelia realized where she'd heard that song before.

This was the song that was playing when they met.

He remembered.

Her stomach fluttered.

The music ended and the crowd cheered. They demanded an encore.

"Guys, we're flattered but that's really all we've got. Thank you. Really," Christoph said, catching his breath as he looked back to the band. "I don't know about you guys, but I'm ready for one of Ray's famous smoothies." He glanced out across the room, searching the crowd until his eyes found the person he was looking for. "Ray, you're the best," he added, nodding toward the owner who approached the stage. Christoph stepped back, and Ray took the mic while the guys disconnected their instruments.

"Let's hear it one more time for the guys!" Ray said, clapping his hands as the crowd erupted again. "They were great! Really—it's always a pleasure having you guys here," he added, giving the boys a warm nod as they exited the stage, instruments in hand.

They headed back toward the café to order their drinks, still riding the high of their performance.

"I wonder who's next?" Christoph asked to no one in particular, grabbing a napkin and wiping sweat off the back of his neck.

"Prepare to be impressed, my friend," Erik said confidently, flashing a smile as they all turned toward the stage.

Ray checked the sign-up sheet and raised the mic again.

"I'd like to call to the stage… Evette Lamoureux," he read. "Is there an 'Evette'?"

"Yup, that'd be me, stud," Evie called out without missing a beat, standing up with her acoustic guitar in hand. She flipped her hair, winked at Ray, and strutted up the stairs like she owned the place. "I'm ready. Let's do this," she said, plugging in her guitar and pulling a chair to center stage like it was an old friend.

Ray adjusted the mic for her height as she strummed once, then again— quick, efficient, confident. She cleared her throat, tapped the mic, and nodded.

"Perfect," she announced, like a diva tuning a luxury car. "I'm Evette Lamoureux. I'm from Avalon, New Jersey, and these are some songs I wrote."

A few in the crowd clapped lightly, not sure what to expect—until she began fingerpicking a haunting, almost sarcastically delicate melody.

"Da Da Da Da Da," she sang casually, almost sweetly.
 "Everyone thinks they know what's best and tell me I need to make up my mind / They tell me how to act, what to say, and I'm not very lady-like / I don't care what they say, I'm just doing my best / If that's not good enough for you, then eat shit and die."

The audience collectively gasped. A few snorted with laughter.

"And I'm not ready to grow up, causing growing ups a load of shit,
And I, I, am ready to fly, fly free where I want to be,
And that's with you!"

"Of all the songs she could've played, she had to play this one first?" Erik groaned, looking to the ceiling like it held divine answers for his suffering.

"I'm just kidding," Evie laughed into the microphone, completely unfazed by the reaction. "Erik told me not to play that song, so obviously, I *had* to play it," she grinned. The crowd chuckled, now warming up to her. She leaned forward, eyes glinting. "Get your cute butt up here and we're going to play what we've been practicing," she said, locking eyes with Erik like it was a dare.

He didn't hesitate. He moved like he was shot out of a cannon, weaving through chairs and people, vaulting up onto the stage behind the drums with the kind of energy that made even the baristas look up in surprise. He dropped onto the stool like it was his throne.

"Alright, let's do this," she said with a wink, turning her focus back to her guitar.

Erik tapped his drumsticks three times.

Then they played.

Christoph strolled over to where Cecelia and Jen sat, their eyes still on Evie up on stage. He slowed his pace as he approached from behind, then carefully tiptoed close and slipped his hands over Cecelia's eyes.

"Guess who," he whispered, his voice low and teasing in her ear.

"If this isn't Christoph, you're getting a black eye," she threatened with a smirk already forming.

He let out a soft laugh and dropped his hands. She turned to look at him, and the moment their eyes met, she lit up.

"Hey, pretty girl," he winked.

She immediately slid out her chair and wrapped her arms around him. "Max, you were incredible! You guys were *brilliant*," she beamed, practically bouncing in place.

"Thank you," he said, grinning wide. "But hey, not so loud. I don't want to piss off Evie while she's playing. She might turn that guitar into a weapon."

He pulled out the chair beside her and sank into it, still riding the adrenaline. "Jen," he nodded to the girl on Cecelia's other side, who was busy tapping away on her phone.

"Hey, Romeo," Jen replied without looking up. "Great job earlier. That last song was actually pretty cool."

Andrew walked up and plopped down beside her, immediately slinging his arm across the back of her chair.

"We all know that was *me*, darlin'," he grinned.

"Pshhh, don't let it go to your head, Sweet Country," Christoph chuckled, tossing him a playful glare. He looked back at Jen and added with a wink, "Thanks anyway." Then his gaze shifted back to Cecelia, his expression softening.

"So… what are you doing afte—"

"Christoph," Sam's voice interrupted as he walked up briskly and clapped a hand on Christoph's shoulder. "Sorry to cut in, but Darius has been trying to reach you. Says there's a situation at the club that needs your attention."

Christoph's smile faltered. He turned slightly, his body stiffening. "What kind of situation?" he asked, voice low.

Sam leaned in, eyes tense. "Fallen."

That one word changed the air between them.

Christoph exhaled, slow and sharp. "Right."

He pushed his chair back and stood. "I apologize, but I'm going to have to excuse myself." He looked down at Cecelia, a hint of regret in his eyes. "We'll continue this conversation another time, pretty girl."

Then he leaned down and kissed her forehead—gentle, warm, but fleeting. And just like that, he was gone.

The moment hung awkwardly for a beat until Andrew cleared his throat.

"Well, I don't know about y'all," he said, clapping his hands on his knees, "but I'm feelin' like pizza after this."

"Oh yeah, pizza sounds like a plan to me," Jen agreed instantly.

"Yeah… pizza," Cecelia echoed, still staring in the direction Christoph had gone. Her lips curled into a soft smile. "Great."

That night, as Cecelia lay in bed, she stared up at the ceiling, earbuds in, letting some lo-fi playlist hum in the background while her brain refused to shut up.

She kept replaying everything in her head like a montage from one of those coming-of-age indie films she secretly loved but would never admit to watching. Evie shredding the guitar like some kind of punk-rock Swiftie with sass. Andrew absolutely *destroying* that fiddle like a cowboy violin god. And Max...

God. Max.

There were a lot of things she realized about Max that evening.

First, he was—unfortunately—the guy of her dreams. Like, literally. And figuratively. Which was inconvenient. And suspicious. And completely unfair. He could sing, play guitar, charm a bookstore owner, and somehow still make her feel like she was the center of the universe with just one wink. One dumb wink. She groaned and covered her face with her blanket for a second.

Was there anything that guy wasn't good at?

She furrowed her brow, thinking harder. Maybe cooking. Yeah. He did say he couldn't cook. She clung to that tiny flaw like a lifeline. One small crack in the otherwise infuriating perfection of Christoph Maximus.

Second, she knew—*knew*—he was hiding something. There was something behind those easy smiles and smooth lines. A flicker in his eyes when he thought no one was watching. A sudden shift in energy when that Sam guy mentioned the word *Fallen*. Cecelia didn't know what it meant, but she saw the way his posture changed, the way the humor drained from his face.

It wasn't something small. It wasn't nothing.

Still… she wasn't exactly in a position to judge. She had her own secrets. Big ones. Old ones. The kind that didn't go away with time. The kind that didn't *want* to.

But here's the kicker—the part that kept her up the most:

She didn't care.

Whatever he was hiding, whatever walls he built around it… she wasn't scared of it. Not anymore. Not after tonight.

Because somewhere between the song and the smile, between the wink and the forehead kiss, Cecelia White had realized the third and final truth of the evening:

She was completely and hopelessly in love with him.

A second-degree black belt. Olympic-level athlete. Top of her class. And she was no match for one ridiculously charming guy with a guitar and a secret.

She sighed and rolled over, hugging her pillow and whispering into the dark like a secret she wasn't quite ready to say out loud.

"Stupid Max."

But her smile said otherwise.

Life, she thought, had a funny way of working things out.

Samuel Wu

Chapter 14

Azazel

Christoph and Sam reached Max Lounge in under three minutes.

They didn't wait for traffic signals. They didn't take the subway. They ran—blurring between streetlights and shadows, legs moving faster than any manmade machine ever could. Whatever had happened, Christoph could feel it pulsing in his chest like a war drum.

Darius stood waiting outside the black-paneled double doors. His usual stoic demeanor was replaced by something more unsettled. For a man built like a tank and calm as a glacier, that meant *very* bad news.

"Darius, report," Christoph demanded, his tone clipped, his steps slowing only when he was in striking distance.

"We caught a small demon patrol doing surveillance on the Lounge," Darius said, his jaw tight. "Three fled. I managed to bring one down. He's secure."

Christoph's eyes narrowed. "They're getting bolder."

Sam, silent at Christoph's shoulder, cracked his knuckles without a word.

"I take it our little 'understanding' with Azazel is officially dead," Christoph said, voice flat. "Show me the demon."

Without another word, Darius turned and led them through the lounge's velvet interior to the staff elevator. The doors dinged open and swallowed them in gold-lit silence.

They descended into the sublevels—below the wine cellars, beneath the private vault rooms, down into a place that didn't exist on any blueprint.

The elevator doors slid open into the cold hush of the lower basement. A vast space stretched out before them, dimly lit and lined with storage crates, empty kegs, and reinforced steel cabinets. At the far end, a metal door embedded with a security keypad stood waiting.

Darius approached, punched in the code. A low, mechanical *click* echoed as the lock disengaged.

With a grunt, he pulled open the freezer door.

Inside, frost clung to the metal walls. Chains hung from overhead pipes like silver veins. A man—if you could still call him that—was strung from a meat hook by his shoulders. Clad in black, his skin was pale and mottled, his eyes twin voids leaking hate.

"I tried to get him to talk," Darius said, arms crossed. "He's stubborn."

Christoph stepped forward, every movement controlled, regal. The air dropped in temperature as he approached the bound creature. He came to a halt just shy of the meat hook, eyes glowing faintly gold.

"Max Lounge is neutral ground," he said quietly. "Protected under treaty by Azazel himself. What was your mission here?"

The demon didn't flinch. He grinned—slow and jagged—as if savoring a joke no one else understood. Then he spit black blood onto the floor between them.

Christoph's jaw tightened.

"I said," he repeated, "what was your mission?"

The demon's grin only widened.

"You're losing your touch, Ceruleus," he hissed, his voice like gravel soaked in oil. "Azazel says you're just a relic now. A pretty face behind a bar. We know what you have… and we've come to take it."

Without hesitation, Christoph's hand snapped out and grabbed the front of the demon's shirt. He yanked him forward until their noses almost touched.

"What did you just say?"

The demon's smile bled into something manic. "Azazel says you're a *washed-up* Archangel. Nothing more than a bartender with a name."

Christoph didn't blink.

He drove his forehead into the demon's face with enough force to crack bone. The demon's head snapped back, his nose crushed. Black ichor ran down his lips like ink. Still, he grinned through broken teeth.

"Fine." Christoph exhaled through his nose, gold light flickering in his irises. "You want to bleed for your master, go right ahead."

He turned to Sam.

"Five minutes."

Sam didn't speak. He just stepped forward, closing the freezer door behind him.

Christoph and Darius waited outside. The heavy *clunk* of the lock engaging behind them was followed by silence.

"…So," Darius muttered, watching frost slowly creep around the doorframe. "What's next, boss?"

"We wait for Erik," Christoph said, brushing a fleck of blood from his knuckle.

A scream—deep, guttural, inhuman—shredded through the thick metal barrier.

Darius blinked. "I thought we had those doors soundproofed."

"Huh" Christoph shrugged. "Guess not."

"So, uh… hungry?" Darius asked casually, as if they weren't standing outside a torture room.

Christoph stretched his neck with a soft pop. "Yeah, I could eat. Fried mac and cheese balls?"

"You read my damn mind." Darius smiled, already turning toward the elevator. "And maybe a milkshake if he doesn't scream again."

Christoph didn't smile.

But his eyes glittered like a storm was building behind them.

Erik walked into the restaurant of Max Lounge, the air immediately cooler, heavier, and glittering with atmosphere. The place was a perfect contradiction—half Gatsby, half enchanted grove—and entirely Max.

Crystal chandeliers dripped from a vaulted ceiling painted like a twilight forest, deep sapphire fading to plum with hand-brushed constellations twinkling faintly overhead. Gnarled silver branches twisted from the walls, wrapped in ivy and hanging fairy lights, their glow pulsing softly like fireflies in rhythm to the jazz-infused music playing from an invisible band.

The staff moved with quiet grace through the room, dressed in signature Max Lounge prep attire: short pleated skirts or tailored pants, crisp white button-ups, slim black ties, and black blazers with silver buttons and the Max Lounge crest stitched over the chest. The look was strict and stylish—but playfully subverted with glittering eye makeup, iridescent nail polish, and the occasional set of elf ears or shimmering hair streaks, giving the waitresses and hosts an otherworldly, fae charm.

At the heart of the room, two Romanesque fountains spilled over with water infused with stardust, mist curling along the edges of the black marble floors like smoke on a moonlit pond.

Erik scanned the room until he found them. Christoph and Darius were exactly where they always were—center of the storm, seated in a high-backed scarlet leather booth that gave Christoph the perfect vantage point. From there, he could see everything. No door opened, no whisper was spoken, without his awareness.

Erik strode past groups of wide-eyed patrons enchanted by the ambiance, slipping into the booth with purpose.

"Why didn't you call me sooner?" he asked, his voice low but edged with concern.

Christoph didn't even flinch. "Didn't want to interrupt your date with Evie," he said, smirking like he already knew the protest coming.

"She would've understood—"

"No, she wouldn't have. Not mid-song. I know what she means to you," Christoph said, his voice softer now, more grounded. "Look, take a seat."

Erik huffed and dropped into the booth beside him, folding his arms on the table. "Alright then. Hit me with the bad news."

Christoph leaned forward, expression serious. "Azazel's scouts were here tonight. Darius caught one casing the Lounge. The others got away."

Darius nodded grimly. "I've been seeing more of them lately. It's not random anymore—it's coordinated."

"Sam's interrogating the one we caught downstairs," Christoph continued. "But if we haven't heard from him yet, that means the bastard's not talking. We're going to need you to pick up his scent and track the others."

"Right. The hive." Erik rubbed his temples. "And I'm guessing you want to wipe it off the map."

"Wipe it clean," Christoph confirmed. "They're stepping out of bounds. No one violates neutral ground without consequence."

"They've been tailing us for weeks," Darius added, leaning back with a tense crack of his knuckles. "We had six following you and Erik through the subway last week. Sam and I put them down, but they're looking for something."

Erik exhaled. "The Key."

"Exactly," Christoph said, his gaze hardening. "They think we have it."

"We *do* have it. You just refuse to take it from Cecelia," Erik said sharply.

"I'm not taking something that belongs to her family," Christoph snapped back. "It's more than an artifact. It's her legacy."

"And you're painting a damn target on her back with your stubbornness," Erik growled. "She's not built for this, Christoph. We can't keep her safe if Azazel's already circling."

"We're the Elite Wing," Darius cut in, voice like steel. "Protecting one girl shouldn't be that hard."

"Yeah? Tell that to the last girl who got caught in one of our wars," Erik muttered.

The silence that followed was heavier than any shout.

Christoph's voice finally broke it. Quiet. Focused.

"After tonight, it won't matter," he said, leaning back in the booth, eyes glowing faintly gold.

"What's happening tonight?" Erik looked back at him curiously.

"Tonight we're taking them out once and for all."

Erik arched a brow. "Oh? A full-blown midnight massacre? Sounds like a great way to spend a Wednesday night."

Christoph gave a humorless smirk. "Got better plans?"

"Honestly, I was hoping to catch the latest episode of *The Bachelor*, but I guess demon-hunting wins out."

Darius snorted. "Priorities, man."

"Hey, I live a complex life," Erik said, grabbing one of the remaining mac and cheese balls from the plate between them. "Step one: cheesy carbs,. Step two: save New York City."

Christoph finally cracked a smile. "Glad to see you're taking this seriously."

"Even Archangels need their comfort food," Erik said, tossing it into his mouth. "Besides, I fight better full."

Christoph stood, adjusting his jacket with slow purpose. "Then let's gear up."

Darius stood beside him, already rolling his sleeves. "Let's show these bastards what happens when you mess with the Elite Wing."

Erik stood last, wiping his hands on a cloth napkin. "Nothing says divine retribution like four angry immortals with a vengeance complex."

And with that, the three of them walked out of the booth and into the shadows of the Lounge—ready to burn every demon between them and the truth.

The elevator doors slid shut with a soft hiss. This time, Christoph reached into his coat and retrieved a matte-black key, small and angular, which he inserted into a hidden slot beneath the keypad. A quiet *click* echoed in the chamber as he turned it, and the button marked (O) lit up with a faint silver glow.

The elevator rose smoothly, and when the doors opened, they revealed Christoph's private office.

Calling it an office felt disingenuous.

The space was part war room, part luxury suite—sharp edges of modern opulence softened by old-world class. A black marble desk commanded the center, its surface sleek and spotless except for a three-monitor setup glowing with data streams. Behind it, two red leather sofas formed a conversational nook beneath an angular brass light fixture, its geometric shadows casting a moody glow.

To the left: a sleek leather sectional, a glass coffee table atop a Persian rug, and a keypad-sealed door. To the right: a floor-length mirror framed in wrought silver, a celestial globe pulsing faint blue, and a marble mini bar fitted with glass shelves and steel stools dressed in black suede.

Christoph strode to the desk and slid into his leather chair like a king returning to his throne. He pulled open the center drawer and tapped in a code on the hidden keyboard. Across the room, the decorative mirror *shivered,* then began to split apart, its halves gliding open like the maw of a beast revealing polished death behind its teeth.

Rows of weaponry gleamed from the hidden arsenal—swords, daggers, kunai, throwing stars, arrows, twin scythes, and more. Every piece carefully cleaned, displayed, and deadly.

Christoph's smile was cold and fond. "Alright, boys. Gear up."

Erik made a beeline for the supply closet beside the desk. He returned carrying four stacks of black tactical gear—leather jackets reinforced with magical thread, Kevlar pants that moved like silk, and lightweight gloves with arcane seals woven into the lining. He tossed the sets onto the couch and began undressing without hesitation.

"You guys do what you want," he said, shimmying out of his jeans. "but I'm changing now. I wore my lucky shirt tonight and I'm not about to mess it up," he said.

"Always the sentimental one," Christoph laughed.

"Hey, you're the one with lucky penguin boxers, bro. I wouldn't talk," Erik retaliated without missing a beat.

"That was a secret!" Christoph feigned betrayal, hand to his heart.

"Hey, we're all brothers here," Darius chuckled and removed a set of golden tomahawks, which he strapped across his back with a click of hardened leather. Next he buckled a utility belt across his large waist and tucked a few knives into it like he was casually packing a picnic basket—if that picnic involved murder. Then he reached to his left and removed one of the quivers already full of arrows and handed it to Erik.

Erik, now in his leather gear, pulled the quiver over his jacket and walked to the wall to pick up a compact bow, black and sleek. He tested its pull before nodding to himself, then took two daggers that he strapped into his boots. He also put one of the utility belts across his waist, filling the various pockets with large black and gold marbles and various sorts of small weaponry— smoke bombs, throwing spikes, vials labeled in Latin. The good stuff.

Christoph took this time to do the same, choosing precision over flash. He moved like someone who'd done this dance a thousand times—quick, exact, and quiet. Daggers were slipped into hidden sheaths on his forearms. Throwing knives were secured to the inside of his jacket. Lastly, he put on a belt, which settled two golden kukri knives above his hips for easy access, the curved blades gleaming in the low light like twin crescent moons.

"How about Sam?" Darius asked, eyeing the remaining stack of gear.

"Erik, bring his gear down with you to the basement. Sam's in the freezer. Darius and I will meet you. We're going to make him a quick to-go bag of his favorite weapons." Christoph said, handing Darius an empty duffel bag.

"He's gonna want the retractable spear and his bow and quiver." Darius said, already filling the bag. "And probably that serrated butterfly knife he refuses to sharpen."

"Obviously," Christoph deadpanned.

Erik nodded and carried Sam's gear with him to the elevator door where he pressed the down button. He looked back at Christoph and snickered. "If I didn't know better, I'd think you were actually enjoying this."

"Me?" Christoph asked innocently. "Never." But a wicked grin pulled at his lips.

And it was the kind of grin that said someone was about to have a very, very bad night.

Back in the basement, the flickering fluorescent light above the freezer cast long, stuttering shadows across the floor. The steel walls were stained with ichor, and the cold air reeked of scorched sulfur and blood. Christoph, Darius, and Erik stood just inside the threshold of the industrial freezer, silent, watching the aftermath unfold.

Inside, the demon was barely hanging on—literally and figuratively.

"My name is Zandolphin. I serve Azazel and the almighty Lucifer who seeks the Key. My name is Zandolphin. I serve Azazel and the almighty Lucifer who seeks the Key. My name is Zandolphin. I serve Azazel and the al—"

He droned on in a loop, voice hoarse and ruined. The same string of allegiance, over and over. A broken record—his mind clearly fractured, whatever will he had burnt out.

"You said five minutes," Sam muttered from the far side of the room. His sleeve was pushed up, a white bandage wrapped tight around his wrist, seeping faintly with golden blood. He didn't look at them—he just kept adjusting the cloth like it could somehow rewind time.

"What did you do to him?" Erik asked, his voice low, taken aback.

Sam finally looked up, eyes tired but sharp. "He told me Azazel put a bounty on your and Christoph's heads. That's all he said. Then he clammed up. Started laughing. I thought you were giving me more time because you knew." His gaze dropped to the ruin of what remained. "I didn't mean to break him this way."

"My name is Zandolphin. I serve Azazel——" the demon rasped again, though the sound no longer came from vocal cords so much as from memory—muscle twitching on repeat.

He hung in torn pieces from the meat hook, his limbs twisted unnaturally. Thin metal spikes were wedged into his joints and under his fingernails. Black sludge oozed from the wounds, bubbling where it touched the floor, like molten oil reacting to something corrosive.

But it wasn't the spikes that had broken him.

Across his chest, crude runes had been etched with precision—sigils scorched into his flesh, glowing faintly. And where the burns ran deepest, there was no mistaking the smell: divine blood. The kind demons feared like fire.

"Sam… did you use your own—" Erik began.

Sam nodded once. "Angel blood's poison to them. Cuts deeper. Hurts more. He wouldn't talk, so I dipped the tips of my blades in it. Drew the sigils with it. I thought it would scare him into talking."

Instead, it had driven him mad.

The demon's face was disfigured—burnt in places like acid had been poured on it. His lips curled back in a twitching, involuntary grin, but his eyes were empty. Whatever consciousness had once been there was long gone.

"We need to do something," Erik said again, quieter now.

Christoph's face was still. Grim. "Just put him out of his misery."

Darius stepped forward, unhooking one of the golden tomahawks from his back. The blade gleamed like sunlight in the dark. Holy. Righteous.

"Allow me," he said, voice steady.

"My name is Zandolphin. I serve—"

The ax cut through the air in one swift stroke.

The head hit the steel floor with a dull, final thud. For a beat, everything was still.

Then the body ignited—not with flame, but with a ripple of black smoke, drawn downward in curling streams. The ash spiraled and melted into the floor as if Hell itself had opened beneath to reclaim its own. Zandolphin was no more.

Christoph stepped beside Sam and placed a hand on his shoulder.

"This isn't your fault," he said. "Don't you dare think for a second that it is. He sold his soul to the Devil centuries ago. This blind obedience—that was the price he paid, willingly."

Sam didn't reply. He simply wiped his bloodied hands with a cloth, still staring at the place where the demon had vanished.

"We can't waste any more time here," Christoph said. "Gear up, Sam. We're going hunting."

Sam reached for the duffel at his feet and unzipped it, the sound slicing through the cold silence.

"About time," he said.

Erik exchanged a look with Darius, who cracked his knuckles and grinned.

Let the hunt begin.

"You sure you have his scent?" Christoph asked Erik, his voice low but charged with anticipation.

"I'm positive," Erik replied. "Once I transform, my senses will heighten tenfold. I'll be able to pick up his trail for sure."

"Alright. Everyone ready?" Christoph's gaze swept across the group, eyes glinting like tempered steel in the dark. "As soon as he shifts, he's going to take off. We stay close. It's been over an hour already—we let the scent go cold, we lose them."

Sam gave a short nod, adjusting the black strap of his holstered blade across his back. Darius rolled his shoulders, the golden tomahawks glinting under the moonlight.

Erik closed his eyes. The street fell silent.

Then, the blue pendant around his neck began to glow—first a gentle hum, then a powerful throb of radiant energy. The light pulsed outward from his chest, racing across his skin like veins of lightning. His form blurred at the edges as the magic overtook him, casting eerie shadows across the alley walls.

There was a sudden *crack*—a sound like thunder snapping through water—and in a burst of cobalt light, the man was gone.

In his place stood a massive black wolf, sleek and powerful, his fur streaked faintly with lines of glowing blue, like constellations traced across his body. His eyes blazed with supernatural clarity.

Then he bolted.

They moved like wraiths through the city—cutting through alleys, vaulting over fences, vanishing into subway tunnels, appearing again like specters in the dark. The wind seemed to bend around them. No footsteps echoed. No one saw them pass. Whatever path these demons had used, they had masked it well, but once Erik had the scent, it was over.

The city blurred past—graffiti walls, rusted stairwells, neon reflections in puddles. Magic danced in the wake of their movement, faint sparks trailing like stardust kicked up by angels on the hunt.

They emerged onto another street. Run-down apartments lined the sidewalks, windows boarded up, metal gates half-collapsed. Burnt-out streetlamps blinked overhead, casting Harlem in an eerie pall.

Darius muttered something under his breath.

"I'm sorry, you say something, Dee?" Sam asked, voice steady but alert.

"We're in Harlem… and not the friendly part," he replied, eyes narrowing.

Christoph's gaze flicked toward Erik—the black wolf had paused, nose to the ground.

"You still have the scent?"

The wolf bowed his head once in silent affirmation.

"Alright, don't let us stop you. We'll be right on your tail," Christoph said with a nod.

Erik barked once—low, sharp—and they were off again, sprinting into shadow.

As they passed the forgotten corners of the neighborhood, Christoph couldn't help but let his mind drift—just for a moment.

The cracks in the sidewalk, the broken homes, the fading laughter of children too used to fear… all of it chipped at him. Even now, centuries after the fall, he couldn't turn off the part of him that *cared.* Angels weren't supposed to. But Christoph wasn't most angels.

This world was never meant to be cruel. But when you're born into a cage, it's hard to imagine anything beyond the bars. Poverty bred desperation. Desperation bred monsters. And yet… so many still clung to hope. That's what made them worth protecting.

Erik came to a halt at the mouth of a narrow alley.

Ahead stood a massive, gated warehouse surrounded by a high barbed-wire fence, rusted and crooked but still intact. A half-lit "NO TRESPASSING" sign blinked in the dark, barely hanging from its bolts.

The wolf's body began to glow again—that same shimmering blue, now brighter. His form pulsed once, then twice, before bursting into light.

And in a heartbeat, Erik stood there once more—broad-shouldered, armed to the teeth, a faint trail of magic still spiraling off his body like steam.

"This is it," he said, his voice low but certain.

Christoph stepped forward, scanning the perimeter. "Alright. Erii and I will run perimeter, scout any outside threats. Wait here a few minutes 'til we get back."

He looked to Erik and pointed to a crumbling multi-story building just ahead. "We'll regroup on the roof of that building. Looks abandoned. Has a good view of the warehouse."

"Ready?" Christoph asked.

"Always," Erik replied, flashing a grin that didn't quite reach his eyes.

In a blur of motion, the two vanished into the night.

Christoph had run his side of the perimeter and scaled the building with his bare hands, fingers biting into stone and steel. He moved like a shadow through smoke—silent, deadly, precise. Erik was already on the rooftop, crouched at the edge, peering over the ledge at the rusted rooftop of the warehouse below, his figure still as a gargoyle.

"I counted three guards on the ground, guarding the inner perimeter. None outside the gate," Christoph said, his voice low and even, like distant thunder before a storm.

"All demons, right?" Erik asked without looking up, his gaze locked on the shadows moving below.

"Yeah. All of them carried that dark aura," Christoph confirmed. He crouched beside him, golden eyes narrowing. "How about you?"

"Same here. One at the main entrance, one at the back, and one covering the side," Erik replied, finally glancing over. The streetlight below flickered, casting strange angles across his face. "Tight but not unbreakable."

"I think going in through the roof is our best bet," Christoph pointed down below. "Two guards stationed at the rooftop entrance. We could descend through the skylights and hit them all at once."

"Oh, I like that. It's like some Batman shit," Erik chuckled under his breath.

"Yeah," Christoph laughed softly. "But I was thinking more like that time in Germany when we stormed that Nazi base."

Erik's smile faded. "Yeah, let's not reminisce about that. Killing humans—even heartless degenerates—never felt right."

"If we hadn't, we would never have retrieved the Mark of Vishnu," Christoph nodded toward the glowing blue pendant around Erik's neck.

Erik instinctively cupped the pendant, its soft hum pulsing between his fingers. "You're right. Who knows what they could've done with it given time to learn its power." He stared down at the warehouse. The wind whipped past them, brushing his coat back like wings. "So, you sure about this?"

"We need to," Christoph said with finality, his voice now carved in stone.

"You realize how big this is, don't you?"

"Yeah, I do."

"Tell me this isn't just about Cecelia." Erik looked at him with concern, a seriousness behind his words that grounded the air around them.

"It's not." Christoph replied, furrowing his brows.

"You're putting on that face you do when you're angry."

"What face?"

"That 'nothing fazes me, self-righteous, going to ruin your world' face."

"There's a face for that?" Christoph smirked despite himself.

"Yeah, I'd show you a mirror right now if I had one."

"Well, I don't." Christoph said, turning his eyes back to the warehouse, "have that face."

"You can't lie to me. I'm your best friend..." Erik stared, voice gentler now. "You love her, don't you?"

"I wouldn't dare." Christoph replied solemnly, his tone heavy.

"You're willing to wage war on Azazel to protect this girl." Erik said, shaking his head slowly. "There are at least five different ways you could have handled this problem—the simplest being retrieving the Angel Key— and you chose to wage war against a Demon General."

"Look at it this way." Christoph put his hand on Erik's shoulder, gripping it firmly. "He put a bounty on our heads. He is sending demons to our club, and whether or not Cecelia gifts one of us her key, eventually they're going to pick up on her Nephilim aura. She's a walking target. I will not have her walking around our city knowing she could be recognized by demons at any given moment." Christoph's eyes flashed gold in anger, his voice vibrating with restrained fury.

"You *do* love her," Erik smiled, nudging his friend lightly.

"I don't know what I'd do with myself if anything ever happened to her," Christoph confessed, his voice quieter now. He stared at the rooftop beneath their feet as if searching for answers in the concrete. Erik patted him on the shoulder in quiet understanding.

Christoph looked up at his friend, eyes burning gold.

"So Azazel has to go."

Sam and Darius had been waiting in the shadows of the alley for some time, the darkness wrapping around them like a shroud. The brick walls loomed tall and cracked around them, graffiti and grime clinging to every surface like memories that refused to fade. A damp chill clung to the air, and impatience gnawed at them with sharp teeth.

"What's taking them so long?" Sam muttered, barely audible, his fingers twitching near the hilt of one of his knives.

"No idea," Darius grumbled. "But next time, we're running perimeter. I'm not built to sit still."

"Yeah, man. Those two always get the fun assignments," Sam sighed, leaning his head back against the cold wall. "Bet they're up there brooding and looking cool while we're down here babysitting rats."

A sudden noise echoed down the alley—sharp and metallic, the distinct clanging of something hitting the ground. Both of them went still.

"What was that?" Sam asked, eyes narrowing as he snapped to attention.

"A garbage can lid," Darius suggested with a shrug, but his hand was already reaching for his tomahawks. "Feel like checking it out?"

"Could be interesting," Sam whispered, a familiar edge of anticipation glinting in his voice like a knife catching light.

"Why are we whispering?" a voice asked suddenly from just behind Sam's shoulder.

Sam spun around, blade drawn in a blur of motion, eyes wide and wild.

"Whoa there, Starshine," Erik said, raising his hands in mock surrender, eyes gleaming with mischief. "It was just a joke."

"You dick." Sam laughed, the tension in his shoulders breaking as he sheathed his blade again. "You nearly got yourself gutted."

"So you guys call running surveillance fun?" Erik teased, eyebrow cocked as he leaned casually against the wall.

"How long have you two been eavesdropping?" Darius asked, narrowing his gaze, unimpressed.

"Long enough to hear about your undying love for Scarlett Johansson," Christoph chuckled as he emerged from the shadows with a casual swagger, his coat catching the wind like wings.

"Undying? Nah, Darius has always had a thing for ScarJo." Erik said, nudging Darius with his elbow. "Since like, 2005."

"One day we'll be together," Darius said with mock sincerity, gazing wistfully up at the cloudy sky like it held his destiny.

"In your dreams, bro." Sam laughed, shaking his head. "And maybe her nightmares."

"Alright, alright, enough," Christoph waved a hand, snapping them all back to mission mode. The lightness dropped from his face like a mask. "Huddle up."

They circled around him, boots crunching softly on the gravel beneath them.

"We need to make as little noise as possible going in," he began, voice low and steady like a blade sliding free from its sheath. "Erik and I will glide from the building behind the warehouse and take out the rooftop guards first. Then you two can join us."

He looked between them, his gold-flecked eyes sharp with focus. "Sam and Erik, you two will work the high ground. There's a skylight Darius and I will enter through. Take out as many demons as you can before we hit the floor. Keep it fast. Surgical."

"Can do," Sam nodded, already running a mental checklist. "But what about the exits?"

"We've got it covered. Erik rigged them with explosives."

Erik grinned, pulling a slim, remote control from his pocket and waggling it like a toy. "The moment you two shatter that skylight, I'll block off their exits. Demon bastards won't know what hit 'em."

"It'll be like shooting fish in a barrel," Sam added, his smile flashing with something dark beneath the surface.

"Right," Christoph nodded once. His voice was flint on steel.

They all nodded in agreement, eyes sharp, postures ready, every breath now laced with anticipation.

"One last thing," Christoph's voice dropped to a growl, his gaze burning. "When we find Azazel... his head is mine."

Now, like all great plans, no matter how many times you go over them in your head or how foolproof they seem, they never go the way you expect.

"Ready?" Christoph asked, looking at Darius, who nodded back. Then he glanced at Erik, standing with the detonator. Erik grinned and pressed the button. A loud bang erupted, and the building shook as the exits exploded simultaneously. Debris flew everywhere, taking out the guards on the outside and sending smoke and ash into the air.

Christoph and Darius descended into the den of demons.

They hit the ground, Christoph drawing his golden kukri knives and Darius his dual tomahawks, ready to strike.

But what they found was not what they were expecting.

All around them were naked, decrepit-looking men and women, running and screaming around tables, counters, and stacks of white-packaged drugs.

"Shit," Christoph muttered.

This wasn't a demon nest. It was a drug den.

Darius Scott

Chapter 15

Those bastards

A barrage of gunfire exploded all around them; arrows whistled past as they zipped through the air, the percussion of bodies like a drumbeat as they thudded against the floor. The clash of steel against steel rang like cymbals, and a chorus of screams filled the room with an audible terror that chilled you to the bone.

The sound of battle was like a bloody symphony.

"We need to find Azazel!" Christoph shouted to his friends through the commotion.

"Don't worry, we've got you covered!" Erik called back.

Sam and Erik were shooting down demons through the broken skylight with pinpoint accuracy, covering Darius and Christoph as they made their way through the chaos-ridden room.

Most of the human workers—sunken faces, hollowed eyes, the drones—knew better than to fight. But those who didn't understand that bullets meant nothing to the Fallen had taken up arms. Gunpowder was useless against them. Their defiance ended in blood and screams.

"Behind you!" Darius roared.

Christoph spun around, whipping his right arm and slicing the head off an approaching demon. With his left, he hurled a throwing knife at Darius. It flew past his friend's head and impaled the demon behind him through the eye.

"You should watch your own back," he smirked and charged forward again, blades flashing.

"Right," Darius grunted. "Thanks," he added, raising his axes to block the crushing blow of another attacker.

Darius was a hurricane in human form. With the brute strength of a god and the technique of a war veteran, he moved like a living battering ram. His golden tomahawks cleaved through necks and torsos alike, sending bodies flying with the brutal elegance of controlled rage. Demons fell before him, shredded and broken, black ichor staining the concrete in spiraling splashes.

"Out of arrows, bro!" Sam called out to Erik.

Erik nodded. "Coming down!" he hollered to the ground below.

In a single move, the two dropped through the shattered skylight, landing with predator grace. They hit the floor, drawing hidden blades in fluid motion. They were outnumbered—but not outmatched.

Sam was known as a tactical fighter, a weapons specialist. Where everyone else had a lane, he thrived in every terrain. He didn't play favorites—he made every weapon his own.

As the tide of demons surged, Sam switched from katanas and throwing knives to a retractable double-edged spear, its obsidian shaft gleaming under the flickering light. He spun across the room like a dancer in a storm, twirling his staff with the dazzling force of a lightning bolt. He treated his weapons like they were instruments of his own soul, and the music they played was *murder*.

An attacker lunged from his left. Sam ducked low, spinning as he moved, sweeping the demon's legs out with the butt of his spear. The creature shrieked and collapsed, but his pain was short-lived. Sam continued the spin, rising smoothly and taking the demon's head in a single, vicious stroke. The body hit the ground and evaporated into ash and shadow.

Erik fought differently. What he lacked in brute strength, he made up for in unpredictability.

He reached into his utility belt and grabbed a set of black pellets. With a modified slingshot, he fired them like bullets, each one slamming into demons and embedding deep in flesh. Their casings dissolved on impact, releasing the cocktail of angel blood, chlorite, and magnesium Erik had specially concocted.

The results were explosive. The demons burst from within—violently—collapsing into clouds of shrieking ichor and blackened bone.

Erik ducked a clawed hand, rolled forward, and lobbed two more pellets mid-tumble. The resulting blasts sent three enemies flying back like rag dolls, crashing into the concrete wall with sickening cracks.

Meanwhile, Darius was mowing through anything in his path. He lifted one demon with a double swing of his tomahawks and used the momentum to throw it across the room like a sack of meat.

Christoph had become a blur of black and gold, blades flashing in the air like vengeful starlight. His kukri knives slashed in perfect arcs, carving down enemy after enemy with clean, brutal efficiency. His face showed no mercy—only the cold focus of war.

In minutes, the warehouse floor was clear. Only the cowering addicts remained—emaciated husks of humanity trapped in the hellish drug den. Their fate would be dealt with later. There were greater evils still breathing.

The four regrouped and moved through a hallway, stepping over bodies that twitched and hissed before dissolving into ash.

"Why is everyone naked?" Erik asked, eyes wide. "What the fuck kind of 'drug smuggling' operation are these perverts running here?"

"They strip them so they can't smuggle the product out." Darius replied.

Erik blinked at him. "And how the hell do you know that?"

"Movies," Darius shrugged.

Erik groaned. "Man, we need new hobbies."

Christoph didn't speak. His blades were already drawn again.

The hunt was far from over.

Sam and Christoph led the way, their blades at the ready. The team moved with the speed and precision of a finely tuned machine, slicing through the darkness like reapers cloaked in vengeance. The air was thick with the scent of blood and brimstone, every step a silent promise of war.

As they pushed deeper into the warehouse, the demon presence thickened. Shadows writhed at the corners of the halls. Red eyes blinked in the gloom, dozens at a time. The Fallen didn't flinch.

They didn't hesitate.

They were death in motion.

The four of them cut through the encroaching flood with ruthless efficiency. Christoph's blades danced like lightning, golden flashes carving a path through the infernal tide. Sam moved like a phantom, blending speed and brutality into a deadly rhythm, his twin blades singing with each stroke. Darius crashed through demon ranks like a battering ram, axes cleaving bone and black ichor in wide arcs. Erik loosed arrows with near-psychic precision, each shot a thunderclap of combustion and light.

They were getting closer. The pressure in the air shifted.

"To the right!" Christoph shouted.

Without hesitation, Erik turned and loosed an arrow. It cut through the dim light like a streak of flame, impaling a charging demon directly through the throat. The creature gurgled and collapsed with a wet thud, its body disintegrating into cinders before it touched the floor.

"Bro, this hall is all clear," Darius announced, lowering his axes. "That was the last of them."

"Dammit," Christoph snarled, slamming his hand against the wall with a sharp crack that echoed through the corridor. "We need to find him!"

"I'll find him, don't worry," Erik said calmly, clutching his pendant. He closed his eyes and let the transformation take hold. A low hum began to vibrate from the crystal. The air shimmered. Then, in a blinding flash of blue light, his human form vanished—replaced by a massive, jet-black wolf with eyes like twin sapphires on fire.

The wolf sniffed the air, his breath curling with heat. He caught the scent.

He looked back at Christoph and barked once—short, commanding—and took off like a bullet.

They chased him through winding halls and decrepit rooms, past piles of broken crates and shattered glass. The air grew colder. More still. Erik darted around corners and veered down a corridor to the left, then another to the right. His paws skidded to a halt before an open doorway. A low, guttural growl rumbled from his chest.

This was it.

The pendant around his neck lit up once more, and in a surge of light, the black wolf was gone. In his place stood Erik, weapons at the ready, his eyes still glowing faintly.

"Through here, guys," he said, voice tight with focus.

They readied themselves and entered the room.

It was cavernous, echoing like a cathedral hollowed out by fire. And in it, standing in neat, rigid ranks, were at least forty demons—armed to the teeth, clad in black armor, weapons drawn, their snarling faces twisted in anticipation.

"Well, I see you've found me," a voice drawled from the shadows. Deep, smooth, and laced with venom.

Azazel.

The bastard stepped forward, wearing that smug, sadistic grin that made Christoph's blood boil.

"Azazel, you bastard," Christoph spat, his grip tightening around the hilts of his kukris. "Come face me, coward."

"Oh, how I'd love to," Azazel replied, tilting his head mockingly. "But I've got to run."

He smirked and turned to his soldiers. "Boys, take care of them, will you? A big promotion—and your own sector in the New Order—to whoever brings me the heads of Ceruleus and Eros."

"Hey, what are we? Chopped liver?" Sam muttered to Darius, who shrugged like this was just another Wednesday.

The demons let out a shriek and rallied, weapons raised, preparing to descend.

"Goodbye, Ceruleus," Azazel said with a mocking bow. "With you out of the picture, that key will be mine."

Then he vanished into shadow—gone in a blink.

"NO!" Christoph roared, fury igniting in his eyes. And then he charged.

The Elite Wing exploded into action behind him.

Erik notched one of his trick arrows—he didn't have time to think. He just let it fly.

It struck the first demon square in the chest.

Boom.

A bloom of crimson-gold flame erupted, launching the demon backward and setting two more ablaze. Arrow after arrow followed, each one an engineered spectacle—miniature bombs laced with magnesium, angelic blood, and divine fury. The explosions lit up the room in strobe flashes of war.

Erik fought like a one-man artillery unit.

Sam dropped from a ledge with a fluid flip and landed in a crouch, blades already moving. His dual katanas sliced the air like golden flame. He moved like a force of nature—controlled, precise, and beautiful in his brutality. Blades sang. Limbs flew. Black ichor splashed across the ground like paint across canvas.

Beside him, Darius became a wrecking ball of divine vengeance. His axes glinted gold as he cleaved through enemy lines with raw force and thunderous bellows. His feet crushed bones. His fists broke faces when weapons weren't fast enough. Demons screamed when they saw him coming—and fell silent when he passed.

Christoph was a storm in flesh.

He cut through the demon ranks like a golden hurricane, spinning and striking in seamless arcs, blades leaving molten trails through the air. His face was locked in righteous fury, his glowing eyes a warning of the wrath to come. Wherever he passed, demons were torn to pieces—smoking heads, severed limbs, and puddles of ash marked his path.

They cornered themselves.

Forty demons had filled the room.

Now, only fear and corpses remained.

The last few creatures fell back, forming a shield wall to block something behind them. Christoph tore through them like paper, his kukris carving golden death through armor and shadow alike. Behind the final demon stood a narrow stairwell—old, concrete, and steep—leading down into darkness.

An escape route.

Christoph didn't wait.

He didn't speak.

He didn't even let his feet touch the steps.

He leapt.

His boots slammed into the ground below, and he took off running, blades low and glowing. His golden eyes flicked around as the tunnel expanded into a vast, abandoned subway system, the walls etched with forgotten graffiti and years of grime.

"This is how they've been getting around," he muttered to himself. "Under our noses."

He stuck to the shadows, moving fast—faster than he thought possible. But it wasn't fast enough. Azazel was a Greater Demon, and if he got too far ahead, Christoph might never find him again.

His chest burned. He pushed harder.

He'd cut down at least a dozen stragglers—demons left behind to stall him. Their deaths were swift and final, black ash curling upward in the dim light.

Finally, the path split.

Two tunnels.

No signs. No scent. No clue. Fifty-fifty.

He could go back. Regroup.

But his fists clenched, and his jaw set.

No. Not now. Not after this.

Cecelia's life was at stake. Every second counted. Azazel had to go.

So he ran. And he searched.

All. Night. Long.

The sun had risen hours ago. Golden light streamed through the tall
windows, casting warm lines across the hardwood floor of Christoph's
Brooklyn apartment. The city was wide awake—horns blaring, chatter on the
sidewalks, life pushing forward—but inside, time felt frozen.

It was lunchtime when Christoph finally walked through the front door,
dragging his feet like a soldier returning from war. His clothes were still
stained with ash and dried ichor, and exhaustion was etched into every line of
his face. His golden eyes, usually sharp and alert, were dulled with defeat.

"Why didn't you answer your phone?" Erik's voice cut through the silence
like a knife—not angry, but filled with the quiet edge of worry. He was
lounging on the couch, eyes fixed on the muted TV screen, which he
promptly shut off with the remote. His jaw was tight, his usual humor
nowhere in sight. "We were worried. We went out searching and couldn't
find you."

"I had him," Christoph muttered. He walked to the kitchen counter, his steps
heavy, and pulled out a stool with a slow scrape of metal on tile. He
collapsed onto it like his bones could barely hold him up. "I had him, and I
let him get away," he added, burying his face in his hands.

There was silence for a long moment. Then a sigh. Erik stood and crossed the
room, boots barely making a sound. He rested a firm hand on Christoph's
shoulder—solid, grounding.

"I'm glad you're okay," he said, his voice low. "Next time, wait for us. We
work better as a team."

"I know," Christoph replied, the words muffled by his hands. He stayed like that for a few seconds, breathing in the stillness, before lifting his head. His eyes met Erik's, stormy with guilt and raw desperation. "But any day now, Azazel could figure out we don't have the key, and then he'll find her." His voice cracked, just slightly. "I can't let that happen."

The weight of those words hung in the air between them. Erik exhaled slowly, walked to the bar, and grabbed a bottle of Honey Whiskey from the top shelf. He poured two glasses, the clink of ice against glass like punctuation marks in their silence. The rich, amber liquid caught the light as it filled each tumbler.

"You need to relax, man," Erik said, walking back over and handing Christoph a glass. "He's not going to find her."

"You're right," Christoph said, taking it. His fingers were still trembling slightly. "Because I'm going to kill him first."

Erik raised his glass, smirking. "To finding Azazel."

"You're seriously toasting to that?" Christoph shook his head, but despite himself, a small smile tugged at his lips.

"To Cecelia, then," Erik corrected, the grin in his voice as he clinked his glass against Christoph's.

"You're an idiot," Christoph laughed, finally taking a sip of the whiskey. It burned on the way down—sharp, sweet, and familiar.

"But I'm your best friend, and I'll always have your back," Erik said, grinning as he slung an arm around Christoph's shoulders. The gesture, warm and brotherly, took some of the weight off Christoph's chest.

"Always?" Christoph asked, one brow raised.

"Forever and always," Erik replied, ruffling Christoph's hair.

Christoph chuckled, the sound low and rough. The weight of the night—of the failure, the chase, the war still looming—didn't vanish. But for a moment, it became bearable.

"I'm going to get some sleep," he said, rising from the stool. "When I wake up, we'll go find that bastard."

"Hell yeah," Erik said, his eyes gleaming with the fire of revenge. "And then we'll blow him to pieces."

"Sounds like a plan," Christoph said, feeling a renewed sense of purpose as he disappeared down the hall toward his room—his shoulders still heavy, but no longer alone.

It had been five days.

Five days.
Four drug warehouses.
Three hundred troops.
Dozens of loyal demons dead.
And all because of four Fallen Angels.

Azazel stood seething in the center of his underground stronghold—an obsidian bunker carved deep beneath the city, where torchlight flickered like dying stars along the stone walls. The scent of sulfur burned the air, and the tension was thick enough to taste. Ancient, cursed relics decorated the room, each one humming with old magic, but none of it could stop the fury rising at the table before him.

He paced with slow, deliberate steps before a blackened steel war table, behind which sat his peers—if you could call them that. Of the five Arch Dukes of Hell, Azazel was the highest. Lucifer's right hand and most trusted general. But tonight, that title felt like a curse more than a crown.

Seated before him were Belial, Abaddon, Asmodeus, and Dagon. They were warriors, tyrants, monsters in flesh—and they looked *pissed.*

"How could we let this happen?" Dagon growled, slamming his spiked fist onto the table with such force that their goblets shook and one cracked clean in half. His sea-wet armor glistened with the sheen of bile and blood.

"This is your territory, Azazel!" Belial snapped. His green eyes flashed like poison in the dark. "You were meant to *control* the East Coast—subtlety, dominion, manipulation—and you let it erupt into war? You let our enemies come to *you*?"

"You should never have put a bounty on their heads, you fool," Asmodeus snarled from his end of the table, elegantly dressed in a velvet coat that looked more suited for a royal court than a war room. He twirled a silver ring on his finger with menace. "It's been centuries since the treaty with Ceruleus and the Elite Wing. What possessed you to break it? What madness made you think *you* could handle them alone?"

Azazel's jaw clenched, but he kept his arms folded across his broad chest, golden shoulder armor faintly glowing with infernal runes. He wasn't ready to admit it—but he had acted selfishly. He had wanted the glory. He had wanted to present the Key to Lucifer himself, to rise even further in their King's favor.

"I had learned there were rumors of an Angel Key," he said finally, voice cold and deliberate. "An Angel Key *here*, in my city. I believed those two Fallen were in possession of it. I thought I could retrieve it quietly—*without* summoning all of Hell into Manhattan."

Murmurs broke out among the four Arch Dukes. A ripple of rage. A stench of betrayal. None of them looked at him the same way they had before.

"You selfish bastard," Abaddon growled, rising to his feet. The horns curling from his temples glowed faintly red, and his warplate shimmered with shifting shadows. "You are a *fool*. Had you told us from the start, this chaos—*this war*—could have been orchestrated. We could have struck from every direction. We could have flanked the Elite Wing. Instead, you sent common demons into a slaughterhouse."

"You underestimated them," Dagon added, voice low and sharp like a blade. "The most elite legion of warriors Heaven ever produced—and you thought *you* could take them down with foot soldiers and bounty hunters?"

Azazel's lip twitched. "I expected them to be *weaker*. They left Heaven. I assumed their power had waned."

"Then you know *nothing* of angels," Asmodeus hissed. "Fallen or not, their loyalty only sharpens their edge. And these ones fight with nothing to lose. That makes them *dangerous*."

For a moment, silence settled over the table like smoke. Then Abaddon stepped forward, hands braced against the steel, voice booming with finality.

"We will stand for this no more. If what you say is true, and these Fallen do possess an Angel Key, then this war no longer belongs to you alone."

His eyes burned with the promise of carnage.

"*Together*," he continued, looking to each of his fellow Arch Dukes in turn, "we will retrieve the Key. And when we do… we will not only rise in Lucifer's favor—but we will *ignite a war*. One this world, nor *any* world, has *ever* seen before."

The others nodded—one by one.

Belial's smile was venomous.
Asmodeus's eyes sparkled with sadistic pleasure.
Dagon cracked his knuckles, eager for blood.

And Azazel, still fuming, gave a nod of his own—because no matter how bruised his pride, he knew this was now bigger than him.

War was coming. And it would be biblical.

Chapter 16

First dates and demon slaying

"Waaaake up♪ Ceceeeeeliaaaaaa♪," Evette's voice came through the blankets like a Broadway overture. "Tiiime♪ for claaasss♪."

"I'm not going," Cecelia groaned, voice muffled by a pillow she yanked out from under her head and smacked over her face. She burrowed deeper into her bed like it might swallow her whole and save her from the pain of consciousness.

"What's wrong with you? You've been moping around like a loser all weekend and all day yesterday." Evie tugged at the comforter like she was starting a lawn mower. But Cecelia held on with the desperation of a girl whose heart had been ghosted by her soul mate. She tucked the blanket under her body and spun herself into a human cinnamon roll.

"It's been almost a week since I've heard from him, *ugh*," she groaned dramatically into the mattress. "What's wrong with me?"

"Nothing is wrong with you," Evie snapped, now gripping the corners of the comforter with the grit of a woman on a mission. "Now *come on*. It's time to get up. *Cecelia*." She braced her feet against the edge of the bed and pulled with the strength of a thousand concerned best friends.

The blanket gave way with a dramatic *snap*, sending Evie flying backwards like a cartoon character. She landed with a thud on the floor, wrapped in sheets like a fallen Greek statue.

"*Oughfff*," she groaned.

Cecelia peeked out from her pillow fortress, blinking.

"Dammit, woman," Evie grumbled, untangling herself. "I was trying to be *nice* and not spoil the surprise, but *I'm done!*" She stood with a huff, hoisting the blanket into a pile and tossing it onto Cecelia's desk chair. "*Get your ass out of bed,* because you have a package."

Cecelia sat up fast enough to give herself whiplash.

Her eyes lit up like Christmas. "A package?"

"*Yeah,*" Evie said, rolling her eyes like she hadn't just been body-slammed by a duvet. She lifted a delicate basket from the desk and carried it over. It was overflowing with yellow blooms and wrapped in shimmering cellophane. "You have an *admirer*. Obviiii," Evie sing-songed and turned away like she wasn't dying to hear more.

Cecelia scooted back against her pillows, legs tucked under her, cradling the basket like it was made of gold.

They were beautiful.

The bouquet was a glowing tapestry of yellow, orange, and sunburst roses, with daffodils curling around a massive sunflower in the center. Her favorite. Nestled delicately in the corner, quiet and striking in contrast, was a single white rose. A whisper of elegance. A message without words.

As she pulled at the knot holding the wrap together, a small envelope slipped out and landed on her comforter. Her heart skipped.

She picked it up, staring at her name inked in impossibly elegant handwriting.

"There's a card!" she called toward the bathroom.

"Don't care!" Evie shouted over the whir of running water.

"Fine, *whatever*," Cecelia muttered with a grin, flipping the envelope over and popping the seal. "Your loss."

It wasn't a card, exactly. Inside was a single piece of thick papyrus, its surface etched with graceful ink like something out of an old love story. On the front it read:

Smile, because it's Tuesday & you're beautiful...

Her breath caught in her throat. Color flushed to her cheeks. She bit her lip trying not to grin like a total idiot—and failed.

She turned the sheet over.

There was more.

Meet me at 7 pm in the lobby for an adventure like none you've experienced before.

— Max

P.S. This is me asking you on a date.

She made a sound that could only be described as a squeak.

"Evie!" she hollered, bolting upright.

"What? I'm showering!"

"I HAVE A DATE!"

SLAM.

The water turned off. Footsteps. Then a scramble. The bathroom door burst open and Evie stuck her head out, wrapped in a towel like a battle-ready queen. Wet, wide-eyed, and ready for gossip.

"What's this about a date?"

"The package was from Max," Cecelia blushed, voice catching on his name. "He said to meet him in the lobby at seven."

Evie's face lit up like someone had flipped the power switch.

"Well, don't just *stand* there like that," she said, throwing the door open fully. "We've got *work* to do!"

"But what about class?" Cecelia asked, suddenly aware she was still in pajama shorts and looked like she hadn't brushed her hair since last week.

"Five minutes ago your brooding ass wasn't planning on going anyway, *dork*," Evie said with a cackle. "So you're going," she declared, pointing with dramatic flair. "You're going, and you're going to have an *amazing time*, and you're going to tell me *everything*—like *everything-everything*—tonight when you get home."

She marched over, put her hands squarely on Cecelia's shoulders, and gave her the kind of best friend stare that could bend fate.

"Got it?"

Cecelia nodded, dazed. "Got it."

Evie narrowed her eyes. "What was that?"

"I got it," Cecelia said again, giggling.

"One more time? I couldn't hear you?" Evie said in a singsong voice, now gently shaking her.

"Alright! *I got it!*" Cecelia squealed through laughter, her chest rising with joy for the first time in days.

Evie finally stopped and pulled her into a hug.

"I promise," Cecelia said quietly. "You're the best. You know that, right?"

"Oh, *I know*," Evie smirked, slipping out of the hug like a satisfied cat. "Now let me go finish up, and then we'll get started on *you*."

She disappeared back into the bathroom and turned on the hair dryer with a triumphant hum.

Cecelia stayed sitting on her bed, still clutching the bouquet. She looked down at the note from Max—at the care, the confidence, the *timing*. She pressed it against her chest with a sigh.

Today was going to be a great day.

"Alright, I did it," Christoph said, walking into the living room, hands in his pockets like he wasn't trying to act nervous.

Erik was sunk deep into the couch, legs sprawled out, a pint of his favorite beer in one hand and a bowl of cheese doodles balanced on his stomach. The Green Bay Packers game played at full volume.

He glanced over, eyes still on the screen. "Good. I'm proud of you. 'Bout time you did something fun for once."

"Yeah," Christoph said, scratching the back of his head. "It was fun setting this up. I haven't planned a date like this in a while." He paused, stepping toward the mirror and fiddling with his dark blue bow tie. "But... are you sure this is a good idea? I mean, Azazel's still out there."

Erik didn't look concerned. He cracked a smile and took a swig of beer. "Yeah, and he's a punk bitch who's been running scared all week. This is *our* city. We took out four of his drug dens, and the guy hasn't shown his ugly face once. We've got him on the ropes."

He leaned over, stuffed another cheese doodle in his mouth, and gestured loosely toward the mirror. "Go out. Have fun tonight. You've earned it."

Christoph smiled faintly and walked over to the couch. "Thanks, brother." He gave Erik a nudge on the shoulder. "So... how do I look?"

Erik muted the TV and sat up straighter, giving his friend a once-over.

"Sharp as a razor," he said, grinning. "You dapper dork."

Christoph huffed a short laugh and adjusted the lapel of his blazer. "Perfect," he said, voice quieter now. "Wish me luck."

Erik leaned back, tossing a cheese doodle into his mouth like it was nothing. "Pshhh, you don't need luck. You've got *game*—you just forgot where you put it. Go remind her."

Christoph chuckled, heading toward the door. Then he paused, hand on the knob.

"Oh man, I didn't even ask—what're *you* doing tonight?"

Erik shrugged, brushing crumbs off his shirt like he hadn't just been watching football in his pajamas all day. "Not much," he said. "Might text Evie, see if she wants to grab food. Maybe swing by the restaurant."

Christoph raised an eyebrow, smirking. "Sounds like a date night of your own?"

"Nah," Erik said, way too quickly. "It's just food." He crossed his ankles on the coffee table and picked up his beer like the conversation was over.

"Well," Christoph said, amused. "Have fun all the same."

He turned back toward the door, but before stepping out, he looked over his shoulder one last time.

"Hey... I'll see you later?"

Erik raised his beer in salute, already half-distracted by the game again. "Later, lover boy."

Christoph rolled his eyes but couldn't help smiling as he stepped out the door.

Christoph stood in the lobby of Goddard Hall, his gaze fixed on the closed elevator doors like they were the gates of Heaven itself. He had already checked his reflection in the glass twice, adjusted his jacket once, and rolled his shoulders back to try to shake the nerves.

"Excuse me, sir," someone called to him in a nasally prepubescent voice.

He turned, a little startled, and looked at the boy behind the front desk. He pointed to himself.

"Me?"

"Yes, *you*," the boy snickered. "Are you gonna sign in or are you just gonna stand there and haunt the elevator?" He popped a bright pink bubble of gum and snapped it back into his mouth with a dramatic smirk. "Because you've been staring at those doors for the past ten minutes and it's starting to creep me out."

Christoph blinked at the kid, momentarily thrown off by the attitude. The boy popped his hip like a mean girl on a CW show and continued picking at his nails like he had somewhere *very important* to be.

"Oh, no." Christoph chuckled, scratching the back of his neck. "I'm waiting for my date. Her name's Cecelia White. She lives here."

"Yeah?" the kid replied sarcastically, chewing louder. "Don't know her. You sure you've got the right building?"

"Pretty sure," Christoph said, rocking back on his heels and slipping his hands into the back pockets of his pants.

And then—*ding.*

The elevator doors opened with a gentle chime.

Christoph turned, and for a moment, the whole world quieted.

There she was.

Cecelia White stepped through those elevator doors like she was walking out of a dream and into reality. Her red skirt caught the light like a flame, her black heels clicking softly with each step. She held a white pea coat draped over her arms, and her long golden blonde hair was curled softly around her face and over her shoulders, which glowed with the warmth of her smile.

Christoph forgot how to breathe.

His heart knocked against his ribs as she waved to him, cheeks flushed in a soft pink that made her skin glow. She looked like something sacred, like the first sunrise after a long winter.

A slow grin spread across his face—one of those rare, unguarded smiles that lit up his whole expression. The kind that said, *there you are.*

He didn't even glance at the front desk kid again. He stepped forward and met her halfway, every thought in his mind narrowed to a single word: *mine.*

"Wow," he breathed, taking her free hand gently in his. He lifted it to his lips and pressed a soft kiss to her skin, his eyes never leaving hers.

It was rare he ever found himself at a loss for words. But tonight? He was *completely* undone.

"Cecelia White," he said, voice rich with awe, "you look ravishing."

Color bloomed across her cheeks once again, and it only made him smile harder.

"Thank you, Max," she teased, curtsying with graceful charm. "And might I say, you clean up rather well yourself."

"Oh, I know, right?" he chuckled, turning and offering her his arm. "Took me almost an hour to pick the right jacket. You're lucky I didn't show up in my penguin boxers."

She laughed, then kissed his cheek before slipping her arm through his.

She didn't know what it was about him, but every time he was near, something changed. She felt taller somehow. Braver. More radiant. Like maybe, just maybe, the world really did hold magic.

"So, an adventure like none I've ever experienced before?" she teased, raising an eyebrow.

"Correct," he said, grinning. His voice dropped just a little lower, more confident. "Are you ready to be dazzled? Amazed? Utterly swept off your feet by a city you *thought* you knew?"

"Oh, but I've been around the city many times, Max."

"Not like this you haven't," he said with a mischievous smirk.

He led her outside to where his sleek black car waited, headlights soft against the sidewalk.

"Now," he said, stepping ahead to open the door for her, "our first stop—Beauty & Essex."

He held the door open with a flourish, smiling like a gentleman from a fairytale.

And Cecelia… she was already halfway to falling for him.

They were near Brooklyn again, on the corner of Houston and Essex Street. He'd parked in a lot nearby and led them across the street to the front door of what appeared to be a pawnshop.

Cecelia raised an eyebrow as she looked up at the lights of the sign. "Well, this is certainly a part of the city I haven't seen before," she teased, reaching for his bow tie and straightening it with a fond smile.

"Oh, pretty girl," he said with a soft kiss to her forehead. "You've seen nothing yet." He winked, grinning like he had a secret he couldn't wait to show her. "After you," he said smoothly, holding the door open with a slight bow.

She stepped inside and immediately noticed the oversized bouncer standing guard over a padded door in the back of the room. The place looked like a run-down pawnshop to the average person, but she already knew—if Max brought her here, there was a reason. And it was never what it seemed.

He took her hand and led her confidently through the shop.

"Hey, Maximus," the bouncer greeted them with a nod.

Cecelia raised a curious brow. "Is there anyone you *don't* know?"

"Strangers," he answered with a grin. "And that's only until I introduce myself."

"Hey Chuck," he added, clapping the bouncer on the arm. "How you doin' so far tonight?"

"Oh, I'm good. You know, same old, same old."

"I hear you, man," Max said with a laugh, like they'd been swapping stories for years.

"Dinner reservations?"

"Of course. And this here," he said, gesturing grandly with a hand to Cecelia, "is my lovely date, Cecelia."

She held out her hand, and the bouncer took it gently.

"Pleased to meet you, Cecelia," he said warmly, then pushed the padded door open for them. "Well, enjoy your night."

Cecelia didn't know what she was expecting walking through that door—but it wasn't *this*.

Instantly, her breath caught. A golden chandelier sparkled above a spiral staircase. Elegant wall tapestries lined the space like art gallery pieces. The golden light fixtures cast a warm, honeyed glow, and everything about the place screamed upper-class speakeasy—like a love letter to the Roaring Twenties.

She blinked in awe.

Okay, so maybe this was *exactly* Max's taste.

And wow… he had good taste.

He led them to the front desk to check in, and the hostess greeted them with a graceful smile. She wore a sleek black dress, her gold necklace and chandelier earrings catching the light with every step.

Cecelia had half a mind to ask her where she got them.

"Right this way, please," the hostess said, plucking two menus and leading them through the velvet-rope entrance. They passed the chic empty bar, down a short hallway, and into the heart of the restaurant.

It was even more stunning in the back.

The roof garden's skylight glowed with soft, natural light. The golden wallpaper shimmered subtly behind potted blooms. The tiled flooring was rich with ornate designs, and each booth was perfectly set with little vases of flowers, dividing the space with elegance. It felt like a hidden garden tucked into the bones of the city.

Cecelia was *giddy*. Every inch of her wanted to take pictures—but she didn't want to embarrass herself. *Later,* she promised herself. *Evie and I are definitely coming back here.*

"Your table," the hostess said with a smile.

Max, ever the gentleman, pulled out Cecelia's chair with a smirk. She slid into her seat, cheeks flushed.

He sat down across from her, leaned back in his chair, and grinned. "So what do you think so far?"

"I think you were right," she said, beaming at him. "This is like nothing I've ever seen before."

"Hm," he winked, picking up his menu. "I think you'll be equally impressed by what they have to order. This menu's basically edible art."

"Oh, I believe I will," she giggled, lifting the menu to cover her suddenly pink cheeks. "You know how I love to eat."

"Which is why I already knew what to get." He waved a waiter over with casual flair.

"We're going to need to have the Lobster Tacos and the Grilled Cheese, Smoked Bacon & Tomato Soup Dumplings to start," he said confidently.

"Wow," Cecelia gasped. "That sounds amazing." She skimmed the menu. "Ooo! And could we bother you for some Tuna Poke Wonton Tacos too, please?"

"Definitely," Max said, nodding without hesitation.

"Of course," the waiter replied. "I'll tell your server to get those started. And can I bring you something to drink?"

"Two Beauty Elixirs," Christoph replied smoothly, as if it were already written in the stars.

"Coming right up," the waiter said, leaving them alone once again.

Cecelia looked up from her menu, playing with a loose curl behind her ear. "By the way, I never got to thank you for the flowers. They were beautiful."

"I'm glad you liked them," he said with a soft smile. "I picked them myself."

Her eyes sparkled. "Really? I'm impressed. How did you know I liked sunflowers?"

"Oh, just a hunch," he replied coolly, swirling his water glass. What he didn't say was that he'd spent an hour going through her photos and posts until he found the one that made him pause—the one of her in the sunflower field. The caption: *In my happy place.* That was all he needed to know.

"Is this the sort of thing you do with all the girls you date?" she asked, leaning in, resting her chin on her hand.

He chuckled. "It's actually been a lot longer than I'd like to admit since I've taken someone out."

"I don't believe that for a second," she teased. "Girls aren't just throwing themselves at your feet?"

"Not that I notice," he said, shrugging. "Erik seems to think I don't make myself very approachable."

She laughed. "And here I had you pegged as a hopeless romantic."

"I am," he said, eyes locking with hers. "But I haven't had a reason to be in a long time."

Her voice was soft when she asked, "And now you do?"

Max didn't hesitate. "And now I do."

He didn't break eye contact.

And Cecelia, completely flustered but absolutely enchanted, realized there was no use denying it any longer.

She was falling—hard.

"Two Beauty Elixirs," the waiter announced from behind Cecelia as he carefully set the cocktails on the table. Each drink shimmered in its delicate martini glass, the bubbly pink liquid topped with a crisp cucumber slice that caught the ambient light just right.

Cecelia tilted her head, eyes dancing with curiosity. "They're… beautiful."

"I wish I could take credit for this more than anything," Max said, lifting his glass with a grin, "but sadly, I cannot. That honor goes to the mixologist. This," he said, holding the drink slightly closer to her, "is the *sexiest* cocktail you will ever taste."

She raised a brow, clearly intrigued. "Hmm. I'll be the judge of that."

They both smiled, their glasses meeting with a soft clink.

"To a wonderful night," she said softly.

"To a wonderful night, pretty girl," he echoed, voice low and smooth.

Cecelia took a sip—and immediately froze. The delicate swirl of strawberries, the fizz of champagne, and that refreshing burst of cucumber—it was like drinking a summer breeze wrapped in velvet. She swallowed and blinked, her eyes wide.

"Max…" she said in amazement, voice dropping into a near whisper. "*Whoa.*"

He laughed, leaning back in his chair like he'd just won a bet. "I *know*, right?"

She took another small sip, savoring it. "Okay, you weren't exaggerating. That might be the best cocktail I've ever had."

He raised his eyebrows smugly. "Told you. I don't play around."

A beat passed, the warmth between them settling like sunlight.

"So," he said, clapping his hands once and resting his forearms on the table, eyes locked on hers, "Cecelia—tell me about yourself."

She smirked. "That's a dangerous request."

"I like danger," he said with a flash of a grin. "Tell me *everything*. Your favorite color, your favorite season, band, book? I want to know why you create the art you do, where you want to go, what you want to see. I want to know your hopes, your dreams..." He leaned in, resting his chin on one hand. "I want to know *you*."

Her breath caught slightly—he meant it. The way he said it, the way he looked at her like she was the only thing in the room—it wasn't a line.

"That's a lot all at once," she said, biting her lip playfully. "But okay. Let's see... Favorite color? Blue. Favorite season? Summer. I love the sun—can't get enough of it. Favorite band? Hmm..."

She paused, then arched a brow. "Actually, you already know that one."

"Oh?" he asked, eyes narrowing in mock confusion.

"Don't think I didn't catch your little shout-out the other night," she said, wiggling her eyebrows. "That playlist wasn't subtle."

He burst into laughter. "Caught me red-handed. I asked Evie."

"I figured," she said, grinning. "Smart move."

He gave a casual shrug. "When in doubt, ask the best friend."

She shook her head, sipping her drink again. "Okay, what else?"

"Greatest accomplishment?" he asked, fingers drumming against the table in anticipation.

"My second-degree black belt."

His eyes lit up. "Really? Why that?"

She paused, her voice softer now. "My first-degree black belt was for my dad. I wanted to make him proud. But that second degree?" She sat a little straighter. "That was for me. I needed to prove to myself that I could do it—that I *deserved* it."

"I like that," he said genuinely. "But what made your dad push you to start in the first place?"

She hesitated, then smiled. "That's a story for another time."

He raised an eyebrow. "Another time, huh? So you're saying there's hope for a second date?"

Cecelia laughed. "Maybe. If you keep impressing me."

"Oh, don't worry. I plan to."

She shook her head, cheeks pink. "Alright, *my* turn."

"Uh-uh," he said, raising a finger. "I'm not done yet."

She crossed her arms over her chest in mock defiance. "Fine. What else do you want to know, *Maximus*?"

"I said *everything*," he smirked. "And I've barely scratched the surface."

"Okay, then what's next?"

"You told me the night we met that you wanted to travel," he said. "So… where do you want to go first? What's your dream destination?"

"Spain," she said without hesitation. "Definitely Spain. I want to see the Dali museum, the Gaudí architecture, and all the art. The culture, the history—it's so rich and expressive. I want to be *in it*—not just read about it, but walk the streets, feel the rhythm, you know?"

He leaned back, smiling wistfully. "I do know. I lived there for a while. Sometimes I wonder why I ever left."

Her eyes widened. "You lived in Spain?"

He nodded. "Barcelona. Madrid. I bounced around a bit. There's something magical about it—how they slow down, how they actually *live*. The colors, the food, the way they talk with their hands. It's... joyful."

"I'd give anything to experience that," she said quietly.

He looked at her for a long moment. "Maybe someday we could go together."

Her heart fluttered. She didn't know if it was the drink, the glow of the room, or just the way he said it—but something about tonight felt like more than just dinner.

She smiled. "Okay. Now *I'm* asking the questions."

He raised both brows in mock horror. "Oh no. I've lost control."

"Tell me something honest," she said, leaning forward.

He blinked, caught off guard—but then smiled. "Alright. Something honest?"

She nodded, gaze fixed on his.

"I don't go on dates like this. Not because I don't want to, but because nothing's felt worth the effort in a long time. But with you?" He reached for his glass, holding it steady. "With you, I *wanted* to plan something. I wanted it to be special. Because… *you're* special."

Her heart skipped, and all she could do was stare at him, stunned.

He took a sip of his drink, casually. "That honest enough?"

She tried to say something clever, but all that came out was a soft laugh and a very real, very happy smile.

"Yeah," she whispered. "That'll do."

Their food arrived, and just like Max promised, it was a *symphony* for her taste buds. Each bite was a new note—crispy, rich, velvety, vibrant. The flavors, the company, the glow of golden candlelight—it all melted together into something unforgettable. They ate, they drank, and somehow the conversation never lost its rhythm.

Cecelia had never talked so much about herself in a single sitting. But with Max, it didn't feel like over-sharing. He wasn't just listening—he was *invested.* His eyes stayed locked on hers like her words were a melody he couldn't get enough of. And just when she thought there couldn't possibly be more questions—he'd surprise her with another, and another.

Time warped around them. The world beyond their booth faded. It felt like they were in a secret universe of their own making—just the two of them.

She told him how painting felt like dreaming with her eyes open. How she got swept away by brushstrokes and background music until hours vanished. She talked about boarding school, about Blake—her loud, hilarious, hopelessly dramatic roommate—and the time they accidentally dyed half their dorm's laundry pink. They shared favorite authors, quoted lines from books they both loved, debated the merits of audiobook narrators versus paperbacks.

She didn't even realize the check had come and gone until Max stood and reached for her hand, his smile soft and inviting.

She slipped her hand into his, and they left the golden warmth of the restaurant behind. The cool night air kissed her skin as they stepped outside, but she barely noticed. She was still floating.

"Damn," she said with a breathy laugh, leaning into him as they strolled. "I meant to ask that hostess where she got her earrings…"

"Next time," he said easily, lacing his fingers with hers. "You've got more pressing matters to attend to."

She tilted her head. "Like what?"

He grinned. "Like the rest of your adventure."

She smirked and tucked herself closer, resting her head on his shoulder. It felt natural—*dangerously* natural. "So where to next, handsome man?"

"The museum," he said without hesitation.

She blinked. "Wait, the museum? It's like… what, 9:30? It's probably closing."

"Exactly," he said, that cocky smile tugging at his lips.

She tilted her chin up to look at him. "I'm sensing you don't do *anything* the normal way."

"Where's the fun in normal?" he replied.

There was something about the way he moved—so smooth, so assured. She never felt rushed around him, and yet he somehow moved through the world like it bent to make room.

They reached the car. Of course, he opened the door for her.

"Well, thank you, kind sir," she teased, curtsying slightly as she slid in.

"My pleasure," he said with a wink that made her stomach flutter.

And somehow—some *magical* how—he was already in the driver's seat, engine purring, by the time she reached for her seatbelt.

How does he do that? she thought. Was he secretly a magician? Or maybe just the kind of guy who knew exactly how to leave a girl wondering.

"Do you want to connect your smartphone?" he asked, handing her the cable.

"Always," she grinned, fishing it from her purse.

"Put on that playlist you had playing at Ray's the other night," he said, glancing at her. "I want to hear that song again. The one with the line about *liquid courage.*"

Her eyes narrowed in playful suspicion. "*Until you let me?*"

"Maybe," he said with a nonchalant shrug, that teasing spark flickering in his eyes.

She laughed. "Okay, okay. Let's see if you can handle it."

She scrolled through her playlists and tapped the track. As the beat kicked in, she glanced sideways at him. "This one?"

He gave a firm nod, revving the engine slightly. "Exactly. *Perfect.* Now," he said, eyes gleaming beneath the streetlight as they pulled onto Houston, "let's get going while the night's still young."

And just like that, they vanished into the city—two hearts caught mid-spin, the stars above them, and the promise of something unforgettable ahead.

"Max, are you *sure* about this? It looks like everyone's leaving," Cecelia whispered as they climbed the grand marble steps of the museum.

"Positive," he said, cool and certain, lifting his phone to his ear. "Hey, Dmitri. We're nearing the front door."

"Ah, I see you guys," came the voice on the other end, warm and familiar.

Max tucked his phone away and gave Cecelia a sly grin as he reached for the brass handle. "You trust me, right?"

She gave him a look. "I'm starting to think that's a dangerous question."

The heavy doors swung open, and they stepped inside the hushed, echoing gallery space—eerily quiet now that the crowd was gone.

"Right this way," said a tall man in a suit with a sleek museum badge clipped to his lapel. His voice was low and polished, his accent faintly Eastern European.

"Hey Dmitri," Christoph greeted, reaching to shake his hand with a friendly clasp. "Thanks again for doing this."

"It's my pleasure, Christoph," Dmitri replied with a smile. "You took care of the Misses and me last week—this is the least I can do to return the favor."

"Dmitri's the museum curator," Christoph said, turning to Cecelia.

"Oh!" she exclaimed, extending her hand. "Hi—I'm Cecelia. It's an honor."

Dmitri shook her hand and gave her a quick but respectful nod. "Nice to meet you, Cecelia. Christoph mentioned you're an art history major?"

"I am," she said, glowing a little. The fact that Christoph had talked about her like that—it did something to her chest.

"Planning to curate one day? Or teach? Perhaps write?"

"I haven't decided," she replied, smiling. "But I'm looking forward to figuring it out."

"That's the right mindset," Dmitri nodded approvingly. He gestured them forward. "Right this way."

They followed him past the empty lobby, silent now, into a dim corridor with a sleek black-glass door at the end.

"This is it," Dmitri said. "Christoph insists he knows what he's doing, so I'll leave you to it. Take all the time you need."

"You're the best, Dmitri," Max said, clapping him on the shoulder.

"Please," the curator chuckled. "You're the one who needs to teach me how to make that cocktail you served my wife. She's been telling everyone it's the best thing she's ever tasted."

"Anytime," Max grinned. "Come by the club next week, I'll walk you through it. We'll make a bartender out of you yet."

Dmitri laughed and stepped away. "Just shoot me a text when you're ready to head out."

"Will do," Max called, then turned back to Cecelia with a sparkle in his eye. "Okay, I need you to close your eyes."

"What? Why?"

"Because it's a surprise," he said, stepping closer and placing his hands gently on her shoulders. "No peeking."

"Fine," she muttered with a playful pout, closing her eyes and covering them with both hands. "But I swear, if this ends up on TikTok—"

He chuckled. "No TikTok. Just magic."

He guided her forward with a careful touch at her elbow. She tried to peek between her fingers.

"Nope," he said, quickly stepping in front of her. "No cheating."

"Ugh, fine," she laughed, letting him guide her as they stepped into the darkened room. The air shifted—it felt cooler, quieter.

"Alright," he said at last, turning her slightly. "Now open your eyes."

She dropped her hands.

And gasped.

It was as if the universe had cracked open just for them. All around her—above, below, to the sides—there was nothing but *infinity*. Endless black, interrupted by shimmering stars. Galaxies swirled in soft, glowing spirals: violet, cobalt, crimson, gold. Points of light blinked and flickered, suspended in the void. She couldn't tell where the floor ended or the ceiling began. She didn't feel like she was standing. She felt like she was *floating*.

"Max…" Her voice was barely a whisper. "This is… *wow*."

"They call it the Infinity Room," he said softly. She turned to find him watching her, hands in his pockets, like he was proud just to see her reaction.

"I wanted to show you something no one else could. Something you'd remember." He took slow, measured steps toward her, as if gravity didn't quite apply. "With everything that's going on… I just wanted one perfect moment. Just for us."

Her chest tightened as he reached her and took her hands. His fingers laced with hers.

"So for tonight," he murmured, brushing a thumb along her jaw, "let's pretend I can stop time."

She looked up at him, eyes wide. "And how would you do that?"

He smiled. "Like this."

And he kissed her.

Her whole world surged.

But it wasn't like the way books or movies described—where problems disappeared and time stood still. It was more. Her heart didn't quiet—it *roared*. Electricity raced through her veins, tingled across her skin. Every inch of her felt like it had just come to life, like she was waking up for the first time in her *entire* life.

His lips were soft and warm and full of purpose. And in that dark star-laced room, surrounded by galaxies, Cecelia knew—*this* was her moment.

Kissing Max wasn't like falling.

It was like *rising*. Into something new. Something impossible.

And

she never wanted to come down.

"So Dmitri said we've got the whole gallery to ourselves. How do you feel about exploring?" Max asked, eyes glinting like he already knew the answer.

"It's what I *live* for," Cecelia beamed, practically bouncing with excitement.

"Then let's go," he said, extending his hand like a prince in a storybook.

She slipped hers into his with ease, and off they went—two silhouettes lost among the masterpieces. Cecelia wanted to see *everything*. Dmitri's staff had long since gone home for the night, leaving only security to patrol the marble halls. The museum was theirs.

Max knew he was going to owe Dmitri *big time*. They were definitely *not* even anymore.

He glanced at his watch. They'd wandered well past the hour he'd budgeted for—he was falling behind on the night's itinerary.

Time for Plan D.

"How do you feel about dessert?" he asked, knowing the bait would be irresistible.

"*Dessert*, you say?" she purred, her finger teasing up his sleeve before poking him right in the dimple. "Tell me more."

He laughed, leaning just out of reach. "There's a place just a few blocks from here. Ever had fried ice cream?"

"Yes—green tea, right?"

"Normally. But this spot makes it with *dark chocolate truffle*." His voice dropped to a reverent hush, as if speaking about sacred treasure. "And they serve it with cinnamon breadsticks and just the right scoop of vanilla bean on the side. Whoever invented it was a truly gifted individual."

She grabbed a fistful of his shirt. "*We need to go. Now.*"

He laughed. "We just need to cut through the park," he said, pointing. "Shortcut that way."

"Well then *move*, Maximus." She pulled him toward the door like a woman possessed.

He managed to text Dmitri a quick thank-you while being yanked into the night.

The air outside was crisp and cool, rich with the scent of autumn. They strolled through the cobblestone path of the park, winding under lamplight and fairy-lit trees shedding copper leaves. Then they reached the fountain—an elegant, angelic statue rising above a cascading pool, glistening beneath strings of holiday lights.

Max paused.

"What is it?" she asked.

He didn't answer. His eyes were fixed on a boy playing violin at the fountain's edge—young, unassuming, but with music that swelled like something ancient and sacred.

"He's… really good," Max murmured, transfixed.

Cecelia watched him watch the boy. There was a tenderness in Max's eyes, a wonder that made her heart squeeze. She laced her fingers with his and gave his hand a soft squeeze, willing dessert to wait a little longer.

Then another musician appeared—a cellist, who nodded to the boy and began to play. The two melodies wound together, slow and aching. Moments later, a flutist joined in, then a guitarist, an oboe, a clarinet. One by one, more musicians emerged from the crowd like whispers of magic answering a call.

Cecelia blinked. "Wait… what is happening?"

The music shifted—more powerful, more deliberate. Then she saw him: Sam Wu, marching into view with a bass drum strapped to his chest like some mythical parade leader, a grin lighting up his face.

She turned to Max—only to realize he'd disappeared.

"Max?"

The crowd had grown, drawn like moths to the music. She searched the faces frantically until—

CRASH.

A cymbal rang out, bright as thunder.

She looked up.

And there he was.

Christoph Maximus stood atop the fountain, golden cymbals in his hands, laughing like a madman under the starlight.

"The only people for me," he shouted over the rising music, "are the *mad* ones!"

He ducked beneath the wing of the angel, spinning like a boy lost in a dream.

"The ones who are mad to live, mad to talk, mad to be *saved*," he called down to her, voice alight with fire. "Desirous of *everything* at the same time!"

She stared up at him, enchanted.

"The ones who never yawn or say a commonplace thing," he shouted, sweeping his arm across the sky, "but *burn, burn, burn* like fabulous yellow Roman candles—exploding like spiders across the stars!"

Oh, *Kerouac*.

She was *swooning*.

He climbed down from the fountain, set the cymbals aside, and strode toward her like he was walking out of a dream.

"And you, Cecelia White…" he said, taking her hand in his, voice softer now, but no less certain. "You are the brightest star I have ever seen."

Her breath caught. He wasn't performing anymore.

This was *him*.

"You may be the most extraordinary human being I've ever met," he said, golden eyes blazing like suns. "And I think I'd like to be your boyfriend."

He spun her once.

She laughed, cheeks flushed, dizzy in the best way.

"Well," she said breathlessly, "I think I'd *really* like to be your girlfriend."

And then he dipped her—slow and sure and cinematic as a fairytale—and their eyes met in that suspended second before the kiss.

"Will you have me?" he whispered.

She giggled, a bright and trembling sound, blushing madly.

"Is that even a question?"

He kissed her.

And the sky answered.

Boom!

Stars burst across the night—*literally*. Sam had popped open his bass drum, revealing a stash of fireworks. One after another, rockets soared into the sky and exploded in wild blossoms of color.

The crowd around the fountain erupted in cheers.

And that was how Christoph Maximus asked out Cecelia White.

With music, fireworks, a fountain angel, and a kiss that made her believe she was born to soar.

"So you totally planned that, right?"

"Absolutely," he beamed, gripping her hand tighter with affection.

She looked at him with a sparkle in her eye and chuckled, still drunk from the effects of their date, the music in the park, and the heat of young love.

"Wait... Oh goodness, Max. How long were those people waiting for us?"

"Oh, not long," he grinned, avoiding eye contact. "Maybe just a few hours."

"Max!" she shoved him, and he let the momentum spin him around, then leaned into her and kissed her on the forehead.

"Don't sweat it, you were worth every minute, pretty girl."

"So we're still getting that dessert, right?" Cecelia teased, but she was completely serious.

"That's where we're headed right now," he said. "You really think I'd be so cruel as to tease you with something like that?"

"No, I suppose not."

"Correct. I live to impress you, and impressed you shall be!"

She chuckled, and he swung their hands as they entered the tunnel—its brick archways painted orange by the passing streetlights, their destination just a few short minutes away.

"You're going to love it. This dish is legend—" he froze mid-sentence, head lifting slightly as he sniffed the air.

The scent of sulfur and brimstone cut through the night like a blade.

"No," he breathed.

A group of four figures dropped from the tunnel exit ahead, landing with sharp, inhuman grace. Their shadows stretched unnaturally against the tunnel walls.

Christoph's jaw tensed. He didn't hesitate—he spun Cecelia around, shielding her with his body as he backed them toward the other end.

But more were waiting. Six more dropped from the opposite end like falling shadows.

Cecelia gasped. "Max…?"

"Stay behind me." His voice was iron. "Keep your back to the wall. When I say run," he looked at her, gold fire erupting in his eyes, "you run."

His hands dove into his coat, and when they reemerged, they were wrapped around a pair of golden throwing knives that shimmered with an otherworldly glow.

"Max?"

"Don't worry. I'm going to keep you safe."

The ten figures moved into position, fanning out to block every exit.

"Ceruleus." one of them sneered, stepping forward. "Give us the girl."

"Max, do you know these guys?" Cecelia whispered.

"Leave now and I'll let you live," Max said, voice low and edged like broken glass. He never looked away from the enemy.

Cecelia looked at Christoph then as if truly noticing him for the first time.

She imagined the crown of ebony curls covering his head, the tattered white clothing that hung from his torn, shattered body.

"Oh Ceruleus, you are alone and outnumbered," the voice chuckled menacingly. "You are the one who will die today."

They began to approach, and Max tapped his left foot in anticipation.

Thump. She'd been dreaming of him for days before they had ever met.

30 feet.

Thump. She'd known those eyes, had seen them in the dark at her empty home in the Hamptons.

25 feet.

Thump. She'd heard that name spoken aloud by angels of the highest order.

20 feet.

Thump. She'd watched as they cut him down and stripped him of all he was.

15 feet.

He looked at Cecelia, seeing the realization as it dawned on her face, and whispered softly, "I'm sorry."

And then—

He exploded into action.

Four knives sang through the air like golden comets, embedding themselves in the skulls of the first wave. Their screams shattered the tunnel silence before they disintegrated into clouds of black ash.

Max moved like lightning. One moment he was beside her, the next he was charging into the fray. He struck like a hurricane made of blades—spinning, slashing, ducking beneath claws, and ramming his shoulder into the gut of a demon before lifting him and impaling him through the chest.

A scream ripped through the tunnel—guttural and raw. Max ripped his blade free, kicked the dying creature into another, and twisted to face the next.

A demon lunged from the shadows, twin bone daggers drawn—but Max ducked beneath the first strike, grabbed its wrist, and twisted. Bone snapped. Max drove his knee into the demon's sternum and followed it with a blade to the heart. The demon screamed and dissolved.

Cecelia was frozen, her breath caught in her throat. The air stank of brimstone and ozone.

She didn't see the one that got past him.

"You're coming with me," a gravelly voice growled beside her.

She spun, but it was too fast. A clawed hand reached for her face—until Max was there, tearing the creature off her like it was paper.

"You stay the hell away from her," he growled, rage burning through his voice. He lifted the demon by the throat, slammed it against the wall, and drove his blade upward through its skull. It burst into smoke.

Only one remained.

Max didn't wait.

He charged, blades gleaming, and leapt—flipping through the air, crossing his weapons in a deadly arc. He severed the demon's head mid-flight. It crumpled to dust before his boots hit the ground.

Silence.

Nothing left but the stink of death and Cecelia's rapid breathing.

He stood motionless for a beat, then calmly sheathed his weapons, tucking them back beneath his blazer like they'd never existed.

Who was he? What was he? She couldn't speak.

He turned back to her, his expression unreadable. Something cold had settled over his face—calculated and ancient. This wasn't the man who danced atop fountains. This wasn't the boy who quoted poetry and kissed her beneath stars.

No.

This was the warrior. The fallen. The one they called Ceruleus.

"I think it's about time I bring you home," he said, quietly.

And without looking back, he turned and began to walk.

She didn't know what else to do but follow.

Chapter 17

Finding truths

The ride back to the dormitory was almost unbearable. The awkward silence hung in the air, so palpable you could taste it. Christoph cursed himself for being foolish enough to think he could be happy with her. That fate wouldn't intervene. That she'd never discover the truth.

Such a damn fool.

"Goodbye, Cecelia," he said, opening the car door for her.

He didn't give her a chance to respond. He couldn't bear it. To hear the words from her mouth, that he disgusted her. No, worse, that he scared her. He was around the car, into the driver's seat, and speeding off down the road before she could make a sound.

It was better this way.

Better to rip the Band-Aid off all at once.

He knew what he had to do now. The demons had found her. She wasn't safe. She wouldn't be safe until Azazel was gone.

Tonight, he was going to find that bastard, even if it was the last thing he ever did.

Evette was sitting on her bed, replaying the perfect evening she had with Erik. The flowers, the candlelight, the fried mac and cheese balls—it was like something out of a movie. She still couldn't believe he'd made it all himself.

Her dreamy thoughts were interrupted when Cecelia burst into the room, slamming the door behind her.

"I take it your night didn't go so well?" Evie asked, raising an eyebrow.

"I don't know!" Cecelia shouted in frustration. She paced back and forth before collapsing on her bed, shaking off her pea coat. "It was amazing. Straight out of a fairy tale. No, scratch that. No fairytale prince could compare to him."

"So why the freak-out?" Evie asked, gesturing at Cecelia's frantic state.

"I'll tell you why!" She was pacing again, speaking with dramatic hand gestures. "Our night was magical. He brought me to this art exhibit. It was like I was standing in the middle of outer-fucking-space, and he kissed me." She lashed out with her foot, in an attempt to kick off her heels. "Ooh it was unbelievably perfect! Ugh!" she tripped, falling back against her mattress and then slid to the floor.

Suddenly, reality hit her like a ton of bricks. She burst into tears, burying her face in her hands.

"Why did everything have to turn to shit, Evie?" she whispered, her voice breaking.

Evie got off her bed and sat down next to Cecelia on the floor, wrapping an arm around her friend.

"There, there. It's okay, Cecelia," she said soothingly.

Cecelia sobbed into Evie's shoulder while Evie stroked her hair. "He brought me to the park," Cecelia continued between sobs. "There was an orchestra, he quoted Kerouac, asked me to be his girlfriend... and then he left me."

"Wait, what?" Evie pulled back, her expression a mix of confusion and outrage. "He left you in the park? I'll kill him."

"No," Cecelia sobbed harder. "He drove me home, but he didn't say a word. He practically shoved me out of the car."

"I don't understand," Evie said, shaking her head. "Your night sounded incredible. That shit was romantic as hell."

"I know!" Cecelia wailed.

"And he asked you out?"

"Yeah," she choked out, tears streaming down her face.

"What could have happened to make him snap like that? It's always the ones who seem too good to be true..."

"He's not crazy; he's an angel!" Cecelia cried.

"He's no angel if that's how he ended your night," Evie said, stroking Cecelia's hair.

Cecelia pushed her off and wiped her eyes. "No, you don't get it," she said, her voice steadier now. "He's an actual 'Angel'."

"Did he tell you this? Wow, I really didn't see this coming. Maybe he is crazy..."

"There were these guys. I thought we were being mugged, and Max pulled out these golden throwing knives, and—"

"Wait, you guys were mugged?"

"Let me finish!" Cecelia snapped.

"Alright, alright. But why does he carry around knives?" Evie asked, exasperated.

"So, we were going through this tunnel in the park on our way to get dessert, and these guys blocked our path." She took a deep breath. "I wasn't scared because there were only four of them." she shrugged, "but then six more guys showed up."

Evie gasped, leaning in closer. "Wait, you weren't scared of four muggers? Cecelia, that's insane! Any normal person would be terrified."

Cecelia paused, realizing how it sounded. "I don't know, I just felt... protected with Max. Like he could handle it."

Evie raised an eyebrow but stayed silent, urging her to continue.

"I thought they were going to mug us, but then they started calling him 'Ceruleus', and he answered. They told him they wanted me and my necklace. Max told me to run."

"What happened next?" Evie was now fully engrossed in the story.

"Max happened," Cecelia stated simply. "He killed them all to protect me."

Evie's jaw dropped. "He killed them? Holy shit, Cecelia!"

"I've never seen anyone move that fast," Cecelia said, shaking her head. "I didn't think it was possible, but I've dreamed about him since before I came to school. And I told you about my family's history with Angels."

Evie was stunned. "I'm confused. Angels aren't real, Cecelia. But back to the part where you said HE KILLED THEM ALL?"

"Yes, they are real, and they were demons. They don't count!"

Evie stood up, grabbing her jacket and boots. Cecelia, realizing Evette must think she was insane, scrambled to her feet.

"What are you doing?" Cecelia asked, alarmed.

"I don't know what any of this means. I don't know if he drugged you, if you've gone crazy, or if he's a murderer and we need to go to the cops. But Christoph is Erik's best friend, and I want some goddamn answers," she explained, pulling on her boots.

"You're going over there right now?" Cecelia asked, surprised.

"Yup. Right now," she said, tying the laces. "You coming or what?" Evie asked, slinging her bag over her shoulder and checking to make sure she had her brass knuckles.

"You know what?" Cecelia said, smoothing out her wrinkled dress. "Yeah, I want answers too. Max owes me that."

Erik was lounging in the living room, catching up on the Packers game he had missed due to his date with Evie. They had just intercepted the ball and were running it past the Patriots when he felt Christoph's presence enter the house. That was the thing about Fallen; they all emitted a unique aura of energy. When you spent such a long time around someone, you learned to recognize it.

Upstairs, Christoph was making quite the racket; metal clinked and clanged as if it were being tossed about.

"You alright up there, bro?" Erik shouted.

"Ugh," was all Christoph said in response.

Guess his date didn't go so well.

Erik stood from his sofa and made his way down the hall to the back elevator. He had a feeling he knew where Christoph was and what he was doing.

He entered the elevator and headed for the training floor. When he exited, he saw Christoph in full gear, readying himself for war.

"What the hell happened?" Erik asked, annoyed. "You're being dramatic."

"Azazel happened," Christoph barked, continuing to fill the duffel bag in front of him with knives, grenades, and other deadly weapons.

"You wanna talk about it?"

"No." Christoph zipped the bag up and went to swing it over his shoulder, but Erik moved in front of him, taking it into his hands. "Let it go."

"No, you idiot," Erik shook his head and placed his hand on Christoph's shoulder. "You're not going after Azazel alone," he said, staring into his eyes.

Christoph turned away and headed back to the weapons vault. He removed more knives, tucking them into his sleeves and the side straps of his pants.

"They attacked us," he said angrily.

"Oh shit," Erik's face dropped. "Is Cecelia alright?"

"She's fine," Christoph paused. "I killed them all."

"Then what's the problem? If no one's left to report, how's Azazel going to know she has the key?"

"He'll find out sooner or later. She isn't safe."

"And what does she have to say about this? What did you tell her now that she knows..."

"It's over," Christoph frowned and looked away, avoiding Erik's eyes. He knew he couldn't hide the pain from his face, not from Erik. "It's better this way, that she doesn't see me again."

There was a knocking at their door two floors down. It was persistent and soon turned into banging.

Someone was impatient.

"Erik, go see who it is."

"Yeah, okay, but don't try and sneak out on me while I'm gone."

"I'll be right behind you," Christoph nodded, giving Erik a look that noted sincerity.

Erik walked back to the elevator and took it two floors down. Stupid Christoph, he thought. Ruining my good vibes. He walked through the living room to the front door, where the incessant banging continued.

"Hey, calm your jets," he called, reaching for the doorknob.

He pulled the door open.

"You don't tell me to calm my jets. You have some explaining to do!"

"Oh shit," his face dropped. It was Evie, and she looked pissed. Behind her was a tear-stricken Cecelia White. Her makeup was smudged, and her hair was a mess. Erik gasped, taking in the sight of her, and then Evie slapped him across the face.

"What the hell was that for?" he asked, rubbing his cheek.

"Your stupid friend made Cecelia cry," Evie shouted.

"Was that really necessary?" he asked, still rubbing his cheek.

"Yes." Evie stated plainly. "Now go get Christoph. He has some explaining to do."

"Alright, just uh, have a seat. I'll be right back," he said and exited the room.

"I thought you said you were right behind me," Erik frowned, watching as Christoph moved back and forth between the vault and a new bag.

"I'm still packing," Christoph grumbled.

"Cecelia and Evie are here. They want to know everything." Erik said, staring cautiously at the long sword Christoph was trying to shove into it.

"Tell them to go away," Christoph answered, clearly not caring about the red handprint on Erik's paler-than-usual face.

"You should really come down," Erik said sternly. "Cecelia is crying, and Evie looks like she's about ready to come drag you downstairs and beat some answers out of you. She hit me," Erik said, pointing to his cheek, hoping Christoph believed him.

Christoph frowned but began to remove the visible knives tucked into his clothes. The truth was, this was killing him. He loved Cecelia more deeply than he had ever loved anything before, but that's why he had to do this. He had to turn her away. Finally, with a cold detachment, he answered, "Fine. I'll deal with this."

When they reached the floor and entered the living room, an angry, red-faced Evie was waiting, practically fuming. She was ready to unleash a tirade, but Cecelia's hand over her mouth silenced her before she could utter a word.

Cecelia didn't know how she let Evie drag her into this. She wasn't big on confrontation. She was the sort who let things go until she couldn't handle them anymore. Her father always taught her, 'Be nice first because you can always be mean later, but once you've been mean to someone, they won't believe the nice anymore. So be nice, be nice until it's time to stop being nice, then destroy them,' but was she really ready to do that to Max?

Cecelia wished life was back to normal, that she had a perfect date with Max, and was in her dorm telling Evie all about it. She wished she didn't know Max was an angel and that they weren't just attacked by demons. Sadly, this was reality. She thought back to the drive with Max, the silence, and soon she was almost as angry as Evie. But she wasn't really angry at Max. She was thankful he had saved her. She was angry at those bastards that attacked them, and she was angry because she understood what they were after. She promised her father she'd protect that key, and she would do anything to keep it safe.

"What are you doing here?" Christoph asked, his voice like a cold slap across her face.

That did it for her. She exploded.

"What am I doing?" she nearly shrieked. She wiped at her wet face with the back of her hands, then slapped her knees and rose to her feet. She didn't deserve this. Her emotions weren't a toy for Max to play with. "No, you don't have a right to ask me questions," she heard herself say. "It's my turn, dammit!"

Evie, who was sitting beside her, was taken aback, but Max stood solid facing her like a statue, cold and unfazed.

"That night at the club," she began, "meeting you wasn't by chance, was it?"

"No," he replied, numbly.

"And last month, before I moved to school, you broke into my house, and you made me believe it was my cat!"

He looked away from her.

"I saw your eyes, dammit! I know it was you. Admit it!"

"It was me," he replied, numbly.

"I knew it! I knew I wasn't crazy!" she looked over at Evie with excited triumph, but Evie, who was completely confused, just smiled encouragingly. Cecelia didn't care. She was confirming all of her suspicions.

"Go home Cecelia, it's over," Christoph told her.

"No, it's not," she said with such force. "I know what you are, and I'm not afraid."

Standing there, with her hair a mess, and her makeup running down her face, she looked worse for wear, but the look on her face, no. That look spoke volumes. That was the look of someone who could take a hit. The look of someone who's been knocked around a few times before. This wasn't her first rodeo. Cecelia was the type that got knocked down, got back up, and gave you hell. Cecelia was a fighter, and to Max, it was the most beautiful thing about her.

"Look," Max said to her, "I have lived thousands of years—" he began.

"Shut up," Cecelia cut him off. "I know how old you are, idiot. I don't care about all that stuff." It wasn't until after she said this aloud that she realized how true it was. It didn't matter to her that Max was an angel, or a fallen angel for that matter. He killed demons, so he couldn't be all that bad. No, what mattered to her was that he tricked her into falling in love with him. Or did he? She wasn't sure, but yes. That's what was pissing her off right now. Those were the answers she needed. "That's not why I'm here."

"What?" This had taken Christoph by surprise. "Then why are you here?"

"Did you trick me into falling in love with you?"

"I'm sorry, what?" His cold exterior started to melt, giving way to confusion.

"Did you, or did you not, trick me into falling in love with you?" she repeated each word carefully to get her point across.

"No, what? No." Her words shattered him. "I love you, Cecelia."

He'd never said it before. Never aloud, and the way he said it was like the air had been pulled from his lungs.

"Then why in the hell did you leave me like that?" she cried, charging at him, and he caught her in his arms.

She crashed against his chest, and he buried his face in her hair, taking in her scent, greedily filling his insides with it.

"I'm so sorry. I thought I'd lost you. That once you found out what I was, you'd be disgusted, afraid—"

She slapped her open palm hard against his chest.

"You're an idiot."

"There are demons in this city that want the key you wear around your neck," he whispered into her ear so Evie wouldn't hear. "You don't know what could happen if they got their hands on it. You aren't safe."

"Actually," she pulled away from him and wiped her eyes with the backs of her hands. "I know a lot more than you'd think."

Chapter 18

Relax and breathe

Erik came by first. Evie opened the door for him.

"I stopped at the bakery on my way over," he said, handing Evie a decorative bag. She set it on the bed and began digging out the boxes inside.

"Oh wow, look, Cecelia!"

Cecelia came over and helped open the boxes. Erik had brought chocolate chip cookies, dark chocolate-covered strawberries, cake pops, pastries, and much more.

"I brought milk too," he said, holding up a gallon jug.

Cecelia was already chewing on a brownie. "You're the best!" she swallowed and bit into another.

"Hey, can I use your bathroom?" Erik asked the girls.

"Yeah, of course. It's right over there," Evie pointed.

"Cool."

Inside, he looked around at the sparkling floors and shiny white sink. The counter was decorated with an assortment of gels, sprays, and lotions that were unfamiliar to him. The hairbrushes, blow dryer, straightener, and makeup all seemed to fit into their own perfect little spots. It was full but it wasn't cluttered. The hand towel was neatly folded to lay against the edge. These girls were neat, and possibly too clean. Professionals could've trained them. He feared meeting Evie's mother. What would she think of him?

Pshhh, she'd love him. All moms loved him.

He took care of his business and washed his hands, careful to fold the towel and replace it the way he found it. Then, as he headed toward the door, he saw it.

"A bathrobe?" he chuckled to himself. He didn't think people actually still wore those. They reminded him of grandmas.

That gave him an idea.

The bathroom door opened. Out came Erik in Evie's bathrobe, wearing a shower cap and a white facial cream mask. Cecelia, who had just taken a sip of her milk, choked upon seeing him. The milk shot from her nose and she doubled over laughing.

"Erik, what are you doing?" Evie snickered. She would not humor him.

"I'm not Erik, I'm grandma," he said, trying to sound like an old lady. "Who's this Erik you speak of, sweetie? Is he your hot new boy toy?"

She shoved him. "You dork, go take that off."

"Come on girls," he sat down between them. "Let old grandma in on the gossip."

Someone knocked on the door. They all looked over.

"I'll get it," Cecelia said, and stood up.

She opened the door, and it was Christoph, holding a bottle of champagne and a playful grin. He took one look at Erik and burst out laughing.

"What are you doing here, grandma?" he asked, chuckling.

"He's your grandma too?" Evie asked.

"I'm grandma to everyone," Erik replied, opening his arms. "So what do you have there, Chrissypoo?"

"I brought Cards Against Humanity," Christoph said, walking over to sit down next to them. "And champagne."

"Oh, my favorite." Erik replied in that old grandma voice.

"It would be, you dirty old perv," Evie laughed, nudging him.

They opened the champagne and passed around glasses. The cards hit the floor, laughter followed, and chaos took root in the best way.

Erik slammed his first card combo down.

"'I drink to forget... the moist remnants of a centaur's colon!'" he announced proudly.

Evie spat her sip of champagne back into her glass.

"Oh my *God*, Erik!"

Christoph wheezed, doubled over, pounding his fist into the floor.

"Why would that even be a card combo?!"

"It's art, it's meant to be questioned." Erik said, placing a hand to his facial mask as if he were pondering Shakespeare.

"Your face mask is cracking," Evie pointed out, snorting.

"Let grandma exfoliate in peace!" Erik scolded, reaching for another brownie.

Cecelia couldn't breathe. Her stomach hurt from laughing. She hadn't felt this light in days.

An empty champagne bottle rolled across the floor. Cookie crumbs trailed along the rug like evidence from a crime scene.

Christoph stood on the bed now—yes, *stood*—wrapped in Cecelia's fuzzy pink blanket like a cape.

"I am the lord of chaos," he declared, holding the Cards Against Humanity box like a relic. "Bow before my collection of inappropriate card combinations!"

"Oh no," Cecelia groaned. "He's entered the theater phase of tipsy."

"I'm here for it," Erik nodded solemnly, eyes wide in admiration. "This is the good stuff."

"Tell the sun and stars hello for me," Christoph said quoting Riordan and falling to the bed dramatically as if he were shot down by Apollo himself.

"Not again," Evie sighed, swiping the empty bottle from the floor. "You remember what happened last time he got theatrical?"

Cecelia just chuckled.

"Good. No memory," Christoph replied, rolling off the bed with a bow. "That's how you know it was a *good* performance."

"Ah the last fudge brownie," Erik declared, holding it above his head like a trophy.

"Oh HELL NO, not if I could help it!" Evie struck without mercy.

Pillows were now weapons. Erik was fending off both girls with a bathrobe tied around his head like a turban, wielding a throw pillow like a sword.

"You'll never take me alive!" he shouted, leaping behind the couch.

"Give up the fudge brownie, Erik!" Evie yelled, chasing him with a cookie box like a hammer.

"You'll have to pry it from my cold, exfoliated hands!"

Meanwhile, Christoph and Cecelia had retreated to the hallway to "strategize" but were now laughing so hard they collapsed against the wall.

"You're seriously not gonna stop them?" Cecelia asked between fits of laughter.

"Are you kidding?" Christoph said, eyes gleaming. "I'm trying to figure out how to *join* the winning side. I want some fudge brownie."

"You're such a menace."

He grinned at her and reached out to brush a bit of cookie crumb from her cheek.

"You smiled again," he said softly.

"I guess I did."

"Good. I live for that," he murmured.

The four of them lay on the floor in a pile of blankets and sugar-induced delirium. Crumbs, cards, and a questionable half-full glass of milk surrounded them like relics of war.

"I missed normal," Cecelia whispered into the quiet.

"You'll never be normal again," Erik said dramatically from the floor. "You know a guy with throwing knives in his blazer and demons at his doorstep."

"And yet," Evie said, curling up beside her, "we're still eating cake pops in sweatpants, so... maybe we're doing okay."

Christoph reached out and took Cecelia's hand. She looked over at him and smiled.

"Yeah," she said. "We're doing okay."

Evie nudged Erik with her toe. "I was going to introduce you to my mom, by the way."

He blinked, caught off guard. "For real?"

"Yeah, for real, doofus."

Erik's face lit up with a slow, surprised smile. "I'd love to meet her."

"I don't even know what the point would be anymore," she sighed. "You're like two thousand years old. It's not like I can marry you," Evie teased.

"Hey, never say never." Erik smirked.

Evie raised a brow. "Okay, so maybe one day then."

Erik smiled—quietly, hopefully. "Then I'll wait."

A beat of silence passed. Then Cecelia rolled onto her back and stared at the ceiling.

"I don't wanna kill the vibe," she said, hesitant but resolute, "but I think we should really talk about my Key. I'm ready now."

The air shifted.

Christoph propped himself up on one elbow, his expression softening. "Alright," he said gently. "Let's start with what *you* know. Then Erik and I will fill in the rest."

Cecelia took a deep breath. "I was told it belonged to Jedidiah—my ancestor. My dad said it held his soul. I always thought it was just some sort of family relic. He told me to protect it, always. But he never mentioned demons."

"He wanted to protect you." Christoph said. "But the truth is... it's so much more than that. The Angel Key is literal. It's a key for one to the Pearly Gates and the only one on Earth right now not bonded to an angel."

Cecelia sat up straighter. "You're serious?"

"As a heart attack," Erik said, nudging a cookie crumb off his hoodie. "It's what Lucifer wants. What *they* all want. With it, they could force open the gates and wage war from the inside."

"Okay... wow." Cecelia blinked, absorbing it. "So if I'm carrying it—"

"Then you're a target," Christoph said. His voice didn't rise, but the weight behind it landed with force. "And so is anyone close to you."

Evie looked up slowly, her eyes narrowing. "You mean me."

"Yes," Christoph said. "Which is why we're not taking any chances."

"We want to train you both," Erik added. "Teach you how to handle yourself in a fight, spot glamours, sense danger before it strikes."

Cecelia glanced toward Evie. "I don't want to drag you into this."

Evie rolled her eyes. "Too late. Also—rude. What, you think I'd let my best friend take on the apocalypse alone?"

Cecelia smiled, a little broken, a little fierce. "So we're doing this?"

"Oh yeah," Evie said, stretching her arms behind her head. "Turn me into a demon-slaying goddess, please and thank you."

Erik smirked. "Be careful what you wish for. By the way—mind if I see that katana Sam said you bought from his shop?"

Evie perked up. "Oh! Yeah, totally." She stood, padded over to her dresser, and returned with the sheathed weapon. With a flourish, she pulled the blade halfway out, letting the light catch the intricate etchings.

"Pretty gnarly if I do say so myself, right?" she said, clearly proud.

"Wicked cool," Erik nodded, examining the craftsmanship. "Mind if I borrow it for a few days? I want to see if there's something I can do to it for you. Something Sam said he already did to the golden knuckles he paired with it."

Evie shrugged, handing it over. "Have at it, angel boy. Work your sexy mystic mojo on it all you want."

Christoph rose and brushed crumbs off his jeans. "I think it's about time we head home for the night." He reached down and offered Cecelia his hand, pulling her gently to her feet.

"It was our pleasure, handsome man," she said, leaning in to kiss his cheek.

He smiled, brushing a strand of hair behind her ear. "I'll see you bright and early, pretty girl."

She narrowed her eyes. "Wait, what for?"

Christoph grinned. "Training starts tomorrow."

Chapter 19

Family

It had been over a month since Christoph started training Cecelia. October had pretty much come and gone. Halloween was in a week, and still no sign of Azazel. She'd been training non-stop, pushing herself to keep up with the Elites. Christoph hadn't taken her request to be trained by him lightly. The very next morning, after their talk, he'd shown up at her dorm room with a bag of workout clothes and a training schedule.

He'd worked into her schedule daily exercise, meals, study time, training, and even breaks for the hobbies she enjoyed. He'd coordinated days of sparring, grappling, weapons instruction, and tutoring. He'd even brought in the other Elites to help with her training.

Christoph was there to work on her sparring and grappling. He'd also been instructing her on knives, but Sam had been handling the majority of her weapons training. In the past days, she'd become very familiar with the katana.

Darius, the largest of the Elites, hadn't done much training with her, but he'd become a familiar face with her and Evie in recent days. She learned that Christoph had assigned him to security detail.

Basically, he'd become their babysitter. She didn't really like the idea of it, but he was surprisingly good company and didn't mind tagging along shopping or really anywhere they wanted to go. He clicked really well with the girls and had a surprisingly great sense of humor. Like, he was really funny. Apparently, on his free nights, he liked to do stand-up comedy. It was interesting how all the fallen angels had such different personalities, but what surprised Cecelia most was Erik.

Erik had been handling Cecelia's education.

Erik had seen a lot in his years and had lived so many different lives. He was, after all, Eros. Being the angel of 'love and mischief,' he'd had such a strong connection to the world and its history. He'd met Cleopatra, had an affair with Helen of Troy, and for a time, lived in Italy under the name Casanova. It was certainly an interesting life.

Erik had taught her all sorts of things about the history of Heaven, Angel Keys, the fall of Lucifer, and the discovery of the Divine Artifacts. He explained the part they played in different religions, how so many great prophets, historical figures, and rulers of the past too, like her, were Nephilim. He taught her how to mix and temper metal with Angel Blood and explained that it was poison to demons who traded their seraphic light away. He explained the elements of Heaven: names like Ithritze, Galilite, and Seraquartz. He educated her on their uses and how magic worked, how to use seraphic scripture, the language of Heaven, to protect herself with runes of power. Last, he explained the Arch Dukes and the names that would haunt her dreams.

There was Asmodeus The Wicked, Dagon The Destroyer, Abaddon The Torturer, Belial The Toxic, and worst of all, Azazel The Ruthless, Lucifer's second in command. At all costs, she could not, under any circumstances, give up her key to one of them. Giving up her key to an Arch Duke would only lead to establishing the certain destruction of the world as she knew it.

This is what she'd been training for: protecting the Angel Key from falling into the wrong hands... and preventing the next war in Heaven. But right now?

Right now was break time.

Training had been brutal—an absolute blur of sweat, bruises, and Christoph yelling. She was half-limping, half-staggering as she collapsed onto the gym mat, her lifeline clutched in both hands: a bottle of Glacier Freeze Gatorade and a half-demolished Big 100 Super Cookie Crunch.

My god, she thought, chewing slowly. *This bar is my pathetic little salvation.*

It was dry. It was dense. It was beautiful.

She'd just started to feel human again when a shadow passed over her, and a voice ruined everything.

"Alright, break's over, pretty girl."

Cecelia groaned, squinting up into Max's face. *That beautiful, smug, infuriating face.* She wanted to punch it. She really did. But she'd only embarrass herself when he dodged without blinking.

"Don't call me pretty right now," she muttered, peeling herself off the mat.

Back to the treadmill she went, dragging her aching body up like a warrior returning to battle. The second she hit 'Start,' the shouting resumed.

"Pick up those knees!" Christoph barked. "Come on—higher! Hiiigher!"

She gritted her teeth and pushed. Her legs were jelly. Her lungs were on fire. She'd already logged *nine* miserable miles today.

When Erik insisted Evie join the training too, she'd assumed they'd be dying side by side. But no—Evie got to do partner stretches and shield practice. Meanwhile, Cecelia was being punished like she'd stolen something from Mount Olympus.

Christoph had her doing side shuffles, sprint ladders, and suicide drills with a weighted sandbag strapped to her shoulders like some kind of divine hazing ritual.

"You think you're going to outrun an Arch Duke?" he shouted. "It hasn't even been ten miles, Cecelia!"

"I'm moving as fast as I *can*, Christoph!" she snapped, barely holding herself upright.

She didn't think she had anything left.

But the day kept moving.

And so did she.

After her run, she'd cranked out an essay on Renaissance art, and then—back to training.

She practiced Krav Maga drills for an hour with Christoph. The same attack. Over and over again. Until her defense became second nature.

Then it was straight into katana forms with Sam.

And Sam was *strict*. Everything had to be perfect. Her knees had to be bent at the right angle, elbows flat when blocking, and exactly ninety degrees before striking. There was no room for sloppiness—not with him.

They gave her a twenty-minute break to refuel, so she scarfed down another power bar and chased it with a protein shake.

Then she was back in the ring—with Evie.

Evie had *serious* hands. Combinations came flying at her face.

Cross, hook, cross!

Cecelia slipped. She ducked. She bobbed and countered. But Christoph wasn't letting her off easy—she was only allowed to counter with her cross punch until the buzzer rang.

Uppercut. Cross. Cross. Feint. Hook!

Evie's hook skimmed the top of her head, knocking strands loose from her braid. She was getting sloppy. Fatigue was dragging her down.

It'd been like this for days.

She was starting to *loathe* one-weapon sparring.

And after this? Grappling. She was pretty sure.

POW!

That's when she saw stars.

She didn't even feel herself hit the floor. Just stars—spinning across her blurred view of the rafters lining the gym ceiling.

Then Evie appeared above her, eyes wide.

"I'm sorry, Cecelia—I didn't think I'd actually *catch* you," she said, frowning with genuine concern.

Then Christoph was there. Not just standing over her—but already crouched behind, reaching under her arms to lift her up.

"Come on, let's go sit down."

Sam handed him a water bottle.

"Here," Christoph said gently, bringing it to her lips. "Drink."

She was too exhausted to argue, and drank greedily. But she knew the truth—his sympathy had a timer.

Ten minutes later, she was back in the ring.

She showered in the training room after practice and was currently sitting in the library, curled up against the cushioned windowsill, with the book 'Emerald Green' in her hands. She'd been there for the past two hours now. For Cecelia, there was nothing quite like snuggling up with a good book in one of those reading nooks at the end of a hard day. Reading had always been her little escape from the world, but recently, it'd become a necessity she craved. Christoph had given her access to the library whenever she wanted, and she had been spending the majority of her free time there. She thought his collection was magical.

The rest of the guys would be coming over later. Christoph had planned a get-together for the night, a little barbecue they'd enjoy around the rooftop fire pit. He was always hosting parties. She'd come to enjoy them very much actually, but right now it was 'Gwyneth Shepherd' time. That was her latest favorite character from the 'Precious Gems' trilogy she was currently finishing. It felt good to read about someone else having to save the world for a change.

"I thought I'd find you in here," she heard Christoph say to her. She pulled a bookmark out that she'd been sitting on and saved her place. Setting her book aside, she looked over and watched him climb the stairs to the floor she was on. She followed him with tired eyes.

"I can tell you're not too excited to see me," he teased.

"That's because I came here to get away from you," she replied, smiling up at him.

"And why would you ever want to do such a thing?" he said, with a sly smile tugging at his cheek.

"Oh, I don't know? Could be because you've been working me to death," she said, shooing away at him, "could be because you smell," she played, holding her nose.

"I happen to think I smell fantastic, though you have wounded me," he feigned pain, holding at his heart.

"We both know that's impossible," she giggled. "I don't believe there's a thing in the world strong enough to penetrate that ego of yours," she said, and winked at him. He walked up to her and kissed her on the forehead.

"Of course, you're right," he said to her, pulling away. "But it's nice to pretend sometimes," he smiled, and sat down beside her. "So, pretty girl. How goes the reading?"

"Oh, it's just getting good!" she said, her eyes began to sparkle. "They've just caught him, and Gideon's pulled his pistol!"

"Goodness, that Gideon sure sounds ruthless," he teased.

"Not at all! Gideon is absolutely wonderful; he wouldn't do such a thing unless it was absolutely necessary, and believe me it is!" she nodded with affirmation. "I don't want to give any away any spoilers but you know the golden rule. Time travelers don't mess with history!" she exclaimed, as if Christoph knew what she was talking about, "the ultime 'no, no'," she shook her head. "This man, he needs to be stopped, Christoph."

"I ever tell you how sexy I find it listening to you talk about books?" he said, gazing at her with his smoldering gold eyes.

"Sexy?" she gasped, holding her hand over her heart. "Me?" she said, fanning herself, "Books?" she pretended to faint.

"Stop goofing off," he laughed, catching her. "The way you get all caught up in your words, pretty girl... you forget you're right in front of me, your eyes sparkle," he said, giving her that smile she so loved. "I can feel the passion radiating off your body. Ugh," he grunted. "I could just pounce you like a puma," he growled.

"Did you just growl at me?" she giggled.

"Yeah?" he grinned. "So what if I did?"

His hands were around her waist and all of a sudden he was on the ground and she was on top of him, suspended in the air on his knees and forearms.

"How do you do these things to me?" she laughed. "You're like a spider monkey, I swear."

"It's Jiu Jitsu," he smiled. "Have you not been paying attention to my lessons these past five weeks?"

"Oh, I have!" she said, wiggling out of his grip. She mounted him, squeezing her knees against his sides and smothering his face with her chest.

"Jesus, I love it when you fight back," he mumbled through her shirt, "especially like this." Little did he know she had snaked her forearm behind his neck, grabbing her other bicep to complete a choke.

"Tap, handsome man."

"Never," he chuckled, blocking her arm and rolling her over. He growled now in the mount. "I told you, like a puma," he said, smiling down at her in triumph.

"Ugh," she groaned. "Not fair. My feminine wares were supposed to distract you!"

"I think they did a pretty good job," he smiled, cupping her chin with one hand and brushing her hair away from her face with the other. She stared into his eyes, admiring the gold flecks swirling around the black in his irises. She thought they moved like stars in a galaxy. She wondered what those eyes had seen. What stories they could tell. She could search for days, weeks, a lifetime, and she'd still never know.

She reached up with her hand and ran her fingertips along his bottom lip. He gasped, and she felt his sweet warm breath tickle her face. She moaned with desire.

In an instant, he was on her, his lips pressed against hers, and she felt her body explode with electric energy. Her hands had found their way into his hair, gripping handfuls of his silky ebony curls. They kissed as though they'd been starved for each other deserts apart, and their love was like the water they needed to survive.

"Wait," she gasped, between kisses. He moved his lips to her neck. "Was there a reason you came looking for me?"

He stopped, as to think for a moment.

"Of course," he said, and rolled over to lie beside her. They both stared up at the ceiling, catching their breath. "But I really can't think of it at the moment," he said, looking over to her and grinning with the most serene of smiles.

"Oh Christoph," she sighed and shoved him with her hand.

He rolled over onto his knees and offered his hand. She took it and he stood, pulling her up with him. "I want to show you something," he said, winking at her and taking her hand. "Follow me!"

She giggled with excitement, and he led her down the stairs and through the main floor.

"What did you want to show me?" she asked, looking behind her at the case of Roman armor she'd seen the first time he'd shown her around the room.

"We're almost there," he replied, looking back at her, and continued forward.

They reached a bookcase at the far left corner of the room. Aged books, with worn bindings covered the entire back shelf. At a closer look, she noticed they were various volumes of religious text. There were copies of The Bible, The Koran, the Talmud, in Hebrew, Latin, and Arabic. There were an assortment of essays collected in binders vaguely labeled "The Fall", "The Sin", "Hell", "Soulless Ones," and one she knew well, "The Great Flood." She pulled a book from the shelf she recognized was in English. It was the Book of Enoch. The seams were filled with yellow post-it notes. Christoph tended to do that with a lot of the books he read. She'd come to notice in the past weeks that was how he chose to mark his favorite quotes and important phrases he came across. Probably so he could come back to them later.

She opened up the book to one of the marked pages and read.

"And Samyaza and his fellow watchers were cast from heaven for taking up human wives...." she closed the book. She recognized this reference in scripture very well. "Christoph, why are you showing me this?"

"Erik and I have been around a long time, and we've seen a lot," he tried to explain, "but we don't know much about light Nephilim. This is all the recorded history we've been able to obtain over the years. This is your history."

She looked at him puzzled. She'd never had questions about Nephilim because she never believed there were any others in the world other than her family. At least that's what she'd been told.

What a self-centered thing to think. How could she have been so delusional?

"The guys won't be here for another hour or so," he said, smiling, "I thought we could check this out together. Maybe try and answer whatever questions you might have."

"Christoph," she went over and hugged him tight. "Yeah," she looked over at Christoph. "Yeah, I think I'd really like that."

They were on the rooftop now, the sky streaked with pink and gold as the sun dipped low behind the city skyline. Christoph stood beside the grill, handing Erik trays of seasoned meat while trying not to catch anything on fire. Erik—thankfully—handled all the actual cooking. Christoph, as everyone had learned the hard way, had the unfortunate talent of incinerating anything he touched in the kitchen.

Tonight's feast was a carnivore's dream. Thick slabs of carne asada tri-tip hissed on the grill, their edges crisping perfectly as Erik brushed them with fresh chimichurri, the garlicky herb sauce glistening in the heat. Lamb kebabs—skewered with bell peppers, onions, and cherry tomatoes—sizzled beside sticky barbecue ribs and rows of chicken thighs coated in paprika, garlic, and just the right amount of heat.

But the sides? The sides were what dreams were made of.

Garlic mashed potatoes, whipped until creamy and smooth, steamed in a serving bowl nearby, flecked with herbs and dripping with browned butter. A tray of spicy mac and cheese—bubbling and golden on top, with crispy jalapeño breadcrumbs—waited patiently under foil. The scent alone made Cecelia's stomach growl.

And then there was the pie.

Sam—of all people—had baked it from scratch. A flaky, golden apple pie with a perfectly latticed top and a hint of cinnamon sugar caramelized across the crust.

"Who knew the 2,000-year-old assassin could bake?" Evie had whispered earlier.

Cecelia had just blinked at the pie, then at Sam. "Honestly? I'm not even surprised. You all should know how to cook by now."

Sam just gave a smug little shrug like *obviously*, and returned to carefully torching the crust with an actual flame spell.

Now, gathered around the rooftop fire pit, Cecelia sat beside Evie, both roasting marshmallows as the savory scent of grilled meat filled the air. Darius was freestyling nonsense lyrics about "divine dinner time" while Sam beatboxed beside him with surprising rhythm.

In the background, Erik and Christoph bickered over flip timing like it was life or death.

"No, no—don't touch it yet, you'll ruin the crust!"

"It's been seven minutes—"

"*Seven minutes is nothing,* Christoph—let it char just a little!"

Cecelia sat back, marshmallow lightly browned on her stick, and let the moment sink in.

This mismatched, ridiculous group—these angels and oddballs—had somehow become her family. In just five chaotic weeks, they'd gone from strangers to something deeper. Something real. It was strange… and comforting. For the first time in a long time, she didn't feel alone.

She felt home.

"Hey, Cecelia." It was Sam trying to get her attention.

She smiled, "Samuel."

"Yeah, so I, uh... I just wanted to apologize," he said, his cheeks turning an uncomfortable shade of red.

"For what, Sam?" she asked, genuinely curious.

"I wanted to apologize for messing with you that first time we met."

"Oh, it's okay," she blushed. "I was really drunk," she admitted, laughing awkwardly with embarrassment as she vaguely recalled the after-party at Christoph's apartment and projectile vomiting all over the upstairs bathroom.

"No, not that," he tried to clarify. "I mean, in my shop... With the fake IDs," he said, as straightforward as could be.

Cecelia remembered the little shop and quite clearly being made fun of by her friends for saying the shop owner wasn't an old man. She remembered her vision blurring every time she tried to get a good look at his face.

She smacked Evie, who was sitting beside her, on the shoulder.

"I told you!" she exclaimed. "I told you Mr. Wu wasn't an old man and you didn't believe me!"

"What?" Evie replied, completely clueless and rubbing at her arm that may or may not now have held Cecelia's handprint. Over the past few weeks, Cecelia had begun letting down her guard, and with it, the usual self-restraint she exercised while masking her unnatural strength.

"Sam is Mr. Wu!" she exclaimed, pointing at Sam. "I told you that day and you didn't believe me!" She stood up facing her, "In your face!" she shouted, pointing at her in triumph. "I want an apology," she demanded, folding her arms smugly.

"You're crazy," Evie giggled, clearly amused by Cecelia's random outburst.

"Nah, she's not..." Sam announced. "It's true," he said, standing up. "I am the infamous 'Mr. Wu,'" he declared, taking a bow, accepting praise for his outstanding performance. Then he made a funny face and put on the unmistakable accent. "You believe me now, tough cookie? Wu gave you gewd deal! Why you no come back?"

Evie gasped. "Holy crap, it was you!" she burst out in laughter, and soon they all did.

"It's probably my bad," Erik said from over at the grill. "I was the one who put him up to it... but hey, if I didn't, we might not be here together right now."

"Aww, I guess I forgive you," Evie sighed.

"Wait," Cecelia exclaimed." What exactly did you put him up to?" she was curious. She had an itching feeling there was something she needed to know.

"Well, uh, you see..." Erik scratched the back of his head, "Christoph wanted to meet you in a place that was safe ground from demons—,"

"Yeah, this is actually my bad. Erii was just helping me out," Christoph cut in.

"Nah bro, but getting Sam involved and the fake IDs was my idea," Erik tried to interject.

"Yeah, but I put you up to it. So really, I'm the idiot here."

"We get it!" Evie silenced the two of them. "Bro-mance... Move on with it."

"I needed you to come to Max Lounge, a place demons couldn't follow. We had a treaty with Azazel and the fallen. They broke it, obviously, but before that, I thought it'd be a good place to talk to you about your key," he sighed. "I meant what I said that night. It was my fault, everything that happened. You don't know how sorry I truly am."

"It's fine, Christoph. I don't want to think about that loser, Brian Watterson. He's not worth it."

"You got that right!" Evie laughed.

"Oh yeah, I can't believe I forgot about that dork," Erik chimed in. "Eves, I told you how he chased me down that day, right?" he laughed at the memory. "Dude's seriously out of shape. He was huffing and puffing like a 50-year-old smoker."

"Hah!" Sam barked. "You guys talking about Brillo-head?"

"Oh my god," Evie laughed. "I knew I got that from somewhere," she chuckled. "Nice one, Sam!" she reached over for a high five.

"Guys!" Cecelia exclaimed. "I said I didn't want to think about him," she giggled. "It's not rip on Brian Watterson hour."

"Yeah, yeah," Evie chided. "Our bad," she shrugged. "But come on!" she exclaimed. "Can we talk about the time Christoph practically made him piss himself in class?" Everyone laughed.

"Okay." Cecelia chuckled. "I can't deny it. That was pretty epic."

Christoph shrugged.

"Some people can't take a hint."

As the evening wore on, Erik glanced over at Darius, who was mid-freestyle—going on about fire-forged friendships and sweet potato dreams.

A mischievous glint sparked in Erik's eyes. He nudged Christoph, who raised an eyebrow in question.

"Watch this," Erik whispered.

He moved casually behind Darius while the beat carried on and, with practiced ease, slid Darius's phone right out of his pocket.

"Bro refuses to set a passcode. It's like he's asking for it," he muttered to Christoph, who was trying—and failing—to keep a straight face.

Erik opened the camera and snapped a pic of Darius mid-verse—mouth open, expression intense. A few swipes later, he added a heavy blush filter, sparkles around the face, and the words *Certified Lover Boy* in bold script across the bottom. It was ridiculous. It was perfect.

He showed it to Christoph, who nodded with a smirk of approval.

Then Erik quietly set it as the home screen and called out loud enough to carry:
"Yo, Darius—some kids were messing with your Escalade down in the lot. One of 'em was trying the handle."

Darius's head snapped up. "What?!"

"Yeah, looked sketchy. Hoodies and everything. You might wanna check it out."

Darius immediately handed his plate to Sam. "Hold this."

He took off toward the rooftop exit, muttering, "Damn kids don't respect luxury anymore…"

Erik sauntered back to the fire pit and casually tossed Darius's phone beside a bag of marshmallows.

A few minutes later, Darius returned, frowning. "There's no one down there. You sure you saw something?"

"Guess they bailed." Erik shrugged, barely holding back a grin.

Darius patted his pockets, annoyed. "Have you seen my phone?"

"I dunno," Erik said, shrugging. "Have you tried the fire pit?"

Darius grabbed it, lit up the screen—and froze.

"What the hell is this?!"

His lock screen now featured a highly filtered version of himself looking like a bashful anime heartthrob, complete with blush and sparkles.

"Who changed my background?!"

Christoph finally lost it, laughter bubbling out.

"Why *Certified Lover Boy*?" Darius demanded.

"'Cause you're a big *softy*," Erik grinned.

"Hey, lemme see that," Evie said, reaching for the phone. Darius passed it over.

"Can you change it back?" he asked, genuinely hopeful.

She took one look and burst out laughing.

Cecelia leaned over and snorted.

Christoph choked into his drink. Sam, who hadn't even seen the photo yet, started wheezing just from the reactions. Evie nearly dropped her marshmallow skewer.

Darius shook his head, a reluctant smile tugging at his lips. "You know, one of these days, I'm going to get you back for all these pranks, Erik."

"Looking forward to it, big guy," Erik said, clapping him on the shoulder.

The laughter lingered, the music kept playing, and no one was in a rush to go anywhere. For Cecelia, it wasn't just a break from training or a rooftop cookout—it was something steady. Something real.

And for the first time in a long time, that was enough.

Chapter 20

No demons, just pizza.

This had been Cecelia's routine for weeks now.

Up at 5:30 with Evie for a morning run—rain, shine, or general exhaustion. It wasn't that she hated it. Honestly, she liked starting her day with movement. But now, the training didn't stop when the run ended. It didn't stop after the showers. It was *all day*, every day—strength, sparring, strategy, survival.

This morning, they were winding through Central Park, weaving past dog walkers, bikers, and the early hustle of New Yorkers. They tried to change up the route often to keep things fresh. The park's shade-dappled paths and skyline peeks made it one of their favorite spots.

A blonde woman with perfect makeup and red lipstick breezed past in a matching tennis set.

"Hey Darius," Cecelia said between breaths, grinning. "Was that your girlfriend?"

"She kinda looked like ScarJo," Evie added, glancing over her shoulder.

Jogging effortlessly behind them in an all-black sweatsuit, Darius didn't miss a beat. "If that's my girl, she *forgot* our anniversary and still owes me a smoothie."

Evie snorted. "You sound so wounded."

"I *am* wounded," Darius said dramatically. "I wrote her poetry once. Didn't even get a 'seen'."

Cecelia laughed. "Yeah, I'm sure she's missing out."

"Please. She's missing out on this cardio king energy," Darius said, striking a mock bodybuilder pose mid-jog. "I'm a limited edition."

"Limited like expired yogurt," Cecelia teased.

"Wow," he said, pretending to clutch his chest. "Attacked on this fine New York morning."

They rounded a bend near the reservoir when a familiar jingle echoed faintly from a street beyond the trees.

Evie's head snapped toward the sound. "Is that an ice cream truck?"

"Focus," Cecelia warned immediately. "We're hitting Chub's after the workout, remember? Eye on the prize, girl."

"But soft serve," Evie whined. "What if he has the SpongeBob bars with the wonky gumball eyes?"

"You can get one after you demolish a sausage egg and cheese."

"*Ughhh,* fine," Evie groaned. "Chub's better be on his A-game."

"He always is," Darius chimed in, jogging a step ahead. "That's my guy. I've been hitting that shop since it was just Chub and a griddle in the back of a bodega. He used to sneak me extra bacon just 'cause I was charming."

"You bribed him," Cecelia said.

"Semantics," Darius shrugged. "Anyway, I'm getting the number three. Hashbrown inside the sandwich, hot sauce, and extra cheddar. Go big or go cry."

"Ohhh the number three," Evie said dreamily. "That's the good one."

"I'm doing the two," Cecelia said. "Avocado, turkey bacon, pepper jack, on a sesame roll."

"Classic," Darius nodded in approval. "Solid fuel."

They passed through one of the stone tunnels beneath the walking path. Their voices echoed briefly before fading into the morning hum of the city. The Bethesda Fountain came into view just ahead, sunlight catching the surface of the water as joggers and tourists began to trickle in.

"That's us," Cecelia said, slowing her pace. "Three miles and done."

"Praise be," Evie muttered, hands on hips as she caught her breath.

They took a second to stretch, sip water, and regroup near the fountain before heading out toward University Place, where the gym waited.

"Alright," Darius said, clapping his hands once. "Let's go lift things and punch people."

"Somebody's excited," Cecelia said, raising an eyebrow.

"Please," Darius grinned. "Y'all are lucky to have me. I'm the whole package—bodyguard, breakfast critic, comedic relief."

"More like gym mascot," Evie shot back.

"I'll take it," Darius said proudly. "Mascots live forever."

And with that, they jogged off toward the edge of the park, the energy between them light, steady, and unshakable.

At the gym, Darius went full beast mode on them.

He didn't ease them in. He didn't warm up to it. He just dropped the Muay Thai pads on the mat with a loud *thump* like it was a challenge.

"Let's go, gloves on," he said, snapping his fingers. "We're starting with five-minute rounds. I want sweat hitting the floor by minute two."

Cecelia was up first, adjusting her ponytail as she slid into her stance.

"Push kick. Slip. Hook. Uppercut," Darius barked. "Now push 'em back and roundhouse to the face! Always clear space for the KO. Again!"

She hit with focus, tight and sharp. Darius nodded but didn't ease up.

"C'mon, Cece—this ain't a turn-based RPG. No cooldowns. You're in a boss fight!"

Cecelia blew a breath out through her nose. "If this is a boss fight, I want to check my inventory for a health potion."

"Too bad. All you got is grit and protein farts. Move!"

Evie wheezed laughing from the sideline.

"Alright, let's go, sass queen," Darius said, pointing. "You're up."

Evie bounced into position, practically vibrating with energy.

"Same combo. Don't be cute with it. Hit me like you're mad the bagel shop was closed."

"Oh, I *am* mad," she said, grinning. "You have *no* idea."

She came at the pads like they owed her rent. Darius absorbed each strike, hyping her up.

"There we go! That's what I like to see! Bring the hunger, baby!"

"You keep yelling food words," Cecelia called from the bench, catching her breath. "You're torturing us."

"Motivation comes in many forms," Darius shouted. "Pain. Passion. Pastrami!"

They rotated rounds and then hit the gym floor.

"You're squatting five. Heavy. No whining," he said, racking plates onto the bar.

"This is like... almost double my body weight," Evie said, eyeing the stack.

"Exactly," he said. "We're building tank stats today."

Cecelia stepped up, tightening her belt. "Do I get a strength modifier for being morally opposed to this?"

"Nope. But you get one extra rep if you stop quoting your D&D sheet mid-set."

She powered through, muscles burning. Evie followed right after with a dramatic grunt on rep four.

"Darius," she gasped, "if I die under this bar, tell Chub's I died hungry."

"I'll put it on your sandwich board," he said.

Next came the ropes. Darius wasn't playing around—minute on, thirty seconds off. No mercy.

"This is how I trained," he said, pacing like a military instructor. "Battle ready. Mind sharp. Body lean. I want you drowning in lactic acid and begging for peanut butter."

"You're a menace." Evie panted, swinging the ropes. "Do all angels train like this?"

"Hell no," he said. "There were fat angels. String bean angels. One dude looked like he was made of breadsticks."

Cecelia barked a laugh. "So not all golden gods and ab perfection?"

"Please. We had one guy who looked like a mattress and still beat the wings off people."

"I like that guy." Evie said. "He sounds like he knows how to live."

"Same," Cecelia added. "Where's his cookbook?"

"Right? Breakfast angels are underrated," Darius said. "Now let's go! One more minute—move like your sandwich depends on it!"

"It *does!*" they yelled back in unison.

Cecelia had never been more grateful to be under a stream of hot water.

She stood in the shower, letting it rinse the sweat and soreness from every inch of her overworked body.

"Jesus," she groaned. "I think my kneecaps are mad at me."

Evie's voice echoed from the next stall. "Girl, that was some serious heat today. I feel like I earned a meal for *three*. Minimum."

"I second that," Cecelia muttered, wiping steam from her face. "I'm pretty sure I just burned off my soul."

Without warning, Evie broke into song.

"I could eaaaat... a double zebra sandwich... a sexy smoothie of banana and blueberries... then gimme doooonuts—Boston crème! That's the dream I wanna seeeeee..."

Cecelia let out a snort. "That could be your next hit."

"I *know*, right? Foodies everywhere would stream it straight off Spotify. Triple platinum by dinner."

Cecelia shook her head, grinning. "Triple bypass, more like."

They finished up, wrapped in towels and sarcasm, and eventually dressed in leggings and oversized hoodies—classic post-gym zombie mode.

As they stepped out of the gym and onto the street, the wind hit their damp hair like a personal betrayal.

"Okay," Evie said, tightening her bun. "Operation: Feed Me Now is officially underway."

"Straight to Chub's," Cecelia nodded. "No detours. No distractions."

"Unless there's a bakery fire and they're handing out free cookies," Evie said.

"Eye. On. The prize."

They walked fast, sore legs be damned, the smell of bacon already taunting them from half a block away.

The bell over the door jingled as they stepped into the warm, bacon-scented haven of Chub's Sandwich Shop. The neon "Open" sign buzzed softly in the window.

"Yo, Chubs, what's poppin'?" Darius called out, striding in like he owned the place.

Behind the counter, their favorite mustachioed sandwich guy looked up and lit up. "Heeeyyy, Big D, my man!" he greeted with his signature thick Brooklyn accent. "Back for more punishment?"

"Let me get two number threes, my guy," Darius said, dapping him up. "And whatever these ladies want."

Chubs squinted at the girls over Darius's shoulder. "Ohhh no You brought Evie *and* Cecelia? I hope your wallet's warmed up."

"Eyyy, keep it to yourself, Chubs," Evie shot back in her Jersey rasp, already beelining toward the counter.

"You two order like you're feeding a family of five. Where does it even go?" he said, half teasing, half amazed.

"Chubs," Cecelia said sweetly, "you should know better than to ask a lady that kind of question."

"Besides," Evie added, tying her hoodie around her waist, "get your notepad ready, 'cause I burned, like, three days of calories and I'm ready to *reload.*"

"Hell yeah," Cecelia said. "You're about to witness greatness."

Evie pointed confidently at the menu. "Alright, lemme get a number three, a number two, an order of fried chicken and waffles, a banana-blueberry smoothie, *and* a matcha latte."

"I'll take the same," Cecelia chimed in, "but swap the smoothie—strawberry banana for me and I need a triple espresso latte because coffee is blood and art is war."

Chubs blinked. "You girls are gonna put my kid through college."

"Happy to help," Evie grinned.

Darius pulled out a crisp bill and slapped it on the counter. "Here you go, Chubs. Keep the change, my guy."

Chubs took the hundred with gratitude. "Now *that's* a man who respects breakfast."

"And who fears starvation," Darius muttered.

The three of them slid into their usual booth, exhausted, sore, and buzzing with the anticipation of grease, carbs, and spiritual rebirth by sandwich.

The smell alone was enough to make Cecelia's eyes roll back in her head.

Crispy fried chicken, fluffy waffles dripping with syrup, spicy eggs piled on buttered rolls, thick-cut bacon still sizzling on the griddle. Chub's didn't just serve breakfast—it delivered spiritual healing on a paper plate.

Evie dove in first, unwrapping her number three like it was wrapped in gold leaf. "God, this sandwich is everything. I'd fight someone for this sandwich."

"You'd fight someone for a cold bagel," Cecelia said, peeling open her own wrapper.

Evie shrugged. "Yeah, but I'd *stab* for this."

"You're disgusting," Cecelia said, eyeing her with mock horror as Evie took a massive bite—and immediately tried to keep talking.

"Sho do you dink Joe's pizza ish shtill doing that afdernoon deal?" Evie mumbled around a mouthful of sausage, egg, and cheese.

Cecelia raised a hand. "Evie. No. You don't get to talk and chew. Pick one."

Darius was already laughing, halfway through his second sandwich. "Nah, let her speak her truth."

"Thank you," Evie said, still chewing. "My truth is pepperoni."

They ate for a few minutes in relative silence—the sacred kind, the kind that comes with really, *really* good food. Nothing but quiet chewing, sips of smoothies, and the occasional sigh of bliss.

Then Darius had to ruin it.

"Y'all remember your biology exam is this afternoon, right?"

Evie groaned, slumping in the booth. "Why would you say that here? This is a place of happiness and waffles."

Cecelia took a long sip of her matcha latte. "I forgot we even *had* an exam today."

"You forget you even *take* biology," Darius said, wiping his hands on a napkin. "This is why I flashcard you people like a maniac."

She gave him a lazy side-eye. "You're too good at remembering this stuff."

He leaned back in the booth, arms stretched across the backrest, smirking. "You're my girls. I make your success my business."

Evie beamed, already halfway through her smoothie. "Aww, look at him being emotionally stable and useful."

She leaned over and squeezed him around the shoulders. "You're the best, D."

Cecelia leaned in too, pressed a kiss to the top of his smooth, bald head, then sat back with a smirk. "We love you, you big softie."

"I know," he said, grinning. "I'm loveable as hell."

"Don't let it go to your head," Cecelia said.

"Too late," he replied, popping the last bite of waffle into his mouth.

Twenty minutes and several food comas later, they stepped out of Chub's, hoods up and spirits high. The early sun glinted off the windows of the black Escalade parked across the street.

Darius clicked the key fob and the headlights flashed.

"First-class ride to campus," he said, pulling open the passenger door like a chauffeur. "Let's get your overfed asses to biology."

"Can't wait to fail with dignity," Evie muttered as she climbed in.

"With snacks in our system," Cecelia added, "we go down swinging."

They slid into the seats, still laughing, still full, still together.

Whatever came next—midterms, demons, or distractions—they were ready.

Or at least well-fed.

And that was a start.

Cecelia stared down at her scantron like it personally insulted her.

The room was silent except for the gentle scratch of pencils, the occasional cough, and someone's leg bouncing like a drum solo under a desk. The giant projector screen at the front of the class blared the instructions in all caps like it was yelling:
 DO NOT TALK. DO NOT CHEAT. FILL IN BUBBLES COMPLETELY.

Evie sat beside her, legs crossed under the desk, chewing on the back of her pencil like it was a snack. Her scantron? Nearly half-filled already.

Cecelia glanced over and whispered, "Are you actually… answering things?"

Evie smirked. "Yup. I'm using my tried-and-true method."

"What method?"

"The Wing It and Pray Method," Evie whispered back confidently. "I go C-B-D-B-A until I feel a vibe change. Then I shake it up."

Cecelia blinked. "You're taking a *vibe check* in molecular biology?"

Evie shrugged. "It's gotten me this far."

Cecelia exhaled sharply and turned back to her paper.

God, she thought. *If you let me pass this test, I promise I'll stop using your name in vain every time I trip. And maybe I'll even stop yelling at Erik. Okay, no. But I'll try. Also, screw demons. Screw everything about demons. I should be eating pancakes right now, not trying to recall the parts of a damn mitochondrion.*

She filled in three answers she felt semi-confident about, then hit a wall at question ten:

"Which organelle is responsible for the production of ribosomes?"

Cecelia blinked. *Why are there so many words in this sentence.*

Next to her, Evie was humming quietly and flipping her paper like she was signing an autograph.

How is she already on the back page?!

Cecelia nearly screamed.

The second they stepped out of the lecture hall, Cecelia groaned into the sky like she was auditioning for a Greek tragedy.

"I think my soul left my body during question fourteen," she said. "Like, I'm not sure I'm here anymore."

Evie adjusted her backpack like she had just finished yoga. "That wasn't so bad!"

Cecelia turned slowly. "Evie. You wrote the mitochondria was the *power plant* of the cell."

"It *is!*"

"It's the power *house.*"

"Okay, tomato tomato," Evie said. "I vibe-checked my way through. We'll be fine."

"We are going to *fail,*" Cecelia hissed. "And I'm going to be haunted by that scantron until I die."

"C'mon." Evie grinned, pulling out her phone. "Let's at least go down with carbs."

She opened their group chat:

Evie:
 JOE'S. 1pm. Bring your appetite and maybe a rosary. I think I failed.

Erik:
What time again? 

Evie:
ONE. Don't be late or I'm ordering your pizza with pineapple.

Christoph:
I'll be there. You owe me a soda, remember.

Cecelia: 🖤

Cecelia sighed as the phone locked. "At least lunch will be good."

"See?" Evie said, slinging an arm over her shoulder. "Vibe check successful."

"You're a menace."

"I contain multitudes."

They reached the academic quad where their paths split.

"Alright," Cecelia said, adjusting her messenger bag, "figure drawing for me."

"Economics for me," Evie sighed. "I'll be sketching little pizzas in the margins while you sketch naked people."

Cecelia smirked. "If they give me a nude holding a slice, I'll let you know."

Evie pointed finger guns. "That's art, baby."

They parted with a mock salute and a promise to meet up at Joe's—hungry, stressed, and still somehow managing to laugh through the mess.

Darius pulled the black Escalade up in front of their building like a personal Uber Black—windows tinted, leather spotless, stereo humming low.

"So ladies, how'd the exam go?"

Evie hopped in the passenger seat, still radiating chaotic confidence. "Biology? Crushed it," she lied with flare.

Cecelia slid into the back, already groaning. "Please. Don't even say the word. I've blocked it out for mental health reasons."

Darius glanced at her in the rearview. "So... not a win?"

"Let's just say the mitochondria might be the powerhouse of the cell, but it is also the destroyer of my GPA," Cecelia muttered, head against the window.

Evie cackled. "You're so dramatic."

Cecelia shot her a look. "Says the girl who answered half the test based on *vibes.*"

"Which, I might add," Evie said proudly, "have never failed me."

Darius shook his head, smiling as he turned down Lafayette. "Y'all are unhinged."

"But we're hot and hungry," Evie said, grinning. "So it evens out."

"And we've got the Max Lounge Halloween party coming up," Cecelia added, pulling her hair into a high ponytail. "I invited Jen and Andrew—they said they're down."

"Oh, I invited Phoebe!" Evie said. "She's so pumped. She's already planning her outfit."

Darius gave a small nod. "Cool. Just make sure to text me their full names so I can flag them with the door team. I don't want any drama if they show up without someone on the list."

"You're the best," Cecelia said.

"The real MVP," Evie agreed, holding up her fist for a bump. Darius obliged.

Up ahead, the glowing red sign of Joe's Pizza came into view, flickering just slightly against the midday sun like a beacon of hope.

"There she is," Darius said, pulling into a parallel spot with expert ease.

Cecelia looked out the window and froze. "Wait… is that Max?"

Evie leaned in. "Where?"

"Right there—walking a husky."

They all turned to look. A tall figure in a dark green jacket strolled down the sidewalk with a silver-gray husky trotting happily beside him.

Evie squinted. "That *does* look like him…"

But when they stepped inside and grabbed their usual corner booth, Christoph appeared minutes later—alone.

"Hey, where'd that cute dog you have go?" Cecelia asked, pointing as he approached. "I swear I saw you outside walking a dog."

Christoph blinked. "Must've been some other ridiculously handsome guy."

Evie rolled her eyes. "Modest, too."

They all laughed as Christoph slid into the booth. The warmth inside Joe's was immediate—walls plastered with celebrity photos, the scent of cheese, garlic, and crisped dough clinging to the air like perfume. The counter was busy, ovens roaring, slices flying out by the second.

Christoph leaned over to whisper to Darius. "Scanned the perimeter. No demons. Erik's giving it another once over on his own. He'll be here soon."

"Got it," Darius whispered back.

Their server—a tiny woman with tired eyes and big hoop earrings—appeared beside the table with her notepad.

"Whatcha having?"

Darius didn't hesitate. "Three plain pies, two pepperoni. To start."

The woman blinked at them like they'd just grown second heads. "You feeding the Knicks?"

"We've got more people coming," Cecelia explained.

"And our metabolisms are elite," Evie added, giving a thumbs-up.

The woman snorted. "Alright, sit tight."

Darius slid a card across the table. "I got the tab."

"Of course you do," Cecelia said.

"'Cause I love you girls and I know you'd sell your souls for pizza."

"You act like that's not already on the table," Evie said.

As if summoned by the scent of mozzarella, Erik strolled in, blue pendant catching the light as he unzipped his jacket and slid in beside Evie.

"Oooh, nice pendant," she said, eyeing the pendant he wore on a leather strap. "What is that? Real sapphire?"

"Oh no, it's a kind of stone."

"Is it new? Where'd you get it?" Evie asked, genuinely curious.

"Nah, I've had it for forever," Erik said, glancing at Christoph with a smirk. "Got it in Germany."

Christoph gave a small shake of his head, amused but silent.

"I *need* that origin story," Evie said.

"Later," Erik replied as the pizzas arrived, hot and steamy. The crust had just the right crunch, the sauce tangy and bright, the cheese pulling in perfect molten strings. The pepperoni glistened with little cups of curled-up spice.

Everyone dove in immediately.

"Jesus," Evie said through a mouthful. "This is actual religion."

"No talking with *your* mouth full!" she warned Evie, who ignored her and grabbed a second slice.

Sam arrived last, slipping into the open seat next to Christoph. He grabbed a plate and started stacking slices.

"Hey Sam," Erik said casually, watching him pile food, "don't look now, but I think your ex just walked in."

Sam's head snapped up. "Wait—what? Who?"

Erik pointed vaguely toward the entrance. "Black top, gold hoops. Back near the soda machine."

Sam turned immediately, scanning. "No way, I think that is her…"

While his back was turned, Erik leaned over and gave one of Sam's slices a generous zigzag of Tabasco straight from his pocket flask-sized bottle. Then he sat back like nothing happened, sipping his soda.

Sam turned back, satisfied. "False alarm. Just some girl with the same style."

"Tragic," Erik said with mock sympathy. "Could've been fate."

"More like I dodged a bullet." Sam picked up his slice and took a huge bite—then immediately froze. His eyes went wide.

"Oh no. Oh no, no, no—DAMN IT ERIK!" he coughed, clutching his throat. "What the hell did you do?!"

Erik shrugged, completely deadpan. "Must be divine punishment. God works in mysterious condiments."

Sam started wheezing. "That's Tabasco, isn't it?!"

Darius, without saying a word, slid his vanilla milkshake across the table with one finger.

Sam didn't hesitate. He grabbed it and downed half in one breath.

Cecelia glanced over, still chewing. "Milk's a base," she said. "Cancels it out. Wish that had come up on the exam."

The whole table cracked up as Sam wiped his mouth, glaring.

"I swear to God," he muttered. "One of these days, I'm getting you back."

"You've said that before," Erik smirked. "Still waiting."

As the laughter faded and more slices disappeared, the topic turned back to the Max Lounge Halloween party.

"You guys know what you're going as yet?" Evie asked.

"I say we all dress up as our favorite book characters," Cecelia said.

Evie groaned. "You nerd."

"Yes," Cecelia replied proudly. "A nerd with taste."

"What are you reading now?" Evie asked, popping the crust of her slice into her mouth.

"*Throne of Glass*," Cecelia said, eyes lighting up. "I just started it."

"Oh, I've heard of that," Evie said. "Isn't that the one with the assassin chick?"

"Celaena Sardothien," Cecelia nodded. "She's the ultimate FMC. You'd love her."

"Hell yeah she is," Christoph said, not missing a beat.

Cecelia looked up, surprised. He just grinned and grabbed another slice.

She smiled.

She *couldn't wait* to finish the book—and talk to him about every single page.

As everyone leaned back in their seats, stuffed and blissfully comatose, Erik nudged Evie with his elbow.

"I've got something for you," he said, voice casual—but his eyes held that telltale glint.

Evie turned to him, skeptical. "What kind of something?"

"You'll see," he said, standing. "Come on. It's in the car."

She narrowed her eyes. "This isn't like... a weird metaphor, is it?"

"Evie," he deadpanned. "I'm being serious for once in my life."

That earned a dramatic gasp. "Someone get their phone out and record this," she said. "Erik just said he's being serious."

The group laughed.

She stood and followed him outside, the late-afternoon sun casting long golden lines across the sidewalk. He led her around the corner, down the block to where his electric blue, fully modded Honda Civic sat gleaming like a low-slung bullet. The paint shimmered, the chrome rims sparkled, and the custom spoiler practically whispered *don't mess with me*.

Evie let out a low whistle. "Still can't get over how stupid hot your car is."

"Don't flirt with my ride," Erik smirked as he popped the trunk.

Inside, resting in a black cloth-lined case, was her sword.

Evie's breath hitched. "Is that...?"

He lifted the lid, and the sunlight caught on the gold blade, casting a faint glow across the lining. It was flawless—sleek, elegant, and humming with barely-contained energy.

She stepped closer, eyes locked on it. "It looks different. What'd you do to the blade?"

"I reforged it," Erik said. "Tempered the steel and reworked the enchantments. I'm sorry the original Chinese etching is gone."

Evie blinked. "What? Why?"

"My essence was a little more powerful than I anticipated," he said with a shrug.

Her gaze snapped to his. "Erik, is that your blood on my blade?"

"Angel blood is poison to demons," he replied, matter-of-fact. "All our weapons are tempered with it."

"I… I don't know whether to be flattered or grossed out."

"Just flip it," he said.

She reached in and carefully turned the blade. Her breath caught again.

Seraphic runes glowed faintly along the edge—etched deep, pulsing like the sword was quietly breathing.

"Whoa. What does it say?" she asked.

"On this side—'Durability. Strength. Bravery.'"

She smiled. "And the other?"

He gave a crooked grin. "Firecracker."

Evie stared at the blade for a long moment, then burst out laughing. "You're such an ass."

"It's your nickname," Erik shrugged. "Tough, loud, and liable to blow someone's head off if they're not paying attention."

She ran her fingers lightly along the hilt. "I love it."

He looked at her—earnest, for once. "I know."

She smiled, then leaned forward and kissed him on the cheek. "You're not so bad, pretty boy."

Erik grinned as he closed the trunk. "Tell that to the next demon who tries you."

They stood there for a moment, street noise humming in the distance, the gold still gleaming faintly in her hands.

Evie wasn't sure what lay ahead.

But now she had a blade—reborn in angel fire, sealed with strength, and marked with love.

And that made her feel ready for anything.

Chapter 21

All Hallows Eve

Cecelia didn't mind coming to the club alone. Evie had left early in the afternoon to go last-minute costume shopping with Erik. Since she already received her costume weeks before, courtesy of Amazon's prime two-day shipping, she agreed to arrive at the club early. She took a taxi, compliments of Max. He insisted on arranging it as a precautionary measure since she refused to let him come pick her up. She figured he knew a guy. He always knew a guy. She knew how busy he was at the club and felt awful tearing him away from it just for a ride. So, taking a cab was a fair compromise.

Cecelia never understood how New York City taxi drivers got a bad rep. She always enjoyed talking to them while they drove. They were such interesting people, full of fascinating stories waiting to be told. This man was paying his way through medical school. His name was Prakesh. He was in love with a woman named Preeti. They were childhood best friends, and she was in love with him too. He was determined to make a career for himself before proposing, and she said she'd wait for him. Cecelia thought that was so romantic.

He spoke highly of Max too, like they were old friends, telling her that she found a good one. If there was one thing you could say about Max, it was he knew how to pick and choose his friends, and Cecelia was always impressed with his choices.

"Thanks!" she called to Prakesh before shutting the door and turning to the building.

"Mmm," she purred. There he was, outside patiently awaiting her arrival, always the gentleman. Ugh, she thought. He was looking more handsome than ever. She climbed the stairs to meet him.

"So you're a Gryffindor?" he asked, commenting on her garb.

"Surprised?" she smirked. "Do you like it?"

You better like it, she thought. She picked it out looking to impress him. She knew how big he was into Harry Potter and thought it whispered his name when she saw it.

He was leaning against the corner of the building near the entrance to his club, smiling at her with that grin of his that drove her nuts. It turned her to liquid. God, did she love that smile. It made her want to shake him, slap him, grab his face and kiss him all at the same time.

"Yeah, of course," he chuckled to himself. His black glittering nail polish caught her eye. "I just always pictured you as a Ravenclaw."

"I'll take that as a compliment," she nodded, knowing Ravenclaws were brilliant.

"I'm actually a Gryffindor myself," he smiled proudly, scratching the back of his head sheepishly, the way he and Erik tended to do.

She adored his little mannerisms. The way he talked with his hands when he was excited about something, the way he quoted his favorite authors with such charisma and enthusiasm—all his little ticks had become ever more endearing with each day spent with him.

"A Gryffindor, you?" she teased.

"Oh, you don't think so?" he raised an eyebrow at her in disbelief.

"Oh no, I believe it," she giggled. "You one hundred percent would be." She smiled, taking him in from head to toe, admiring the blue suede shoes, slim-fit grey dress pants, and navy blue smoking jacket he had on. His face was done up like an 80s runway model, with blue sparkly makeup around his eyes, darkened brows, and sparkling glitter in his hair.

"So you really went all out, didn't you?" she said, nibbling on her lower lip. She thought he looked sexy, uncomfortably so.

"You were the one who suggested we dress as our favorite book characters," he replied, winking at her. "I couldn't let you down," he said, taking a step back and bowing to her. "Magnus Bane. The pleasure is all yours," he snapped his fingers, and blue sparks flickered above his hands.

"Whoa! How'd you do that?" she gasped in surprise, genuinely curious.

"A magician never reveals his tricks."

"Wait, Fallen Angels can do that?"

He chuckled. "I wish I could say it's magic, but it's just a slight of hand," he opened his palm to show the rough diamond-like surface on the outsides of the rings he was wearing. When he snapped his fingers again, the blue sparks formed from the friction.

"I ordered them from a special effects shop in Cali. They make all sorts of props for movies. I figured they'd be the guys to go to, and they didn't let me down."

"Most certainly not, that's absolutely brilliant," she grinned with approval.

"Thanks, pretty girl," he winked. "Now come on, let's go inside. I want to show you what I've been up to the last couple of days."

He took her hand and led her through the sliding doors.

The hallway was dark and smoky, with fluorescent black lights lighting a path along the ceiling and floor. The walls were covered in webs; the material glistened in the light. Animatronic spiders climbed up and down the web with such authenticity it was chilling. They reached the front desk where a large executioner stood guard. A hood masked his face in shadows, and in his hand, he held a large executioner's axe. It looked deadly real, which made his costume ever more convincing. There was an open coffin to his left. It was creepy and looked like it came from a funeral home. Max had a thing for the theatrical. She wouldn't be surprised if there were a body waiting inside ready to jump out. She decided she wasn't going to check. Better she didn't find out.

"Hey Cecelia," she was startled by the deep voice coming from behind the mask of the executioner. "You look really cool," she recognized it with instant relief.

"Darius? Is that you?"

He nodded.

"You look absolutely terrifying," she giggled.

"I try," he shrugged.

"Dammit, D. I told you not to break character. What the cheese, bro?" Christoph looked at his friend in mock disapproval.

"Oh yeah. My bad, bro," he chuckled.

"Well, don't do it again, big guy. I want this to be believable," he turned to leave but looked back. "Come on, Cecelia, you haven't seen anything yet," he said, smirking, and walked past Darius through the smoky doorway into the unknown.

"Christoph, you must be breaking so many fire violations here, it's not even funny."

"What did I tell you, pretty girl? This is my city, so I make the rules."

The smoke cleared, and she saw what he was talking about.

"Whoa," she gasped. "Christoph, you've really outdone yourself."

The club had been completely transformed.

The room was eerily lit. The bar had been covered in webs, glow-in-the-dark spiders caught in between them. She was fascinated by the red-lit jack-o-lanterns on the back shelves scattered between the top-shelf liquor bottles, their glowing surfaces carved with faces that screamed in agony. On the countertop were skulls with open jaws filled with napkins, and smoking cauldrons stood between them, likely filled with dry ice. Pier 1 imports would be impressed; she knew that's where he liked to shop for his decorations.

She looked up to the ceiling where giant spiders hung above the bar and dance floor. Circus equipment also hung from the rafters. Things like shiny hooks and long pieces of silk material. Christoph must have had it set up for an aerial arts performance later that night.

Looking back down, she spotted stripper poles on four small stages he must have had built specifically for tonight. They were lit by purple fluorescent spotlights and set around the dance floor. There was a girl sitting on one of them. Cecelia hadn't noticed right away. She was surprised with herself because this girl was dressed in black lace lingerie and was finishing her body paint. She must have been there a while. Her limbs were done up in neon colors to look like a skeleton. Oh, and she was drop-dead gorgeous.

Cecelia felt a pang of jealousy come over her. Christoph had hired girls like this for his party, and here she was standing there in her Hogwarts robes.

She paused to look around as Christoph walked behind the bar to grab some cocktails he must've prepared earlier. "So where is everyone?" Cecelia asked when he returned with two glowing drinks.

And like on cue, someone answered.

"Up here," she heard and looked up to see Evie smiling down at her from the top railing. "Whoa, Christoph. You look like Adam Levine," she smirked. "Hot!"

"Evie!" Cecelia squeaked in excitement. "How'd you beat me here?"

Erik, who was beside her, nudged her shoulder.

"What?" she shrugged. "We just did?"

"Hey, I thought we said we were dressing up as our favorite book characters," Cecelia popped her hip out at them. "What gives?"

"We never said any of that, that was all you and Christoph," Evie replied smugly.

"Holy smokes," Christoph choked on the cocktail he'd been sipping. "Evie, are you The Doctor?"

"You bet your sweet ass. Number 10," she preened, throwing her trench coat open with her hands on her hips. "Tenant will always be my Doctor," she smiled, removing her blue sonic screwdriver from her inner coat pocket.

"Oh sick!" Christoph noted with enthusiasm.

"Thanks, Erik got it for me," she smiled proudly, lighting it up.

"You nerds," Erik chuckled to himself.

"Shut up, Erik. You're a bloody beer can. You can't say anything," Christoph chided.

"They have beer in movies, books, and TV," he smiled. "I win you all. You're just jealous."

"He has a point," Evie shrugged her shoulders.

"Alright, fine. You win," Christoph smirked. "Now get your butts down here. Let's get you set up before Darius opens the doors." he said, smiling. He turned to Cecelia. "So, Erik and I wanted to set you up with a table for the night. How many of your friends are coming by again?"

"It's just five of us. Evie and I invited Jen, Andrew, and Phoebe," she blushed.

"Excellent, follow me, pretty girl."

It wasn't long before Cecelia's friends arrived, their expressions of surprise and excitement revealing their impressed reactions. Bottle service was a hit, giving them their own private corner with comfy leather couches and little coffee tables. Erik had already sent over food without asking, and Evie attacked it like a starved animal.

"I told you it was all about the fried mac n cheese balls!" she declared between bites.

"Mmm, I hear ya," Andrew replied. "Damn this place is fancy. These tuna taco wonton things are incredible, and I have no idea what I'm drinking, but it tastes like the sweet waters of heaven," he said, holding up his drink.

It was purple and bubbling, the rim lined with watermelon pucker and coated in blue-raspberry pop rocks.

"Christoph calls that one 'Witches Brew'. It's made with strawberry champagne, blueberry vodka, and muddled blackberries. Here," Cecelia said, handing him a menu. "It's one of tonight's specials."

"Well my Peach Candy Cocktail tastes better than trick or treating," Jen declared holding her class up to Andrew and then taking a bite at one of the candy rings along the rim.

"Goleee. I've got to try that next, sugar!" Andrew said raising his glass to toast with her.

People started arriving shortly after. Cecelia enjoyed watching their faces light up with sheer amazement as they entered the transformed club. The space filled with conversation, energy, and excitement. Music pulsed through the speakers, and the dance floor became an ocean of bodies moving to the rhythm. Cecelia was captivated by the dancers on the poles, their movements so skilled and passionate that it was hard to look away. They were magnificent.

"Hey, did you hear Christoph booked Lancifer for tonight?" Evie shouted over the crowd.

"Huh?" Cecelia asked, breaking out of her reverie.

"Lancifer, he's like 'the tits'."

"Oh yeah, ha. Max loves him! He's always playing his music in the gym."

"Yeah, well he's about to come on."

She looked toward the main stage. Smoke appeared, and purple lights flashed. A figure emerged from the rafters.

"Happy Halloween, New York City!" he shouted.

The crowd erupted in applause.

The lights illuminated the figure dressed in a blue British Naval jacket, gold shoulder pads shimmering.

"Who's ready to party?" he asked, stepping off the rafters, suspended by an invisible wire. The crowd cheered as he was lowered through the smoke onto the main stage.

"I'm Lancifer, and this song's called Bring Your Bass!"

The music blasted through the speakers.

DooDooDebadodo DooDooDevadodo, the synth was like lasers, and then came the bass.

The walls are shakin'/From the vibrations that the DJ's makin'/ Got everybody in here conversatin'/ 'Bout what we're doing all across the nation/ Tonight's a celebration!

The crowd sang along with him.

Let's get this party poppin'/ We got a bass let's drop it/ From Tokyo to Costa Rica all the way to Compton/ And no we won't be stoppin'/ Let's dance like no one's watchin'/ Turn up the volume everybody just a couple notches!

The music ignited the crowd. Cecelia and Evie let the beat take control, jumping and dancing along with everyone.

Lancifer was amazing.

When the first song ended, Evie took the opportunity to pull Cecelia aside.

"Time for drinks!" she announced, leading Cecelia to the bar.

There was Erik.

"Hey there little Erii." Evie said, leaning on the counter to get his attention.

"Ladies," he winked and knelt down, reaching into the fridge. He brought out a tray. "Tonight, I present to you a foreign delicacy, BRAINS!" he cackled maniacally.

The girls laughed.

"Those look really cool!" Cecelia said excitedly.

"Oh yeah, they better," he chuckled. "They were a bitch to make," he held out the tray. "Take one."

"What are they?"

"Jello shots, Obviiii, Cecelia." Evie teased, taking one. "No finger scoop required," she winked. "Come on, let's do it!"

They took the shot. The fruit-flavored explosion was electrifying.

"YES! You made them strawberry-watermelon! You listened!" Evie was so excited she could squeeze him. "Oh god," she realized. "You need to cut me off after four. I'm going to eat these things like candy."

Erik laughed. "Alright, Eves. You got it," he winked and took the tray away. "It's crazy busy here, but text me if you need anything and I'll send someone over."

"Alright! Thanks, hot stuff!" she hollered, turning to Cecelia. "Hot stuff? Did I seriously just call him 'Hot stuff'?"

Cecelia shrugged.

"God, what's happening to me?" Evie laughed.

"You're in looooove," Cecelia teased. "Come on, let's get back to the table."

Evie pushed her, then froze.

"Shit, don't look now, but Shrek alert at your 6 o'clock."

Cecelia turned slowly.

"Brian," she choked.

"Yeah, how the balls did he sneak into here?"

It felt like someone punched her in the chest. The air had been sucked out of her lungs.

"I don't know," she whispered, then saw who Brian was talking to.

Phoebe. Shit-faced-drunk Phoebe.

"OH HELL NO." The air returned to her lungs. Anger ran like fire through her veins. She grabbed Evie by the wrist and pulled her hard. Through the crowd they went, Cecelia pushing people aside, manhandling them with unrestrained strength.

"You're so hot!" Brian said to Phoebe, grinding on her from behind, his grimy hands on her hips keeping her from falling.

"Phoebe? How did Phoebe get so drunk?" Evie asked Cecelia. "Are you okay, Phoebe?"

"This guy's been buying me drinks! His name's Brin! I mean Bryyyannn," she slurred.

"You know these broads?" Brian asked, still grinding.

"Yeah, these are my friends!"

"Phoebe, come on, let's go. He's bad news," Evie said, taking Phoebe's hand.

"OKAY!"

Brian held on.

"Come on babe, I thought you wanted to come back to my place?"

"OKAY!" Phoebe slurred, spinning around and almost falling. Brian caught her by the hips. Cecelia had enough.

"Sorry, Phoebe, but this guy's a creep," she reached for her hand, and Phoebe took it.

"OKAY! Thanks for the drinks, Brin!"

"You fucking tease! Just 'cause you didn't want none of this doesn't mean you have to be a cockblock!"

Evie walked over to help Cecelia support Phoebe. She was practically falling over.

"Fuck off, Brian, you rapey bastard." Evie chided. "How the hell did you even get in here?"

"I had VIP tickets, slut."

"Liar." Cecelia spat. "Darius would never let you through the door."

Brian pulled down the Batman mask he wore.

"They didn't ask me to take it off, not my problem," he laughed and pulled it back up. "Come on, sexy, last chance to come home with a real man."

Cecelia felt bile rise in her throat.

"You disgust me."

"You jealous, Cecelia? You know you liked it. You want some more?"

It was the color of her pulse, the thought of his hands snaking up her back made her body quake. It was the color of anger so raw hell could not contain it. She looked to Evie.

"That's enough."

"Knock him the fuck out, Cecelia."

She turned so fast, anyone watching could barely see her fist connect with his jaw, but they saw the impact as his body swung around and hit the floor.

Red was the color that broke from his nostrils and pooled on the floor.

"You piece of shit!" Evie wound up and kicked him square in the family jewels, his body convulsed and curled into a ball.

"OH SHIT!" someone shouted. It was Lancifer. The music kept playing. "Anyone else here just see Harry Potter and Doctor Who knock Batman the FUCK OUT?"

The crowd cheered!

"Damn this party's lit!"

Christoph and Darius appeared through different corners of the crowd. Without a word, Darius picked up Brian Watterson and threw him over his shoulder. With a nod from Christoph, he quickly disappeared through the crowd.

"Are you okay, Cecelia? Ladies?"

"Yeah." Cecelia calmed down. "Yeah, we're okay. Phoebe's really drunk though and needs to get home."

"Do you want me to call an ambulance for her?"

"No, she's drunk but it's nothing we can't handle. She hasn't thrown up or anything," Evie replied.

"We can take her up to the office. Keep an eye on her. If anything happens, we'll take her straight to the hospital," he assured Evie and then looked to Cecelia.

"I'm calling a friend at the police station and having him send a squad car around. I'm not letting this kid get away with this."

She didn't argue. She was done with Brian.

Erik came over and helped Evie take Phoebe to the office, where they looked after her for the remainder of the night. When the party was over, and Phoebe had long passed out, Evie insisted on taking her back to their dorm. Darius offered to drive them and personally ensured they'd reach their room safely. Cecelia offered up her bed to Phoebe, and Evie was grateful.

"Love you, Evie. I'll see you tomorrow morning."

"Love you too, CeeCee," she waved goodbye as Evie shut the door and they drove away in Darius's black Escalade.

"Why don't you and Erik head back?" Max suggested. "I'm gonna stay here and help Jax and the rest of the staff close up."

"Okay," she said and hugged him tight. She pulled away to stare into his warm golden eyes and smiled. "Don't stay too late."

"I'll be back before you know it," he kissed her and walked back into the club.

Cecelia
As a Gryffindor

Christoph

As Magnus Bane

Evie
As The 10th Doctor

Erik

As Beer

THE MARK OF VISHNU

Chapter 22

To catch a Nephilim

All Hallows Day

The personal library of Christoph Maximus was truly something magical. Books collected over thousands of years, some so delicate they had to be kept behind glass . . . and then there was this.

You'd think it funny that an immortal fallen angel would be into fiction, but he had cases upon cases filled with Mythology to Science Fiction, Fairy Tales to Urban Fantasy, Shakespeare to Dan Brown! Titles she recognized like *Dante's Inferno*, *A Midsummer Night's Dream*, *The Mortal Instruments*, wait.

It was all starting to make sense. That conceited bastard, she giggled. It was funny how little things like this made her giddy after only a few drinks at the club.

These were all books on Heaven and Hell. She picked a book off the shelf and opened it to a page he had marked with a post-it note. She recalled how he recited writers like Bukowski, and Kerouac, and quoted heroes from Clare, and Riordan on occasion. The majority of his books were riddled with these little yellow things. She found it quite endearing how he loved his quotes.

"Though rather despite myself, I thought him a pretty bit of poison to start with, but I have come around. There is a soul under all that bravado. And he is really alive, one of the most alive people I have ever met. When he feels something, it is as bright and sharp as lightning." – Magnus Bane, Clockwork Prince - Cassandra Clare

Oh Max, she sighed.

Cecelia liked to believe that you could learn a lot about a person from looking at the books they read, but it wasn't so easy with him. He was... complicated.

Though tonight, he didn't seem so brooding. Tonight he was something entirely different. What a magical night it was. The music, the dancing, the décor, ugh. He had transformed that club into another world. The haunting costumes, the people, the drinks! The night was alive with celebration, and Max was behind it all. She just wished he didn't have to be so responsible, closing up with the staff.

She giggled, what a selfish thing to think. She wanted him here with her. To run her hands through his thick hair, take in the smell of cucumbers and that cologne he always wore, and to taste his sweet—

Her thoughts were interrupted by a loud noise coming from downstairs.

The hell? She thought.

It sounded like someone was pounding on the front door, but she was four floors up, they had to be hitting that thing pretty hard for her to hear all the way up there. Crazy drunks, she tried to rationalize it. It was almost 4 am after all, who else would it be?

Then a powerful explosion resounded throughout the building and shook the floor beneath her feet. Oh, these weren't drunks. Dammit. She reached into her pocket for her phone to call Max, but it wasn't there. Shit. I left it in my purse downstairs. No time now, I've gotta hide!

SCREECH, it was a sound like metal being torn apart like paper. She could feel the hair stand up on the back of her neck. They were peeling apart the fireproof door!

There was a pop, followed by a loud crash, and then thundering footsteps beating up the stairs. Oh shit! Oh shit! It's too late, she realized. I need a weapon. She dropped the book she'd been holding and ran for the door. I need to get upstairs to the training room!

Erik poked his head through the library doors then and she stopped in her tracks.

"Hide!" he demanded.

She looked at him dumbfounded. What did he think she was trying to do?

"It's an ambush, dammit! They're here, Cecelia," his brow furrowed angrily. "Hide, and I'll try to hold them off."

She'd been right. Demons. Demons had come for them.

He secured the doors and then rushed around the room, moving too fast for her eyes to see. He lifted furniture, moving it and stacking it in front of the library doors. First a desk; then a sofa, then more desks, propping chairs against them, and Max's mini fridge? She looked around and found Erik pulling a large bookshelf past her and leaning it against everything he had used to barricade them in. She had to prepare herself for the inevitable. They were coming for them, and she wasn't going to let them take her without a fight.

"I don't know how long this will hold, but it'll buy us some time."

There was a loud rapping at the doors. "Eros, we know you are there," called an unfamiliar voice. It was sweetly smooth, like silk. "Let us have the girl and go, this does not concern you," it said so convincingly.

"Over my dead body, Azazel," Erik replied, undeterred.

"Oh, that could easily be arranged," Azazel threatened, as if it were a simple thing, like adding it to his daily planner.

There was a loud crash, like a dozen bodies slamming against the door at once. The barricade shook nervously.

Then there was silence.

"Maybe they gave up," she said, but there was no confidence in her voice.

"No, I don't think they'd give up that ease—,"

Light slowly began to form behind the barricade of furniture, and shined through the empty spaces.

"Dark Magic," Erik choked.

"Shit," Cecelia replied. "Wait! What the hell is that?"

The furniture shook, began to topple, and from the light a figure too large to have walked through the doors of this apartment began to form.

Cecelia instinctively dropped to the floor as the barricade burst apart. A bookcase sailed through the air and into the back wall with a loud crash. Everything had gone flying, like a hurricane was let loose in the room. Furniture flew around viciously, leaving destruction in its wake. The demons had broken through.

The floor beneath her splintered and she looked up to see what had emerged surrounded by waves of dark mist that smelt like sulfur and brimstone.

She gasped and crawled back on her hands and feet.

It was insect-like with clawed feet that led up to coarse muscular legs, with skin like that of a rhinoceros, and it had a deadly scorpion stinger for a tail. It had a face like a beetle with pincers and hollow holes for eyes that seemed to radiate with flames.

This was hell spawn, and it brought backup. Demon foot soldiers formed beside it flanking it.

Erik appeared from behind a shelf. He was wielding a crossbow set to fire, and in his other hand, he had his next bolt ready to reload.

"You brought a fucking Goliath Demon into my house?" he shouted in anger and surprise. "I swear to God, Azazel, when I get my hands on you, you're dead."

Erik burst into action. He fired his first bolt straight into the eye of the Goliath demon. It screeched and thrashed its weight about, tearing up the wooden floor and smashing into bookcases.

Erik didn't wait; he leaped into the air, notching his next bolt. He sailed over the demon and fired into its second eye, landing on the base of its skull. With his free hand, he reached behind him and pulled a sword from his quiver. The demon, now blinded, screeched and thrashed about with its stinger, taking out foot soldiers Azazel had brought with him. They screamed as they were tossed about and torn apart by the sharp appendage. Erik kept his balance the whole time and raised the blade true above his head. He may have been known as a prankster, but deep down in his bones, he would always be an Archangel, and he wasn't going to let anyone forget it.

"Get the hell out of my house!" he shouted and drove the point of the sword into the demon's head, through its armored skull, and into its brain. The demon gave one last scream of agony and then began to crumble. Erik leaped from its head before it collapsed to the ground in a pile of smoke and ash.

The demon foot soldiers advanced on him quickly.

Cecelia ran.

She needed to find a weapon. She needed to help. She hadn't been training with them like crazy for nothing.

Rome, she remembered Max telling her. *These twin daggers were from my time in Rome.* She raced through the aisles heading for the case that held those daggers.

Demons were now airborne, flying above the library, their black bat-like wings beating powerfully as they searched her out. She moved against the shelf, making herself as small as possible, and continued forward. She was almost there! She looked up and saw they were getting closer.

Shit! Shit! Shit!

She heard a deep growl, and a large black wolf leaped out from the aisle in front of her, snatching one of the airborne demons between its jaws. It was enormous and like none she had ever seen, her savior! But the demons didn't waste time. They were on it before it could strike a killing blow.

The wolf twisted and turned, snapping at their wings. Two of the demons grabbed it by the hind legs, lifted, and then slammed it against the floor. It connected painfully, splintering the hardwood beneath it, but it was back on its feet in seconds.

The wolf was fast, dashing away, dividing, and singling out the demons. It leapt into the air and began to glow. The glow came from the blue pendant it wore around its neck like a collar. The effervescent blue spread across its body until it became so bright she had to look away. When she turned back, the wolf had disappeared, and in its place was a large golden eagle that clawed at the demon's face, blinding it.

That pendant, her eyes lit up with understanding.

Erik wore that pendant. It was his Holy Relic, she remembered. Holy shit, it's Erik!

She wasn't going to let him do this on his own. She turned for the case and charged, smashing it with her elbow. She cleared the broken glass away with her shirt and reached inside the case to remove the twin golden daggers.

Erik had now taken the form of a grizzly bear and was mauling two demons at once.

With the daggers in hand, she raced to the fight and hit the ground like a batter stealing third right between the grizzly's legs. She rolled to her feet, and then the two of them were back to back, Cecelia slicing with her daggers, and Erik striking with his powerful claws. But how long they could keep this up, neither of them knew.

They were soon divided. She caught one of the demons in the leg. She smiled triumphantly watching as he fell to the floor clutching at the sizzling wound. She moved to finish it off, and was confident in her stride—

He came out of nowhere.

A large demon struck her in the side with great force, and she went sailing across the room. She collided with a bookshelf and heard a sickly snapping sound. Bone and muscle were torn apart in an instant. She felt the burning in her leg before she hit the ground. Then the massive bookshelf fell over on top of her.

Dazed, she struggled, despite the pain, to crawl from beneath it, pushing books aside. She'd made it clear, but her leg. Her damn leg was busted. She tried to lift herself, but couldn't budge as she looked on helplessly watching Erik fight the demons alone.

She could tell he was losing energy fast because he was back in his wolf form. He managed to tear an arm from one of the demons, but then another two struck him in the side and sent him slamming against the face of a bookcase.

Their assault was relentless.

All at once, four demons were on him, punching, kicking, and stabbing at the cornered wolf. Then a demon Cecelia hadn't seen before, different from all the others, stalked across the room and to the fight. The other demons turned to see him, feeling his dark presence radiating from his evil form. Cecelia felt it herself. It seemed to suck all the warmth from her body.

His slicked-back dark brown hair, pointy cheekbones, and chiseled jawline reminded her of a young James Dean. He had on a leather biker's jacket and walked toward Erik like a bully in a schoolyard, playing his audience. He was not at all what she imagined. No pointy ears or sharp devil horns. He was handsome, like the fallen angels she'd grown to know so well. But there was one distinct difference.

When she looked at his eyes, she saw flames. His body was empty of his once golden angelic aura. It was empty and on fire with rage.

This was Azazel.

They ceased all movement and stared at him like obedient dogs. Like a trainer, he waved his arms, and the demons spread apart revealing Erik, back in his human form, lying motionless on the ground.

Erik, who loved to play practical jokes— Erik, who once made her laugh so hard that milk came out of her nose. The boy who stole her best friend's heart, and who Christoph loved more than his own.

"Ah, Eros, the great Angel of Love and Mischief," Azazel said mockingly. "You're no Ceruleus Maximus, but your eyes would still make for a mighty prize! Ha!" he laughed menacingly. There was something sinister in the way he stared at Erik. He reached down, snatching the pendant from around his neck. "The Mark of Vishnu," he eyed it resentfully, like it was some garbage he'd picked up off the street. "You rogues and your relics! Well, God's little trinkets can't save you now," he crushed it in his hand and reached for his sword. He raised it above his head.

"Oh, how I love to watch the mighty fall," he grinned looking down at Erik, taking pleasure in watching his lifeless form.

He grinned, and his smile was something truly wicked.

It enraged her.

Cecelia didn't even think, she didn't remember climbing to her feet, feeling the blade move in her hand till her grip was perfect, or raising her arm above her head. She just let it go, and her dagger sailed through the air, end over end until it hit its mark.

With a sickening thud, the demon Azazel staggered backward and looked down to his chest to find the golden dagger embedded in his heart.

"You stay the hell away from him!" she shouted.

"You bitch!" Azazel dropped to his knees, clutching his chest. The wound where the dagger lay embedded was now smoking, "What have you done?"

"Metal tempered by angel blood, asshole. It's poison to demon scum like you," she spat. She moved to charge, ignoring the pain in her leg, but then—

"What kind of Greater Demon would you be, if you let a little Nephilim like this best you?" Cecelia heard a deep, haunting voice say from behind her that sent shivers down her spine and raised her hairs on end. He had her by the shoulders.

She was too focused on Azazel to notice him sneaking up behind her.

She'd gone stark white, frozen in fear. He dipped his head and sniffed her hair. "Never smelt one like you before, Nephilim of light," he spat.

Azazel reached for the dagger in his chest and pulled it free. Black ichor sprayed from the fresh wound onto the floor, and he laughed.

"Of course not, Abaddon, now quit your toying and be done with her," he winced but put on a front that echoed irritation.

Cecelia felt a sharp blow at the back of her neck, and she went weak in the knees.

"Leave him for Ceruleus to find," she heard Azazel command as she hit the ground.

"A message."

And then there was only darkness.

The Staff of Moses

Chapter 23

The Staff of Moses

As Christoph locked the club's front door and punched in his security code on the touchpad, a flash of movement caught his eye—an all-black Mercedes GL slowly rolled past the sidewalk, its windows so dark they might as well have been painted.

Those creeps.

His jaw clenched. He knew that car.

They can't take a damn hint.

He watched it crawl by, the engine a low growl, like a predator sizing up prey. For a split second, he felt their eyes—whoever was inside—staring him down. Then it sped off without a word.

"What the hell was that about?" he muttered, scratching the back of his neck, unease prickling down his spine.

He turned the corner toward his block, reaching into his coat for his keys—then stopped cold.

His front door, the reinforced fireproof slab of steel he'd had installed just last year, was shredded. The hinges were torn out. Splinters of what used to be the frame littered the front steps and yard like kindling.

His heart detonated in his chest.

Shit.

"Cecelia," he breathed, his voice raw. In the next instant, he was sprinting. The keys were forgotten. He barreled into the wreckage, already drawing a set of throwing knives from his inner coat pocket. The apartment was silent, too silent.

He flew up the stairs—five at a time, barely touching the rail—until he burst into the living room.

It looked like a bomb had gone off.

The couch was upside down. The flat screen was shattered on the floor. There were deep gouges in the walls, broken beer bottles glinting in the carpet, glass crunched beneath his boots as he stepped in.

This wasn't a robbery. This was a message.

He moved like a storm through the apartment. Guest room—empty. The window open, the fire escape visible, untouched. Maybe she got out. Maybe—

But he already knew better.

"Dammit," he growled, tearing through the closet, tossing a broken lamp across the room as he bolted back into the hall. His last hope was the library.

She always liked that room best. If she had any chance at all, it would've been there.

He shoved open the door—and stopped.

It had been torn apart. The walls scorched. Bookshelves toppled. A chair was broken in half, and deep claw-like marks raked the floorboards. The air reeked of sulfur and brimstone.

The smell of demons.

Why did I let them go back without me? Why did I think they were safe?

He tore through debris, blood pounding in his ears, every nerve screaming for any sign of life. "Come on. Come on, come on—"

Then—

A thud.

Faint.

A heartbeat.

He didn't think. His body just moved. He ripped back a collapsed bookcase with a snarl, throwing it aside—and what he saw nearly buckled his knees.

No.

No no no no no.

Not Erik.

Lying there—bloody, pale, still—was his best friend.

His brother.

He wasn't breathing. His skin was cold. His lips were blue. Gold blood soaked his clothes and pooled around him.

"Erik?" Christoph rasped, dropping to his knees. He shook him. "Erik, wake up."

Nothing.

"Come on, man. You're not doing this. Don't do this to me."

He slapped him—once, then again.

"Wake up!"

No response.

"DAMMIT, WAKE UP!"

His voice cracked.

Nothing.

This isn't happening. No, no, no—this can't be real. He was just cracking jokes earlier, teasing Evie. He was fine. He was—

Christoph's breath turned ragged as panic flooded his veins. His hands hovered uselessly over Erik's chest, shaking. His mind was spiraling.

I don't know what to do.

Sam.

He grabbed his phone, fingers trembling as he dialed.

The line rang.

"Bro, I'm asleep, what do you—?"

"Sam!" Christoph's voice came out high, panicked. "You need to get here—now. Call Darius. Tell him to get the Staff from the vault."

"The Staff? What the hell's going on?"

"I NEED it!" he snapped. "They came to my house—they took her. Erik's down, Sam. He's not breathing. There's so much blood—so much goddamn blood—"

"Have you tried closing the wounds?"

"He isn't breathing, Sam!"

"Then shock him!"

"Just get here!"

"I'm on my way."

The line disconnected. Christoph threw the phone aside and dropped to Erik's side again. He tore Erik's shirt from the neckline and stared at the wreckage of his friend's body.

Focus. Close the wounds. Get his heart beating.

"I need this to work. Please let this work."

He grabbed one of his knives and sliced a clean line across his own palm. His other hand smeared the blood across Erik's chest in careful, desperate strokes—drawing healing runes, one after the other, glowing faintly as they activated.

They flickered—struggled—fought to stay alive.

But it wasn't enough.

The wounds didn't close.

"No. No no no—dammit!" He slammed his fists against Erik's chest, tears threatening to burn through his lashes. "Don't do this to me!"

He listened.

Nothing.

Christoph tilted Erik's head back, cleared his airway, and breathed into his mouth. The chest rose, then fell.

Still no heartbeat.

He began compressions—thirty, then another breath. Then thirty more.

The silence screamed in his ears.

This is my fault.

They did this for me. They left him like this so I would find him. So I'd break.

His little brother. The only constant in his life. From the moment they found each other again in Egypt, he had never left Christoph's side. Every impossible mission. Every decade lived under another name. Their days as merchants in Italy. That chaotic Vegas stint—Erik kicked out of the casino for counting cards, laughing the whole way.

That insane weekend down the Shore when Erik tried to cheer him up over a girl he had to leave—cheap beer, fireworks, Erik dressed like a pirate trying to duel random frat bros with glow sticks.

Erik had always been there.

His truest friend. His reckless idiot. His anchor.

And now—

He was slipping away.

He wouldn't give up.

He would never give up on him.

When Darius and Sam arrived, Christoph was still going—still pumping Erik's chest like time itself was on the line.

"God, no…" Darius whispered, nearly stumbling at the sight of Erik's lifeless body. His voice cracked as he dropped to a knee beside them.

Christoph didn't even glance up. "Clear me a perimeter. I need space. Now."

Fifteen, sixteen, seventeen… His voice was hoarse, every number rasping through clenched teeth as sweat poured from his temple.

Darius and Sam moved fast, shoving back toppled furniture, clearing bookshelves, broken glass, and splintered wood until a rough fifteen-foot circle of open floor surrounded them.

Christoph held out a bloodied dagger to Sam.

"Sam. Don't question anything I'm about to ask you to do. Just *do it*. Please."

Sam swallowed hard and nodded, worry creasing his brow. Christoph never sounded like this—shaky, scattered, broken. He was always the calm one, the tactician, the one who never lost control.

But right now… he looked like a man standing on the edge of the world.

"You got it," Sam said quietly.

Christoph's voice was barely audible now. "Cut your hand. Draw a healing rune. Center of his chest. Darius, you're next."

Sam obeyed, slicing into his palm with a hiss, then knelt beside Erik and drew the rune in his own blood—each stroke trembling.

"Darius," Christoph said without looking. "Hand me the Staff."

"Here, bro." Darius stepped forward and passed it reverently. Then he took the dagger from Samuel and did the same.

The runes were still glowing faintly—but they weren't closing. Erik's body had accepted the marks, but there was too much damage. Too much blood loss. Not enough time.

Christoph stared down at his best friend's face—colorless, lips bluish-purple, eyes half-lidded and empty

Then he did something he hadn't done in a long, long time.

He dropped to his knees, gripped the Staff of Moses with both hands, and bowed his head.

And he prayed.

Not the hollow kind. Not the whispered gratitude before a mission or the silent hope before a fight.

This was the kind of prayer that came from the pit of a broken soul.

"In my entire existence," Christoph whispered, "I have never questioned you. Not when Michael betrayed me. Not when they ripped my wings from my back. Not when you cursed me to walk this earth alone while everyone I've ever loved turned to dust." His voice cracked.

"I never asked you for anything," he whispered, eyes filling. "Not once. But I'm asking now. No—I'm *begging*."

Tears slid down his cheeks, splashing onto Erik's skin.

"Don't take him from me. Take *me* if you have to. Take my soul. Bind it. Burn it. Use it however you want. Just don't take him. Please."

His hands clenched around the Staff. His voice rose.

"Grant me the power you once gave your prophets. Let the power in this Staff—*your* Staff—bring him back!"

He pressed it to Erik's chest.

The room was silent.

Then a flicker of light sparked beneath the Staff—just a glimmer at first, like a candle being coaxed to life.

Then it burst.

A golden, blinding radiance enveloped Erik's body like a sun igniting from within. The wounds sealed in seconds. The bruises faded. Color surged back into his cheeks, and the gold sheen of his blood shimmered with renewed vitality.

Darius shielded his eyes. Sam stepped back in awe.

They watched, breathless, as a miracle unfolded in front of them.

Then—he breathed.

Just one.

A faint rise, then a fall.

"Erik?" Christoph gasped. "Erik, open your eyes—please."

There was no response yet—but his chest rose again, steady this time. His heart was beating.

Sam blinked, stunned. "I don't know how this works. I've never *seen* this before… but he's breathing again. We brought him back."

Christoph lowered the Staff, breath ragged, forehead glistening with sweat, his cheeks tear stained. His hands were still shaking. He stared down at Erik like he didn't dare look away.

It was enough.

He was alive.

And then—another memory cut through the fog in his brain like a dagger.

"Cecelia," he said aloud. His eyes shot to Darius. "They took her."

Darius nodded once. No hesitation. "Let's move."

"Sam," Christoph said, already pushing to his feet. "I need you here. Stay with him. I don't think they'll come back after this mess, but someone needs to be here when he wakes up."

"Of course," Sam said, kneeling back down. "I'll hold the line."

Christoph looked at Darius. "You know we're walking into a trap, right?"

"I know." Darius's voice was hard steel.

"And you're still going?"

"I told you I'd protect her. I wasn't there. Erik was." Darius glanced at Erik, then back. His voice cracked just once. "Look what happened."

Christoph clenched his jaw. "It's not your fault. It's *mine*."

Darius shook his head. "No. It's *his* fault. Azazel's. And he's going to pay."

Christoph looked him square in the eye. "So you know the plan, D?"

Darius cracked his neck. "Walk in. Fuck shit up. Leave."

A grim smile broke across Christoph's face. "That's right, big guy."

He didn't wait.

He was already moving—into the training room, where weapons lined the walls like an armory of vengeance. He stripped off his blood-stained shirt, changed into tactical black: military pants, boots laced tight, leather jacket zipped high to his throat and grabbed a duffle bag to fill with weapons.

No guns. No explosives.

Quiet.

Efficient.

Deadly.

He filled the bag efficiently with what he needed. Slid his twin gold daggers into the sheaths strapped to his shins. Tucked throwing knives into both sides of his coat. Then reached for the final weapon—the Staff of Moses— strapping it across his back like a promise of pain.

In the garage, he moved past the Camaro, past the dirt bikes, straight to the covered tarp in the corner.

He yanked it off.

The sleek black Ducati gleamed in the low light like it had been waiting for this moment.

He secured his duffel bag on the back.

Ran a gloved hand along the chassis.

"Athena," he murmured, "be with me."

Then he threw his leg over the seat and kicked it to life.

The engine roared like a beast set free.

Darius wasn't far behind heading to his black Escalade.

The garage door opened, flooding the dark room with city light.

And the two of them pulled into the night—riding straight into Hell.

Arch Duke
Abaddon

Chapter 24

The Reckoning

The wind tore at him like claws as he ripped through the city on Athena, his jet-black Ducati slicing through the darkness like a blade. Headlights flared and blurred, horns blared in the distance, but Christoph barely registered the noise. He moved with brutal precision—low, fast, unyielding.

Riding Athena always felt like flying.

Tonight, it felt like war.

He leaned into the curves like he had wings again, banking hard as the machine purred beneath him, responsive to every shift of his weight. He wasn't just moving—he was hunting.

Find her. That was the only thought in his mind, the only command burning through every synapse.

In the last month, he and the Elites had razed Azazel's world to the ground—every warehouse, every lab, every shadowy backdoor op—turned to ash. He'd followed every lead, shaken down every demon stupid enough to cross his path. And one by one, the dominoes fell.

Azazel had nothing left.

Nothing… except the girl. His girl.

The only place he could be hiding now was his last stronghold—the forgotten veins beneath the city. The old subway system. Abandoned. Unmapped. Reinforced. And if the rumors were true, cursed to hell.

But Christoph didn't care if it was a death trap.

They came for Erik.
They took her.

And now he was coming.

The Staff of Moses was strapped across his back, humming faintly with an ancient, holy energy. He wasn't sure how much power it still held—or how much of his soul it would cost him to unleash it—but if this was his final hour, he'd make it count.

They reached the bay.

Christoph slowed the bike and kicked it into a slide, veering off onto the crumbling service path near the edge of the compound. He killed the engine, swung off, and stood still in the darkness—listening.

The night was quiet. Too quiet.

Then came the low rumble of a larger engine.

A pair of headlights crested the hill behind him, sweeping across the broken pavement. Darius's Escalade pulled up beside the bike, tires crunching gravel. The SUV rocked to a stop, and the door opened.

Darius stepped out, massive and ready for war.

"Took you long enough," Christoph muttered without looking.

"I was right behind you the entire time hoping you wouldn't do anything stupid until I got here. Now, are you ready to do this?"

Christoph nodded once. A cool and deadly look in his eye.

And then, without another word, the two fallen advanced—boots hitting dirt, the weight of vengeance in every step—as they approached the edge of the compound.

The place was dead quiet.

Two guards loitered outside the rusted access gate—smoking, bored, completely unaware of what was coming. Beyond them was nothing but shadows and silence.

Too quiet.

"This has trap written all over it," Darius muttered, his voice low and grim.

Christoph's golden eyes didn't blink. "I know, big guy."

"They'll hit us hard once we're inside."

"They're going to try," Christoph said, and his smirk wasn't cocky—it was lethal. He reached behind his shoulder and gripped the Staff like a sword forged in Heaven. The weight of it grounded him. Fueled him.

"Darius," he said, tilting his head toward the dark below, "what's the best way to put out a fire?"

Darius cracked his knuckles. "Smother it."

Christoph nodded once, his jaw tight. "Exactly."

Inside the decrepit station, the stench of sulfur clung to every surface, thick as rot. Cracked tile walls were illuminated only by flickering lights bolted high into the ceiling, casting warped shadows that danced across the faces of the demons inside.

They were gathered in a makeshift war chamber, pacing, snarling, drunk on victory and the scent of spilled angel blood.

"He was nothing!" one demon cackled, his claws still stained gold from the earlier fight.

"I watched him grovel beneath my heel," another lied, slamming his fist against the wall, cracking the stone.

"Let Ceruleus come!" a third snarled, pacing in wide circles. "Let him come for his little whore. The Elites are broken. Their time is over!"

The crowd roared in agreement, pounding fists against weapons, feet against the ground. Their battlelust was at its peak—unhinged, frothing.

Azazel had promised them a shattered Ceruleus. A broken angel. A man undone by grief and failure.

But that's not what was coming.

Not even close.

From the shadows, a deep voice cut through the noise like a blade. "SILENCE."

The demons froze.

A broad-shouldered, gleaming figure stepped forward into the half-light—his bald head catching the glow, his massive arms crossed like twin tree trunks. Abaddon.

He didn't need to shout again. The room obeyed.

"Soldiers," he said, voice like gravel dragged across iron, "can you feel that?"

He stalked through them slowly, eyes narrowed, each step deliberate. His boots crushed glass and bone without pause.

"That weight in the air? That static crawling across your skin? It's not fear... not yet. That's the storm, boys. The calm before it hits. At any minute, Ceruleus Maximus is going to come crashing through those doors like a force of Heaven itself, and when he does—we take his head."

His voice thundered now.

"Say it with me! Bring me death! Death to Ceruleus! DEATH!"

"DEATH TO CERULEUS! DEATH! DEATH! DEATH!" the soldiers echoed, fists raised, howling. The war chant rattled the walls, a guttural, demonic battle cry bouncing through the underground like a drumbeat of doom.

And then—
 Drip.

A single drop of water struck Abaddon's scalp.

He paused, mid-chant. Reached up. Touched it.

Another drop.

He looked up.

"General!" a demon near the front barked, eyes wide. "Water! Beneath the door!"

Abaddon took a slow step forward. "Water?" he repeated, frowning.

Then came the sound—subtle at first. Pipes creaking. Groaning. Somewhere in the walls, something cracked.

Then—

BOOM.

The entire station shook with the thunder of a colossal crash at the front gate. Lights flickered. Dust rained from the ceiling. Screws spun loose from overhead beams and launched like shrapnel. Bolts exploded from pipe seams, ricocheting like gunfire.

"FORMATION!" Abaddon roared.

But the demons hesitated.

A low rumble pulsed through the floor like something ancient awakening. Then the walls screamed—steam hissing, pipes bursting—and suddenly a flood of scalding water erupted from the entrance, smashing through the gate like a battering ram of divine wrath.

The deluge hit them like a tsunami.

Screams rang out as the water surged forward, hurling soldiers like ragdolls. It slammed them into walls, pinned them to ceilings, filled their lungs before they could even scream a second time.

Abaddon turned to flee, but the wave crashed over him too, dragging him under.

And then—
 silence.

Water rippled, steaming in the ruin. Bodies floated. Moans echoed like ghosts.

And at the door stood Ceruleus Maximus.

The Staff of Moses glowed in his hand. His jacket dripped with steam, shoulders squared, golden eyes blazing with vengeance. Righteous. Divine. Terrifying.

He didn't speak.

He didn't need to.

The water around his feet parted.

With a flick of his hand, the flood drained as if commanded by Heaven itself, sweeping away debris and revealing the carnage left in his wake.

Abaddon gasped, coughing as he crawled from the wreckage. He forced himself upright, every muscle trembling. And then he saw him—standing at the gate, unscathed, unmoved, unfazed.

Ceruleus gave a slow, savage smile.

It sent a chill down the demon's spine—the first he'd felt in centuries.

It filled him with rage. He watched as Ceruleus raised the staff before him and slammed it to the ground.

Then came the lightning.

It had been quiet for nearly an hour.

Too quiet.

Cecelia hung from the ceiling, arms stretched above her head by thick iron shackles that bit into her wrists. Her muscles had long since stopped burning. Now they just trembled. Her throat was raw, scorched from all the screaming—hoarse cries that had echoed endlessly off stone walls until they faded into silence. She wasn't sure when she'd stopped. Maybe her body had made the choice for her. Maybe she'd simply run out of voice.

She was certain the damage was permanent.

Every part of her ached. Her shoulders felt like they were being slowly torn from their sockets. Her legs dangled uselessly beneath her, numb from lack of circulation. A deep, bone-heavy exhaustion weighed on her like a second body. It was the kind of fatigue that blurred the line between sleep and surrender.

And still, the room remained silent.

A predatory silence.

Even the demon soldiers standing guard moved like shadows now—eerily quiet, never speaking, just watching. Like they were waiting. Smiling inside. This was Azazel's game. Psychological warfare. After the pain, after the torture, after Abaddon, he wanted to starve her spirit.

Break her in silence.

She didn't flinch anymore when the shadows stirred. Didn't blink when one of them came too close. There was nothing left they could take from her body that hadn't already been offered in screams and blood.

And yet—

She had not broken.

Time passed slowly. Warped. She drifted in and out of awareness, her head slumping forward, hair falling across her face like a curtain. Her lips were cracked. Her skin sticky with sweat and dried blood.

But behind her swollen eyes…
 Hope.

Small. Faint. But alive.

She gripped it the way a drowning person clung to the surface of the water—desperately, defiantly.

They'd underestimated her. Thought pain would shatter her. Thought fear would erase who she was. They didn't understand. When pain had stripped her down to nothing… hope was what remained. That unrelenting whisper in the back of her mind telling her: *He's coming.*

Maximus is coming.

And when he did, this whole goddamn place would burn.

It was only a matter of time.

He had killed them all.
Drowned them.
Burned them from the inside out.

Slit their throats for good measure.

He'd do it again in a heartbeat if he could.

Those bastards.

They all deserved to pay for what they did to Erik. He was here to collect.
He'd left Abaddon behind, broken and bleeding—for the other Dukes to find.
A message in black ichor.

Where was she?

Him and Darius tore through the tunnels like predators, every footstep
thunderous, echoing like war drums through the abandoned subway system.
His grip tightened around the staff in his hand, knuckles white with fury. He
could barely think straight. His mind kept circling back to her.

He wished Erik were with him—Erik would've found her by now. No one
tracked like he could. But Erik…

He shuddered at the thought.

If what they'd done to Erik was any indication of what they were capable of,
he didn't want to imagine what they might've done to his Cecelia—his sweet
girl.

He scanned for signs—any sound, any scent—but the maze was deliberately
confusing. Muffled acoustics, branching paths, echoes that looped back on
themselves like whispers in a nightmare. Whatever Azazel had planned, it
wasn't just a trap. It was a spectacle. One designed to break him.

Room after room, hallway after hallway—nothing. Empty spaces. Blood
smears. Chains. Too quiet.

Then—he stopped.

A flicker. A whisper on the air.

Burnt lilac.
Cheap whiskey.
And death.

Azazel.

He turned.

Azazel's voice slithered out of the shadows like oil. "Oh, *Maximus…* Have you and Darius finally come to *die?*"

Christoph spun on his heel, and there he was—standing smug in the doorway of a room they'd had already cleared.
He should've known. Demon illusions. Veils over space. They were *always* playing dirty.

"Where is she, you piece of shit?" he growled.

"Oh, she's just hanging around," Azazel chuckled, as if he'd just told the funniest joke in the world. "But that's no concern to you, seeing as we have you surrounded."

Christoph's jaw flexed. Darius stepped beside him, back to back, axes drawn. Their formation was instinctual—years of brotherhood turned into choreography.

One by one, the others emerged from the dark:
Dagon—scaled, slitted eyes gleaming, twirling his golden trident like it thirsted for blood.
Asmodeus—clad in jagged crimson armor, dragging his massive double-edged sword with casual menace.
Belial—silent, grinning, licking the edge of his kukri as if he were tasting a memory.

"You've been a real nuisance," Azazel sneered. "Did you really think you could keep that Angel Key away from me forever?"

"From Lucifer," Christoph corrected. "And yeah. I think I did a pretty damn good job. Especially since I don't sense it on you."

Azazel stiffened.

Christoph grinned. "That's what I thought. She wouldn't give it up. Which means... she's still alive."

"Fool! After I kill you, just like I killed that pitiful prankster Eros, I'll get the truth out of her. I'll find it!"

"I'm going to stop you right there." Christoph stepped forward, his voice a razor. "First off, don't you *ever* speak about *my* best friend like that again. He's alive, by the way—sorry to ruin your little victory party—but you're going to pay for what you did to him."

Azazel's cocky demeanor faltered.

"He... *lives*? How?"

"I'll get there," Christoph said, his voice dropping to something dark. "You just sit tight, sweetie."

He raised the Staff of Moses. It pulsed in his grip, responding to his fury.

"Oh, you think you scare us?" Azazel barked, but the confidence was slipping. He glanced at the other Dukes.

"Haven't you ever wondered why Michael was so desperate to get rid of me?"

Azazel sneered. "Humor us, Ceruleus."

Christoph smirked, and the light around him began to shimmer.

"I was meant to *replace* him."

The silence hit like a slap.

"He was afraid of me," Christoph said softly. "And you know what?" His grin sharpened. "You *should* be *too*."

He raised the staff, white fire already forming along the runes.

"HEAVENLY FIRE, I BESEECH YOU!"

The power exploded—raw, divine, unforgiving. A tidal wave of holy flame surged forward like the wrath of Heaven itself. Darius caught Christoph as the recoil sent him stumbling back. The fire consumed the tunnel. The Dukes *screamed*, tried to flee, but there was no escape.

When the light cleared, the chamber was scorched black.
 No trace of the Dukes.
 Not a single ash left behind.

The Staff of Moses cracked in two as it hit the floor.
 Christoph collapsed in Darius's arms.

"You did good, bro," Darius whispered, hoisting him up onto his shoulder. "Rest. I'll find her. You'll get her back."

Darius carried Maximus over his shoulder like he weighed nothing. With his senses honed and his grip firm on the axe in his right hand, he tore through the underground maze, crashing through demon after demon like they were made of glass. Every enemy that came at him fell hard. He didn't stop. Couldn't stop. The swarm meant he was close.

Little bitches, all of them.

Then—he saw it.

Guarding the next door stood a Baramous demon. Its hulking body rippled with muscle beneath spotted fur, its dragon-like claws scraping at the stone, maw glowing with flame and lined with jagged obsidian teeth.

It growled low.

Darius lowered Christoph with care, setting him down gently against the wall.

Then he reached for his other axe.

This wouldn't be any different.

The creature launched forward. So did Darius.

It swiped—he ducked, drove his boot into its gut, and sent the beast slamming into the ceiling. It crashed hard, but landed on all fours with a snarl.

He spun his axes in both hands. A grin pulled at the corner of his mouth.

"Let's go, ugly."

It charged again. He met it head-on.

Its claw came down, but his axe came up first—cleaving through bone and muscle, severing a massive paw in a spray of black ichor.

It roared and belched fire.

Darius spun, both arms a blur, creating a vortex of steel and force that smothered the flames like snuffing out a candle.

It lunged to bite.

He dodged left, then countered with a brutal uppercut. Its head snapped back. Before it could recover, he spun with the other axe and took off its head clean. The body dropped, twitching before it turned to dust returning to the pit from whence it came.

Demons poured from the open doorway behind it.

Darius didn't blink.

The first leapt—and caught a side kick that launched it backward into the others like a living cannonball, sending them sprawling like bowling pins.

He surged forward like a cyclone of devastation. Axes flashing, arms sweeping in brutal arcs. Limbs flew. Bodies shattered. Black ichor painted the walls.

When it was over, the silence was deafening. The last demon dropped in pieces at his feet.

Darius stood still, chest heaving, axes dripping. Then his eyes shifted—back to Christoph.

Maximus was slumped against the wall where he'd left him, head bowed, the Staff of Moses cracked beside his boots. The fire in him—gone. His shoulders didn't rise. His aura, once blinding, now flickered dimly like the last embers of a dying forge.

He looked like a fallen statue. Empty.

But not broken. Not yet.

Darius exhaled through his nose, wiped his blades clean with one fluid motion, and marched over.

"Alright, that's enough laying around."

He crouched low, sliced open his palm with his dagger, and let his golden ichor pool into his other hand. It shimmered unnaturally bright, casting dancing reflections across the blood-slicked floor. With careful strokes, he painted a glowing rune across Christoph's chest—Shared Strength—a symbol born from brotherhood and forged in celestial war.

The second the rune locked into place, it pulsed with energy—once… twice… then lit like a spark catching fire.

Darius pressed his bloodied hand to Christoph's sternum and leaned in close.

"You're not done, Maximus. She's close. I need you back on your feet."

No response.

So he slapped him.

Not hard. Not gentle either.

Christoph gasped, golden eyes flaring open like he'd been struck by lightning.

"There he is," Darius smirked, crouched beside him. "Welcome back, sunshine."

Christoph groaned, blinking hard as strength surged back into his limbs like a warm current. "What… happened?" he rasped.

"Oh, not much," Darius said, casually flexing his knuckles. "You torched the Staff of Moses, might've disintegrated some Arch Dukes, and then collapsed like a drama queen."

Christoph winced, dragging a hand down his face. "How'd we get here?"

"I carried your ass like a sack of potatoes. Took out a small army and a Baramous demon while I was at it. Real highlight reel stuff."

"A… Baramous?"

"Big, ugly, claws like razors, teeth like a blender? Yeah. Kicked it into a wall. Then took its head off."

Christoph blinked. "You're serious?"

"Deadly."

"Did you find Cecelia?"

"We're close," Darius said, his voice shifting—serious now. "I can feel it. But I need you on your feet."

"Right." Christoph smacked his cheeks lightly, forcing the fog from his brain. "Okay. I'm good."

Darius offered his hand. "Then let's go get your girl."

Christoph clasped his forearm and hauled himself up, swaying once before finding his center.

Their eyes met. The fire was back.

Side by side, they turned toward the corridor ahead—two brothers on a mission. One fueled by fury. The other by love. And together?

They were unstoppable.

It felt like a dream.

She heard his voice through the darkness, clear as a bell, calling her name.

She must be asleep again, she thought. Just another cruel trick of the mind.

An image flashed before her: Darius placing Maximus on the floor, slicing open his palm and drawing glowing seraphic runes across Max's body in strokes of golden ichor.

"My power will be your power," Darius whispered, his voice full of conviction. Max's body glowed, faint at first—then brighter. "We're here, bro. I found her. Time to wake up and finish this."

His eyes shot open. A blaze of gold. He sat up with a sharp inhale, nodded once, and rose like a man reborn.

"Let's finish this."

Cecelia's breath hitched.

Maximus.

No. It couldn't be. It had to be another hallucination—another trick Azazel's demons had planted in her head.

But then she heard him again, louder this time. Urgent.

"CECILIA!"

That voice. That fire.

"CECELIA, I'M COMING!"

Her eyes snapped open.

And then all hell broke loose.

The heavy iron doors burst inward in a deafening explosion of light and rubble. Darius came in first—bruised, bloodied, axes already soaked with ichor—and behind him, through the dust and fire—

Maximus.

No longer just a man, no longer just a fallen angel, but a storm. A divine inferno in motion.

The horde reacted immediately—at least forty demons strong, all armed, all ravenous, all standing between him and her. She saw one of them turn pale at the sight of Max's glowing skin, etched in radiant gold seraphic symbols like ancient war paint. They charged.

So did he.

His twin daggers flashed, carving arcs of molten gold through the dark. He moved like a shadow cast by lightning—blindingly fast, brutally efficient. One slash took off a demon's arm. A spinning elbow shattered another's skull. He ducked under a cleaver, drove his knee into a gut, then brought both daggers down like fangs into the back of a neck.

Black ichor sprayed the walls.

Darius wasn't far behind—spinning in brutal circles, his twin axes humming through the air like death bells. He caught one demon in the chest, cleaved through another, then used a reverse grip to sweep an entire row of them off their feet like weeds.

Demons surrounded them—left, right, behind. Didn't matter.

Max dropped to one knee, swept a blade through a demon's ankles, flipped it, and finished it mid-air with a slash across the throat. Another came at him from behind—he turned and drove a dagger into its mouth before it could even scream.

She lost count of how many fell. Her vision swam with fire and blood and light. The horde that had haunted her dreams was being annihilated before her eyes.

"Cecelia!" he roared, and she saw him—burning with purpose, slashing through the last wave between them. The two guards beside her stepped forward, blades drawn.

"He'll never make it to you, *whore*," one spat, but she saw the tremble in his grip, the quiver in his voice.

He was wrong.

A flash of gold. A blink.

Both demons dropped—daggers in their throats. They disintegrated into ash before they hit the ground.

And then Maximus was there—his hands cupping her face, those golden eyes locked to hers.

"I've got you. You're safe now. Everything's going to be alright."

Her tears came hot and heavy, blurring the vision she'd begged the heavens to see.

Behind him, Darius limped in, covered in gold blood and black ichor, breathing hard, a satisfied grin on his face.

She reached for Max's hand, and he took it gently, reverently, like it was the most important thing in the world. Then she heard it.

"CERULEUS!"

The voice she feared most. Deep. Familiar. And full of rage.

Abaddon.

He emerged from the far side of the chamber, half-charred, half-mad, his armor in tatters, face twisted with fury.

"Ceruleus! Come face me!"

Max didn't flinch. He knelt beside Cecelia, slicing his palm and pressing it to the chains. Golden blood hissed and sparked, carving radiant symbols of release into the metal.

"You thought you could get rid of me?" Abaddon screamed.

Max ignored him. His hands trembled as he freed her wrists, as he held her bloody palms in his.

"What did they do to you?" he whispered, horrified. "I'm so sorry, Cecelia. I'm so—"

"CERULEUS!" Abaddon bellowed again.

Darius stepped forward, shouldering his axes.

"I'll take care of it," he growled.

"Darius, no—" Max finally looked up from Cecelia, voice tight with concern. "I used up so much of your power. Are you sure about this?"

"Bro," Darius said, steel in his voice. "I've got this." He nodded once, eyes fixed on the hulking demon across the room. "He made this personal."

The matter was closed.

Max turned back to Cecelia, his expression softening. "Cecelia, you have to talk to me. Your bones are broken—I need to set them before I can heal you. Is that okay?"

She opened her mouth. No sound. Her throat had given up long ago. The cords were shredded, muscles torn. Still, she tried. She wanted to speak—for him—but nothing came.

His eyes brimmed with pain.

"Cecelia… please."

She couldn't answer. Couldn't even lift her arms to hold him. She sagged in his arms like a doll, limp and broken. So he cradled her, held her like something sacred. And behind him…

Darius marched forward like a god of war.

He faced Abaddon, unflinching. The ground cracked beneath his feet.

"You going to fight all Ceruleus's battles for him?" Abaddon sneered, his monstrous frame towering like a nightmare given form—spikes jutting from his shoulders, chest glowing faintly with molten veins, jagged teeth bared.

"You hurt my friends," Darius growled, twin axes sliding from his back like guillotines ready to drop. "No one hurts my friends."

Gone was the lovable giant. What stood now was a weapon sharpened by centuries of war—one of Heaven's greatest.

Abaddon snarled. His body convulsed, spikes shooting from his forearms like shrapnel. Darius deflected with a quick spin of his axe, but the shockwave sent him skidding back.

And then—

Abaddon punched the ground.

A wave of fire burst forth, racing like a tidal surge. Darius dropped to a knee, slammed both axes into the floor, and held—gold ichor bleeding from his palms into the weapons, anchoring him against the heat.

When the fire cleared, he rose.

Scorched, pissed, and grinning.

He charged.

They collided with the force of titans, the shockwave splitting stone. Abaddon clawed at him with molten talons, and Darius answered with a flurry of strikes—one axe spinning low, the other cutting high. Sparks flew. Metal bit flesh. Ichor sprayed.

Abaddon laughed, razor fangs gleaming. He grabbed Darius by the throat and slammed him into a pillar. Spikes burst from his shoulder again—but Darius ducked, twisted, and brought his knee up hard into the demon's ribs.

CRACK.

The monster grunted.

Darius didn't let up. He smashed the hilt of one axe into Abaddon's face, head-butted him square in the chest, then spun and swept his legs out from under him. The giant fell with a roar that shook the walls.

"Lucifer will return, Darius," Abaddon hissed, ichor foaming between his teeth. "And there's nothing you or the Elites can do to stop it."

Darius stood over him, face battered, body heaving, one axe raised high.

"Well," he said, spitting blood. "Tell Lucy he can kiss my black ass when you see him."

The axe came down.

It was the last thing she saw before the world faded to black.

Chapter 25

To heal and regroup

Christoph carried Cecelia's limp form in his arms, her head resting against his chest, her body light as air and heavy as death. Darius had already pulled the Escalade around, flinging open the back as Christoph climbed in. Together they secured her as gently and quickly as they could, and then Darius hit the gas, tires screeching against the broken asphalt as they tore out of the underground ruins. Max Lounge was closer than the apartment—and better equipped. It had supplies, space, and privacy. Everything they needed. Christoph didn't waste a second. He mounted his Ducati and tailed the SUV like his soul was tethered to it, weaving through traffic like a shadow chasing light, praying to whatever remained of Heaven that they weren't too late.

"Darius. Clear the table."
 Christoph's voice was low, urgent, and laced with panic he refused to show.

Darius didn't question it. With one sweep of his arm, he sent everything—plates, menus, spare bar tools, a speaker—clattering to the floor. The silence that followed was broken only by the shallow, uneven breaths of the girl in Christoph's arms.

Cecelia was barely conscious. Her weight slumped against him like dead stone, but he clung to her like she was the last piece of the world worth saving. Her pulse flickered faintly against his wrist—there, but thin. Fragile. He didn't like the way it felt.

He laid her down gently, as if the wrong touch might shatter her. Her body was broken—her skin a patchwork of deep bruises, her arm twisted unnaturally, her leg slack and bent in three places. Her golden glow had dulled beneath the purple of trauma. His stomach churned at the sight of her.

"I don't know how much longer this sleeping spell will hold," he said, brushing a lock of hair from her cheek with a shaking hand. "We have to work fast."

"On it," Darius said, already sprinting into the back.

Christoph rolled up his sleeves and pulled open the medical kit when Darius returned, every movement clinical but charged with barely restrained emotion. He couldn't let his hands shake. Not now.

He reached for her dislocated shoulder first. "Hold her steady."

Darius nodded and anchored her down.

"One… two…"

A sickening crunch filled the room as he popped the joint back into place. Cecelia whimpered in her sleep.

"I'm sorry," Christoph whispered, then began scrawling glowing sigils across her skin in golden blood. The runes shimmered, easing the swelling and coaxing the magic into her bones.

Her breathing remained shallow. Too shallow.

"Her ribs are bad. I think… one might've punctured her lung." He felt along her side, wincing. "Shit."

"She's strong," Darius said quietly, placing a hand on Christoph's shoulder. "She made it this far."

Christoph nodded, jaw clenched. "Darius. Syringe."

"Syringe," Darius echoed, handing it over.

"When magic fails…" Christoph muttered, injecting the anesthetic into her side, "let there be science."

He made the incision with practiced speed, holding his breath as he carefully removed the splintered bone fragment from her lung. There was blood—too much of it—but he worked quickly, pressing his hand over the wound and whispering a healing incantation as he sealed it with his blood. The runes blazed gold, then faded into her skin.

It took an hour. Maybe longer. Time meant nothing while she lay so still.

When it was done, Christoph leaned against the bar, his hands bloodstained, his expression hollow.

"She's stable. But she's not out of the woods yet. She needs time for her Nephilim blood to fully accept my angelic blood."

Darius watched him silently, waiting.

Christoph finally spoke. "We need to leave. Get out of the city—tonight. If they come back… for her, or for the relics, we won't survive it. I'm too beat up. So are you."

Darius gave a slow nod. "Montauk?"

Christoph nodded back. "Yeah. The house is shielded. We'll regroup there."

"I'll call Sam," Darius said, already pulling out his phone. "Tell him to get Erik and bring Icarus. We'll load up the relics and get moving."

Christoph turned back to Cecelia, brushing her cheek again with bloodstained fingers.

"Hold on, sweetheart," he whispered. "We're not done yet."

She woke up to the gentle vibration of the road beneath her and the low hum of tires on pavement. Disoriented, Cecelia ran her fingers through her hair in a half-awake attempt to fix it—only to discover it was a full-blown disaster, like a bird's nest had crash-landed on her skull and declared war.

She blinked hard. She was in a car.

Her clothes had been changed. She wore a worn gray sweatshirt that smelled faintly of cucumbers and clean musk, like men's cologne and... Max. Her fingers tightened around the fabric.

Max.

She turned her head.

He was right there beside her, eyes closed, chest rising and falling with the soft, steady rhythm of someone at peace. His face looked younger in sleep, less burdened. Erik was on the other side of him, arms crossed and head tilted against the window, also out cold.

It all hit her at once—like a punch to the chest.

The library. The demons. Azazel. The fight. Erik—bleeding out.

Abaddon.

Her throat closed at the memory. But the pain she remembered so vividly… it wasn't there. Not really. Her body still ached, but it was distant, muted. Must be healing magic, she thought.

And then she remembered Max. That blur of gold and shadow tearing through monsters like they were paper.

She looked forward. Sam was driving. Darius, in the passenger seat, had his head tilted back and was snoring softly. She swore she saw him drooling.

She turned back to Max.

He yawned just as she did. His eyes fluttered open.

"You're awake," she whispered.

"I'm awake," he replied, yawning again and closing his eyes like he was deeply offended she'd disturbed him.

"Am I really here?"

He cracked one eye open. "Yep."

"Is this real?"

"Also yep."

"Abaddon?"

"Dead."

"Azazel?"

"Unfortunately, still breathing."

"Where are we going?"

"Away. Somewhere safe."

"Your apartment?"

"Gone. Completely wrecked."

She swallowed. "And Erik? He's okay?"

"He's alive. Hasn't woken up yet. But we got to him in time."

"Thank God," she exhaled—and then her stomach betrayed her with a dramatic, roaring growl.

Max grinned, eyes still half-lidded. "Hungry, pretty girl?"

"Starved," she admitted, covering her face with her hand.

"Sam, hit the next drive-thru," Max called up front.

"There's a Wendy's in about five minutes," Sam said, tapping the GPS. "If we don't die of starvation first."

"Bless you," Darius murmured without opening his eyes.

Ten minutes later, they pulled up to the glowing menu board like a pack of wolves rolling into a buffet. Sam rolled down the window and didn't hesitate.

"Yeah, we're going to need nine Junior Bacon Cheeseburgers, twelve spicy chicken sandwiches, fifteen five-piece nuggets, and twenty large fries."

He looked back. "Christoph, anything else?"

Christoph gave him the most offended look possible without actually moving his face. "You forgot the milkshakes."

Sam laughed. "Right. Five milkshakes, five cokes, and don't be stingy with the barbecue sauce."

Bzzzt... The speaker crackled. A nervous teenage voice responded, "Uh... sir? I'm gonna need you to pull up."

Sam rolled forward like a man who'd done this many, many times before.

He leaned toward the window as the gangly kid inside peered at them with wide eyes. "We're not high," Sam said preemptively. "We just have a lot of friends waiting back home."

"It's not that," the teen stammered, adjusting his glasses. "It's just... that's gonna take a while."

"I'll tip you twenty if you throw in some extra ranch," Sam offered.

"Wow dude, for that I'll give you my employee discount," the kid replied seriously.

"Deal."

They waited in the parking lot, the heavenly scent of fast food finally hitting the car like divine ambrosia when the bags started rolling in.

"You know," Cecelia said between bites of her second spicy chicken sandwich, "I don't think we ordered enough."

"You're absolutely right," Darius said, inhaling fries like a vacuum. "I could eat twenty more nuggets easy."

"Don't worry, big guy," Max mumbled through a mouthful of burger. "You can make up for it at second dinner."

Darius beamed, already reaching for another sandwich. "Now *that's* what I'm talking about."

Cecelia leaned back in her seat, letting the warmth of food and laughter wrap around her like a blanket.

They reached the Montauk house just as the horizon began to smudge with light. Dawn painted the sky in bruised shades of lavender and gold, casting long shadows over the coastal driveway. Erik's seaside estate—normally a vacation haven—now looked more like a sanctuary under siege.

Sam eased the car to a stop, and they spilled out one by one like survivors of a warzone, bone-weary and running on fumes. The ocean wind bit at their skin, but it was oddly comforting.

Christoph didn't speak. He moved on instinct, cradling Erik's unconscious form like it weighed nothing. Darius and Sam followed close behind, lugging duffels filled with medical supplies, weapons, and the last remaining relics of their crumbling sense of order.

Inside, the house was still. Echoey. The large windows in the living room caught the sunrise and splashed it across the hardwood floors like liquid gold. The sea outside whispered against the cliffs, pretending none of them had just fought demons in the belly of New York.

Christoph brought Erik to the guest room beside his own and laid him down gently, adjusting pillows, checking his pulse. Cecelia hovered in the doorway, clutching the sleeve of Max's hoodie as if it were armor. Her eyes never left Erik.

"He's stable," Christoph said quietly. "I think his body just needs time."

He didn't add that time wasn't something they had an abundance of.

Cecelia nodded, but her eyes lingered on her friend's face like she was afraid to blink and miss something.

Back in their shared room, Cecelia sank into the mattress like it might swallow her whole. Every inch of her body screamed with fatigue, but her heart was still thundering. Christoph sat beside her, brushing a tangle of hair off her forehead. She closed her eyes at his touch.

"You're safe," he whispered. "Rest. We'll figure out the rest later."

Across the hall, Sam didn't bother unpacking. He walked into the nearest guest room, kicked off his boots, and fell face-first into a cloud-soft bed with a dramatic *oof*. Darius grunted something unintelligible, shut his door, and passed out halfway through removing his shirt.

For a few short hours, the house exhaled.

Until—

"Evie..."

The name rasped out like a secret. Erik's eyes blinked open against the soft dark of the room, glassy with confusion.

"Evie?" he croaked louder this time, eyes darting.

"Erik!" Christoph appeared in the doorway a second later, Cecelia right behind him.

"Where is she?" Erik pushed himself up weakly, panic rising fast. "Where's Evie?"

Christoph's stomach dropped. He hadn't thought—no, they *hadn't thought*. In the chaos of escape, they had left her behind.

"Sam! Darius!" Christoph's voice cracked like thunder down the hallway.

The two emerged quickly, groggy but alert. One look at Erik told them everything they needed to know.

"We have to go back," Erik pleaded, voice shaking but eyes clear. "She's still out there. I *felt* her."

Sam didn't hesitate. "Then we're going."

"Tonight," Darius added, already turning for his gear. "We don't wait."

Later, as the house quieted once more, Christoph and Darius sat in the living room under the silver wash of moonlight. A bottle of aged whiskey sat between them, already half gone. The tide whispered beyond the windows, too calm for the storm brewing inside them.

"We can't keep running," Christoph muttered, staring into his glass.

"Who's running?" Darius grunted. "We've been fighting on the back foot. Time to flip the damn script."

Christoph nodded slowly. "Dagon. Belial. Asmodeus. Azazel. They die."

Darius raised his glass. "And when Lucifer crawls out of whatever hole he's hiding in, he goes next."

They clinked their drinks—glass on glass, resolve on resolve.

This wasn't just vengeance.

It was a promise.

They would get Evie back. They would tear through Hell itself if they had to. Because what they were fighting for now wasn't just survival.

It was family.

Arch Duke
Asmodeus

Arch Duke
Dagon

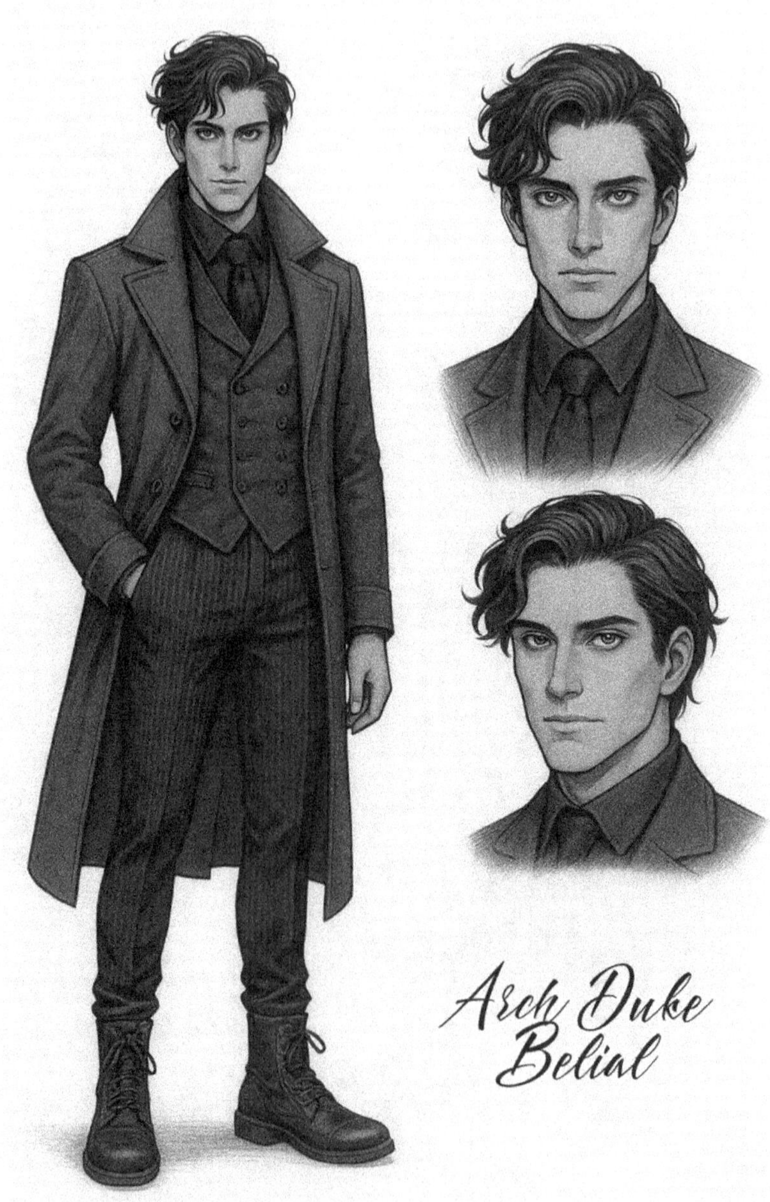

Arch Duke
Belial

Chapter 26

Deep dark revenge

Deep within the labyrinthine tunnels of their lair, the Arch Dukes gathered, their malevolent presence casting long shadows across the damp, decaying stone walls. The flickering light from the torches barely penetrated the oppressive darkness that filled the cavernous hall. The air was thick with the acrid scent of sulfur and burnt flesh, a suffocating reminder of their defeat. The walls wept with moisture, as if the earth itself recoiled from their shame.

Dagon, his serpent-like features contorted in agony, sat slumped against the cold stone, his scales charred and blackened from the holy fire. His usually smooth, greenish skin was split and bubbling with burns, the result of divine flames that had licked at his body with righteous, merciless fury. Each breath was a hiss of pain. He writhed as Belial worked, the latter's expression unreadable—equal parts frustration and contempt.

Belial crouched low, muttering incantations in the old tongue, the syllables guttural and throbbing with forbidden power. His hands smeared black salve over open wounds, smoke rising as it met scorched flesh. Magic pulsed beneath his fingers, stitched into every herb and root, every whispered curse.

"Hold still." Belial growled, voice tight with suppressed fury. "If you keep squirming, this will take even longer—and you'll live to regret it."

Dagon bared his fangs but obeyed, trembling with barely contained rage. His glowing eyes locked forward, wild and murderous. "That cursed Ceruleus will pay for this," he spat, voice low and venomous. "I'm going to rip out his fucking spine and use it to stir the ashes of his little whore."

Asmodius, tending to Azazel, looked toward Dagon with a scowl. "We underestimated them," he growled, the words grinding like stone. "That mistake won't happen again."

It had been millennia since the treaty with the Elite Wing. Once, they'd clashed in blood and fire—brother against brother, angel against fallen. But when it became clear the Elites had fallen too, shunned from the Host, the Arch Dukes chose distance over war. They saw the Elites' disgrace as weakness. They assumed time would finish what Heaven had started.

Azazel sat against a cracked pillar, motionless as Asmodius continued to stitch charred flesh along his ribs with black sinew. The thread cut deep, but Azazel didn't flinch. His eyes, glowing like dying stars, stared into nothing. He felt the pain. He welcomed it. He deserved it.

The loss of Abaddon pressed down on his chest like iron. He didn't like the brute, not really. But there was a time—another life, another war—when Abaddon had been his closest friend. They had fought side by side in Michael's legions, bled for Lucifer's cause, and defied the Host together when the world still had wonder. That version of Abaddon had been brash, blunt, and loyal to the end. Azazel had always valued that. No sycophancy. No fear. Just truth, no matter how ugly.

And now? His old friend was gone. Darius had removed his head like he was cutting through nothing. All because Azazel had broken the treaty.

"This is on me," he muttered.

"Ceruleus and his pathetic Elite Wing think they've won," Azazel snapped suddenly, louder now, voice ragged with rage. "But they've only bought time. We will bring them to their knees and make them beg for mercy before we grind their bones to dust."

Belial rose, finally finished with Dagon. His face was unreadable, his eyes like pits in the earth. "Asmodeus is right. We underestimated the Elites," he said flatly. "But that's your fault, Azazel."

Dagon growled in agreement. "It's been millennia since they sealed Samael. And we forgot what they were capable of. We let our pride rot our memory. We thought because they had fallen, because they lost their wings, that they were weak."

His eyes narrowed, pupils slitting like blades. "But Darius—he cut Abaddon down like a butcher. Sent him screaming back to the Pit. You made that call, Azazel when you broke the treaty."

"It doesn't matter what mistakes were made," Azazel snapped, rising now, his voice cold and clear. "There's no undoing it. We shattered the treaty because that Angel Key is out there with them—and it will be ours even if we have to kill every last one of them to get it."

Asmodius crossed his arms, expression grave. "There are losses on both side. Think. If we're here licking our wounds, where are the Elites? Where would they run, where would they hide? You destroyed their home. Tried to kill Eros. Tortured the Nephilim girl. They'll be regrouping somewhere they find safe while they heal too."

Azazel's cruel smile slowly returned. "Somewhere safe. Somewhere they never expected us to touch."

His eyes gleamed.

"Max Lounge."

Asmodeus's mouth twisted into a grin. "Exactly. They've used that place like a sanctuary for years. It was neutral ground, protected by that flimsy accord. Well, that accord is ashes now. Let's send them a message they won't forget."

"We burn it to the ground," Azazel said. "And if they're inside?"

Dagon's laughter slithered through the chamber. "Then we pick them off one by one as they flee. Like rats."

Asmodius stopped pacing, his voice sharp. "And if they're not there, we gather our troops—demons, beasts, every corrupted soul loyal to the cause.

No more half-measures. No more waiting. We will find them. We will bring a war to their doorstep and drown them in blood."

Dagon stood, his healing complete, his body still wreathed in the stink of smoke and fury. "We will show them what real fear is," he hissed. "They forgot what we are. They forgot Hell."

The four Arch Dukes faced each other now, their dark auras colliding like storm fronts, the power in the room coiling around them in suffocating waves. They had been humiliated, but not broken. They had bled, but not fallen. And now the fire of vengeance burned brighter than ever.

Ceruleus and his Elite Wing had no idea what was coming.

As their schemes took shape in the shadows, their minds filled with fire and ruin. They saw Max Lounge engulfed in flames, heard the screams of innocents, and tasted the blood of their enemies.

They would not strike quietly.

The Arch Dukes would have their revenge, and it would be glorious.

Max Lounge was no longer safe ground.

They took two cars, Darius and Sam in one, Christoph, Cecelia, and Erik in another. The journey was tense, every passing mile a reminder of the danger they faced.

Erik tapped his fingers anxiously against the steering wheel, knuckles white. He put the phone on speaker, dialing fast.

"Come on, pick up," he muttered.

It rang once, twice. Finally—"Hey Erik?" Evie's voice filtered through, "What's going on?"

"Evie, listen to me. You're not safe." Erik's tone was urgent, almost pleading. "You need to pack. Right now. Grab your bag. Don't open the door for anyone. We're coming to get you."

Evie didn't hesitate. The calm in her voice didn't match the pounding of her heart. "Okay. I'm on it."

Evie didn't waste a moment. She grabbed her duffel bag and began throwing clothes into it. Her eyes fell on the katana she had bought from Sam's shop in Chinatown, the one with the intricately designed hilt. She grabbed it along with the gold brass knuckles he had sold her, their weight reassuring in her hands.

"I'm packing now," Evie said into the phone, her voice steady despite the adrenaline coursing through her veins.

"Good. Just stay put," Erik replied, his voice softening. "We'll get you out of there."

When they arrived at Evie's apartment, she was already waiting in the lobby by the door, her bag slung over her shoulder. She quickly jumped into the Escalade, her heart pounding with both fear and relief.

As they drove off, they passed by Max Lounge.

The sight that met their eyes was pure devastation.

Flames devoured the building—bright tongues of fire licking up the walls, swallowing the once-vibrant marquee in smoke and ash. The windows had shattered inward, the front doors blown open like the jaws of a beast mid-scream. The restaurant was unrecognizable. A blackened, burning corpse of what it once was.

Erik and Christoph sat frozen in the front seat, their faces carved in shock. Heartbreak flickered behind their eyes—not just at the loss of the building, but what it had represented. Their dream. Gone.

Christoph was the first to speak, his voice raw and strained. "I'm just… relieved it was closed. I called the staff this morning. Told them we were shutting down for a few weeks to deal with a family emergency."

His words hung heavy in the silence, like ashes in the air.

Erik nodded, slow and numb, his gaze still locked on the burning wreckage. "We should've seen it coming," he muttered. "We gave them an opening."

No one argued. There was nothing left to say.

They turned away, the burning ruin shrinking in the rearview mirror but seared into memory.

The ride to Montauk was quiet, tension twisting through every silence. Evie sat curled in the back seat, staring out the window as trees blurred past.

When they reached the house, no one rushed to unpack.

They moved like ghosts.

Evie settled into one of the guest rooms, the soft hum of ocean wind outside her window offering the faintest illusion of peace.

But they all knew better.

This wasn't over. Not by a long shot.

They sat in silence for a while.

The firepit crackled, casting flickering gold across tired faces. The ocean whispered somewhere in the distance, a dull echo behind the aftermath. The Montauk house was quiet—almost too quiet after everything. For the first time in what felt like days, no one was bleeding.

Cecelia leaned into Evie under the blanket. Her body was healing, but her soul hadn't caught up. Evie pulled her closer, arms around her like armor.

"I'm sorry I wasn't there," Evie said quietly. "But I'm here now. And I'm not going anywhere."

Cecelia didn't answer. She didn't have to. The silence between them was thick with everything they couldn't say. The bruises on Cecelia's face had faded, but the memory of chains, cold stone, and screaming still lingered behind her eyes. Her fingers dug into the fabric of the blanket.

Evie held her tighter. "They don't get to break you," she whispered. "You're still here, Cece. You're alive. That's more than they deserve."

Across the fire, Darius exhaled slowly, staring into the flames. "The one who touched you is gone," he said, voice low. "I made sure of it. But there are four more—and they'll come. We didn't just kill Abaddon. We humiliated them. And demons don't forget."

Evie looked up, firelight dancing in her eyes. "Good," she said. "Let them come. I've trained for worse than nightmares in nice clothes. No one fucks with my best friend or my boyfriend and walks away."

Darius cracked a smirk. "Now that's the spirit."

Sam set down a wooden crate by his feet, its silver clasps worn from age. "I brought the relics," he said, voice calm but cold. "Every weapon, every enchantment we had locked away. If they come again," he said tapping the crate below him, "We're throwing everything we have at them... We end it once and for all."

Christoph sat back, a glass of honey whiskey in one hand, his other still wrapped from the fight. He hadn't spoken much—not since the building went up in flames. But now, his voice cut through the night like a blade.

"They're coming," he said, eyes sharp. "They want the Angel Key. And now that we've taken one of their own, and they won't stop for anything until it's theirs."

He glanced at Cecelia, then Erik. "They think they can take what's ours. They think they can scare us. But they forgot who the fuck we are."

Erik tossed back a shot, setting the glass down with a heavy thud. "We built that place from the ground up," he said. "It wasn't just a restaurant—"

"We can rebuild," Christoph said. "Buildings don't matter. People do. As long as we're still breathing, they haven't won shit."

Erik nodded with understanding.

Sam looked to Christoph. "This isn't over. It's just beginning."

Darius stood, stretching his shoulders, eyes burning with the promise of violence. "We've bled before. We'll bleed again. But if they think they're getting anywhere near her again—" he gestured toward Cecelia without saying her name, "—they're dead already. They just don't know it yet."

The fire cracked louder, the flames rising in the wind as if stirred by something divine.

Christoph lifted his glass. "To the Elite Wing."

Erik, Darius, and Sam raised theirs in unison, eyes hard with fury, loyalty, and the ghosts of everything they'd lost.

"To war," Sam muttered.

"To vengeance," Darius growled.

"To making them pay," Erik added, lips curled into something more animal than human.

Evie leaned in to Cecelia, her breath warm against her friend's ear. "They've got each other," she whispered. "And they've got us. They're not ready for what's coming."

Cecelia didn't smile. But she nodded.

The Elite Wing had been tested. Fire hadn't broken them.

It had forged them sharper.

As they drank, a shadowy figure watched from the treeline. The demon scout, hidden from view, observed the group with keen interest. He pulled out his phone and quickly typed a message to Azazel.

"They are in Montauk. Preparing for battle. Awaiting your orders."

With a smirk, he sent the message and disappeared into the night, knowing that the Arch Dukes would soon bring the fight to the Elite Wing's doorstep.

The walls of the chamber pulsed red with flame and shadow, each beat echoing the heartbeat of Hell itself.

A summoning circle, drawn in blood and scorched bone, stretched across the black stone floor of the Arch Dukes' hidden war chamber. Ancient glyphs shimmered and burned, writhing like living things. Waves of heat distorted the air. At Azazel's feet, a rift opened—vomiting forth a tide of demons.

They came in droves.

Hulking soldiers in obsidian armor stomped through first, brandishing swords wreathed in fire. Winged fiends with jagged horns and smoke trailing from their eyes hissed as they flew in overhead, their talons raking the cavern walls. Towering goliaths emerged last—slow, massive things that dragged chains behind them and snarled with hunger. All of them dropped to one knee before the Arch Dukes.

Azazel watched them with a cold, calculating gaze, his armor scorched from his last battle, but his pride intact. He stepped forward, the blood in the circle licking at his boots, feeding off his rage. The smell of ash, iron, and death filled the air.

This was no longer about a petty retaliation.

This was war.

A sudden buzz broke the moment—his phone.

Azazel plucked it from his hip and read the message. One line, sent by their scout.

"They're in Montauk."

He smiled. Not a pleasant one—this smile was jagged, bitter, unhinged.

"They think they're safe," he said aloud, low and venomous. "They think they can hide."

The other Arch Dukes were scattered across the chamber, preparing for blood.

Belial stood at the far end, sharpening his twin kukris with a whetstone carved from demon bone. "Let them think they can hide," he said with a dry chuckle. "We'll gut them where they sleep."

Dagon crouched at the edge of the circle, eyes glowing with a poisonous sheen. His scales had mostly healed, though the holy fire had left deep grooves along his side. "Start with the girls," he hissed. "The mortals. Let them scream. Let the Elites watch as everything they love turns to ash."

Azazel's expression didn't flinch. "This isn't about fear anymore," he said. "This is about pain. They killed Abaddon. One of our own."

There was silence for a breath. Heavy. Measured.

Belial sheathed his blades. "He was a bastard," he said. "But he was our bastard."

"They humiliated us," Asmodeus growled. "They burned us with holy fire. And they reminded us why we were fools to forget who they were."

"No," Azazel corrected, eyes burning. "I forgot. I led us into that slaughter. I underestimated Ceruleus. I underestimated Darius. I let pride blind me, and it got Abaddon killed."

He looked at each of them in turn, fire reflecting in his gold-ringed pupils.

"I won't make that mistake again."

The demons in the circle hissed and stamped their weapons, snarling and foaming, awaiting command.

"Prepare the legions," Azazel said, voice rising with dark promise. "Tonight we burn Montauk to the ground. If the Elite Wing is inside, we'll catch them in the flames. And if they run—we'll butcher them in the streets."

"Let's remind them what real war feels like," said Asmodeus, hoisting his twin-bladed glaive. "Not these skirmishes. Not these petty ambushes. War."

"Let the humans scream," Dagon said, lips curling. "Let the angels bleed. Let the world watch."

Azazel took one last look at the demonic army kneeling before him. Then he turned back to the others.

"When the Elite Wing falls, we take the Angel Key. And with it—we open the gates."

A sick smile pulled at his cheek.

"And Heaven burns."

The four Arch Dukes stood at the edge of the summoning circle, flames bathing their faces in hellish light. Around them, the army of the Pit waited—ready to march, to rise, and to slaughter.

Azazel looked down at the text message once more, then crushed the phone in his hand. Sparks hissed between his fingers.

"Montauk," he whispered. "Let's finish this."

Chapter 27

The Battle of Montauk

Christoph's eyes flew open.

Not from a sound. Not from a dream. From instinct.

The air was wrong.

The faint, acrid sting of smoke clung to the back of his throat—charcoal, sulfur… fire. He sat up fast, muscles already tense, fingers reaching beneath his pillow to close around cold steel.

"They're here," he said aloud, voice low and certain.

He was already moving. In one fluid motion, he swung his legs off the bed, yanked on his leather jacket—knives lining the inside—strapped on his belt with twin kukris, and had a second blade sheathed at his thigh. Two minutes. That's all he needed. He was trained for this. Born for this.

Beside him, Cecelia stirred, eyes flashing open, heart pounding. She didn't ask what was happening. She didn't need to. She grabbed her own belt from the nightstand, slid twin daggers into place, pulled on her leather jacket, and reached for the blade sheathed beside the bed. Her boots were already laced. Knives slipped in.

No words were exchanged. They didn't need them.

Christoph moved fast, sweeping out into the hall like a phantom.

"Get up!" His voice boomed down the corridor. "They're here!"

In the adjacent bedroom, Erik was already on his feet. Leather jacket on, his quiver of trick arrows and sword were strapped across his back in one swift motion. He tucked his reinforced slingshot into his belt and jammed a pouch of metal pellets into his jacket pocket. His expression was steel—focused and ready. No hesitation. No fear. Just cold, methodical resolve.

Evie was just behind him—sliding into her boots, and zipping up her jacket fast. They'd practiced this. She grabbed the golden angelic blood forged brass knuckles from under her pillow, slid them onto her fists, then took her katana from the nightstand and secured it with a strap to her back. Her jaw was set. She was done running.

In less than two minutes, they were armed to the teeth—no panic, no wasted movements. This was what it meant to be the Elite Wing. They were ready for war.

The hallway lights flickered once. Then again. A low vibration passed through the floorboards.

"They're close," Christoph said, his voice gravel.

No one questioned him.

The demons had found them—but this time, the Elite Wing would be waiting.

Demons burst through the doors and windows, shattering the calm of night with splintering wood, guttural howls, and the stench of brimstone. Fire licked up the drapes as the first floor descended into violent chaos.

Sam and Darius met the wave head-on.

Darius was a force of raw destruction, his twin axes already in motion—spinning, cleaving, shattering demonic limbs and bone with terrifying precision. He moved like a wrecking ball, slamming one demon through the foyer wall with a crunch that shook the foundation, then pivoting to hack the next in two. Blood and black ichor sprayed across the marble floors as he tore a brutal path through the invaders.

Sam was chaos incarnate.

Twin swords flashing gold, he hacked through bodies like they were made of paper. A roundhouse kick sent one demon flying through a window. He stabbed another in the gut and shoved him backward into the flames. "COME ON THEN, YOU UGLY BASTARDS!" he roared, laughing, eyes wild. "WHO WANTS TO DIE SCREAMING?"

He was a whirlwind—cutting, kicking, slashing, yelling curses that made the demons flinch even before his blades reached them.

"GET THEM OUTSIDE!" Azazel's voice boomed from the treeline, dripping with venom. "I WANT THEM BLEEDING IN THE OPEN!"

Demons poured in, their grotesque forms flooding the halls, trying to push the Elite Wing toward the open yard—toward the ambush waiting beyond the burning house.

Upstairs, Christoph and Erik burst through the second-story window, landing hard on the first-floor roof. Christoph's blades were already coated in blood, his jacket bristling with weapons. He moved like a predator, eyes scanning, jaw clenched.

Erik grinned like a madman, drawing a trick arrow with a crimson fletch and loosing it into the yard.

BOOM.
 An explosion rocked the earth—five demons incinerated in a ball of fire.

"Hell yeah!" Erik laughed, notching another. This one exploded mid-air, showering the enemy in golden ichor shrapnel. The demons screeched as it burned through their skin like acid.

"Eat celestial shrapnel, bitches!" he yelled, firing again.

A sonic arrow hit the next group—*KRAK*—the blast ruptured their skulls with a shockwave so loud it dropped others to their knees.

Below, demons screamed and scattered.

From behind Erik, Evie vaulted down from the balcony to join them with her katana drawn, gold knuckles clenched tight on her left hand. She landed in a crouch, then rose with a slash so clean it split a demon open from neck to sternum. Her brass knuckles crushed the skull of the next with a sickening *crack*.

Cecelia landed beside her, blades already slicing. Her twin daggers danced in her hands like extensions of her arms. One demon lunged—she spun, caught it in the neck, and buried the second blade in its gut.

"Try me, you demonic pricks," she spat, eyes blazing.

On the roof, Christoph's voice rang out like thunder, his rage unmistakable. "AZAZEL! YOUR HEAD IS MINE!"

And below, in the burning yard, a pack of snarling demons stared up at them—dozens of them—waiting, crouched, ready to strike.

But the Elite Wing was ready too.

And this time, they weren't running.

Erik's quiver was empty. Smoke stung his eyes as he let the bow fall from his hands, the once-beautiful weapon clattering against the scorched roof. His chest rose and fell with ragged breaths, sweat soaking through the collar of his shirt. Around him, flames devoured the rooftop, the shingles popping, the wooden beams groaning and cracking beneath their feet.

"Roof's giving out!" Christoph shouted, already moving. "We need to get down—*now!*"

The roof buckled with a sudden *snap*, and all four—Cecelia, Evie, Erik, and Christoph—launched into motion. Christoph leapt through the gap in the collapsed roof, blades drawn. Erik followed, twisting midair and landing hard on the first floor. Cecelia and Evie landed in tandem, their boots hitting debris-strewn tile just as the roof above them collapsed in a roar of flame and falling timber. They charged into battle.

Darius stood in the remains of the living room, panting like a beast, gold blood and black ichor splattered across his chest. An entire section of wall had been demolished—torn down by brute force and rage. His twin axes dripped with black blood as he turned to them.

"Through here!" Darius barked, motioning to the gaping hole.

But the moment they moved—hell struck again.

A fresh swarm of demons flooded through the breach, screeching with bloodlust. Clawed hands reached. Fangs snapped. Cecelia and Evie didn't hesitate.

Evie was a blur of motion, her katana whistling through the air, carving into torsos and necks with surgical precision. She ducked a swipe, pivoted, and drove the blade clean through a demon's throat. Black ichor sprayed her cheek. She didn't blink.

Her left fist cracked into another creature's jaw, brass knuckles shattering bone on impact. She moved like she'd been born to fight, fluid and vicious, painting the living room floor with the pieces of her enemies.

"Holy *shit*, Evie," Erik muttered, eyes wide as she beheaded a snarling brute and kicked the body into two more. "That's my girlfriend."

"*Focus, Erik!*" she yelled, kicking a demon in the chest and impaling the next without missing a beat.

Erik snapped to, unsheathing his golden samurai sword. The blade shimmered like liquid sunlight in the smoke-filled room. He charged.

His first strike cleaved a demon clean in half. The next parried with claws, but Erik countered with a flurry of slashes that ended with his blade embedded deep in the monster's skull. He yanked it free and spun, carving through two more. The golden blade hissed and sparked as it kissed ichor and bone.

Demons fell around them in a storm of fire and fury—but they just kept coming.

Darius was a juggernaut, swinging his twin axes like a god of war. He cleaved through a horned beast's ribcage and grabbed another by the throat, slamming it through a burning table. He moved like nothing could stop him—covered in cuts, growling like a wolf, his axes an extension of his rage.

Sam appeared behind them like a storm, blades flashing in either hand. His eyes were wild, mouth twisted into a savage grin. He hacked down a demon, then kicked another so hard its spine snapped against the wall.

"COME ON THEN!" he howled. "IS THAT ALL YOU FUCKERS BROUGHT?!"

He was a whirlwind of steel and fury, cutting through flesh like butter, every move laced with deadly precision and sheer brutality.

Erik fought at his side now, covered in ash and blood, laughing like a madman.

"Who wants the last dance?!" he shouted, slicing open a demon's belly, then ducking under a claw to stab upward into its jaw.

Then—A flicker in the smoke.

A shadow moved like oil.

And Erik saw him.

Dagon.

He towered over the chaos, serpent-skinned and smiling with venomous satisfaction. His eyes were fixed on Evie as he stepped through the flames, fangs glinting, claws twitching.

He towered over the chaos, serpent-skinned and hulking, his scales shimmering with sickly iridescence in the firelight. Smoke curled around him as if Hell itself exhaled through his lungs. His vertical-slit eyes locked onto Evie, and his forked tongue flicked at the air like he could already taste her blood.

"Well, well," Dagon hissed, stepping through the blaze. His claws twitched with anticipation. "Let's see what that pretty little wench can do without her precious angel protecting her."

Evie stepped forward, unshaken. Her katana glinted in her grip, the golden blade catching the light of the inferno. "You want to go, snake boy?" she snapped. "Let's *go.*"

Dagon's lip curled back into something inhuman. "I'm going to *break* you, *little* girl," he growled. "Ruin that little body of yours and kill you *slow.*"

"My name isn't *little girl,*" Evie said, her voice as sharp as her sword. She squared her shoulders, eyes blazing. "It's *Evette Renee Angelique Lamoureux,* you sick, twisted *fuck.* And you can take your beastiality fantasies and *choke on them in Hell.*"

"*DAGON!*" Erik's voice ripped through the chaos. "You stay the *fuck* away from her!"

Dagon didn't listen.

He struck—faster than lightning, cobra-fast—but Evie didn't flinch. She pivoted and sliced, her katana singing as it bit into his chest. Golden metal tore through scale and sinew, and Dagon screamed—a high, ragged sound not meant for mortal ears.

"AHH—WHAT IS THIS BLADE, YOU UNHOLY WENCH?!"

Evie's lips curled into a grin. "A present from my *boyfriend*," she spat, yanking the blade free, her stance already resetting for another strike.

Dagon's tail whipped around with a crack like thunder. Evie barely saw it coming—too fast. It caught her midair and sent her crashing into the side of the hallway, knocking the breath from her lungs.

"*EVIE!*" Erik roared, and the fire in him *snapped.*

He launched himself at Dagon, sword forgotten. His hand slashed open with practiced precision, blood spilling like gold across his palm. Dagon turned just in time to see Erik slam that glowing hand into his face.

The result was *instantaneous.*

The holy blood *burned through him*, sizzling through scale and bone like acid, boring a hole through Dagon's face as he shrieked in agony. Smoke poured from his eyes, his jaw cracking open in an inhuman scream that rattled the walls.

Erik *held him down* with his entire body, gritting his teeth as the Arch Duke writhed and thrashed, trying to escape the searing purity tearing through his cursed form.

"BURN, you fucker!" Erik growled through clenched teeth.

Evie staggered up, blood on her face, eyes locked on Dagon. She limped forward, katana gripped tight, her whole body shaking—but not from fear.

"Erik—*ROLL!*"

Erik shoved off just as Evie brought her katana down with every ounce of fury and fire in her body.

The blade *screamed* as it cleaved through the already-burning flesh, severing Dagon's head clean from his shoulders.

The body convulsed violently, black ichor spraying like molten ooze before erupting into flames. The fire devoured him whole—flesh, bone, essence—until there was *nothing* left but ash and the echo of his final scream.

Silence.

Heavy, crackling silence.

Evie collapsed to her knees, breathing hard, her sword still smoking in her hands. Erik crouched beside her, pulling her close. His hands trembled as he touched her cheek, brushing away the blood and sweat.

"You good?" he asked softly, eyes wide with disbelief.

Evie looked down at the pile of ash and whispered, "That's for touching my friend."

The beach was a warzone.

Flames crackled from the ruins of the Montauk house behind them, casting a hellish glow across the sand. Smoke rolled out into the night, mixing with the salty breeze as the crashing waves hissed nearby.

Darius stood with his twin axes clenched tight, chest heaving, blood trickling down his arm. Sam stood beside him, shirt torn, Herculean Whip dangling from both hands—its clawed, electrified chains humming with teal energy.

Across from them, Belial and Asmodeus emerged from the smoke, walking side by side like nightmares. Belial's skin glistened with acidic sweat, his veins glowing a toxic green. Asmodeus's armor pulsed red, his double-edged blade dragging through the sand, sparking trails of fire behind it.

"You bring holy relics to a demon's war?" Belial sneered, his tongue flicking like a serpent's. "Cowards."

Sam grinned, blood on his teeth. "You bring nothing but hot air and a shitty attitude. And now you're afraid of a little god-gifted steel? Also, can't forget to mention you brought an army to fight six of us," he scoffed. "Ask yourself, who are the real pussies here?"

With a scream of fury, Asmodeus charged first—hellfire erupting from his blade as he swung it like a scythe. Sam met him mid-charge, his whip flashing forward in a wild arc. The electrified claws cracked across Asmodeus's chest, sending a burst of teal sparks and black ichor spraying through the air.

At the same moment, Belial lunged for Darius, spitting a stream of acid that sizzled into the sand. Darius rolled to the side, surged forward, and slammed one axe into Belial's side. The demon shrieked and grabbed Darius by the arm—burning flesh with a touch that made Darius grit his teeth through the pain.

They all fought like monsters now.

Sam was a hurricane, spinning, whipping, striking like a blur—his chains wrapping around Asmodeus's legs, yanking him off balance, then slashing deep across his chest. Asmodeus roared, raising a hand to unleash another wave of flame, but Sam was already on him, flipping over his back, landing behind him, slashing the whip across his spine.

Darius slammed his second axe into Belial's knee, twisting it as the demon shrieked in agony. Belial retaliated, grabbing Darius's throat and spewing acid point-blank into his shoulder. The skin sizzled, the smell unbearable.

"DARIUS!" Sam shouted, seeing his friend stumble.

Darius didn't scream. He didn't back down.

He saw red.

With both axes in hand, Darius let out a guttural roar and went berserk. He threw one axe into Belial's gut and used the other to slam the demon backward into a jagged rock along the shoreline. Belial crumpled to the sand, coughing black ichor.

Sam had his own problems. Asmodeus had caught him mid-swing and drove his flaming blade deep into Sam's back. Sam collapsed with a strangled cry, coughing gold blood onto the sand.

"NO!" Darius breathed, his voice shaking.

He turned just as Asmodeus stood over Sam, raising his sword for the killing blow.

Darius moved like a force of nature. He crossed the beach in seconds, tackled Asmodeus, and without hesitation, grabbed him by the ankle and tore the Arch Duke of Lust in half with his bare hands—from groin to chest. Asmodeus didn't have time to scream. The demon's body exploded in fire and ash, his sword clattering to the ground, extinguished.

The beach fell silent.

Belial scrambled to his feet, black blood pouring from his gut. His face twisted in horror as he looked between Sam's fallen form and the blood-drenched, panting Darius.

"You—you're insane," Belial hissed, backing away.

Darius's eyes glowed white.

"You're *next*."

Belial turned and fled into the shadows, leaving a trail of ichor behind him.

Darius dropped to his knees beside Sam.

"No. No. No," he muttered, tearing open his own palm with one of his axes. Blood flowed freely.

He pressed his glowing palm to Sam's wound, whispering the seraphic healing spell. Light flared from the contact, searing through the darkness, and Sam gasped as his lungs filled again.

"Shit," Sam croaked, coughing. "I thought I was a goner for a second there."

"You're not allowed to die," Darius said, voice ragged. "Not on me. Not tonight."

Sam let out a groan. "You ripped a demon in half for me?"

"Wouldn't be the first time."

Sam chuckled weakly. "I fucking love you, man."

Darius just nodded, watching the flames behind them as they rose higher into the night.

The night exploded into new levels of horror.

Goliath Demons thundered down the dunes, their massive rhino-like bodies shaking the earth with each stomp. Black armor fused with bone covered their frames, segmented scorpion tails twitching and coiled to strike. Their heads—jagged, insectile horrors—snapped mandibles in anticipation.

"YOU HAVE GOT TO BE KIDDING ME," Sam roared, barely getting to his feet as one of the beasts barreled toward him.

Darius stepped in front of him, blood dripping from his hands, axes raised. "Alright then," he growled. "Let's dance."

The first Goliath Demon struck like a freight train. Darius sidestepped at the last moment, his axe cleaving into its knee joint. The monster shrieked, tail whipping around like a battering ram. Sam ducked low and sprang forward with a warcry, Herculean Whip glowing, both chains spinning into a whirlwind of clawed fury.

The whip wrapped around the creature's throat. Sam yanked, jumping over its back and slicing downward in a blur—electric teal energy surged, frying through muscle and bone. It dropped, crashing into the sand with a roar that echoed across the shoreline.

Another Goliath charged. Darius caught its tail mid-swing, teeth clenched, and slammed his axe down at the base, severing it clean. Acidic black ichor sprayed through the air. Sam jumped onto its back and unleashed divine rage, carving along the spine with both chains. The creature bucked once… twice… then collapsed, twitching.

"Two down," Darius panted.

"Twelve to go," Sam muttered grimly.

Across the yard, Erik and Evie were fighting sky-born nightmares. Winged fiends—thin, sinewy demons with torn bat-like wings and claws as long as daggers—circled overhead like vultures.

Erik was laughing.

He stood in the middle of the field, arms raised, slingshot glowing. "Bring it, you ugly bastards!"

He loaded a golden pellet—his own angelic blood sealed within—and fired. The projectile slammed into a demon's chest and exploded, golden light bursting outward in a scorching wave. The fiend shrieked and disintegrated midair, ash raining down like fireflies.

Evie moved like death incarnate. Her golden katana spun through the air, carving an arc of holy destruction as it sliced the wing off a descending demon. It crashed to the ground, shrieking, and she drove her brass-knuckled fist into its throat, crushing its windpipe with a sickening crack.

"Evie, left!" Erik shouted.

She turned just in time to duck a swooping talon. Her response was swift—a spinning backfist with her brass knuckles, sending the demon hurtling back with smoke pouring from its ruptured face.

Another winged demon dove for Erik. He launched a sonic blast pellet—the moment it hit, the fiend's head popped like a watermelon, golden ichor misting through the air.

"God, I love these things!" Erik cackled, loading another shot.

Evie rolled her eyes, slicing the leg off one demon and impaling it through the gut with her katana in the same motion. "Less flirting with your slingshot, more killing, loverboy."

"I can do both!"

They fought back-to-back now, sweat and blood painting their skin, golden weapons gleaming in the firelight. Every movement was honed, perfected—a dance of violence performed by two warriors who had everything to lose.

The skies were streaked with smoke. The beach was soaked in ichor. The demons kept coming, wave after wave.

But so did they.

Cecelia and Christoph fought like fire and wind—unrelenting, untouchable, and untamed.

Back-to-back in the chaos, they moved as one. Christoph's twin kukris flashed in tight arcs, slicing through demon throats and rib cages. Cecelia's Roman daggers darted like golden serpents, precise and deadly. A slash to the neck, a stab to the heart—she was poetry in motion, eyes burning, breath steady.

A soldier lunged. Cecelia dropped low into a sweep, Christoph vaulting over her shoulders mid-spin, both blades dragging across two demon skulls in perfect unison.

Another came from behind—they locked forearms, pivoted together, and kicked outward, launching the attacker through the air like a ragdoll.

It was a dance of violence. A symphony of carnage. The crack of bones, the hiss of ichor against steel, the rhythm of footsteps weaving through blood and flame. Their bond, forged in fire, had become a language all its own.

Then it emerged.

A Baramous Demon.

It snarled as it pounced into the clearing—leopard-like in form, massive and fast, black fire seething from its throat. Dragon-like claws scraped deep furrows into the earth as it circled them, the ground sizzling with every step.

Christoph let loose a barrage of throwing knives and they sang through the air meeting the beast but they landed harmlessly only leaving smoking trails where they embedded into the monster's skin. "Shit," he scoffed.

It exhaled—a plume of fire that roared toward them. Christoph grabbed Cecelia's arm and twisted her behind him, raising a crossed X of kukris to block the heat. The flames parted just enough for her to roll under it.

Cecelia burst forward, sliding beneath the Baramous, her daggers flashing. A slice—one, two—its hind legs buckled.

"Now!" she shouted.

Christoph leapt.

A somersault through the air, kukris reversed, and he drove them both down into the back of the beast's skull with a roar.

The Baramous shrieked and collapsed, flames sputtering out as it convulsed, bursting into flame until it was nothing but dust and shadows.

Christoph looked to Cecelia and nodded but there was no time to breathe.

A wave of fiends barreled toward them, a tide of teeth and claws.

They fought back-to-back again—slashes and strikes, ducking and spinning, but there were too many.

From the corner of his eye, Christoph saw them—two winged fiends sweeping in low like vultures. One tackled Cecelia from behind.

"No—!" he lunged, but the second one slammed into his chest, knocking him back.

Cecelia screamed as the creatures seized her, dragging her across the bloodstained sand.

"CECILIA!" Christoph roared.

He slashed wildly, trying to reach her—kukris tearing through demon flesh, his body covered in blood, eyes frantic. He surged forward only to be dogpiled by a dozen demon soldiers, their claws dragging him down.

"NO! LET HER GO!"

He reached an arm toward her, but she was already airborne—her figure disappearing into the night, kicking and thrashing, daggers still swinging until she vanished behind the treeline.

Christoph's voice cracked with rage and despair.

"CECILIA!"

But the demons didn't stop. They wanted him down. They wanted him broken.

And he wasn't about to let them have that.

Cecelia thrashed violently, boots slamming into ribcages and wings as the winged fiends dragged her higher into the smoke-choked sky. The distant cries of battle echoed from the beach below, but her fury drowned out everything else.

"LET ME GO YOU DISGUSTING CREEPS!" she screamed, twisting in their grip, slicing one across the thigh with the blade she had managed to draw mid-flight.

They didn't respond.

They just dropped her.

She hit the ground hard, rolled, and sprang to her feet in a combat stance, both Roman daggers in hand. The sand beneath her was blackened and scorched, littered with ash and broken beams—all that remained of the Montauk house.

She barely had time to adjust before she heard the slow, deliberate clap.

Azazel stood before her, tall, sharp, monstrous—and smiling like the Devil himself.

"Well, well," he said, voice dripping with venom and mockery. "Just the beauty I've wanted to see. At last we meet again, my darling."

Cecelia spat in his face.

"Go to Hell."

Azazel didn't flinch. He dragged a gloved finger down his cheek where her spit landed, then licked it off slowly.

"Oh, I have a trip planned," he said. "But not there. Somewhere else. Somewhere much nicer. And you, my dear, are the key to getting in."

Her grip tightened on her daggers. "Try me."

Azazel's eyes glittered with madness. "No need to be coy. Just hand it over."

"Never."

He tilted his head with a grin. "Then let's dance for it."

"In your dreams."

With a chuckle, Azazel unsheathed a pitch-black blade, its surface glowing faintly with emerald runes that pulsed like a heartbeat.

"This," he whispered, holding it up reverently, "was a gift. Forged by the hands of Lucifer himself. He called it *Zanfa*. It drinks angelic blood. Burns it. Feeds on it. Want to see what it does to a Nephilim of Light like you?"

Cecelia stepped back instinctively. Her breath hitched, just for a moment— but her stance remained firm. The dagger in her left hand was reversed, ready to block. The one in her right, steady at his chest.

Azazel lunged, faster than she expected—a blur of blade and hate.

She brought her daggers up just in time—

Steel screamed against steel. And the world exploded into motion.

Christoph burst from the crowd of demons like a comet of wrath—lightning streaking from his fingertips, shadows trailing behind him like tattered wings. He carved a blazing path across the beach, his skin glowing where he'd sliced himself open, golden light pouring from the wound.

It was the only way.

His divine magic, once sacred and sealed, now burned freely through his veins—unstoppable, unsparing. He wouldn't survive this. He knew it. But he didn't care.

He'd burn every last ounce of power left inside him if it meant reaching her.

Demons exploded to ash in his wake, their bodies disintegrating as the raw force of heaven and hell merged into one devastating blaze. Goliath demons crumbled beneath his twin kukris, their black blood hissing into vapor as lightning scorched the earth. A wave of aerial fiends dove from above—he raised his hand, summoned a vortex of shadows that blanketed the sky in darkness. Then, with a roar of pure agony, he unleashed a lightning storm within the void, frying every last one of them mid-air.

His body was cracking apart from within—he could feel it—but still he ran.

Through the smoke and ruin, he saw her.

Cecelia.

Locked in a brutal clash with Azazel.

And then—Azazel lunged.

Christoph flashed between them just in time, his daggers crossing Zanfa with a shower of sparks that lit up the night.

Azazel grinned. "*Ceruleus.* You've finally come… to *die.*"

Christoph's jaw was clenched tight, his voice ragged and shaking with fury. "Wrong. Tonight, you fall, bitch."

Their duel erupted.

Daggers versus demon blade. Sparks flew with every clash. Azazel swept with wide arcs of void magic, dark slashes of unholy flame—Christoph countered, his blades glowing with white lightning, blocking, parrying, striking back.

Azazel struck low—Christoph jumped, spinning in the air and kicking him across the jaw. Azazel rolled, and came up swinging. Christoph dropped to one knee, skidding beneath it, slashing upward in a flash of gold and black.

"You should've stayed buried, angel," Azazel spat.

"You should've stayed in Hell," Christoph snapped back, crackling with energy.

Azazel grinned as they circled, blade clashing against blade, the sound ringing like a war drum over the crashing waves.

"That key will be mine, Ceruleus," he sneered, stepping in with a wide slash. Christoph met it with both daggers, locking their blades in a brief, brutal stalemate. Sparks flared between them.

Then Azazel smirked—and broke the pattern.

He *faked* a strike toward Christoph's right shoulder, but at the last second, he twisted his hips and *lunged past him*—blade aimed *straight for Cecelia.*

Cecelia barely had time to raise her daggers.

"CECELIA!" Christoph roared.

He flashed forward, catching Zanfa mid-thrust with the crossed edge of his twin kukris. The sheer force of it sent a shockwave rippling through the sand.

Azazel laughed as their weapons locked again. "Still so predictable, Ceruleus."

"You'll never touch her again!" Christoph growled, forcing Azazel back.

But the Arch Duke wasn't finished.

He took a step back, eyes flaring, and *faked again*—a flourish of Zanfa toward Christoph's chest—only to *open his mouth and unleash a torrent of hellfire directly at Cecelia.*

"NO!" Christoph moved faster than thought.

He spun and threw himself in front of her, arms wide, body crackling with divine energy. The fire slammed into his back like a hurricane of flame. It hit *hard,* engulfing them both in a wall of blinding red and orange.

Cecelia screamed behind him.

Christoph's skin began to *burn,* divine light seeping from the cracks as his angelic power strained to contain the infernal blaze.

Azazel emerged through the smoke, a shadow with a blade. He struck again—this time, *through the fire*—and *drove Zanfa straight through Christoph's back,* piercing through his ribs and into his heart.

The blade pushed out through his chest—right above Cecelia's shoulder.

His eyes went wide.

His body froze.

A choking sound escaped him.

Lightning flickered.

Shadow spilled from his mouth.

Time seemed to slow.

Cecelia screamed, catching Christoph as he collapsed, Zanfa still protruding from his chest. Azazel laughed, and twisted the blade.

"Oh, how *I love* to watch the *mighty* fall," Azazel sneered, placing his boot on Christoph's back and yanking the blade free. "You were always weak, Ceruleus."

He smiled and laughed, raising the blade up high.

But the laughter didn't last.

Erik's voice split the air: "NOOOOO!"

A flash of steel—then silence.

Azazel's head hit the ground a half-second before the rest of him.

Erik stood behind him, sword dripping in black ichor, his face frozen in horror and rage.

But it was too late.

Christoph collapsed into Cecelia's arms, golden ichor pouring from the wound. His skin, once glowing, now flickered like a dying star.

"So this is what it feels like to die," he smiled wistfully, gazing into the gray of Cecelia's eyes. His voice was quiet, almost reverent, like he was tasting the final note of a symphony only he could hear.

"No, Max. You can't. You can't die," she gasped. "You're not going anywhere. You have to stay with me," Cecelia cried, her voice cracking beneath the weight of her heartache. "You have. To stay. With me."

In his time on Earth, he'd watched more lives pass than anyone should ever see. Lovers clinging to last words, warriors taking their final breath. But he'd always wondered what it would feel like to *pass on*—to *finally let go*.

"I will not let you go. Stay with me, Max. Stay with me." She pressed her hands against the wound in his chest, already slick with his golden blood, trembling as she tried to hold him together with nothing but hope and desperation. "Max, Max—" she choked, tears falling freely, "don't go. We have so much left to do. You were going to show me the world, remember?"

she pleaded, as if words could keep his soul from slipping through her fingers.

"I know, pretty girl," he whispered, his smile barely holding. "But that's going to have to wait for another time, and another life."

He lied, of course. He knew what he was. Fallen. Forsaken. There were no second chances for beings like him. But she didn't need to know that. She only needed his smile.

"This is it for me."

"No, no it can't be. No, it's not." She looked at him, then to Erik, panic blooming like fire across her face.

"Cecelia…" Erik's voice was low, broken. "You have to say goodbye. This might be the last chance you get. Our kind don't come back the way yours do."

A single tear escaped Erik's eye and fell like a blessing onto the bloodied chest of his best friend.

Cecelia looked down at it, then at herself. That's when she noticed it—resting on her chest, glowing softly with celestial light.

Her Angel Key.

Its silver filigree shimmered like it knew.

"You're not going anywhere, handsome man," she said, brushing her tears away, her voice steadying with purpose. "I love you too damn much."

"Stop it, Cecelia," Erik said, his voice tense with fear. "We don't know what that could do to a fallen——" she didn't listen.

"With an open heart, and everything I am," she said, removing it from her neck, her voice shaking now with reverence instead of grief. "I, Cecelia White, gift to you, Christoph Maximus, this Key to Heaven."

She placed it gently around his neck.

He stared back at her with sorrow and pain in his golden eyes. Tears had filled hers as she watched him struggle.

He smiled up at her, wiping a tear away. "It was a privilege loving you," he exhaled softly, "pretty girl," and then his eyes closed for the last time—*he was gone.*

"No!" she cried. "NO! This was supposed to work." She gripped Max's shirt. The agony was raw in her voice. "This should have *worked*, dammit!" she looked at Erik with dread in her eyes.

Tears streamed down his face and he fell to his knees. She put her arms around him and a sobbed wrenched itself from his body.

Then a gasp escaped him. Cecelia pulled away, turning to look back at her Maximus.

His body started to glow. Slow at first and then it ignited in golden light, radiant and pure.. Cecelia stumbled back as the brightness enveloped him, lifting him slowly from the earth until he hovered there—*weightless, timeless*—his body suspended in the air like a constellation come to life.

For one sweet, blissful moment, he stood as a man-shaped flame of gold, light pouring from every inch of him, his wings—no longer fallen, but reborn—unfurling behind him in a silhouette.

Then—

He shot upward like a streak of light, a golden comet bursting into the sky.

Ash and light rained down like blessings.

She looked to the ground, to the blood-soaked sand where he'd been and she saw there was nothing left.

"Where did he go?" she whispered. Her voice was barely a breath, cracked and hollow.

"Erik…" she turned slowly, trembling. "Where did he go?"

"Home, Cecelia," he said, stepping beside her and placing an arm around her shoulders. "He's gone home."

Chapter 28

The Last Will & Testament of Christoph Maximus

Cecelia hadn't left her bed in days.

The world outside moved on—bells rang, professors lectured, students laughed in the courtyard—but inside her room, time had stopped. The curtains remained drawn. The light refused to enter. The air was heavy with a silence that swallowed everything whole.

Evie had tried—she brought food between classes, warm meals that went untouched, boxes she carried out just as full as when she brought them in. Cecelia didn't move. She didn't speak. She barely breathed. Her body remained curled beneath the covers like a shadow of the girl she once was.

She wasn't sleeping. She wasn't crying.

She just… stopped.

Darius came by. He stood in the doorway for a long time, saying nothing. Just watching her with hollow eyes. He called her name once, gently. She didn't answer. Didn't even flinch.

Sam tried next. He cracked jokes. Sat on the edge of the bed and told her Christoph would be pissed to see her like this—that he'd want her to throw a punch, not a pity party. But her eyes stayed fixed on the ceiling, glassy and lifeless. It was like talking to a ghost.

Eventually, he left, too.

Evie didn't know what else to do. She sat on the bathroom floor that night and cried until her lungs ached, until Erik found her and held her against his chest. That's when she whispered the only thing she could think of.

"We need to give him a funeral."

It turned out Christoph *did* have a plan.

Of course he did. It was Christoph Maximus. The man didn't just wing things—he choreographed life like a cinematic trailer. So when their lawyer, Marcin, reached out, no one was exactly surprised. Appalled by the drama? Yes. Surprised? Not even a little.

Apparently, Max had left behind a full-blown, notarized, leather-bound *Last Will & Testament*, complete with monogrammed bookmarks and a playlist titled "If I Die, Play These."

He had requested to be cremated, and for his ashes to be placed in the roots of a sapling—a weeping willow, specifically—to be planted in Central Park, right across from the fountain where he'd once asked Cecelia to be his girlfriend. Max insisted it had to be the Bethesda fountain. He'd settle for nothing less. *But* not near the hotdog carts. He *hated* the way they smelt.

But—because Max planned for every outcome—in the event that no remains were recovered (which, of course, happened), he'd left behind a vial of his blood in a secured case labeled *In Case of Eternal Incineration*. The instructions were clear: pour the blood onto the roots of the sapling and let him grow. A new kind of life. One that would outlast them all.

He left the task to Erik first, but with a contingency list of successors—Sam and Darius—because, in his words, *"Let's be real, the Creator only knew those two would outlast them all."*

It hurt—*achingly*—for Cecelia to climb out of that bed.

Her legs felt like lead. Her chest was cracked porcelain. Every movement made her bones scream. She didn't even turn the water on in the shower at first. She just sat there on the tile floor, hugging her knees, until the numbness finally gave way to tears. When she did turn the water on, she let it rain down on her for what felt like hours, the steam doing nothing to warm the frost clinging to her soul.

Evie had already picked out her dress. The red one.

"Max asked for it," she whispered softly.

Cecelia choked at his name.

Evie forced her into a chair and sat in front of her with mascara in one hand and sheer will in the other. "He'd want you to be beautiful today," she said. "For him."

Cecelia sat like a doll, silent, motionless, while Evie did her hair, her makeup, her nails. It was easier not to fight. Fighting would mean she still cared enough to hurt. Right now, she just needed to survive the hour.

Darius came to pick them up. He didn't say much—just helped them into the black Escalade like it was a funeral chariot. They rode in silence, the streets of Manhattan blurring past the tinted windows, until they reached the edge of Central Park.

Now they stood there. On the lawn across from the fountain. The one that had changed everything.

Sam and Erik had already dug the hole. The sapling stood beside it—small, delicate, trembling slightly in the breeze. A weeping willow, just like Max asked.

Erik turned to Cecelia and gently handed her the vial. "Do the honors?"

She stared at it like it was a relic. Her hands trembled. To hold a part of him again, even this small, was almost too much. For a second—just a wild, intrusive second—she thought about downing it. Making him a permanent part of her. Like blood and memory fused.

But no. That was unhinged, and she was grieving—not insane.

She uncorked the vial and knelt down, slowly pouring the shimmering golden liquid into the roots of the tree. It soaked into the soil like it belonged there.

A part of him did.

As Darius lifted the sapling and set it into place, Sam turned toward Erik and squinted.

"Hey… how exactly did you get *permission* to do this?"

Erik gave him a sideways smile. "Permission?"

Sam blinked. "Oh no."

Darius just grinned as he patted down a clump of dirt. "Don't worry. I took care of it."

"You *what*—"

"I took care of it," Darius repeated, without elaboration.

Erik laughed, clapping him on the back. "Thanks, D."

They all took turns packing dirt around the base, their hands smudged with earth and grief. Erik knelt last, pressing the soil tight.

The willow stood tall. Fragile, but proud.

Just like Max had always been.

Erik cleared his throat.

He didn't step forward so much as drift, like the weight of the moment was pulling him by the collar. His hand raked nervously through his hair, and for a second, it looked like he might not say anything at all. But then he exhaled and spoke.

"I, uh… I never thought I'd be doing this," he said, voice cracking at the edges. "Christoph was like a rock for us. For me."

He looked down, pressing his lips together as his throat tightened.

"I just want to say thank you," he continued, softer now, "for being you… and for loving me no matter what crazy or stupid ideas I had—or trouble I got into. You *always* had my back. And you knew I had yours. I promise you, I'll try to be that for the others now. I'll try to be someone you'd be proud of."

A silence hung. Heavy and still.

Then Erik let out a small breath of a laugh and added, "I should probably share a story now. Christoph probably wouldn't want me spilling his dark secrets but, uh—here we go anyway."

That earned a few smiles.

"It's the story of the first time Christoph bailed me out of trouble. Not the last, not even close—but the first."

"I was training to be a healer, right? But I always wanted to be a warrior. Don't ask me why. I guess I just idolized this archer named Sariel. He was a legend—quick, precise, kind of dramatic. My kind of guy. And when he passed during the Great War, I thought, well, now's my chance. But no matter how hard I trained, how many times I asked… Michael wouldn't take me."

Erik shrugged. "So naturally, I did what any angry little shit would do."

Evie gasped preemptively.

Sam grinned. "Oh no."

"I decided to teach him a lesson. One day, after the Golden Hand got back from a mission, I 'volunteered'—" he made air quotes with his fingers—"to polish their armor after my squad healed them. And when Michael wasn't looking, I took his sword. *Glorious.* And I hid it."

Evie slapped a hand to her mouth.

Sam laughed. "You *what?*"

"I panicked, okay? I got maybe ten feet down the hall before I heard Michael shout. I was *dead,* like *dead dead.* But then there he was—Christoph. He stepped out of nowhere, took the sword from me, and just… hid it behind his back like it was no big deal."

Erik shook his head in disbelief, even now.

"Michael stormed by, fire in his eyes, and the sword? Gone. I didn't know at the time that Christoph could cast cloaking spells—*no one* did—but he cloaked it. Just like that. Then, like ten minutes later, he snuck it back into the weapons room like *nothing* happened."

"I bought him drinks that night," Erik said, smiling at the memory. "And we've been best friends ever since."

Darius chuckled. "That was classic Christoph. He didn't need to know someone to have their back. He just always did what was right."

"Man," Sam said, shaking his head, "Michael really was such a prick, bro. What do you think he would've done if he *had* caught you?"

Erik raised an eyebrow and gave a knowing smile.

"Well… he did catch me eventually. For something else." He held out his arms and gave a half-bow. "And, well… here I am."

There was a beat of silence. Then Sam cracked up, nearly doubling over. "I *knew* it!" he shouted. "I *knew* that was you! I always thought that fire in Michael's quarters was a little too poetic!"

"I set fire to Michael's room for *him*," Erik confessed, finally. "Lit it up like it was Judgment Day."

Even Cecelia cracked the faintest, fragile smile.

The laughter didn't last long—but it didn't need to. It was enough to remember him with joy, even if only for a moment.

Sam was next. He stepped forward slowly, silver hair catching the late light, eyes a little red—but steady.

"I remember the first time Max saw me train," he began, voice low and rough around the edges. "He watched in silence, arms crossed, probably judging me, like he always did when he was pretending not to be impressed." A soft chuckle passed through the group.

"He waited until I'd run through all my sets—daggers, blades, spearwork—then finally said, 'You fight like an angry poem.'"
Another chuckle.
"I asked if that was a compliment and he said, 'It is now.'" Sam looked down, his fingers tightening into fists. "He made me feel like I belonged—like being skilled at *everything* wasn't just chaos, it was a gift. He trained with me. Believed in me. Fought beside me like I was his equal, even when I didn't believe I deserved it."

He stepped back, nodding once before quietly saying, "Miss you, brother."

Darius came forward next, shoulders broad and posture solid, but his voice was gentler than anyone expected.

"I met Max back in Heaven. Before the fall. Back when we were all a little less... jaded."

A pause.

"We didn't bond over training or missions or anything serious like that. We bonded over jokes. The dumb kind. The kind that make you groan and laugh at the same time. I used to throw punchlines at him like darts, and even when they didn't land, he laughed anyway. Not because they were funny—but because *I* thought they were."

He smiled to himself. "He was my first audience. And my favorite one."

He rubbed the back of his neck, looking up at the tree. "So, uh… Max, if this sapling ever starts telling jokes? You'll know why."

A few tears, a few laughs, and then he took his place beside Sam again.

Evie stepped up, her expression soft but proud.

"When I first suggested adding Brian's face to the wall of shame," she said, "Christoph didn't just say yes—he ran with it like it was the greatest idea he'd ever heard." Her voice cracked through a smile. "He had someone *blow up* Brian's face, Photoshop Shrek ears on it, and mount it on the lounge wall like it was divine art."

Laughter broke out around her.

"And when I asked if this was a thing now, he said, 'It is now. Thanks to you.' He always made people feel like their weirdest ideas were genius. Like you were one of the greats just for *being* you."

She stepped back, eyes misty but glowing, her arm brushing against Cecelia as she returned to the circle.

Then all eyes turned to her.

Cecelia was last.

Cecelia stepped up slowly, her fingers curled tight around the edge of her sleeve. She didn't look at anyone. Just the tree.

"I don't really know how to do this," she said, her voice barely above a whisper. "But… I guess I'll start with a quote from *The Fault in Our Stars*. Ceruleus Christoph Maximus was the star-crossed love of my life."

Her lips trembled, and she looked up for a moment like she was trying to hold herself together.

"Our love wasn't normal. It wasn't simple. It didn't start with flirting or numbers exchanged or awkward first dates. I met him in a dream. I saw him… as angels were clipping his wings. And somehow, I knew him—before I even knew his name."

She gave a small, shaky laugh. "That sounds insane, right? But when I met him in real life… it felt like the universe just clicked. Like my soul had been waiting for him. And when we kissed—it wasn't just sparks. It was electricity. It was like he gave me wings to soar…"

Her voice caught. She wiped her eyes, but the tears kept coming.

"We were both book nerds. He loved quoting his favorite authors like he was living out some epic fantasy… and I think that's what we were doing. Living a story. Our own little fairytale. And somewhere along the way, I gave him my heart before I even realized it."

She looked at the sapling now, her eyes soft and far away.

"He ruined me. In the best way. Because now that I know what that kind of love feels like… I know I'll never find it again. I don't want to. No one else could ever be him. And I'll carry that… for the rest of my life."

Her voice dropped lower.

"He was my home. And now that he's gone… everything feels cold. Empty. There's this huge hole in my chest where he used to be. And I don't know how to fill it. I don't think I ever will."

She stepped back, her arms hugging her own ribs like she was trying to hold herself together.

"I miss you, Max. I'll miss you forever."

There was silence.

Not the kind that demanded words, but the kind that held grief like a heartbeat. A moment where no one dared move—because if they did, the spell might break.

Then Evie stepped forward.

She didn't say anything. She just wrapped her arms around Cecelia and held her like she could soak up some of the pain. One by one, the others followed—Darius with his quiet strength, Sam with a hand on her shoulder, Erik with tears in his eyes but none falling.

No one said "it's going to be okay." Because they all knew it wasn't.

They just stood there—together, holding each other, like maybe that could keep them from shattering.

After a while, Erik stepped back and pulled something from his coat. A small silver flask.

"Jack Daniels Honey," he said softly, unscrewing the cap. "Max hated it. Said it was for posers. But he always drank it anyway, because it's what *I liked.*"

He poured a slow stream onto the soil beside the sapling.

"For our brother," he said, his voice thick.

Sam took the flask next. "For our shadow and our light. The best of us."

Darius added, "For Max. For the real ones. Always."

Evie wiped her face. "For her Max. The only man who ever got my best friend to skip class."

And then Cecelia. She took the flask in both hands, like it was something fragile. Sacred.

"For my everything," she whispered. "For the man who made me feel like I was finally awake. Forever and always."

"Forever and Always," they toasted.

They drank, and stood there, letting the breeze carry the silence between them.

Then, slowly, they turned to go—leaving behind the young willow, golden blood in its roots, already reaching for the sky.

They were just renting the place—nothing like the five-story brownstone where Cecelia had first met them all—but it was still lovely. Cozy. Lived in. Safe.

Darius had been dating an interior designer, and she'd gone all out on the four-bedroom Brooklyn home. Modern industrial with soft touches—candles in wall sconces, leather seating that somehow didn't clash with the velvet pillows, a dining table long enough for all of them.

Now they were out on the back deck, the late summer sun melting behind the trees. The sky had turned that soft purple-blue haze and the string lights overhead buzzed to life. They were sipping cocktails and eating their way through the feast Erik's chefs had whipped up. The club was gone—burned to a shell—but Erik had found temporary jobs for the entire kitchen staff.

Cecelia stared down at her plate: Mongolian beef bao buns, sriracha honey wings, chicken satay skewers with spicy peanut sauce. It was almost offensive how good it all looked. Hard to stay depressed with food like that.

Erik stood and tapped a knife to his glass—a smoked mezcal and fig old fashioned.

"Alright, people," he said, his voice warm but steady. "I have before me the final will and testament of the late, Magnificent Christoph Maximus." He raised his drink. "Let us toast the man, the myth, the bastard who somehow made the rest of us look like amateurs."

Cecelia raised her peach mango mojito and managed a real smile. "To Max," she said softly.

"To Maximus," the others echoed, glasses clinking.

Erik opened the envelope, unfolding the thick parchment-like paper with theatrical flair. "Okay, first line—'To my dearest friends, I hereby divide my wealth six ways. To Erik, Cecelia, Darius, Sam, Evie... and Rule.'" Erik blinked. "Wait—who the fuck is Rule?"

Everyone looked at each other.

"I don't know," Darius shrugged. "But I guess that's one-sixth we don't touch until we find out."

"Fine, fine," Erik said with a smirk. "The mystery heir. Classic Max."

"Wait, I'm getting money?" Evie asked, wide-eyed.

Erik held up the will, squinting dramatically. "Yep. Says it right here."

Evie nearly dropped her drink. "Holy shit, I don't have to worry about student loans anymore! This is—this is life-changing!"

"Babe," Erik said, nudging her, "I told you I got you."

"Yeah, but now I got me too," she grinned. "It's like double got."

"Alright, alright," Erik said, waving the paper. "Let me finish. I'm getting to the good stuff."

He cleared his throat, then continued, his voice gentler now. "'To my best friend Erik, I leave my legacy, with the words: Live our best dream, brother.'"

Erik looked up at the darkening sky, holding back the catch in his throat. "I've got you, bro," he whispered.

He swallowed and went on.

"'To Samuel, I leave my knives—of which you know I hold dear.'"

Sam raised a triumphant fist. "Hell yeah. I always told him I'd be the one to sharpen them if he ever died."

"Pretty sure he knew you'd turn it into a shrine," Darius muttered.

"Damn right."

"'To Darius,'" Erik read, "'I leave my records. You always knew how to appreciate good music—and better jokes.'"

Darius gave a quiet nod, his smile bittersweet. "Thanks, brother. I'll keep spinning 'em."

"'And to Cecelia…'" Erik looked at her. "'I leave my books.'"

Her breath caught.

He had thousands. Shelves that stretched floor to ceiling. A library curated over centuries. Dog-eared favorites. First editions. Annotated spines and secret notes left in margins.

"Thank you, Erik," she whispered. "I... I'll take good care of them."

She didn't know where she'd put them. But it didn't matter. They were pieces of him.

"I wasn't done," Erik added, scanning the page. "'And my house in Spain.'"

Cecelia gasped.

"He remembered," she said, her voice cracking. "He told me once he had a place near the coast... he said we'd run away there someday, if it all ever went to shit."

Everyone went quiet again.

But this time it wasn't grief. It was reverence.

Because even in death, Christoph Maximus had found a way to take care of them all.

Epilogue

The return of Archangel Ceruleus Maximus

The ethereal glow of Heaven was a sight to behold, its radiant splendor a stark contrast to the tumultuous world below. Clouds of incandescent light drifted lazily, casting a serene, celestial aura over the realm. Angels moved gracefully, their wings shimmering with an otherworldly brilliance. The grand hall of Heaven stood tall and majestic, its golden spires reaching towards the heavens, a symbol of divine authority and peace.

Yet today, the serene tranquility was shattered by a flurry of whispers and urgent murmurs. Angels clustered in groups, their eyes wide with disbelief, their voices tinged with astonishment and excitement.

"Have you heard? He's returned."

"Impossible. Ceruleus Maximus? But how?"

"He broke through the gates. He's coming for Michael."

The whispers grew louder, echoing through the hallowed halls. The news spread like wildfire, and soon every angel in Heaven was abuzz with the astonishing revelation. Archangel Ceruleus Maximus, the once-mighty warrior and leader of the Elite Wing who had been cast out, had returned.

In the heart of the celestial city, the grand hall loomed, a testament to divine power and authority. Its doors, intricately carved with scenes of creation and grace, were a barrier that few dared to breach. Inside, the council of archangels convened, a gathering of Heaven's most powerful beings. At the head of this council stood Michael, the highest of archangels, his presence commanding and resolute.

But even Michael's calm demeanor wavered as the heavy doors of the grand hall burst open with a resounding crash. Every angel turned, their eyes widening in shock and awe.

Standing in the doorway, bathed in a radiant, golden light, was Ceruleus Maximus. His presence was overwhelming, a force of nature that demanded attention. His wings, once stripped from him in disgrace, had been restored to their former glory, their golden tipped feathers shimmering with divine energy. His eyes, burning with righteous fury, scanned the hall, searching for the one who had betrayed him.

Gasps and murmurs filled the room as the angels took in the sight of their long-lost brother. Ceruleus strode forward with purpose, each step resonating with power. The archangels, including Gabriel and Raphael, watched in stunned silence, their expressions a mix of awe and apprehension.

"Ceruleus," Gabriel whispered, his voice barely audible over the din. "It can't be."

But it was. Ceruleus Maximus had returned, and he was not the same angel who had been cast out. His time on Earth had changed him, tempered him with the fire of mortal struggle and the pain of loss. He was stronger, more resolute, and he had come with a purpose.

As he reached the center of the hall, the angels parted before him, creating a clear path to the throne where Michael stood. The tension was palpable, the air thick with anticipation.

"Michael!" Ceruleus's voice rang out, a clarion call that silenced the hall. "I know what you did. Come out and face me!"

Michael, his face a mask of controlled fury, stepped forward, his gaze locked with Ceruleus's. The two archangels stood in stark contrast—Michael, the embodiment of divine authority and order; Ceruleus, the symbol of rebellion and justice.

"What is this madness, Ceruleus?" Michael's voice was cold and measured, but there was an undercurrent of fear that he could not entirely hide. "You have no place here. You were cast out for your defiance."

"And I have returned for the truth," Ceruleus retorted, his voice unwavering. "You betrayed me. You feared my power, my loyalty to the Creator. You conspired to have me cast down because you saw me as a threat."

Gasps and shocked whispers rippled through the assembled angels. The council, usually a place of serene discourse, was now a battlefield of raw emotions.

"Your lies will not sway us," Michael said, but there was a flicker of uncertainty in his eyes. "You are a fallen angel, tainted by the mortal world."

Ceruleus took another step forward, his golden wings spreading wide. "I have seen the truth, Michael. I have walked among humans. I have fought beside them, and I have learned what it means to sacrifice for love and justice. I am not tainted—I am renewed. And I will not rest until the truth of your treachery is revealed."

Michael's composure cracked, his eyes narrowing in anger. "You dare to challenge me here, in the heart of Heaven?"

Ceruleus's gaze was steely, unyielding. "I dare because it is my duty. I dare because I will no longer be silent. I am Ceruleus Maximus, Archangel of Justice, and I will see you answer for your sins."

The grand hall fell into a tense silence, the angels watching with bated breath as the confrontation between Michael and Ceruleus reached its boiling point. The fate of Heaven itself seemed to hang in the balance, the return of Ceruleus Maximus heralding a new era of truth and reckoning.

Bonus Chapter

Evie & Erik's Date Night

The door clicked shut behind Christoph, and Erik sat in silence for a moment, staring at the muted TV. The Packers were about to score again, but suddenly, he didn't care.

He glanced down at the cheese doodle bowl sitting crooked on his abs. Lame.

His eyes flicked to his phone on the coffee table.

Screw it.

He grabbed it and opened a new message.

Erik: Hey, what are you doing tonight?

The dots started blinking almost immediately.

Evie: No plans yet. Hbu?

He grinned.

Erik: Have dinner with me at Max Lounge?

There was a beat of hesitation. He sat up, wiped his hands on his sweats, and stared at the screen like it might bite him.

Evie: Yeah. That sounds fun.

His grin deepened. He didn't even realize he was sitting up straighter until he caught his reflection in the dark TV screen.

Erik: I'll send a car for you. 7 sharp.

He fired off the text, then tossed the phone on the couch beside him. He pushed the half-eaten snacks aside, stood, and stretched like a man with purpose.

Yeah, it wasn't a date.

It was just food.

Totally casual.

Except… she said yes.

He smirked to himself as he headed to the bedroom to get ready.

"Fuck it," he said to himself with a smile. "I'm going all in."

Time to suit up.

By 7:30, the black car pulled up to the curb, and Evie stepped out looking like the night had been waiting for her. She smoothed her soft white off-the-shoulder blouse, its gathered sleeves brushing just beneath her elbows, and adjusted her signature gold hoops with a confident smirk. Her brown waves were pinned loosely back on one side, the rest cascading over her shoulder.

She barely made it past the velvet ropes before a host with pointy elf ears and glitter-dusted freckles greeted her like royalty. "Miss Lamoureux," they said with a knowing smile, "this way, please."

The dining area was pure magic—half 1920s speakeasy, half enchanted forest. Twinkling fairy lights dripped from the ceiling like stardust, weaving through artificial tree branches that curled around golden chandeliers. Moss-covered archways framed each booth, and clusters of soft candlelight flickered atop art deco tables, illuminating glassware like stardust in motion. The jazz band was setting up in the distance, their instruments catching the glow of floating orbs that pulsed with the rhythm of the room.

She was led to a semi-private table for two, framed by ivy and copper roses, and there he was—Erik Taylor… and damn he looked *good*.

He was already seated, his dark blue pinstripe suit catching the ambient glow. His white button-up was open at the collar just enough to look intentionally undone, and his chestnut waves were slicked back effortlessly. *Of course he looked like that.*

She wanted to jump his bones.

He stood when he saw her and gave her that annoyingly charming grin. "Wow," he said, taking her hand. "You look… beyond beautiful."

Evie raised a brow, lips curving. "Don't think I don't know you practiced that line in the mirror," she teased.

He chuckled. "Would you believe me if I said it came naturally?"

"Not even a little." As much as she liked him, she couldn't let it show. Obvi. That was weak girl stuff and this Evie Lamoureux was a force.

He grinned and gestured for her to sit, sliding into the booth across from her. Before she could ask for a menu, he held up his hand.

"I already ordered for us," he said smiling proudly.

Her eyes widened. "You what?"

He better have gotten her those Mac n cheese balls, she hoped. There were going to be words if he didn't.

"Trust me," he said with a wink. "You'll like it."

She narrowed her eyes playfully. "Just this once, Little Erii. You mess up, I swear on that sweet saint Cecelia, you'll never get a second date."

He held up both hands in surrender and chuckled. "Deal."

Evie leaned back and let her eyes wander around the room, trying to hide the excitement in her expression. "I can't believe I'm finally eating here," she whispered. "When Brian Watterson mentioned it at the start of the semester, I thought he was just trying to flex. That jackass couldn't even get past the bouncer."

Erik smirked. "That jackass is still on the banned list. Tried sneaking in last week dressed like one of the hosts. Fairy ears and all."

She burst into laughter. "You're lying."

"I wish I was."

A server strode over with such grace, Evie thought she might actually be a real fairy. She placed two glowing cocktails on the table, each one shimmering like bottled aurora borealis.

Evie took one sip and her eyes went wide. "Okay. Alright. That's actually dangerous. I love this."

"Told you to trust me," Erik said with a smug tilt of his glass.

As the cocktails worked their magic and the jazz band warmed up in the background with smooth trumpet trills and the soft shuffle of brushed drums, Erik leaned forward, resting his elbows on the edge of the table.

"So," he said, eyes flickering with amusement, "tell me about school. Classes. Hobbies. Nerd stuff."

Evie squinted at him like he had two heads. "You're asking me about school?"

"Yeah, why not?"

She took a long, dramatic sip of her glowing drink. "Fine. I'll bite."

He smirked, waiting.

"Biology?" she groaned. "Nope. Absolutely not. I'd rather be stung by a swarm of bees. Algebra is just… barfsville. Econ's fine, I guess, and Modern Euro—well, let's just say Cecelia deserves a medal for carrying me through that one."

"You two are dangerous together," Erik said, grinning.

She nodded. "We really are. But Music Theory 101? Chef's kiss. I live for it. Like, genuinely forget-the-rest-of-the-world love it."

"You've definitely got the ear," he said. "And the voice. Plus, let's not lie— you've got stage presence for days."

Evie gave a half-shrug, trying not to look too flattered. "Thanks, hot stuff. I was hoping to get signed before graduation, but if that doesn't work out, I've been thinking about editing. Maybe producing. You know, like you."

Erik's smile curved slow and confident. "Funny you mention that. I think I can help."

She arched a brow. "Oh yeah?"

"Yeah." He leaned in, voice low like he was letting her in on a secret. "Consider your internship next semester locked."

Her eyes went wide. "No way. Seriously?"

"Hell yeah."

"You're not just saying that because I look like a snack in candlelight?"

"That's a bonus," he said, raising his glass.

They clinked again, the glowing liquid swirling like bottled moonlight.

Conversation rolled into surfing next—Evie's eyes lit up as she told him about her childhood chasing waves. How she thought she'd go pro one day, how sponsors looked great on paper but the reality was way rougher.

"I won almost every comp on the East Coast," she said casually. "Even have a couple broken boards hanging in my mom's garage."

"That's so badass," Erik said. "But also very on-brand. You give surfer chaos energy."

"Thank you. I am *mostly* chaos."

Evie took another sip of her glowing cocktail and set it down with a sigh. "Okay, I'll admit it. You were right. This thing's addictive."

Erik raised his glass with a smug grin. "Told you. It's dangerous."

She laughed, swirling the drink. "So. You ordering for me, mixing magical cocktails, and playing my favorite song at open mic night—you trying to win points or just show off?"

He leaned back in the booth, his eyes gleaming. "Can't it be both?"

She arched a brow. "You played Fall Out Boy on purpose, didn't you?"

"I did."

Evie narrowed her eyes. "Because…?"

"Because you told me in the studio that Fall Out Boy was your number one," he said smoothly. "And that if someone didn't know the full From Under the Cork Tree tracklist, they weren't worth your time."

Her mouth curved into a grin. "I did say that."

He nodded. "So I figured, what better way to prove I am worth your time than belting out 'Sugar, We're Goin Down' in front of your closest friends," he laughed.

"Off key."

"Off key," he agreed proudly. "But with soul."

Evie laughed. "You're such a dork."

"An observant dork," he countered. "I listen when you talk. Even when you're yelling at me."

She smirked and leaned forward. "Fine. One point to you."

Erik looked mock-offended. "Just one?"

"Well," she said, dragging out the word, "depends on how good these mac and cheese balls are."

He held up a hand. "Patience, young padawan. They're coming."

Evie swirled the glowing cocktail in her glass, eyes twinkling with mischief. "Alright, Mr. Fanboy—what's your favorite Fall Out Boy song?"

Erik didn't even blink. "Get Busy Living or Get Busy Dying. Easy."

She nodded slowly, impressed. "Solid choice. That bridge hits hard."

A grin tugged at his lips. "Always loved that line: 'I'm falling apart to songs about hips and hearts.'"

"Oof. Yeah. That one cuts."

He leaned back in the booth, tipping his glass toward her. "I used to think it would make a killer name for a restaurant."

Evie snorted. "That'd be such a long-ass name."

"No, not the whole lyric. Just 'Hips and Hearts'. Clean. Emotional. Weirdly poetic."

She tilted her head. "Okay, you might be onto something. Bonus points if the cocktails are all named after break-up songs."

Erik smirked. "I like the way you think."

She rested her chin on her hand. "But seriously, that album is their best. No skips. Front to back perfection."

"That tour was insane," Erik said. "Every show was chaos—in the best way. Patrick had laryngitis by week three and still nailed every set."

Evie narrowed her eyes. "You talk like you were there."

"I was."

Her brows rose. "Wait… were you there?"

"I followed them for a few summers," he said, sipping casually. "Road-tripped between shows. Helped with set-up once. Pete still owes me twenty bucks."

Evie stared at him like he'd grown a second head. "Okay. No way. You talk like you were friends with them."

He grinned. "We are."

She blinked. "Bullshit."

Erik just shrugged. "I actually founded their fan club."

Evie gawked. "No. You didn't."

"Did," he said, like it was the most casual thing in the world. "It started as a blog. Next thing I know, I'm printing shirts and moderating meetups."

"You're lying."

He pulled out his phone and tapped through his camera roll. "Scroll left."

She took the phone—and blinked. There he was, a scene looking Erik Taylor, arm slung around Patrick Stump at Angels & Kings, both mid-laugh, beer pong cups in the background. Another shot with Pete Wentz flipping off the camera. Another of Erik mock stage-diving in the tiny bar's corner stage.

She looked up slowly. "What the actual hell. Who are you?"

He leaned in, grinning. "I'm Erik fucking Taylor, remember?"

She shook her head, laughing. "I'm going to need, like, twelve more cocktails before this makes sense."

Before she could interrogate him further, their food arrived—golden mac n' cheese balls stacked like treasure, crispy sriracha wings, and glistening satay skewers lined with peanut drizzle. A fairy host placed it all down like sacred art, then vanished without a sound.

Evie's attention locked instantly. "Oh my God. Are those—"

"Yup," Erik grinned. "The famous mac n' cheese balls."

She squealed. "I've been dying to try these since I saw them on a yelp review! They smell illegal."

She grabbed one and took a greedy bite. The crispy shell gave way to molten cheese, creamy with a subtle kick of heat. Her eyes widened in real-time.

"Okay, wait," she said, half chewing. "Why do these slap? Is that a hint of buffalo I'm tasting?"

"Use the sauce," Erik said, sliding over a small ramekin.

She dipped. She tasted. She blinked like she just saw God.

"What is this? Some sort of spicy aioli voodoo?"

"My own vodka sauce recipe."

"You're full of it."

"Okay, I stole it from the Cheesecake Factory… and then fixed it."

"These blow theirs out of the water."

"I know."

She pointed a fork at him. "If you're not careful, I might fall in love with you over these mac n cheese balls."

He leaned back in his seat with a smirk. "That was always the plan."

Evie polished off the last of the mac n' cheese balls with zero shame and not a hint of remorse. Not a single one made it to Erik's side of the table.

He didn't seem to mind. He was fully invested in the honey sriracha wings—his fingers sticky, his smile satisfied. There was hot sauce glistening near the corner of his mouth, and he clearly didn't care.

A waitress strolled over mid-bite and handed him a moist towelette with a smile so casual it felt rehearsed.

Evie cocked her head, amused. "Is that, like… standard procedure?"

Erik wiped his hands and shrugged like this happened all the time. "Comes with the territory. Perks of being the boss."

She rolled her eyes, half-laughing. "Of course it does."

He flagged down another round of drinks without missing a beat. When they arrived, Erik was handed something golden brown with a smoky citrus curl, while Evie's came in a tall glass that looked like a purple dream. It was pale lavender at the bottom and deep violet at the top, layered with crushed ice and garnished with a sprig of rosemary and a few sugared blueberries.

Evie lit up. "Oh my god, this is gorgeous. You really are trying to impress me, huh?"

"Not me. Christoph makes the cocktails. That one's called the Blueberry Lavender Lemonade."

She lifted the glass carefully and turned it slightly in the light. "It's almost too pretty to drink."

"Almost," he said with a smirk.

"Hold on," she said, pulling out her phone. She snapped a quick pic, adjusted the angle, and then took another. "Okay. Now it's fair game."

She sipped. Her eyes widened immediately.

"Ohhh—okay," she said, nearly laughing. "This tastes like… like if a garden threw a party in your mouth."

"Good party?"

"Elite party," she confirmed. "This might be my new favorite cocktail."

"Damn," Erik said, raising his glass. "Should I be jealous?"

She squinted at him playfully. "Maybe. What's yours called?"

"I call it a Honey Vanilla Roman," he said. "Jack Daniels Honey, vanilla vodka, apple cider, splash of ginger ale. It's cozy. Tastes like a hug."

Evie smiled, biting her lip. "You really are the sweetest sometimes. I hate it."

"You love it."

"Shut up."

Just then, their entrees arrived. The server set down a steaming plate in front of Evie, and she leaned in immediately, eyes going glossy.

"Short rib?" she guessed, already clutching her fork like it owed her money.

"Braised for eight hours," Erik said proudly. "On top of cheesy garlic mashed potatoes, finished with a cabernet rosemary glaze."

Evie inhaled. "Oh wow."

The scent was heaven—rich and savory with hints of garlic, butter, and wine that rose from the plate in warm, mouthwatering waves.

She sliced into the short rib and gasped when the fork slid through like silk. The first bite hit her like a slow-motion movie moment—tender meat that melted, tangy red wine reduction balanced with just enough salt and garlic to make her toes curl.

Her head tilted back slightly, eyes fluttering shut. "Oh my god."

Erik grinned. "That good?"

She held up a hand, eyes still closed. "Don't talk to me. I'm experiencing something."

He laughed softly, resting his chin in his hand as he watched her savor the next bite.

"No, seriously," she said, finally looking at him again. "This is insane. The potatoes? The sauce? You didn't tell me food like this even existed outside of my dreams."

"I'm full of surprises," he said, clearly enjoying every second of her reaction.

She stabbed another forkful. "This is like… marriage material. This is how you trick people into commitment."

He shrugged. "Hey, I just feed people. What they do afterward is on them."

Evie looked across the table, suddenly serious. "I'm not even kidding. If the dessert is as good as this, you're in dangerous territory."

Erik gave her a slow, knowing smile and leaned in slightly.

"Wait till you see dessert."

The waitress returned to clear their plates, but before Evie could even mourn the last bite of that short rib, a tall French chef in a pristine white jacket emerged from the kitchen—personally carrying a plate like it was a holy offering.

She straightened in her seat, watching in awe as he gently placed it down.

Macaron ice cream sandwiches.

No, not just any macarons—these were borderline mythical. Lavender, blush pink, deep violet, and golden honey shells stacked high, each one filled with swirled gelato and sprinkled with edible gold flakes. A delicate drizzle of honey trickled down one, and whole sugared pansies and blooming roses adorned the plate like edible couture. It looked too perfect to eat… and yet.

Evie's jaw dropped. "What is this sorcery?"

Erik leaned in, clearly proud. "Handmade macaron ice cream sandwiches. Lavender blueberry with sugared violet petals… Mexican chocolate and honey… and that one's strawberries and cream. All house-made. Every single one."

Evie decided then and there she was going to date him so hard and then marry the shit out of him.

No, she was serious. Like—lock it down, change-her-last-name serious.

She couldn't wait for Scarlet to meet him. That was her mom, of course. On second thought… maybe not. Scarlet might fall in love with him too, and then what? She'd have to duel her own mother. She didn't want to fight her mom to the death, but for him? She just might.

She took one bite and her entire heart did a somersault.

The lavender blueberry macaron was chilled perfection—soft floral notes balanced by the juicy punch of berries, wrapped in a cloud of creamy gelato that melted the second it hit her tongue. The next one was Mexican chocolate with honey—spiced and warm and deep, like the first bite of a secret you're not supposed to know. And the strawberry one? Summer in a dessert. Rich, nostalgic, and so good it made her want to write poetry.

She put her fork down and stared at him.

"Erik. Erik, I don't know any other way to say this…" she took a dramatic breath. "But I don't think I could imagine a life without this food. I think—" she shook her head slowly, "I think this is it for you. I hope you don't mind settling for me."

He blinked, caught off guard—and then grinned, eyes sparkling.

"Evie," he said, leaning forward. "I don't think anyone in their right mind would ever consider you settling."

He picked up his spoon and pointed it at her like a mic drop.

"You're the Super Bowl of babes."

Evie snorted, nearly choking on her next bite of strawberry cream. "That is—without a doubt—the most ridiculous thing anyone's ever said to me."

"But also accurate," Erik added, sipping his drink like he just told the truth of the universe.

She laughed, full and bright, and took another bite of that lavender blueberry one. She didn't know how the night could possibly get better.

But knowing him?

It probably would.

The last bite of strawberry cream still lingered on her tongue when the jazz band shifted to a slower tune—sultry horns melting into a low upright bass groove. Warm, golden light flickered through the enchanted forest ceiling, casting shadows that swayed like fireflies.

Erik stood, sliding out of his chair with a quiet confidence, and extended his hand to her.

"Dance with me."

Evie raised a brow. "What, like right here?"

"Right here," he confirmed, palm still outstretched, his voice smooth as the bass line.

She smirked, placing her hand in his. "If you step on my toes, I swear to God, I'll hip toss you so fast."

"I believe you," he laughed.

He led her gently onto the open space beside their table, just between two mossy archways lit with soft candlelight. The band's trumpet crooned something old and romantic, and Erik eased a hand to her waist. She followed his lead, her heels clicking lightly against the floor as they began to sway.

To her surprise, he actually had rhythm.

"Okay, okay," she murmured, eyes narrowed in mock suspicion. "You've done this before."

"Maybe once or twice," he said, teasing.

With a grin, he spun her out, fingers still laced with hers, then pulled her back in. She twirled right into his chest and couldn't help the breathless laugh that escaped her.

They fell into the music easily, two beats syncing like they always belonged together.

Her eyes drifted up to his, catching the shimmer in them, and suddenly she remembered the first time she'd ever seen him—standing in the back of Max Lounge, arms crossed, sleeves rolled, blue eyes dark and brooding.

She remembered thinking they looked like the ocean after a storm.

Erik held her gaze like it was the only thing keeping him tethered to the world. The way she looked at him—it shattered something inside him every time. Like she saw past the cracks. Like she didn't care he was more than he seemed.

She was a firecracker in a thunderstorm—and with one look, she lit up his world like it was the Fourth of July.

He leaned in slowly, his hand gliding from her back to her waist, guiding her into a low dip. Her head tilted back with trust, hair falling like silk, the world going quiet.

Then he kissed her.

Soft at first, reverent. Like he was afraid she might vanish. Then deeper—warm and lingering, tasting of strawberry and honey and all the chaos she brought into his life. Her hand slid to his chest, fingers curling into the lapel of his jacket as she kissed him back like she meant it.

When they finally pulled apart, she was breathless.

"I can't believe you just did that," she whispered, eyes still closed.

"Believe it," he said, pulling her back upright and brushing a stray strand of hair from her cheek. "I've been wanting to do that all night."

And maybe longer.

Outside, the night was crisp and humming with the quiet magic of fall. Leaves rustled in amber clusters along the sidewalk, and the breeze carried a faint scent of cinnamon and cold concrete. The streetlamps glowed warmer than usual, like they were trying to fight off the chill.

He walked her to the curb, where his fully modded, blue Honda Civic waited under a flickering streetlight like a wolf in disguise. Sleek rims, blacked-out windows, the low growl of the engine warming the air.

Evie paused. "Okay, I'm not gonna lie—this is sexy."

He grinned. "Fixed it up myself."

"Of course you did."

He opened the passenger door with a mock flourish. "M'lady."

She slid in with a laugh. "You're lucky you're cute."

The drive back to her dorm was cozy, the windows slightly fogged from the temperature drop. City lights blurred past in a mosaic of gold and orange.

Inside the car, it was just them—Fall Out Boy playing over the speakers, their hands brushing now and then between gear shifts and glances.

When he pulled up in front of her building, he didn't rush. He parked, then turned to face her, eyes a little softer in the glow of the dash.

"I had a really good time," he said, voice low.

Evie leaned in and kissed him again—shorter this time, but just as electric.

"So did I," she whispered.

She opened the door and stepped out, hugging her coat a little tighter as the breeze nipped at her heels. She paused on the curb, looked back with that signature smirk. "Night, Little Erii."

He watched her until the building doors clicked shut behind her, then leaned back with a slow, easy grin.

"Super Bowl," he said to himself, his voice full of something more than charm. "Yeah. That's my Super Bowl girl right there."

And with that, he shifted into gear and rolled off into the amber-stained night.

I hope you enjoyed reading *Maximus - The Key to Heaven*. This book holds a special place in my heart, as it was written during a time of profound loss after my best friend Erik passed away. Through this story, I sought to create a new world where he could continue to live on with me. The vibrant personalities of the characters mirror the close friends and the bonds we shared, capturing who we were back then. The places depicted are manifestations of the dreams we shared and hoped to one day create together. Thank you for joining me on this journey and keeping his spirit alive.

Let's Call This a Bio and Be Done With It

I love to read. I love adventure. I love honesty, the cruel, brutal and beautiful kind. I love romance, comedy and music. I'm a strong believer in the idea that there is a perfect song to be played behind every situation and if I could, I'd soundtrack my own life. I love the rain. I love movies and the wonderful way they can captivate you and inspire you. I love food with my entire being and I promise you, I will never give you a poor recommendation. I love wine. Oh, how I love wine. Every Wednesday should be Wine Wednesday. I love to run, I love the feeling of freedom and the wind against your face. I love Tuesdays, they're my favorite day of the week and I don't care what anyone else has to say about it. I love to love because I'm full of it and I believe we all have so much to give and only so little time to do so. I consider myself lucky. It's a good life.

Thank you for taking the time to read my work and thank you so much more if you are willing to leave a review! It's greatly appreciated more than you could know.

- Christopher M. Shamoun

@SeraphicNovels

Acknowledgements & Shoutouts

First and foremost, I want to thank my dear friends and original editors, Ray Paul Muniz and Cheryl Tegan Crumpler-Hall. You helped me untangle the wild storm in my head and shaped it into the urban fantasy world you now hold in your hands. I am forever grateful for your guidance and patience.

To my original core ARC team — Kristen, Ramya (Mia), Marina, Tara, Jenny, Catherine, Candice, Nova, and Gaby — thank you for being the first to believe in this story and for walking with me through its earliest steps.

To my Maximus 2025 ARC Team — Georgiana, Alisha, Nikky, Sharon, Vanessa, Sarah, Sahar, Debbie, Riya, Stevie, Vivien, Melinda, Chhaya, Bella, Isla, Alysen, Anna, Natalie, Tori, Amanda, Rachel, Alex and my boy, Jad — your support, feedback, and enthusiasm mean the world to me. You've helped breathe life into this book in ways I could never have done alone.

Special shoutouts to my Elite Wing and friends who agreed to be featured in this story: Samuel, Darren, Tim, Jen, Yale, and Ray. Thank you for letting me immortalize pieces of you within these pages.

To my literary inspirations — Cassandra Clare, Rick Riordan, Becca Fitzpatrick, Susan Ee, Wendy Higgins, and Jennifer L. Armentrout — your worlds lit the spark that inspired me to create my own. Reading your stories gave me the courage to believe in mine.

And then there are the little things that carried me through the writing process:

- *Book 1 Cocktails as they appear in order:*
    - Berry Blast Mojitos
    - This One's a Dinger
    - Fizzy Bubbly
    - Cupids Love Potion (my version of Beauty Elixir)
    - Witches Brew
    - Peach Candy Cocktail
    - The Brains (a Jello shot recipe)
    - Smoked Mezcal and Fig Old Fashioned

- ○ Peach Mango Mojito
- ○ Blueberry Lavender Lemonade
- ○ Honey Vanilla Roman
- **_Cited quotes woven throughout this book for your reference:_**
  - ○ "My problem isn't that my favorite characters aren't real. It's that I'm not fictional… I don't want them to be real. What I desperately wish is that I could be fictional with them. It's not that I want them here with me, in this mundane and ordinary world… it's that I want to join them in their extraordinary one." - Author Unknown.
  - ○ "I think the world would be a much better place if there were no guns. Then we could finally focus on things, like sword fighting, and how to kill a man with one punch." - Author Unknown.
  - ○ "The only people for me are the mad ones! The ones who never yawn or say a commonplace tuning, but burn, burn, burn like fabulous yellow roman candles-exploding like spiders across the start." - On the Road by Jack Kerouac.
  - ○ "…be nice first because you can always be mean later, but once you've been mean to someone, they won't believe the nice anymore. So be nice, be nice until it's time to stop being nice, then destroy them." - A Stroke of Midnight by Laurell K. Hamilton.
  - ○ "Though rather despite myself. I thought him a pretty bit of poison to start with, but I have come around. There is a soul under all that bravado. And he is really alive, one of the most alive people I have ever met. When he feels something, it is as bright and sharp as lightning." - Magnus Bane, Clockwork Prince by Cassanda Clare.

- **_Cited songs throughout the book as they appear in order:_**
  - ○ The First Single - The Formatt
  - ○ Let Me In - Grouplove
  - ○ Shimmy Shimmy Quarter Turn - Hellogoodbye
  - ○ Of Monsters & Men - Little Talks
  - ○ Four Years Strong - Heroes Get Remembered, Legends Never Die
  - ○ While I'm Alive - STRFKR
  - ○ You, Me, A Hurricane - Cecelia
  - ○ Sugar We're Goin Down - Fall Out Boy
  - ○ Unit You Let Me - Oh Honey
  - ○ Lancifer - Bring Your Bass

        o   The Last of The Real Ones - Fall Out Boy
        o   Valencia - Still Need You Around (Lost Without You)
        o   Get Busy Living or Get Busy Dying - Fall Out Boy

- *Cecelia's reading list as it appears in order:*
    o   Obsidian - Jennifer L. Armentrout
    o   Onyx - Jennifer L. Armentrout
    o   Opal - Jennifer L. Armentrout
    o   Origin - Jennifer L. Armentrout
    o   Opposition - Jennifer L. Armentrout
    o   Ruby Red - Kerstin Gier
    o   Sapphire Blue - Kerstin Gier
    o   Emerald Green - Kerstin Gier
    o   Throne of Glass - Sarah J Maas

A very special shoutout to Erik's sainted mother, Janet — I love you.

Finally, to the ones who've been the soundtrack to so much of my life — Fall Out Boy: Pete, Patrick, Joe, Andy, and the OverCast Kids — thank you for reminding me that music and stories are two sides of the same magic.

References

We are thrilled to share that the people, places, and events in this adventure are inspired by real life! Below, you'll find the names and addresses of actual locations you can visit to immerse yourself in the story.

Beauty & Essex
146 Essex St, New York, NY 10002

David Zwirner's Gallery in Chelsea
525 W 19th St, New York, NY 10011

The Bethesda Fountain
Central Park, New York, NY 10019

Joe's Pizza
7 Carmine St, New York, NY 10014

You'll also be delighted to know that although the location is not yet real, the recipes and cocktails from *Max Lounge*, and the restaurants *Hips & Hearts*, and *Novela* from Book 2, Eros - The Great Cataclysm are and can be found in the companion guides:

"A Max Lounge Bartender's Guide"

AND

"A Hips & Hearts Recipe Book"

Also by Christopher M. Shamoun

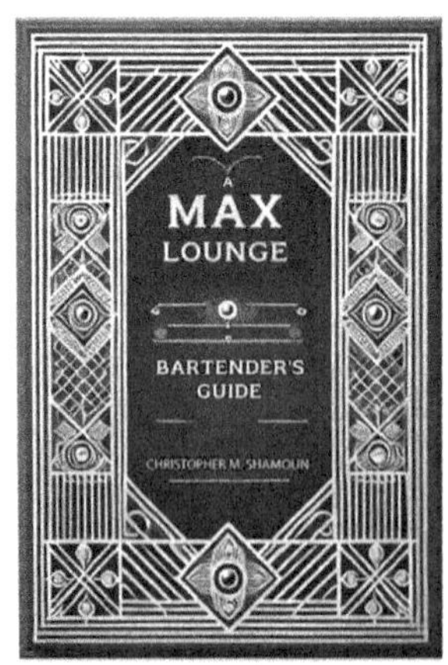